Split Decision 2

The Comeback

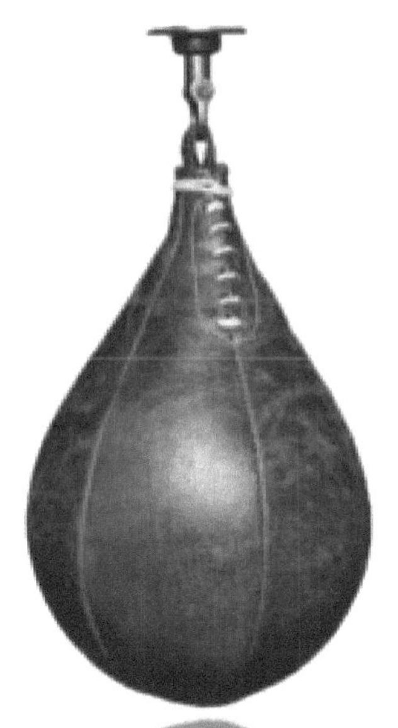

Marc A. Beausejour

S.H.E. PUBLISHING, LLC

SPLIT DECISION 2 | *The Comeback*

For information contact : www.shepublishingllc.com | info@shepublishingllc.com | Tel: 219.515.8032

Edited by D.A. Goodwin | Front Cover photo by ID 48584570 © Ammentorp | Dreamstime.com
Library of Congress Control Number: 2024932784
ISBN: 978-1-953163-95-0 (paperback)
Second Edition : February 2024

1   2   3   4   5   6   7   8   9   10

Acknowledgments

I would like to thank the Lord, first and foremost, because without Him, none of this would be possible.

In a journey that started with my first self-published book, WORDS ON HIGH, there were many people that God has sent along the way and I've learned a great deal from them. Although, I have not seen her in decades,

I would like to thank my third-grade teacher from Public School 50, Mrs. Bess for instilling the love of reading within me early in my life.

I want to thank my parents, Jean and Lineda Beausejour for the vision of a productive life that they had since emigrating from Haiti.

I want to thank everyone that I grew up with in New York from P.S. 50Q to JHS 217Q and my church family, Bethany French Baptist Church.

I would like to thank my Georgia family, from my friends that I went to high school and college with, many of whom I still communicate with today.

A special thanks goes out to my friend and editor, Dawn "D.A." Goodwin, for taking the time to edit this book. Since 2018, when you edited, Fires of Justice, I felt that it took my writing career to another plateau, and there are not enough words to describe my gratitude.

I would like to thank my cover designer, Mr. Clinton Holmes, whom I had the pleasure of working with for the first time; for doing an exceptional job with the front and back cover design.

If I have not mentioned anybody else in the acknowledgements, just know that if I've had the pleasure of communicating with you and you've encouraged me throughout the journey or you've supported by purchasing my books, you are appreciated. Thank you all!

Preface

Book #7! Wow, it certainly took plenty of prayer, hard work and perseverance to make this project happen. Sub- consciously, we're all fighting an internal battle, whether some of us are contending with the COVID-19 virus or contending spiritually within ourselves. My hope is that this book serves as a reminder never to concede when things do not go your way. Continue to fight, even if you have absolutely nothing left. God bless everyone and stay strong!

M.A.B.

Prologue

January 19, 2019

I shouldn't be here…how did I find my way back here?

These thoughts burned through the mind of 28-year-old Sylvio Dominique as he found himself lying on his back in agony. But he wasn't lying on the streets of a secluded alley, where he'd almost lost his life six years earlier. Often, he has visited the very location where his life changed and where he tragically lost his best friend. Omar shouldn't have been out there with him that night, and although it seemed like ages ago, Sylvio's guilt never left.

Sylvio could still see traces of blood on the pavement where the life had drained out of him and Omar. The city did all it could to erase and scrub out the remnants of the horrific shooting, yet the pavement still bore the discolored blood plasma from that fateful evening.

Sylvio was now lying in a place where he never thought he would return: the center of the ring. A few minutes earlier, he'd heard the deafening roar of over thirty thousand people attending his fight at the Staples Center in Los Angeles. But that was all before his body hit the canvas with such force that he could no longer hear the crowd. Instead, he heard a loud ringing in his ears, and his eyes rolled back into his head. Blood was pouring out of his nose and mouth, and for a while, he was not fully aware of his surroundings.

Over in Sylvio's right corner, his trainer Jim Shaw, along with a couple of his cornermen, were shouting at the top of their lungs, urging him to get back up. At least that's what he was able to make out by their lip movements. Their words went unheard by their fallen fighter, who was dazed and stunned by a right and left jab combination to the face and jaw.

Six years ago, I was the man. I was barely hurt in the ring. I was fast, ferocious, and feared. They called me "The Wolf" for that very reason. I was the champion of the world at one point. Now, I'm nothing. I'm just a bum like the rest of 'em.

With Sylvio's vision partly blurred, he barely made out the image of the referee standing over him counting to ten, and he couldn't tell how much longer he had before he'd be counted out. Reaching up to his face with a gloved hand, Sylvio gingerly tried to push his mouthpiece back in, but the moment he nudged his chin, he felt another rush of pain and a sensation like his lower gumline was unhinged. He knew right away that his jaw was broken. He had heard the injury was common in boxing, but never had he felt the excruciating pain and foreign sensation that it carried.

Jim was all too familiar with the injury, having endured a few broken jaws himself. But he and fellow cutman, Harry Delmond, had guarded and protected his fighter from any serious injury in the ring. Therefore, he knew as soon as the punch landed squarely on Sylvio's chin that his jaw had snapped.

In a twisted sort of way, Sylvio thought that it was ironic that he was in this position. The once invincible Sylvio Dominique, who knocked out many a fighter before his prime, was now the one knocked senseless. Upon instinct, Sylvio closed his eyes and immediately thought of euphoria, a dwelling where pain and suffering no longer existed. He fed his mind with thoughts of his scars dissipating and Omar smiling and joking like he normally had done.

Then Sylvio's thoughts turned to her. The woman that many had thought deceived him. But she'd never left his side. The beautiful Valentina Cruz slid into his subconscious, and he wanted to touch her, smell her, and taste her. He wanted her soft hands to gently massage his sore shoulders, back, and legs. He wanted to feel her warm skin against his own, and he wanted to hear her encouragement again. Sylvio wanted Valentina to kiss his wounds and to reach over and make sweet love to him as she had done over the years. But he was not sure where they stood. He still loved her, but did she love him? Would she have understood why he was compelled to return to the game that nearly killed him?

Sylvio knew his father, Jacques, was watching him as well. For years he had worked on rehabilitating the broken relationship with his family. At times they may have felt that he was alienating them, but were they privy to the thoughts and concerns that ran through Sylvio's mind then? Sylvio could not allow them into his world because he knew he would one day be putting them in danger. He couldn't afford to lose any more family or anybody else because of his choices, so he had no choice but to return to the fight game. But Sylvio didn't have to look far to see a mirror image of an individual who suffered because of his choices.

Jim knew all too well about the pain of losing a loved one, and he has had difficulty expressing or letting on how he felt because in boxing it was equivalent to weakness. Fighters were not meant to feel or be sensitive to others. They were warriors, modern day gladiators, that had weapons at their disposal, and it was that very mindset that they needed to carry to the ring.

"GET UP, WOLF!" Jim yelled as he urged his fighter to beat the ten count.

Come on, Sylvio, get back up. You heard Jim. It ain't over till you can no longer fight. Your face is busted in, your jaw's broken, and your mind's all over the place. But whatever you do, get back up. It don't matter if your family left you or if your girl left you and nobody believes in you. The only thing that matters is that I believe in you.

With those thoughts and all his remaining strength, Sylvio gathered himself, forcing himself to rise when the referee was almost at the count of ten. *It's me against time. It's me against him. It's me against myself…*

Chapter 1

Two Years Earlier | Upon arriving at the Los Angeles International Airport, Dr. Liu Zhang parked in the lot and made his way over to the terminal to await his son's arrival from China. Although he couldn't have been more excited at seeing his son, Jun Zhang, the doctor was also nervous. This was the first time in five years that Jun would be staying at home. To most parents, having their children at home with them was routine, but Dr. Zhang's son was no ordinary child. Jun was a top-ranked, mixed martial arts fighter who had recently dominated the sport. In just four years, he had managed to work his way to the top of the MMA division, as he regularly outsmarted and outdueled his opponents in less than three rounds.

When he wasn't at the hospital with a patient, Dr. Zhang was watching Jun dominate, night after night, in the octagon. The UFC was the sport that was steadily growing in popularity because of the full contact physicality that it allowed. While many of the fighters were highly skilled at their craft, Jun was special. Having trained with legendary trainer, Chao Yong, Jun was often flown back to his parents' homeland where Chao would train him using ancient methods. Those methods not only preserved Jun's health, but they kept him in peak physical condition. Therefore, he was rarely hurt.

Finally arriving at his son's gate, Dr. Zhang saw that his son's plane hadn't arrived yet. Wondering if he had arrived too early, the doctor stared at his watch. Where is he? His flight should have arrived by now.

No sooner than five minutes later, the passenger jet landed. As Dr. Zhang watched the throng of passengers exiting the flight, his son finally emerged. Standing at six-foot-four with rippling muscles and carrying a Nike duffel bag, Jun's face exuded one of extreme focus and concentration, even when he wasn't in the octagon. When he saw his father, his face relaxed, flashing the grin his father had seen so frequently when he was growing up.

"Why the long face, man? You look like you're about to hurt somebody," Dr. Zhang laughed, hugging his son.

"Come on, Dad. You know me. I gotta stay focused all the time. Thanks for waiting for me," Jun replied as he embraced his father.

Together, they walked to baggage claim to pick up Jun's luggage before heading to the U.S. Customs office. It had always been a tedious process in past years, but the lines doubled in the wake of the current U.S. government. The officers were not taking any chances, checking to confirm that all immigrants or children of immigrants were properly documented.

Afterwards, the father and son headed back to Dr. Zhang's car. "So, how's Mom?" Jun asked as they entered the car.

"She's doing well. Working as usual," Dr. Zhang replied as they drove out of the parking lot.

It was barely noon when they left LAX, and the sun was shining brightly. Jun let his window down to take in the sight of palm trees and feel the Pacific breeze. He was still a young fighter, only twenty-two years of age, but he learned at a young age to appreciate everything in life. It was a key value bred inside him by his parents, who were Chinese immigrants who came to America for a better life and job opportunities. Jun's mother was an elementary school teacher in the Riverside School District. For as long as Jun remembered, she always stressed education and upholding the family name and traditions.

Mrs. Zhang was not too thrilled that Jun had decided to make his living fighting in the UFC, yet she didn't stand in the way of his success. Still, she worried whenever he faced off against an opponent. She didn't have the same zeal Dr. Zhang had whenever Jun's fights came on TV.

Jun was actually coming to a crossroads in his career. There was no denying the reports and the rumors that swirled about his future in MMA. Although he was the top-ranked fighter slated to be on the card to fight for the UFC title, Jun was given an offer to go over to professional boxing.

Dr. Zhang knew his son was still mulling over his options, but he couldn't understand why Jun wanted to switch over, especially at the early stages of his career. "You know, we have much to discuss," he finally said after a moment of silence.

"Yeah, about what?" Jun asked.

"This boxing thing you want to do. Are you sure that's the direction you want to go to?" his father asked.

Jun laughed. "So, you heard about it too, huh?"

"Who hasn't heard about it? Everybody is wondering what the hell you're thinking about."

"I know, Dad. But believe me, this is the direction that I want to take. The UFC has been great, and I've done a lot in that arena. But I want a different challenge, to do something new and fresh."

"Look, son, don't give me that 'something new and fresh' stuff. It's gotta be more than that, right?"

Jun gave his father a look Dr. Zhang recognized from years of scolding his son whenever he misbehaved. It was a sheepish look of guilt that may have been spurred on by the fact that Dr. Zhang knew what Jun was up to.

"I spoke with my manager, and he said that I could make more money switching over to light heavyweight boxing," Jun confessed.

"So, Kim Li's been the one putting these ideas in your head. Boxing is limited to just using your fists and nothing else. No kicking, no grappling, nothing like that. Seems kind of inferior to MMA if you ask me," Dr. Zhang remarked.

"That's not the point, Dad. Kim is showing me the numbers. Do you know I'm only worth a million dollars right now, and I've fought over thirty fights? I could make twice as much per fight if I switch to pro boxing now."

"Every decision you make can't be based solely on money."

"You don't understand, Dad. I'm doing this for us too. Boxing is making waves, and they're still selling out fights in big arenas, and I could see the kind of payday that I wouldn't see if I stayed in one spot. I got to move around."

"So, moving around means putting yourself at risk trying to fight their game?"

"I know what it sounds like, but I'm ready for this new challenge. I've already scouted the talent they got there," Jun said smugly.

"And what if it fails? What if you get hurt?"

With pure determination, Jun's intense eyes locked in on his father's. "Trust me, nobody's gonna be able to touch me inside that ring."

One Year Later | As he drove to the Shaw-Dominique Community Center, or the SDCC, Sylvio Dominique rolled the windows of his Toyota Camry down. Normally, the weather would be unbearably cold, and the ground would be covered with snow or some type of dew that would frost overnight. Not today. Today was unusually warm for the month of February.

Six years removed from the historical middleweight championship fight versus Felipe Maximo, Sylvio finally felt the peace he hadn't felt in a long time. Doubts crossed his mind after his abrupt retirement from boxing at the age of twenty-two in the aftermath of his friend Omar Keaton's murder.

Boxing was all that Sylvio knew, and when he bowed out of the sport, he struggled to find his purpose in life. He knew he wanted to help others avoid the same mistakes he made as a young, brash boxer. He also wanted to give back to the people in his neighborhood and do anything he could to help the next generation. So, the plan was put in motion to build the SDCC, which he would co-own with Jim Shaw. After the community center was completed, the doors finally opened to the public, and the support Sylvio received was paramount.

After his retirement, the Showtime Network did reach out to him to appear as a guest analyst on their networks. Sylvio accepted the invitations and early on. He often re-appeared as a guest analyst, covering other boxers. But before long, Sylvio realized he was slowly being drawn back to boxing. The last decision he wanted to make was to return to the sport that nearly destroyed everything he held dear and almost took his life. Instead, he was content with managing the daily routines of the community center.

Sylvio re-enrolled in Queens College, taking online courses in sports management and organizational skills. He learned to use his celebrity to attract clientele and other residents to his center. To most people in the tri-state area, Sylvio was a draw, still signing autographs whenever he could.

Jim and his brother, Kevin, handled the financial books for the center, often aided by Sylvio's friend Gary Williams, who was a member of Sylvio's old boxing entourage, the Wolf Pack. Gary worked full-time at the community center as a boxing trainer.

Sylvio's childhood friend Alfred DeWitt, or "A.D." as he was known as throughout the neighborhood, worked there part-time. But A.D. was beginning to see opportunity in his budding career as a music producer and sound mixer and was getting calls from rap acts around the area. As a result, he barely had time to work at the center because he was working at gigs to support himself and his girlfriend, Monique Sinclair.

While working at the community center, Valentina, a graduate of the New York Film Academy, began to appear in commercials and small sketches on streaming services. Just recently, she'd received a call from her agent, Rosa Evans, stating that she was invited to audition for a role in a YouStream series being filmed in Atlanta, Georgia. Valentina flew down and auditioned for the role, and not only did she secure it, but she also became a regular character on the show. She still desired to work at the center, but with constant filming on her schedule, Sylvio, Jim, and Valentina had to hire a replacement interim director for her position over the drama program.

Yolanda Jennings interviewed for the job in front of Sylvio and Valentina, who watched her interview via Skype. Both were awed by Yolanda's charisma, charm, and energy with the young children. Much like Valentina, Yolanda studied drama, but she attended the University of Columbia, earning her bachelor's degree in sociology.

Aside from the regular criteria necessary for the position, Sylvio saw that Yolanda had another great trait. Standing at five-foot-seven with light brown skin and a toned figure, but with some curves as well, she was quite the eye candy. Therefore, Sylvio took great pleasure in gazing upon her and often found it difficult to concentrate whenever he was at the office and she walked by with a short skirt on warm days or leggings on cold days. Several thoughts would cross Sylvio's mind at the slightest glimpse of Yolanda as she made her way over to the theater. And sometimes, he was happy Valentina wasn't in New York because she might have had suspicions.

Yet, Sylvio kept it professional and did not attempt to make a move on Yolanda. The Wolf may have tried to play the game, but Sylvio was working on restraint and seemed content at just observing the drama director's beauty. His office was adjacent to the theater, so it was easy for him to survey it whenever Yolanda and the kids worked on a stage production. The community center already held two plays since its inception, with the most successful production being the rendition of Motown's "The Wiz." Valentina was still working there then, and she did such a masterful job directing the kids that it earned her standing ovations after each showtime.

But the main event came just a couple of months after the fireworks that took place in the Dante Shaw Boxing Gym.

The current middleweight champion, Barry Taylor, stormed SDCC to challenge Sylvio to a one-round sparring match. Sylvio, who had not fought in years, did everything he could to avoid fighting the younger boxer, but when his adversary continued deriding him,

Sylvio finally put his gloves on and proceeded to give Barry a lesson.

Barry managed to get a couple of headshots in, but Sylvio realized Barry was super raw with no concept of slipping jabs or ducking quick head shots. Sylvio kept the champion off balance with stinging jabs, which infuriated him, and when Barry went for the knockout and lunged forward, exposing his chin, Sylvio delivered a shot that sent him to the canvas.

Members of Barry's entourage scrambled to erase the tape and any footage of the current champ being knocked down by a retired former champ. Meanwhile, Barry sulked out of the gym while Sylvio once again had to dodge questions about a possible return to the ring. But he made it very clear. He was not going to fight ever again. It wasn't worth the risk.

Unbeknownst to anyone present that day, Sylvio's right hand swelled up after the shot to Barry's chin, so much so that he had to go to the doctor to have it examined. After applying medication for a few weeks, the swelling finally subsided, but it was yet another confirmation that Sylvio's time in the ring was over.

As he parked across the street, Sylvio saw a few kids heading into the center, but most were walking past it. To him, that seemed to be the first sign of trouble. SDCC had been slipping in terms of clientele as well as in employees and members. New York's price inflation certainly didn't make matters any easier for the community center, which had seen a decrease in attendance over the past couple of months. Sylvio knew that if the center's financial budget didn't clear within the next few months, they would end up losing it and would be forced to sell.

With those thoughts in mind, Sylvio got out of his car and strolled inside.

"Yo, Wolf, what's good, man?"

"Here comes da man!"

"Yo, lemme get a round wit' you real quick, Wolf!"

Boxing gym members greeted the ex-champ as he entered the building. "What's up, fellas? Yo' I'll holla at ya' later alright?" Sylvio replied as the members went back to the Dante Shaw Gym to continue working out.

Walking upstairs to the second floor, Sylvio looked inside the computer lab. To his dismay, it was empty. A few months back, there would have been a few kids in the lab studying the CISCO systems and learning computer technology. But for some weeks now, the seats had been routinely unoccupied.

Soon it won't be long until I sell the computers and use this as just a storage room. Sylvio turned off the light switch and closed the door before heading to his office.

"Hey, Mr. Dominique!" a female's voice called out.

Sylvio turned and saw Yolanda easing over to greet him, smiling warmly. "Hey, Yolanda, what's up? You just now coming in?" Duh, of course, she's just now coming in. Why are you asking a stupid question like that?

"Yeah, I always arrive about an hour before my drama students come in. I take the time to do some meditation and get my mind right before the day, you know?"

"Yeah, I feel you. I need to do some meditation myself, to be honest." Man, she looks beautiful in them snug jeans and that top. Come on, Sylvio, you got a girlfriend. Get yo' mind out the gutter. Fuck that...I can't. There are so many things I wanna do to her. I mean, it's been a long time since Val and I got down. I got needs.

"So, were you just in the computer room?" Yolanda asked, snapping Sylvio from his internal lustful battle.

"Yeah, I was," Sylvio replied. "Can't believe that room is empty again. At this point, I just think it's taking up useless space, and we ain't got money to keep things we ain't using. I was thinking about selling the computers and maybe turning that room into a larger dressing room for your students."

"That would be cool."

"Yeah, I'll keep you posted on that."

"Okay," Yolanda smiled.

They both stared at each other for a quick second before Sylvio broke their trance. "Anyway, I gotta get to the office. I'll catch ya' later," he said.

"Okay, bye!" Yolanda waved as she entered the theater.

Sylvio stared, longing for what he couldn't have.

Chapter 2

Opening her apartment door, Gabrielle stormed into her living room, and began to pace back and forth. Her boyfriend, Anthony, followed a few moments behind her. Gabrielle was beyond infuriated after discovering Anthony had been sleeping with other women behind her back. While accompanying her shopping at the mall, Anthony made the critical error of leaving his cell phone unattended as he was trying on a new pair of sneakers. Without warning, his phone vibrated. It was there that Gabrielle saw texts and picture messages sent to Anthony with details about his latest sexual romp.

The messages were enough to drive Gabrielle crazy with rage, but when Anthony returned to her side, she played it off and placed the phone back where he left it, leaving him unaware that his secret life had been exposed. After the silent—yet tense—car ride, Gabrielle was now back at the apartment they shared, although she wasn't sure how long he would be around after making the discovery.

"Baby, what's up? You been ignoring me since we got back from the mall. You wouldn't even tell me what you think of my new kicks," Anthony said.

But Gabrielle continued pacing and ignoring him for a few more moments before speaking. "So tell me, how long have you been seeing her, Tony?" she asked.

"Seeing who? I don't know who you talkin' about." Anthony pretended to be oblivious to Gabrielle's anger and resorted to deflection tactics.

"You know damn well who I'm talkin' about. Who the hell's Kamiya, and why you got her naked ass all up in yo' phone?"

"Hold up. You been checkin' out my phone behind my back?"

"I wouldn't have had to check nothin' if yo' side chick hadn't sent me pictures of her titties with messages about what went down wit' ya'll the other night."

"Okay look, baby. I know this looks real bad, but I can explain everything, okay?"

"I don't wanna hear nothin' you gotta say to me, okay? You think I'm out here being a ho' behind yo' back? Why would you do me like this?"

Anthony backed away from his fuming girlfriend and sat down on the couch, realizing he had been exposed.

"Look, Kamiya was just someone I met at work. We also work out at the same gym. It wasn't supposed to go down the way it did, but she called me ova' to her crib. Said she needed help moving some heavy furniture. Then one thing led to another and..." he paused, unable to finish his explanation.

This was the pause Gabrielle was waiting for to confirm Anthony's guilt. "I mean, what was it, Tony? Was it them tight-ass leggings that she was rockin' at the gym?"

"Nah, it wasn't nothin' like that. I swear...I had no idea Kamiya was a freak like that."

"You mean a freak like you?" Gabrielle bit back. "I can't believe you would sleep wit' her behind my back. I mean, what does she have that I don't have?"

Anthony got up from the chair. It was time for him to go on the offensive side of the argument. "Okay, you really wanna know what she got? She's real chill, and she listens to what I gotta say. I ain't gotta jump through no hoops to prove nothin' to her. You're always testing me. Every time you go somewhere, I gotta roll wit' you, just like that sip and paint event last weekend. I ain't even wanna go, and you still dragged my ass over to it."

"So, your solution was to see somebody else behind my back? Just to satisfy yo' weak ass ego? You ain't shit! You know that?"

"Okay, fine. You got me. Is that what you wanted to hear? I don't deserve a girl like you, right? You used to the high-end life—never had to struggle for nothing. You don't know what it's like for me, and you know why? You never bothered to find out what kind of man you got."

"You're so right, and you know what? Guess now I'll never know."

"Wait, what you sayin'?" Anthony asked.

"I'm sayin' that we through, Tony. Apparently Kamiya knows her way around you better than I do, so you two are perfect for each other."

Gabrielle began to walk to her room, but suddenly Anthony snatched her arm from behind. "Don't leave me now, Gabby. I need you. Look, I know I fucked up, okay? But let's not overreact. I got a lot goin' on in my life right now, and I need you by my side."

"Don't you mean, you need Kamiya by yo' side? I mean, it wasn't my ass that was on that picture message. So let me go!" Gabrielle struggled to free herself from Anthony's tight grip on her arm.

"Not till you say you forgive me," Anthony replied angrily.

"I said, 'Let go of me!'" Gabrielle demanded, trying to snatch from his grasp, but Anthony was not letting his girlfriend go easily.

Dragging her to their bedroom, he tossed her onto the bed. "You could've made this easy. Instead, you decided to make it hard for yourself. So, I'm gonna give you a choice," Anthony said grimly, opening a dresser drawer.

To Gabrielle's horror, he pulled out a small handgun.

"We could let this whole thing go. I'll break it off with Kamiya, and we could get down like we used to," Anthony said, pointing the gun at Gabrielle's head.

Terrified and nervous, Gabrielle began to cry. She was looking insanity and death in the face. "So, you gon' shoot me now, Tony? Is that it?"

"If I can't have you, I don't think anyone else can. I'm sorry you saw those pictures on my phone. I made a terrible mistake, but I could be a better man if you give me a chance."

The last image Gabrielle had of her boyfriend was a depiction of a roving madman brandishing a deadly weapon to prove his point. "And I ain't even got a choice in the matter?" Gabrielle was sobbing and hoping her life wasn't about to end in the apartment.

"Afraid not, Gabby. I neva' wanted it to go down this way, but you forced my hand. I got a rep to maintain, you know. Mama always told me never hurt a woman, but I will kill a bitch if I have to." Anthony exuded pure insanity.

Suddenly, a loud voice yelled, "CUT! Alright, folks, that's a wrap! Great scene, guys!" said the director, Anderson Jacobs, as the other actors, cameramen, and producers clapped their hands, snapping Valentina Cruz out of character.

Wiping the tears from her eyes, Valentina stood up from the bed and hugged her co-star, Robert Yates, who played her psychotic and unhinged boyfriend, Anthony Jenks, while she portrayed the young, resourceful but impressionable, Gabrielle Flores. Together, they were lead stars in a new drama series titled "You Thought You Had Me," which aired on YouStream, a new cable streaming service that aired new soap operas, sitcoms, and movies.

It was Valentina's first major role in a recurring drama series, and they had just completed their fifth episode. For years, Valentina had been cast in commercials and small movie parts while also working at SDCC with her boyfriend, Sylvio, and his old trainer, Jim. She was extremely thankful that Sylvio was supportive of her dreams. He helped her hire Rosa Evans, who had been working relentlessly to book Valentina for auditions in different movie projects and shows.

Valentina caught a break when Rosa called her to audition for Anderson and other producers and writers of an upcoming suspense drama series. Although the auditions were held in Los Angeles, the series was filmed in Peachtree Studios in Atlanta. Valentina auditioned and left feeling good about her performance, but she remembered the scores of women that showed up to the audition, and although she held out hope she would secure the role, she had her doubts.

But one morning, Rosa called her, stoked to share the news that Valentina had been selected to play Gabrielle. Valentina was truly beside herself. She'd studied for years at the New York Film Academy. Her hard work had finally paid off. She flew down to Atlanta where she met the other stars of the show during the first table read.

Robert was one of her favorite actors. He had appeared in other movie projects and sitcoms and was a veteran in theater. As hard as he worked to play an antagonist in the series, Robert was the opposite of his alter ego, Anthony. After filming an episode, Robert would spend hours helping Valentina and the other castmates understand the nuances of acting and getting into character.

Valentina was very pleased that the series was paying a princely sum of about $900,000 per episode, and it was already trending in social media. There were many instances where she would walk downtown, and people from all walks of life were approaching her to get an autograph and take selfies with her.

Those experiences made Valentina grateful that she worked on her goal and ignored all her doubters. She often recalled how much attention Sylvio received from his boxing career and recalled times where they would be at dinner and people would ask him for autographs. These days, she would chuckle to herself upon thinking that now it was her turn to be the celebrity in the relationship. However, her budding career was not without its challenges.

Due to the hectic filming schedule, Valentina had to move to Atlanta, where she rented an apartment downtown, near the Four Corners. The apartment, located on the 30th floor, had a great view of the Atlanta skyline, especially at night. But Valentina felt lonely there and often wished Sylvio was sharing it with her. They video-messaged each other religiously, and she was delighted to hear that Sylvio was a fan of the show. Often, they discussed the previous episodes that aired, while also discussing Sylvio's day at SDCC.

The final scene of the fifth episode was filmed in a high-end apartment facing Peachtree Studios across the street. After greeting everybody on set, Valentina made her way outside to cross the street so she could go inside her dressing room. She was also anxious to call Sylvio via Skype. She had just made it to her dressing room when she felt the sensation that she was being followed.

Instinctively, she turned around and saw that it was Robert, smiling at her.

Valentina breathed a sigh of relief. "Rob, are you following me? You just as psychotic as Anthony," she joked, as she opened her dressing room.

"Nah, I can't be nowhere near that level of crazy. To keep it one-hunnid, I don't even like guns like that," he replied.

"See, that's what I respect about you. I would've neva' known that if I just seen you on the show."

"That's what all my friends be sayin' all the time," Robert laughed. "But anyway, since we wrapped early, Sal, Asia, Paul, and I were goin' to the city to grab a bite to eat. You down?"

"I wish, but I gotta call my boyfriend in New York. You know, I gotta check up on my man," Valentina replied. "Where ya goin' though?"

"I don't know. We were feelin' somewhere between Chinese food or pizza."

"Yeah, better roll with the Chinese food cuz I'm extra picky about my pizza. And we don't play when it comes to pasta in New York."

"Here we go with the New York comparisons again," Robert laughed. "Come on, girl, you gotta open your mind down here. This is the South, baby. I'mma convert you one of these days."

"Yeah, good luck wit' that. I'm a New Yorker till I die, feel me? Anyway, bring me back some chow mein or something. I gotta go call Sylvio."

Robert stuck his hand out. "Um, ain't you gon' give me the money to buy you chow mein?"

"Nah, can't you buy it for me? I thought ya was on that Southern hospitality tip. Where that hospitality at?"

"Oh, you got jokes? Aight, I got you this time, but you payin' up next time," Robert said as he exited the dressing room.

After he left, Valentina took out her MacBook laptop and opened Skype to call Sylvio. After three rings, she finally saw his image populate on her screen. "Hey, baby, what's up?" she cooed as her boyfriend adjusted his screen for a clearer picture.

"Chillin' like a villain, you know. Wishin' you were next to me right now," Sylvio replied.

"Aww, me too, baby, but I'm mad busy right now. They got me filming six days a week. There's supposed to be twelve episodes this season, and we've only finished episode five so far."

"Damn, that's crazy. But I see you doin' yo' thing though. I'm feelin' Gabrielle, but I think she can do better than Anthony. Dude is way too smooth. Either he runnin' game on her, or he low-key crazy. Can't wait for the next episode to come out."

"Oh, trust me, shit gets deep next episode. You got no idea!"

"Oh word? What happens next episode?" Sylvio asked.

"Uh-uh. You know I can't spoil it now. You just gon' have to tune in," Valentina teased.

"Oh you gon' do me like that? But I'm yo' man though. I don't get no preferential treatment?"

"Come on, Sylvio. I don't even tell my brothers what's gon' happen next."

"I feel you. How are your brothers doing?"

"They're good. I think they're hella happy to get outta New York since things got hot with them and the Serps," Valentina explained, referring to her ex-gangbanger brothers, Juan and Bruno Cruz, who were both associated with the 85th Street Serps.

The gang had been working in covert gambling operations, coercing, maiming, and even killing violators or people they perceived to be a threat to their operation. It was the Serps that took the life of Sylvio's friend, Omar, and they had an insider in Sylvio's boxing circle that turned out to be none other than Sylvio's longtime friend Kyle Green.

But karma soon caught up to Kyle. Right after Omar's death, Kyle was found dead a week later. Two members of the Serps, along with the gang leader Pedro Quinones, were charged for the murders and sentenced to life in prison. Without Pedro's firm leadership, the gang disbanded. It was later discovered that Bruno and Juan turned on the Serps and acted as informants for law enforcement to bring down the rest of the operation.

Unfortunately, the Cruz brothers were targeted by the other free members. After receiving death threats, they finally packed up and moved to Miami Beach. Sylvio, with the help of Jim, was able to provide Juan and Bruno some money to start their new lives in Florida. To Sylvio, it was a token of gratitude towards the Cruz brothers because if they hadn't frantically returned to warn their sister of the planned hit on him, he would've died the evening after winning the belt.

"Glad to hear they're doing good," Sylvio replied. "Damn, I miss you, girl. I'm so tense from all this work. What I wouldn't give for a good shoulder and neck massage right now."

"Hmmm, I think you want more than just a massage." Valentina laughed because she knew what massaging Sylvio normally led into: intense sex.

"You ain't lyin'. You got 'dem hands of magic, girl. But I got some magic of my own for you too now," Sylvio chuckled.

"You got a freaky mind, baby. It's way too early in the day to be this horny."

"Sorry, can't help it. You know I'm always gon' be a wolf. It's part of the territory. One day, I'm gonna fly down to the A, and put it on you. You can believe that."

Valentina covered her mouth as she tried to stifle her laughter. *Sylvio can be so lame sometimes.*

Sylvio laughed before letting out a yawn.

"Are you sure you okay, baby? You look tired."

"I'm good, Val. Just got more work than usual at the center."

"Yo, I miss the center so much. Sometimes I wish I could go back and work with the kids. How's Yolanda doin' though?"

"Oh, she holdin' it down for you, Val. No doubt, girl's got some acting skills. You better hold on to that Gabrielle role cuz she could be comin' for your job," Sylvio cracked.

"Whatever. I seriously doubt that. Them kids know that I'm still runnin' thangs up there. Yolanda's a nice girl or whatever, but she can't outdo or out-class yo' girl, you feel me?"

"Damn, Val, head's swole a bit much? You've only been runnin' for five episodes. Get a season under you first. Then talk smack," Sylvio laughed.

"Shut up, boy! Anyway, how's Jim doing?" Valentina asked.

"Well, you know the old man. He could never stay away from the fight game. He trainin' young pups at Dante Shaw Gym downstairs."

"I guess he's trying to make more Sylvio Dominiques, huh?"

The question struck Sylvio like a dart. Whether rhetorical or not, he did not want any of the young boxers to endure what he had to endure during his career. It was true that Jim couldn't stay away from teaching the game, but he could offer alternatives to the kids. There were other avenues of education in the center.

"It's not that I'm discouraged by what he's doin', but I wish these kids were more into technology, books, and other things. I just walked by the computer lab, and it was empty for the sixth week in a row," Sylvio said.

Valentina sensed the discouragement in her boyfriend's voice. "Really?"

"Yeah, it's getting to the point where I feel like just scrappin' the lab and selling the computers. I mean, why waste money on systems that ain't being used?"

"Sylvio, you sure you want to do that?"

"I don't know. It's just an idea. I'm gonna review our finances with Kevin in a few days. If we can clear our budget, maybe the lab stays. But if we come up short, we gon' have to cut back somehow."

"I got you. Anyway, I gotta log off, baby. Sounds like the gang came back with my food. I'll holla at you lata'." Valentina logged off before Robert returned with her lunch.

A few hours after his video chat with Valentina, Sylvio walked downstairs to visit the Dante Shaw Boxing Gym. Named after Jim's late son, it was an indoor boxing haven for young up-and-coming pugilists and trainers. Adorned with street art murals of famed boxers such as Rocky Marciano, Sugar Ray Robinson, Muhammad Ali, and Mike Tyson, the gym was never short of potentials who walked in to receive training from experienced managers and cornermen. Although he was part owner of the SDCC, Jim Shaw could be found in the gym training other young boxers. Sure enough, as Sylvio opened the gym doors, he found his old trainer working hard at his craft.

"All right now. One, two, one two...gimme two jabs!" Jim barked out to a boxer, appearing no older than sixteen years of age. Holding a glove pad in both hands, Jim absorbed the boy's punches.

"Good work. Now gimme two hooks to the body."

The boy listened and delivered two crisp hook punches to the glove pads.

"Use your hips, man. Put more power behind them hooks," Sylvio said, smiling as he approached.

Jim turned around after hearing Sylvio's advice. "What's up, Wolf?" Greeting Sylvio, Jim shook his hand.

"Not much, partner. Just workin' and maintaining. Who you workin' with today?" Sylvio asked.

"Oh, my bad, lemme introduce ya'. Sylvio, this is Kwame Turner. Kwame, I think you know who this is," Jim said as Kwame took one of his gloves off to shake Sylvio's hand excitedly.

"No doubt, B.! The Wolf of Queens, Sylvio Dominique! Former middleweight champ...it's definitely an honor, man!" Kwame exclaimed.

"Take five, Kwame. I'mma holla at my man real quick," Jim instructed as Kwame went to search for his water bottle. "So, what's crackin' man?" he asked Sylvio.

"Shit, nothin' much. Stay workin'. You know how it is."

"You ain't never lied. How's Val doin'?

"She's good, man. You know, still workin' on the show, getting' her Hollywood on. You ain't check the show out yet? She all ova' YouStream, man."

"Man, you know I ain't got time fo' all that."

"Come on, why you buggin', man? You know, one day I'mma put you on to that show. Best believe that."

"I ain't got time for all that trash on TV anyway. In case you ain't noticed, a brotha's been a lil' occupied lately," Jim explained slyly.

"Occupied? What you been doin'? Lemme find out that you actually got a life outside of the gym, old man!"

"You betta' watch it, boy. I ain't too old to whip yo' ass."

"Alright, so what's her name?"

Jim shook his head. "How do you know it's a woman?"

"Cuz I know these things, bro. It don't take rocket science to figure that out," Sylvio laughed as he jokingly threw his arm around Jim's shoulder.

There were moments when Sylvio didn't look at Jim as just his trainer or his friend, but as a father figure he lacked during his younger years.

Realizing that Sylvio would not budge, Jim finally cracked. "Okay, her name's Charlene, alright? We met at Key Food a few weeks ago when I was in the produce section. Fine lookin' thing too."

"Did you go for cucumber or eggplant?" Sylvio asked mischievously, hoping Jim would get the inappropriate innuendo.

"Eggplant," Jim replied as they both laughed.

"I'm tellin' you, Wolf, she was bad. She had a body like you wouldn't know, and she's into sports too. She was talkin' about all yo' fights."

"I'm impressed, Jim. At yo' age, you still pullin' chicks? I gotta give you props, man. Yo' brother was tellin' me how you was the man back in dem days. Looks like you still got it."

"I've been had it, youngblood. I was a wolf before you was even an embryo, son."

"Oh, you gonna go there? You gon' put our age into this? I don't think you wanna take it there, Jim," Sylvio laughed. "So, what ya got planned?"

"Well, I got two tickets for the 'Raisin in the Sun' show on Broadway this weekend. Turns out, she loves theater too."

"That's what's up, man. Yo' on the real, I'm happy for you, Jim.

I hope it works out."

"Yeah, it's good that I got more time to hang with her since I don't have to train any big-headed boxers anymore," Jim replied subliminally.

"Whatever, old man. You miss the old days. Admit it. Hell, I ain't afraid to admit it. Walking in here always brings back them memories. But that was all in the past. Gotta look ahead now. I'll catch you later," Sylvio said, leaving.

After finishing a day at the gym, Jim returned to his one bedroom flat in Woodhaven, Queens. Taking his shoes off, he pressed the button on his answering machine to listen to his voice messages. *Damn credit card scammers.* The machine played one pointless message after another.

Taking a whiff of his armpits, he recoiled in disgust. Twenty minutes and a shower later, Jim re-emerged from the bathroom and made his way to the bedroom, when he heard a knock on his door. Staring at the clock, he realized it was ten minutes after eleven in the evening.

Who's knocking this late at night? He walked over to look at the peephole. Maybe it's Charlene. She might have left something when she was here the other night, or it might even be Kevin. Better not be Sylvio.

Among all other pet peeves that Sylvio knew about Jim, one was that he hated being disturbed late at night. But upon staring at the peephole, Jim couldn't believe his eyes as he unlocked the door to face his surprise visitor. It wasn't Charlene or Kevin. It wasn't even Sylvio.

Chapter 3

As Jim opened the door to welcome his surprise visitor, there was no denying his astonishment. In his front doorway was a woman standing about five-foot-six with a light skin tone and complete business casual mode: a dress shirt with a black blazer complete with a knee-length skirt. She would have been a welcome sight for many men, but Jim was struck with suspicion because he knew her all too well.

It was none other than his ex-wife, Natalie Brown. The previous time they had stood face to face was more than twenty years ago when she walked out on him after the tragic death of their son, Dante. Yet, there she was, causing Jim to have a rush of mixed emotions.

"Natalie?" he asked blankly, as if he expected her to be a mirage.

"Hey, Jim, how are you? It's been a long time—"

"Twenty-two years, to be exact. What you doin' here?" Jim interjected sternly, cutting her off.

Natalie hung her head for a moment, albeit a very quick moment. "Mind if I come in?"

Jim was visited by the urge to kick the woman who broke his heart off his doorstep, but he decided that it wasn't worth the trouble. "Yeah, sure. Come in. Make yourself at home," he said, inviting her inside his flat.

"Not bad, Jim. This place is really you," Natalie said, looking around.

"Yeah, I know it ain't much, but you know me. I was never the one for all the flash," Jim said.

"You sure wasn't. You were always down to earth. That's what I liked about you," Natalie said as she sat down on Jim's couch.

"Um, so don't take this the wrong way, but how did you know where I stayed at?" Jim asked.

"Well, your brother was never great at keepin' secrets," Natalie replied.

Jim shook his head. *Kevin. Boy, I can't wait to get my hands on him. Fool had the audacity to tell my ex-wife where I live and didn't even tell me she was coming.* But Jim kept his thoughts to himself because he knew he had to play this scenario out. "Well, since you came to visit, would you like something to drink?"

"Yeah, I'd like that. Thank you."

Jim went to the fridge. *What do I have in here?* He had some bottles of water, juice, and a couple bottles of red wine for the nights he and Charlene shared. Shrugging, he grabbed one of the bottles, took out two glasses, and poured the wine. Walking over to Natalie, he handed her a glass.

"I don't remember much these days, but I do remember that you had a fine taste for red wine," he said as Natalie took a sip.

"Mmmm, you ain't lyin'. So, you mean to tell me that you been by yourself all this time, and you just happen to have a bottle of Sutter House wine in your fridge? So, I see you've moved on. She must be pretty fine," Natalie said furtively.

Jim wasn't playing her game. "Okay, but you never fully answered my question. Why'd you come back, Natalie? Why now, after so long?"

"I can't just drop by and visit my ex-husband and friend?"

"Do you know how many times I called you after you left me in '96, begging you to come back? All the voice messages and the letters I sent you, and you ain't answered not one of them," Jim said, and realizing how high his temper rose at times, he paused to take a sip of wine to calm himself down.

"Jim, I know this visit is random, and I'm so sorry I left you hanging all these years, but I really was an emotional wreck after our son's death," Natalie confessed.

"And I wasn't? Dante's death tore me up inside. You don't think I was hurtin' too?"

"I never told you this, but after I left you, I went to seek therapy and grief counseling for years. Those sessions made me realize that Dante's death wasn't your fault. I blamed you unfairly for months, and I've stayed away. But I got the help that I needed, and I wanted to offer you the same help," Natalie replied.

"I'm handling it day by day, okay? I don't need help from any counselor or any therapy session," Jim said firmly.

"Hmm, is that why month by month, you go back to P.S. 11 and walk the grounds? Alienating everyone that you grew up with? Or is that why you're passing by various schools picking up bullied kids and takin' them to your gym because your guilt won't allow you to let go?"

Jim knew Natalie was right, but she knew more than he expected. "Ain't there anything Kevin didn't tell you?"

"He didn't have to tell me, Jim. I know you. I know that you wear your emotions on your sleeve, and I know how you cope with pain. You immerse yourself in this boxing, hoping that it can massage your guilt away."

"What, you a therapist now?"

"As a matter of fact, I am one." Natalie handed Jim her business card. "My office is in Yonkers. I used my experiences to help others heal after tragedy."

"Well, as I've told you before, I don't need help. I'm fine."

Natalie stood up from the couch and walked over to a shelf that contained Jim's amateur boxing trophies as well as old photos and pictures of himself and Sylvio during his boxing tenure. Natalie was particularly interested in the photo of Jim and Sylvio. "He's a nice-looking boy. Is he the new Boom?"

Jim chuckled at the mention of his old nickname. "I ain't heard anybody call me that in years, since I stopped fighting. But he went by the name 'Wolf.' He's accomplished a lot in the fight game."

"Yeah, I know. Sometimes, I would order a fight and watch him. He moves just like you used to in that ring. I even watched his title match with Maximo. You've done an excellent job molding him in your image, Boom. Seeing the success that he had was another reason that I wanted to come visit," Natalie confessed.

"Look, if you came to hop onto the Sylvio Dominique gravy train, you late by about six years."

"I know. I saw his announcement when he retired from boxing, and I couldn't help but have a feeling of déjà vu. You were young when you stepped out of the ring too," Natalie pointed out.

"Yeah, but he had his reasons. Someone almost took him out, and I was nearly too late." Jim turned his head as a tear fell from his eye. "I almost had another Dante in my hands. I supported Sylvio's decision to step out of the ring, even if he took a lot of flack for it."

Natalie placed her hand on Jim's shoulder. "It's okay. You were a great father to Dante when he was alive, and you are a great mentor and father figure to Sylvio. But you can't save all these kids, Jim. Not everyone needs your help, and one day, you might find yourself in over your head. I'm not trying to tell you how to run your life, but I sense that these school wanderings and picking up kids and taking them to the gym is a psychological response to your grief."

"Why are you so hung up on what I'm doing on my time? You have your way of healing, and I have mine," Jim shrugged.

While Natalie was looking at the shelf, her eyes fell upon another picture. "Oh my God, you still have this?" she asked, holding a photo of herself and Jim with a couple other boys that was taken during the early 1980s.

"Yeah, that was a couple months after we first met." Jim smiled at the photo. "There goes Tavion's goofy ass, and Alan's there too. Man, we were thick as thieves back in dem days," he reflected.

"Look at the clothes we had on. And look at my hair! We swear we looked fly back in dem days," Natalie said, laughing.

"Yeah, I still ain't forgotten that lil' headband phase you was on for about a year," Jim laughed.

"Oh my God, that headband. Lookin' back at it, that was definitely a fail. Don't judge me, okay? Everybody was rockin' that Lisa Lisa look back in those days. Let's not forget your lil' Cameo/Big Daddy Kane look. You was workin' that high top box fade to death, remember?" Natalie shot back, laughing.

"Hey, I won't front. I was bent on keepin' my joint fresh every day. Tavion eventually had them Jheri curls, and he was over-greasing that joint. Shit was so slick, I thought he was gon' cause car accidents with all the grease that was drippin' on the streets," Jim laughed.

At that moment, all the awkward tension flew out the window

as Jim and Natalie continued browsing old photos.

Jim took out an album that he kept in storage in his closet and opened the cover. There were pictures of his mother, Janice, and Kevin. There were no pictures of Jim's father. He had been locked up for much of Jim's childhood.

"But before we had all our styles, we were just three nappy-headed boys from Fort Greene just tryin' to find ourselves."

"Do you remember the first day we met? Of course, you weren't a pro yet back then," Natalie smirked.

"Nah, I wasn't. But I was building up my rep. 'Boom' was on his way," Jim replied as he reflected on the day that he met Natalie Brown. It was also the day that he almost lost everything.

Thirty-Six Years Earlier | It was summertime in Brooklyn, New York. That day was recorded as one of the hottest of the whole year. Fire hydrants were turned on as kids ran under the cool waves, showering themselves under the spray. Kids played hopscotch on the pavement and jumped rope. The older boys were at the parks playing basketball or enjoying other amenities there. It was a joyful day for a town that had otherwise been inflicted with urban blight and poverty.

Government policy and low wages rendered many adults unemployed, and searching for outlets, some began to deal and use drugs. There was always fear of gangs, crime, and robbery in certain areas, but to 14-year-old Jim Shaw, it was home.

Walking from the park with Tavion Graham and Alan Rollins, Jim was counting the money he'd earned from his bare-knuckled boxing exhibition in the park. Growing up in the boarding house projects on DeKalb Avenue, Jim discovered he had quick hands. With no father raising him, he took the mantle of being the man of his family, working part time at the corner bodega store. In the hood, kids always tested each other's mettle, so Jim learned to defend himself and his brother by knocking down any assailant that came at him or his friends.

Having been bullied before, Jim watched old boxing tapes and would often shadow box on his own. He wasn't very tall or strong, but he was resourceful and always discovered ways to protect himself. Recently, he had been looking for a challenge and boldly, perhaps unwisely, he placed a bounty on his own head, challenging any kid in the city to a three-minute boxing session. If they won, he would have to pay them five dollars. If he won, the loser would pay him double that amount, and to date, Jim had not yet lost. The extra money he earned fighting helped buy food for another few days.

Jim's reputation grew, and throughout middle school, kids feared the boy whom they called "Boom" since it was exactly what he guaranteed: to drop any challenger who stepped before him. Emerging from the park after knocking down a kid named Alvin Waters with two punches, Jim was counting the spoils.

"Ayo, put that shit away, son. I ain't tryin' to get jacked out here," Tavion said, nervously eyeing the money.

"Ten bucks, my nigga. That makes fifteen. I need more bustas to fight," Jim bragged confidently as they approached the intersection.

"What you need to do is chill wit' this boxing, man. What if you challenge somebody and they come at you wit' a gatt?" Alan asked.

"Man, scared money don't make no money. I made it clear on my challenge. No weapons, just using yo' fists, and it's just a couple minutes. It ain't like I'm wasting their time," Jim said.

The three boys turned on Dekalb Avenue, when they suddenly heard a melody coming from an ice cream truck. Jim turned to his friends. "Mr. Softee just got hea'. Ya' got money?"

"Nah, I'm broke as a joke, man. Anyway, you the money maker. We should be askin' you to buy something for us," Tavion replied smartly.

"Alright, cool. What you want?" Jim asked, as he was about to jog toward the direction of the truck, knowing if he didn't arrive in time, the ice cream man would drive away. He didn't like to stay in the neighborhood too long.

"Get me a chocolate blast," Alan replied.

"What you want, Tay?"

"Get me a strawberry shortcake cone."

"That don't surprise me. You look like a fruit cup," Jim joked, pointing at Tavion's multicolored, striped shirt.

"Fuck you, man. Just get my shit," Tavion replied laughing.

So sensitive. Jim ran to the block where he heard the music. But he wasn't the only one who heard it. Scores of kids were making their way over to the truck. Rushing to beat them there and make it to the front of the line, Jim bumped into a girl who was right in front of him. She lost her footing and fell down, sending nickels, quarters, and dimes flying everywhere.

"Oh no...look what you made me do!" the girl said as she began to scramble to pick up her loose change.

Feeling a pang of remorse, Jim stayed back to help her catch the coins before they rolled into the gutters. "I'm sorry. I didn't see you there," he apologized before looking up.

Upon seeing the girl's face for the first time, Jim was transfixed. She appeared to be about fourteen years old with brown eyes and light skin, and she was wearing denim shorts with Chuck Taylors and a shirt that she tied as a midriff, exposing her belly button.

"Hello, can you hear me? I said I got it," she said, snapping Jim back to reality.

"Oh, right," he finally replied as he watched her continue to pick up the change.

"Great, I lost a couple quarters. Now I don't have enough money to get a cone," she sighed.

Jim hung his head in guilt. He wanted to make it up to her. "Hey, look I'm really sorry about that. I got some money. I'll buy you what you want."

The girl's face lit up. "Really?"

"Yeah, it ain't nothin'. I got you."

"Wow, thanks. I'll pay you back."

"Don't worry about it. Um, my name's J-Jim by the way," he stammered. Great, the one time I see a beautiful chick, and I babble like a mindless idiot. She probably thinks I'm stupid.

But, thankfully, the girl didn't tease him. "My name's Natalie."

"I ain't seen you around hea' before. You just moved to Brooklyn?"

"Yeah, I just moved here from Mount Vernon."

"Word, from all the way there? That's cool. So, what high school you gon' be goin' to?"

"Brooklyn Tech."

"Seriously? That's where I'm goin' too. Maybe we have the same class or something."

As they made their way over to the ice cream truck, Jim and Natalie talked about their families and their hobbies. They managed to arrive at the truck right on time, and as they emerged from the throng of kids still waiting on their cones, Jim held his own sprinkled vanilla ice cream with two other cones for his friends, as he walked back up Dekalb Street.

Natalie eyed Jim curiously as she ate her chocolate ice cream. "Are you gonna eat all of those by yourself?"

"Oh, nah. These are for my boys. They ova there waitin'," Jim replied, gesturing to his two impatient friends.

"Damn, man, it's about time," Tavion said when Jim and Natalie approached them. "Gimme that. Look see, it's meltin' all up in ya hand now," he said, taking his cone, before he finally saw Natalie. "Yo, what's up, girl? Who you be?" he asked, winking at her, but it became clear that Natalie was turned off by Tavion's catcalling tactics.

"Yo, Natalie, don't mind these two buttheads ova' hea'. This is Alan, and this is Tavion," Jim introduced.

"Nice to meet you. Hey, Jim, I gotta get back home, but thanks again for the cone. Maybe we'll run into each other at school," Natalie said, waving as she turned back to head home.

The three boys watched her walk back across the street. "Damn, mack daddy. No wonder you took so long to get back. You was out here trying to get your pimp on," Alan laughed.

"Man, it ain't even like that. I bumped into her by accident, and she lost her money, so I bought a cone to make it up to her. Don't mean nothin'," Jim said.

"Okay sure...right. Whatever. I'd like to bump into her too. Only it wouldn't be an accident...you know what I'm sayin'?" Tavion laughed and fist-bumped Alan.

Jim didn't find it humorous. "Yo', chill, son," he said, serious.

"What's up wit' you? A nigga was just playin', man. You act like you gon' marry this chick or somethin'. Man, don't let a ho make a ho outta you. You da Boom, baby. Gotta be harder than that."

As they walked, Alan said, "Yo', Jim, while you were getting the ice cream, we heard dat fool Grant Butler bumpin' his gums, talkin' mess about you. He wanna take you up on that challenge."

Jim turned to face Alan. "Grant Butler? Tall, lanky ass lookin' muthafucka? Somebody need to tell him to quit while he ahead. He don't need to be fightin' me. I need someone worth my time."

"Yeah, but he issued the challenge. Can't back down now. You still got a rep," Tavion said.

After finishing his cone, Jim asked, "Where he at?"

A small crowd gathered at Fort Greene public park where Jim made his way to go toe to toe with Grant Butler. Grant was over six-foot-two as an eighth grader and virtually towered over all his peers, but Jim knew full well that although Grant was taller than he was, it didn't necessarily make him a threat in any form or fashion.

As soon as he saw Jim and his friends, Grant started laughing with the throng that accompanied him. "Yo', that's him? This is the guy ya call 'Boom'? He don't look like nothin' to me," he bragged as Jim approached. Grant was either ignorant of Jim's reputation, or he just wanted to talk to save face.

"Grant, look, man. Obviously, you must be new to the game, so I'm gon' tell you what's up. We go at it for three minutes, straight boxing, no kicks or low blows. If you beat me, I'll pay you five bucks. If I beat you, you pay me ten. Got it?" Jim's jaw was taut as he waited for his opponent's reply.

"Whateva', man. Let's go to the grass so you'll have something soft to land on after I drop you."

Warily following Grant, Jim looked around for any signs of law enforcement. During his challenges, he had been successful in keeping the encounters brief and discreet as to not draw attention to himself. But Grant seemed hell-bent on centering the entire situation around his perceived success.

As soon as they got onto the grass, Grant struck Jim with a closed fist just above Jim's eyebrow. It came exceedingly quick, and Jim was not fully prepared for the punch. The crowd gasped at Grant's quickness on the first punch, and they were convinced he would hurt the young upstart. But although Jim was struck in the face, he did not drop to the ground. When he placed his hand over his eye, he saw that Grant had drawn blood.

With his fists still up, Grant began taunting Jim in front of the crowd. "See, I told ya he ain't ready for this."

But Jim's heart was pumping with adrenaline. Now he was bent on destroying Grant. Jim lunged at his opponent, responding with a punch to the gut and then Grant's right cheekbone. Grant doubled over in pain, but Jim did not intend to let up on his retaliation. He continued striking Grant over and over in his face and chest area, capitalizing on his opponent's poor lateral movement.

After blackening Grant's eye, Jim continued applying body shots to Grant's chest. "I don't hear you talkin' now!" Jim taunted as he punched Grant uncontrollably.

But when Jim struck Grant just above his heart, Grant's eyes widened, and his body started convulsing. "Yo', man, what's wrong with you?" Jim asked when Grant's body doubled over, and he began foaming at the mouth as he fell to the grass. Jim suddenly heard blaring sirens.

"Yo', let's go. Five-O 'bout to roll up," Tavion warned.

A wave of fear swept over Jim, and he backed away from Grant. *If he dies, I'm responsible.* "Come on...let's go," Jim said as he quickly ushered Tavion and Alan away from the park.

A few hours later at the Carnasie Boys Detention Center, Jim paced back and forth inside his isolated room. After witnessing

Grant's spastic episode, Jim and his friends had retreated to Alan's house, but it didn't take long for police to track Jim down because of his reputation in the neighborhood. And in less than thirty minutes, he was placed under arrest and was on his way to the detention center.

Rubbing his sore knuckles, Jim was in a state of helplessness, as he found himself in the very predicament he swore he wouldn't end up in, and that was police custody. He could only imagine what his mother would say once the news got out in the streets about his arrest.

With his father already incarcerated, there would be talks that the apple did not fall far from the tree. In people's minds, since Jim's father was a criminal, it would only be a matter of time until his offspring fell into the same trap. Reaching into his pockets, which were now empty, Jim knew that once he managed to get out of the detention center, he would need to search new ways of making money. He could no longer do the boxing challenge, and he couldn't help his mother with the bills based only on his paycheck from the corner store. Then, once word spread about his arrest, there was no guarantee that he would remain employed there. He would most likely be fired, and without the second income, Jim's family would be at risk of getting evicted from their apartment.

I could always join the dope game. It's not like I'll be using it anyway. I'll just sell it. Quick money and no one has to know...

While those thoughts ran in Jim's mind, an officer opened the door to his cell. "Shaw, you're going home. Let's go." The officer gestured Jim out of the closed cell and out into the lobby.

Jim half-expected to see the disappointed look on his mother's eyes in the detention center, but to his astonishment, his mother was not the one waiting for him. Instead, a middle-aged, stocky black man stood up and greeted him.

"Jim Shaw?" he asked.

"Who wants to know?" Jim asked suspiciously, as the man signed his release forms.

"Your mother sent me here to bail you out. Let's go," he said as he and Jim walked out of the detention center and down to the man's car, parked nearly two blocks from the detention center.

"Who are you?" Jim asked.

"Name's Flip Timothy, son. I work at the same office with your mother. After she heard of your arrest, she asked me to come spring you."

What the hell kind of name is Flip? "Why? I don't even know you."

"But I know you, young brother. Your reputation as Fort Greene's 'Boom' precedes you. Word on the street is that you terrorizing folk everywhere you go and takin' their lunch money."

"Man, it ain't even like that," Jim replied angrily. "It was a lil' hustle...that's all. Just showing how quick my hands were. It wasn't like I was bullying anybody."

"I don't think that's the way Grant Butler sees it," Flip said, looking at Jim's eyes.

Jim avoided his gaze. "Look, I told him what it was. He kept poppin' off at the mouth, and he hit me wit' a cheap shot. What you want me to do, back down?"

"No, brother. I want you to use your head. He was goading you to a fight cuz he knew you would lose your head. From what I heard, you nearly killed him."

Jim shook his head. "How is he? He's gon' be cool, right?"

"Yeah, he'll live. He had an epileptic seizure while you were beating him, but luckily help arrived in time."

"Man, it wasn't even supposed to go down like that. But he pushed me, and I don't play that."

Flip chuckled.

What the hell's so funny?

"Everyone likes to play the tough guy in these streets, and when shit hits the fan, they ain't nowhere to be found."

"Yeah, well I ain't everybody. Look, man, thanks for getting me out and all, but I don't need your help."

"I think quite differently, brother. You do need my help. You got anger. That's good. You got aggression. That's great. You got boxing skills...there's no denying that. But unless you do something other than robbin' other folks in the street, you ain't gon' be out in these streets long enough to change your mentality."

"Do it look like I have a choice?"

"We all have a choice, Jim. It's up to us to make the right one." Taking out a business card, Flip gave it to Jim.

"What's this?" Jim asked, reading the card.

"It's the gym that I work at. Flatbush Fists. I train a lot of potential boxers such as yourself. All that anger, aggression, and rage, I can teach you how to harness it into a machine inside the ring."

Jim eyed Flip and mulled over his options. With his life going on a fast track to nowhere, life as a boxer seemed best compared to that of a hustler, gangbanger, or drug dealer. "This looks real, man. But I ain't got no money, and I'm probably lookin' at assault charges right now."

"Let me handle the charges. But you gotta promise me one thing. If I do you a solid on this, you gotta stay dedicated to the fight game and stay off them streets because, if you don't, you will end up back here. Or, even worse, you'll end up dead. Understand?" Flip asked gravely.

Jim nodded. As they drove back to Fort Greene, he didn't know what to expect in the coming days, but he knew that his fortunes would improve for the better.

Chapter 4

Four Years Later | The two boxers circled each other, each searching for an opening inside the other's guard at the Prospect Park Coliseum. Eighteen-year-old Jim Shaw was fighting his first professional match against rangy Italian middleweight Lorenzo Mateo. From the onset of the fight, it was clear that Lorenzo was the more experienced boxer. He was giving the young fighter a thorough lesson.

Under Flip's training and management, Jim had become one of the best young amateur boxers in the country, only losing one match at the Golden Gloves Amateur Competition. But only a few weeks earlier, after graduating high school, Jim had declared that he would fight professionally. Money was becoming scarce, and Janice had picked up another job just so she could pay the rent and mounting bills. Jim wanted to help in any way possible.

With his little brother, Kevin, still in high school, the choice to go pro was not a difficult one for Jim. But he was facing his first test in fighting against Lorenzo Mateo, who was not only stronger than him, but he also had more experience in the professional ranks, having fought for three years.

At Jim's corner along with two other cornermen, Steve Furlong and Joseph Channing, Flip was frantically trying to hurl advice at their novice fighter, who was behind on the scorecards because of Lorenzo's long arm wingspan. That's what kept Jim from getting inside to pound away at his body, and with his long reach, Lorenzo was able to keep Jim off balance and prevent him from landing his best shots.

By the end of the seventh round, Jim was starting to pant heavily as he made his way over to his corner. Lorenzo, on the other hand, looked fresh. Although Jim's jabs had found their mark on his face, he was barely hurt while Jim had a cut underneath his right eye. Joseph worked to stop the bleeding.

"Okay, Jim, listen to me. You have got to pick up the action. Slip his jabs. Don't wait for him to go off on you. I know he has a long reach, but keep workin' to get inside to the body. Keep your gloves up, and protect the eye. Remember, kill the body, and the head will fall. Slip, bob, and weave. Now let's go," Flip said, putting Jim's mouthpiece back in as the bell rang, signaling Round 8.

The spectators, many from Brooklyn, were cheering for Jim, including his mother and younger brother who sat close to ringside. Jim got back in the ring where Lorenzo was waiting for him. That's when Jim devised a tactic to pull Lorenzo toward the center of the ring. Lorenzo, sensing that he could get Jim against the ropes, began to throw head shots, hoping to knock out the inexperienced boxer, but he made a crucial mistake when he swung a wide right hook that gave Jim the split second he needed to duck under the punch.

Once inside, Jim landed a combination of blows to Lorenzo's midsection, and as soon as the punches made contact, Lorenzo's mouthpiece nearly flew out his mouth from the force of Jim's punches, which made him grunt in pain. But Jim wasn't done yet. He threw two more jarring hooks to Lorenzo's side with a force strong enough to drive the challenger to the ropes. Once against the ropes, Lorenzo attempted to tie Jim up with his long arms, but Jim avoided the tie-up just as the bell rang again.

"That's what I'm talking about, baby! Now you boxing," Flip said, taking Jim's mouthpiece out again to give him water. "Stay on him like a gnat. Don't let him free to use that power against you. You have your own power. Keep chopping away, and once you see an opening, hit him wit' the boom," he said, referring to a knockout punch.

The bell rang for Round 9, and Jim got back to the center of the ring with renewed energy as he continued pressuring Lorenzo. Lorenzo was clearly getting upset that he was being upstaged in the later rounds by the young upstart, and he was beginning to miss his punches. All Jim needed was another split second to get inside the body. Sure enough, after Lorenzo missed more punches swung out of frustration, Jim ducked under and hit Lorenzo with three more body shots. And then when the opportunity came, Jim threw an uppercut and left hook combination to Lorenzo's chin, instantly dropping the Italian fighter.

"BOOM!" the crowd yelled in unison as Lorenzo hit the canvas. As the referee began the count, Jim waited in a neutral corner, and when Lorenzo couldn't make the ten count, Jim raised his hands in victory.

"That's the way to do it, Boom!" a fan yelled from ringside.

Flip jumped to the center of the ring and hugged Jim as the crowd chanted "Boom! Boom! Boom!"

Although he was in the moment, Jim could hardly believe that he had managed to score a knockout in his first professional fight.

"Trust me, brother. This is only the beginning," Flip said as Jim walked over to Lorenzo's corner and in a gesture of sportsmanship, shook his opponent's hand before stepping down from the ring.

A few minutes later, as Jim rested in the locker room, Steve began to remove his gloves and padding. "Good shit today, man. With them skills you got, you gon' be champ in no time flat," he said.

"Whoa, whoa, let's not jump ahead now," Flip said, entering the locker room after talking to members of the press. "It's true. You won your first pro fight in dramatic fashion, but you ain't done nothin' in this division yet. We still got work to do. The one thing that you must remember about the fight game is that you must never be satisfied with just winning one fight. You have to come into each fight with a chip on your shoulder."

Jim nodded. "Yeah, you right. I gotta come back harder than this. But a knockout on a first pro fight is impressive though. Don't you think?"

"Don't mean a damn thing to me. The same way you knock an opponent out could be the same way you get knocked out if you don't keep ya' edge."

"Okay, I got you Flip," Jim replied. There were times when Flip was completely uptight and was a stickler for details.

"And when are you gon' cut that thing down?" Flip added, referring to Jim's new hairstyle—a high-top box fade, which had slowly become the new fad.

"Cut it down? C'mon, Flip, you know I can't touch the box," Jim said, patting his hair while looking in the mirror.

"You feelin' yourself too much, bro," Joseph said.

"Yeah, well the girls don't think so. They diggin' this here new style," Jim bragged as he headed toward the shower.

Later the next day, Jim walked into the neighborhood bodega and was immediately approached by other Brooklyn residents that had watched the fight or heard the results from the fight. Jim was overwhelmed with pens, small napkins, pads, paper, and other items they wanted his autograph on. *Man, I could get used to this life.*

Leaving the bodega with bags of chips and dip, Jim made his way over to Greg Shepard's apartment for a house party. Greg was one of his classmates at Brooklyn Technical High School. He lived on the first floor, and the added luxury was the spacy basement under his apartment. That's where he was hosting the party that evening. Then Jim's friends Tavion and Alan would be attending, and there would be no shortage of women.

In the last three months, Jim had been involved with a girl name Sharonda. She was beautiful but heavily insecure. And while she wanted to pursue a relationship with Jim, he did not wish to pursue one with her. The reason was not physical because there was no question that with hazelnut brown skin and a body that would drive any man crazy, Sharonda was gorgeous.

But Sharonda was rumored to be a woman who loved to test the waters frequently. And as a man who didn't like his woman to be spontaneous, especially with the HIV epidemic going on, Jim chose to move on from Sharonda and test the waters himself although there was only one girl that he would love to dive into. They shared a few classes together in school, but Jim never gathered the courage to ask Natalie out, and she never asked him out.

The two were cordial with each other, and even though she would never admit it to him, Jim knew why he and Natalie never dated. When word spread about Jim's fight with Grant Butler four years earlier, Natalie's parents—strong devout Christians— thought Jim was a hoodlum and would be a bad influence for their daughter. So even though they lived on the same street, Natalie and Jim barely spoke with each other.

As Jim continued to Greg's apartment, he heard footsteps behind him. Quickly turning around, he realized it was Kevin. "Man, what you doin' behind me?" Jim asked his 16-year-old brother.

"What you think I'm doin'? I'm goin' to Greg's crib for the party too," Kevin replied.

Jim rolled his eyes. "Whateva' man. But this party ain't no child's play. Some shit always be goin' down, so keep your head low, mind ya' business, and you'll be straight."

Five minutes later, they arrived at Greg's apartment. Right away, they saw the smoke coming out of the small window. After they knocked on the door, Greg let the brothers enter the basement. The boom box was playing different tapes with tracks by Run DMC, Whodini, Fat Boys, Full Force, and many other artists. And Greg's basement was so spacious that breakdancers were on the middle of the huge mat on the floor spinning on their heads like spinning tops.

Jim dropped off his bags of chips on the food table in the corner and grabbed a beer.

"Ayo, Boom!" a voice yelled from the opposite end of the basement.

When Jim turned around, he realized it was Tavion and Alan. Both had girls sitting on their laps and were all smoking marijuana. Like Jim, Alan also had a small box fade, but that stood in contrast to Tavion, who sported a Jheri Curl. With constant sheen spraying, Tavion was able to maintain his curls.

"What's up?" Jim said, greeting his friends.

"What's good, Boom?" Alan greeted.

"Yo' I heard you beat ole' boy today," Tavion said, while taking a drag of his joint.

"Yeah, but it wasn't easy. Mateo was no joke. That pro level is somethin' serious," Jim said.

"That's the way it is, dawg. It ain't the pro level unless shit gets real, you know what I'm sayin'?" Tavion said.

"True. Yo' lemme hit that one time," Jim said as Tavion passed him the joint. Jim normally didn't do drugs, but if he was at a party or a free social setting, he was not one to turn down a hit of weed. He just had to make sure it was out of his system before the next fight.

"So, what's yo' names?" he asked the girls.

But before they could respond, Tavion spoke for them. "This sweet thang hea' is Kyra. The other one is Monica, and no you can't have either one," he laughed.

"Man, whatever. I can pull plenty of Monicas and Kyras all day. Don't even play me like that," Jim laughed.

Tavion looked at Alan before laughing sarcastically. "Yo', you hear this?" he asked. "You talkin' big for a nigga who couldn't even pull a girl from his own block. Natalie was her name, right? What happened to that, homeboy?"

"Man, you know her daddy don't want me datin' her. He still sees me as that nappy-headed boy in handcuffs," Jim replied.

"For real? Yo', people still buggin' over that Grant Butler shit? They need to let that go. He started it, and you ended it. No big deal. If he knew what was good for him, he wouldn't have scrapped wit' you," Tavion said as Alan took out another dime bag and started rolling up again.

"Damn, ya got stash for days. Who's yo' plug?" Jim asked.

"Big Earl from out in Queens," Alan said.

"Oh yeah, I heard of that dude. But didn't he get busted last year cuz one of his dealers snitched on him?" Tavion asked.

"Nah, that ain't the way I heard the story. One of Big Earl's dealers was fuckin' wit' one his bitches, and Earl beat his ass and killed the girl. Got away before the po-po arrived though. The guy that got jacked up by Earl was arrested and sent upstate. At least that's what they said went down," Alan explained.

And to think that I once considered dealing drugs. Glad Flip found me when he did.

Tavion said, "Yo', Boom. There go ya' girl right there," he said, pointing at the front door.

Jim's mind started racing as he turned and saw Natalie entering the party with two of her friends. Her hair was tied back into a side ponytail, and she had on a T-shirt with leggings. She didn't cover her face with huge amounts of makeup, which was one of the traits that Jim liked about Natalie. And while she wasn't flashy, she wasn't a Plain Jane either. She was all about balance.

"Better get to it before I do," Tavion warned jokingly before being slapped in the chest by Kyra.

"See that, son? That's what happen when you don't shut up," Jim laughed.

While making his way over to Natalie, Jim saw her eyes scanning the party floor before meeting his. Suddenly, his heart skipped a beat. It was like entering the boxing ring against an unknown opponent all over again. Turning away from Natalie's gaze, he did a quick breath test against his hand and realized that his breath reeked of marijuana.

Reaching into his pockets, he pulled out a pack of Tic Tacs that he bought at the bodega and popped a few in his mouth. With his breath finally smelling like peppermint, he continued to the other side of the floor. Natalie was busy talking with friends until she felt a tap on her shoulder.

"Hey, Natalie, what's up?" Jim greeted.

"What's up, Jim?" she greeted back, slightly louder after the music volume increased.

"I didn't think you'd come out here tonight," he said.

"Me neither. To be honest, Teresa was the one that dragged me here," she said gesturing to her friend, who took one look at Jim, and her mouth fell open in surprise.

"Natalie! How come you ain't told me that you knew 'Boom'?" she asked.

"Boom?" Natalie asked blankly.

"Yeah, it's kind of my nickname in the boxing ring," Jim explained.

"Oh, you're a boxer?" Natalie asked.

"Yeah, I just turned pro a couple weeks ago. I won my first fight today," he said.

"Wow, that's crazy. I had no idea," Natalie said, clearly impressed.

"Yeah, a lot has happened since I got arrested. I'm sorry I ain't get the chance to tell you sooner, but I thought if you knew that I fought for a living, you wouldn't wanna talk to me," Jim said.

"Why would you think that?" Natalie asked.

"Well, I know your parents didn't want you around me after I got arrested, so I thought they wouldn't let us hang out," Jim admitted.

"Well, my dad maybe would've been buggin', but my mom wouldn't have minded. She knows you ain't no thug who gangbangs, hustles, does drugs, or smokes weed."

Jim's eyes shifted sideways, nervously. "Yeah, I got too much goin' on right now anyway."

"So, have you decided what college you wanna go to yet?"

"Um, well I was accepted to a couple schools, but I've decided to hold off from college right now, at least until I'm through wit' this boxing gig."

"Really?" Natalie sounded shocked and somewhat disappointed.

Jim was no fool. He picked up on her disapproving tone. "Look, I just have a good thing goin' on right now. I just started my pro career, and I'm making more money now than I would have if I worked a desk job."

"I mean, ain't nothin' wrong with workin' a desk job, Jim. Lots of people do it, and you ain't gonna be a boxer forever," Natalie said.

"True that," Jim agreed. "I mean, not unless they make some type of chamber to regenerate my body so that I never age. I'mma die young," he laughed, and he was relieved that Natalie laughed also. "So, where you plan on goin'?"

"Columbia University. I'm planning on being a psychiatrist one day. I wanna help people who are goin' through stuff in life and understand how the mind works," she replied.

"That's cool. I dig that," he said.

While Jim and Natalie continued talking, he caught Tavion's facial expression out of the corner of his eye as his friend started pointing toward the front door. Jim turned around and saw Sharonda entering the party. *Damn. I gotta get up out of here.*

Sharonda was the last person he needed to run into, and if she saw Natalie with him, there was no doubt that she would cause a scene. By then, the breakdancers had stopped performing and only a few or the partygoers remained on the dance floor.

"Uh, Natalie, I gotta go. Gotta get up early in the morning to work out, you know what I'm sayin'?"

"Yeah, I feel you. This party's gettin' kind of old, anyway," she agreed. "Teresa, you ready to go?" she asked her friend, who had been chatting with another friend.

"What? Go where? Girl, we just got here. You trippin'," Teresa replied derisively.

"Well, I'm gonna go. I'll talk to you tomorrow," Natalie said.

"So, you leavin' by yourself?" Teresa asked, while Jim listened intently.

She's right. I can't let her walk through the hood by herself. "Nah, I'll walk her home," Jim interjected.

Natalie smiled at him. "Yeah, Jim will walk me home," she confirmed.

Teresa shrugged although she shifted her eyes between Natalie and Jim, insinuating a possible romance.

"Okay, Boom, go on and take her home, but don't try nothin' funny on my girl now. She'll tell me everything."

"Don't worry. I got you," Jim said, and he and Natalie made their way out of the basement, even managing to sneak past Sharonda, who was busy talking to her friends, oblivious that her ex-boyfriend exited the same area with another young lady.

As they headed home, they talked more about their ambitions, future goals, and wealth they wanted to generate for their families.

"Ugh, you ain't neva' lied. I'd do anything to get my parents out of here," Natalie said in exasperation.

"That's why I work so hard in the ring so I can get my lil' brother and my mama out of here," Jim said, before coming to a stunning realization. *Aww, man, I left Kevin at the party. Oh well, his narrow behind can find his way home. He ain't about to ruin this for me.*

On that cool summer night, Jim felt a strong connection with Natalie, one that he hadn't felt with anybody else—not even Sharonda.

"So, how do you like boxing?" Natalie asked.

"Boxing's great…when you're winning, of course."

"You ever lost a fight before?"

"Oh yeah. I've lost my fair share of rounds in amateur boxing, but I've still been able to dominate," Jim boasted.

"I just don't know how ya' could continue taking punches to the face and head. I'm sure that you can get a lot of brain damage from takin' all them hits."

"Yeah, if you ain't careful. But that ain't neva' gon' happen to me. I was built for this."

"You sound confident for a brotha' whose head looks like a pencil eraser," Natalie laughed, making fun of Jim's box fade haircut.

"I know you ain't talkin' wit' yo' fake side ponytail. I see you ain't rockin' the headband tonight," Jim countered, laughing.

"No, the hair band was gettin' played out anyway, just like that haircut will."

"Yo', why you actin' like you don't like it? You know it looks smooth on me. If I'm gon' knock anybody out, might as well do it in style, right?"

Natalie shook her head. *This boy got an ego. I don't like men with egos, but there's something different about him.*

"You know, you should come watch my next fight," Jim said.

"For real? I ain't never been to no fight before."

"Trust me, it's not as bad as some people make it out to be. Well, it won't be bad for me cuz I know I'll win anyway."

"Hmmm, well I guess I can try to come. Where's it gonna be

at?"

"Nassau Coliseum in Long Island. Gotta fight a cat by the name of Horace Tucker."

"Are you nervous?"

"Nah, I don't get nervous anymore. My trainer said fear, as all other things, are often an illusion. Can't get nervous in this game."

As they arrived at Natalie's brownstone building, Natalie turned to Jim. "Thanks for walking me home," she said.

"No problem," he replied.

Natalie leaned forward and kissed Jim on the cheek. "Well, I guess I better get inside before my parents flip," she said, as she started walking up the stairs to her door.

"I guess I'll see you at the fight then," Jim said.

"You know it. Good night, Boom," Natalie said, heading walked inside.

"Good night," Jim said.

And as the door closed, and he began to walk home, Natalie watched him from her living room window.

As the sixth-round bell rang at Nassau Coliseum the following Saturday, Jim jogged to his corner, feeling confident and upbeat. He had thoroughly dominated his opponent in the early rounds, and he knew he was ahead on the judges' scorecards. Horace Tucker was a mediocre boxer and did not have the hand speed, dexterity, or ring sense to make the fight a contest. His poor ring performance stood in contrast to Jim's brilliance, as he boxed soundly and used his long reach to keep the rangy boxer off balance.

By Round 5, Jim had blackened one of Horace's eyes, and red marks and bumps revealed the spots where Jim's gloves had landed. As Jim sat in his corner, getting wiped down by Flip and the other cornermen, he looked into the stands. Although there was a large crowd of spectators at the fight, he was able to find Natalie sitting nine rows from ring center. By looking at her, Jim could tell she was impressed. He wanted nothing more than to put on a show for her, and there was no better stage than the ring.

Jim knew Flip was talking to him, but he was oblivious to what his trainer was saying. All he could do was stare at Natalie. Her blouse was partially open, revealing some cleavage, which was quite enticing. At this point, Jim had to make a quick decision.

Okay, time to end this fight cuz I'm trying to get physical outside the ring with Natalie.

The bell rang for Round 7. Jim sprang up out of his corner stool and returned to the center of the ring. Horace attempted to throw his best hooks and jabs, but Jim was too swift, and he easily slipped the challenger's punches. Jim then returned two jaw-jarring overhand jabs, stunning Horace and sending him to the canvas.

"BOOM!" the crowd roared after Jim delivered the crushing blows.

Retreating to his corner while the referee performed the mandatory ten-count, Jim told Flip, "Pack it up, man. It's a wrap."

"C'mon, Boom, let's wait for the ref to finish counting," Flip replied annoyingly, but there was no need to wait as was confirmed by the deafening roar of the crowd when Horace was counted out.

"Didn't I tell you it was over?" a smug Jim asked, grinning at Flip.

Raising his hands in victory, the spectators were chanting, "BOOM! BOOM!"

But the only person that seemed to be in the coliseum was the only one that mattered to Jim, but to her, he was just Jim Shaw.

When Jim and Flip walked back to the locker room, Flip lauded his young fighter. "That's what I'm talkin' about, Boom! Gotta make 'em feel ya! You gon' be champ one day, son. Best believe that!"

After Jim's gloves were removed, and he showered and put on fresh clothes, he began to make his way out of the arena when he saw Natalie near the exit. Smiling, he asked, "So, what you think of the fight? Bet no one else could put on a show like that." He figured Natalie didn't know much about boxing, and he expected a short answer.

"Eh, it was okay," she said. "You were flat footed in the sixth round, and your hands weren't always busy, and your left hooks were weak."

"Damn, girl, like that? Thought you said you ain't know too much about boxing."

"I said I ain't never been to a fight before. That don't mean I didn't know anything about it, genius," she laughed.

"Oh, so you played me. Is that it?" he asked, laughing.

"Well, you just assumed I didn't know about it," she replied.

"Well anyway, I won, so yo' boy's still undefeated," Jim laughed as he and Natalie headed out of Nassau Coliseum. Jim didn't know if she initiated the act or if he initiated it, but suddenly, they were holding hands. "So, if you want, I can get Flip to give you a ride back home," he offered.

Natalie had other plans in mind. "Home? Don't you want to celebrate your win?" she asked teasingly, and from the look that she gave Jim, he knew that going home wouldn't be an option for the evening.

A few hours later at the Nassau Motel, Jim and Natalie rented a room and barely opened the door before their lust overtook them. Kissing her relentlessly, Jim carried Natalie to the bed and with his large hands, he undid her blouse and bra while cupping her breasts in his hands. Natalie unzipped Jim's pants and pulled them down as he spread her legs apart and proceeded to remove her panties. He worked his tongue down from her chest to her naval, then even lower. Natalie moaned in pleasure as she released her sensual body fluids. Jim finally arched his back, preparing to enter Natalie's sweet nectar. Relishing the sensation—the sweet pleasurable escape—Natalie and Jim were enveloped in each other's arms as the night gave way to morning.

Chapter 5

Jim's boxing career was off to a stellar start as he reeled off four more victories against other middleweight challengers. Because he'd built the reputation of a knockout artist, his opponents became more wary about challenging him. But the most reservation came from the seasoned boxers. To most of them, facing Jim Shaw was a risk. If they won, they wouldn't earn much money because Jim was still relatively unknown outside of the northeast region. At the same time, if they lost, they faced scrutiny and public humiliation at the hands of the media, sportswriters, and their constituents.

Jim remained unaffected by the decisions of his opponents, particularly because he looked at every fight the same way. It was his road to the middleweight belt and an opportunity to make money for his family. With more wins came more of the financial reward. Jim was being offered endorsement deals from athletic apparel companies, and his stock began to rise. He attributed much of his success to Flip, but his inspiration was Natalie Brown.

Since Jim's second fight, she had shown up to each one in support of her new boyfriend. Jim didn't know what it was, but Natalie unleashed a part of him that compelled him to win every single time he stepped into the ring.

When Flip got wind that Jim was dating Natalie, he was none

too pleased. He wanted Jim to focus on his budding career, and he couldn't allow any distractions to sway his phenom. But Flip couldn't deny the affect that Natalie had on Jim. Jim was more focused in the ring, and he was deftly knocking out his opponents within the first few rounds. On the other hand though, Jim wouldn't explain to his trainer why he desired to end each fight early.

After every win, Jim and Natalie would begin with a midnight meal. Then they would follow it up by making love, which drove Jim to end the fights even earlier than expected as he anticipated his reward at the end of the evening. There was no better feeling than touching Natalie's soft, delicate skin after mixing his up with other boxers.

One day, on Jim's free weekend, he took Natalie to a place on Canal Street called Tom's Grille. While Natalie was happy that Jim treated her to lunch, she seemed preoccupied with her own thoughts, and Jim noticed.

"Hey, Nat, what's up? Burger's too cold?" he laughed as Natalie just sat in front of her uneaten food.

"No, it's not that. I'm just not that hungry today," she replied as she stared out the window.

Jim took her hand and caressed it. "Hey, if something's bothering you, talk to me about it. Is it family trouble?"

Natalie looked at Jim for a split second before lowering her gaze. "You could say that."

"C'mon, Nat. You can tell me. If anyone's bothering you, let me know. They betta' recognize," he bragged.

Natalie managed to crack a smile. Jim's ego knew no boundaries, and she loved his brash personality. "How long have we dated each other now, Jim?"

"I would say about seven months, right? Damn, time flies when you're with someone you love. I ain't even realize it's been that long."

"How would you feel if a third person was involved in this relationship?"

Jim was completely thrown off by the question. *I didn't know Natalie gets down like this. If she wants a threesome, shit, I'm down with it long as it's another woman...anything to spice up a relationship.*

"And, no, I ain't talkin' about no threesome with some other girl, so you can wipe that smirk off yo' face." Natalie immediately shot that notion down.

Damn.

"Okay, so if you're not talking about another woman. Then, what do you mean by third person? I know it ain't another man," Jim said seriously.

Natalie's gaze dropped again. "Not exactly."

"Okay, baby, I'm confused. You over hea' talking about a third person in this relationship, and you making me jump through hoops and play guessing games—" Jim protested before Natalie interrupted him with a bombshell revelation.

"I'm pregnant, Jim."

Upon hearing those words, Jim dropped his burger. His appetite suddenly left him, and he felt as if air was sucked from his body. It was news that he wasn't ready to receive. "Are you sure?"

"Yeah, I'm sure, Jim. I missed my period, and just the other day, I went to the doctor's office for my routine checkup, and the doctor confirmed it himself," she replied as she studied Jim's reaction to the news.

Jim was still processing the information. Here he was, on the rise in his boxing career, and just as he was starting to make a name for himself, it was revealed to him that he was going to be a father at the age of nineteen.

"Well, ain't you gon' say anything?" Natalie asked.

Jim suddenly thought about his own family—his brother and mother. How would they take the news? "Did you tell your parents about it?"

Natalie's parents were all but unaware that their daughter was dating a man whom they once saw as a hoodlum in the streets of Fort Greene, Brooklyn.

"No, I didn't tell them yet. They would lose their minds if they knew about us, and the baby. I'm gon' get the standard lecture about how I'm supposed to wait till marriage and how I ain't ready for all this. I just wanted to tell you first."

The image of Jim's father flashed before his mind. He had only seen Braxton Shaw as a younger boy before he was locked up in prison for his part in the drug game. Since being locked up, Braxton had not had any communication with his sons or his wife. Jim's mother attributed Braxton's lack of communication to his debilitating drug habit, which included crack/cocaine and other drugs that added to his state of paranoia and left him unavailable for his own family.

Jim didn't even know if his father was alive or not. And after observing how his own father was absent in his life, Jim couldn't disappear on Natalie or their child. He couldn't be another Braxton. "Don't worry about anything. I'll take care of us," he reassured Natalie.

"Really? You ain't gon' get mad and leave me?" she asked.

"Nah, I can't do that. My father wasn't around for me and Kevin. I wanna be wit' you every step of the way, and I wanna be the father that the kid deserves."

"I don't know if we're ready for this, Jim. I mean you have your boxing career, and I got plans to go to school, and now with this baby, I don't know."

Jim took Natalie's hand and held it tightly. He realized that his girlfriend's hand was quivering slightly. "Nat, there ain't any obstacle we've faced that we haven't been able to knock down yet. We've made it because we stuck together through the noise. I can't see myself with anybody else but you. I wanna be there for you and the baby."

Natalie then hugged her boyfriend. Jim returned the hug, secretly wondering what he was going to do next.

Early the next day at Flatbush Fists, Jim was working on the heavy bag, but Flip knew that his focus wasn't all there. "C'mon, Jim, more power. I want to see you hit that bag! C'mon, one-two-one!" he yelled as Jim worked on his combo.

Then they commenced to jumping rope. Jim usually excelled at jumping consistently, but on this day, he couldn't prevent the rope from tangling on his feet at times, which threw him off rhythm. The worst of it came when he sparred with Darryl Blain, one of his usual sparring partners. Jim normally dominated the sparring sessions, but Darryl had the upper hand this time and managed to catch Jim awkwardly slipping, leaving his left cheek open for Darryl to catch him with a right to the left side. Jim went down but got back up and continued sparring.

As soon as the session concluded, Flip walked over to Jim. "What's goin' on, man? You don't look right. Is everything okay?

You've been a step slow since you walked in here. Talk to me, man."

"Natalie's pregnant, man," Jim said, taking off his headgear.

The news surprised Flip although he'd already sensed his fighter was too involved with his relationship. "Really? Well, no wonder you couldn't focus today, Boom. Congratulations, brother!"

"Thanks, man. I appreciate it. It took me by surprise when she told me. But, man, I don't know if I'm ready for no child," Jim said.

Flip sat next to Jim in the ring. "Since you were a boy, I taught you how to take care of yourself and how to be a man out here in these streets. You've been a fighter since you were a kid, so I have no doubt that you're gonna raise your child to be the same type of fighter as you."

"Nah, I ain't raising my kid to be no boxer. If it's a girl, I'm gon' be mad overprotective of her, keeping all them thirsty boys away from her, and if it's a boy, I'm gon' make sure that he has nothin' to do wit' this fight game."

"C'mon, man, you gon' have to teach him how to get tough and defend himself. Create another 'Boom,'" Flip joked.

"If there's one thing you've taught me about the fight game, it's that it doesn't stay legit all the time. Whoever my kid turns out to be, I'mma make sure they street smart, so they don't get suckered into the drug game either," Jim vowed.

"As I knew you would," Flip said.

They walked into the locker room. "So, have you talked with Gus Pendleton yet?" Jim asked, referring to the current fight promoter.

"Yeah, I talked to Gus, and he said that there are no offers for a title shot," Flip replied.

"Why not?" Jim asked.

"Look, Jim, in order to be considered as a contender for a middleweight title, you gotta get yo' rep up even more," Flip explained.

"C'mon, I've been faithful to the game for four freakin' years, man. Right now, I'm undefeated since going pro. There's gotta be a title shot waiting in the cards," Jim protested.

"And one day, there will be. Just gotta keep working, and you'll get that opportunity. I promise you, man." Flip patted Jim in the back as Jim headed for the showers.

"Damn, son, you got the bitch pregnant?" Tavion asked as they sprawled across his room floor, playing cards. "I knew you wanted to sex her up, bro, but I would've thought you'd be more careful."

"Man, I thought I was being more careful, but it happened, and I decided we're gonna have the baby," Jim said.

"You gotta be kiddin' me, son. As far as I'm concerned, that ain't yo' baby. You ain't got no obligation to that situation, Boom," Tavion replied.

"Do you hear yourself when you speak? I got every obligation to my kid, man."

"Jim, you are one of the best boxers to come out of this area. You at the top of yo' game man. You can't let her come in here and fuck all that up with a baby. For all you know, you might not be the daddy."

"What you talkin' about, man?"

"I'm sayin' Natalie ain't the saint that everybody makin' her out to be. You think you the only dude she fuckin' wit' right now? She probably been with every other brotha' at Brooklyn Tech. Only reason she wit' you is cuz you makin' bank. That's why."

Jim turned to his friend. "You wrong bout that, man. She ain't like them other hoes out there, B. She different."

"Yeah, okay. Keep tellin' yourself that. Maybe you'll convince yourself to believe that fairies and Santa Clause exists too," Tavion said.

Jim playfully pushed his friend's head from the back of the couch. "Whatever, man. Just quit gettin' Jheri Curl juice all up on the couch. Grease stains are hard to clean," Jim laughed.

As Tavion adjusted himself, Jim noticed the small pipe fall out of his pocket along with a few hundred-dollar bills.

"Yo', man, what's this?" he asked although he knew what it was.

"It ain't nothin' man," Tavion replied furtively.

Jim didn't let up on the questioning. "So, you doin' crack now or you sellin'?"

"Man, don't worry about it," Tavion replied with a hint of annoyance.

Jim was no fool. He had been around the streets long enough to recognize a drug dealer, or dope boy.

"What you mean 'don't worry about it,'? You out hea' sellin' shit that's gonna kill our people, and you okay wit' that?"

"Man, how's that different from what you doin'? I'm makin' money just like you, homeboy. Alan got his football thing, and you got yo' boxing gig. I ain't got the athletic skills ya got, and if this is what I gotta do to make money, then so be it."

"C'mon, Tavion, don't go out like this. When I was in juvey four years ago, I had the same choice. This game out here will kill you!"

Tavion threw his cards down in fury, stood up, and started pacing the room. "Who are you to talk? You out here fightin' and bustin' yo' ass for the white establishment for a few dollars while they make money off you. But best believe, when you lose, they gon' move on to the next one. They'll use you up until they can't make money off you, and once they get bored with you, they'll throw you away."

Jim stood up and dropped his cards to the floor. As far as he was concerned, the game was over. "You trippin', B. Flip ain't gon' let that happen."

"Here we go with Flip again." Tavion rolled his eyes. "Boom, the man ain't God. He ain't nothin' but a puppet, and the boxing division's pullin' them strings. You think he cares about you? All he cares about is his bottom fuckin' line. Don't believe me? When is he gon' give you a shot at the title?"

"I've only had six pro fights under my belt. He'll set me up for a title fight when he thinks I'm ready."

"Yeah, okay. Is that what he told you?"

Jim didn't immediately reply, and Tavion felt that Jim's silence validated his argument. "You gotta remember one thing, man. Flip works for you. You fighting is doing nothing more but putting millions in yo' pockets and billions in their pockets. He owes you that payday, kid."

Despite Tavion's abrasive tone, Jim couldn't help but wonder if his friend had a point. "Look, man, I gotta go. I got workouts this afternoon. Gotta get ready for the next fight."

"Alright, man. Peace. Think about what I said," Tavion replied as Jim walked out of the apartment.

Surprisingly, Flip didn't keep the same enthusiastic energy the way Jim thought he would after he told him the news about the baby earlier. The next day at the gym, he just wore an expression that Jim couldn't read.

"You gotta stay hungry in this division. I told you so many times to steer clear of them girls, and you go and do this. First it was Pam. Then it was Sharonda, and now it's this Natalie chick. Guess she the one that hit the jackpot, huh?" Flip said.

What's that supposed to mean?" Jim asked.

"It means you're a public figure now, Jim. Believe it or not, you got eyes watching you everywhere, and if you slip out here, you could lose endorsement deals, and we're talkin' millions of dollars down the drain."

Jim stared at his trainer. The more he talked, the more he began to see what Tavion meant about his trainer using his success and his marketability for financial reward. "So, you think me being a father is going to hurt my chances of being a champion?"

"Man, I'm tellin' you like this. Life is a beautiful thing, and I'm happy for you and Natalie. But this moment only comes once in a lifetime for fighters like yourself. You got to stay ahead of the game, and kill all distractions."

"So, you can keep bankin' off me, right?" Jim asked.

Flip looked at Jim as if he didn't recognize him. "That's not true, Boom. We've been a team since you were fourteen years of age, and since then, I've never abandoned you or left you hangin'. I've been like the father you never had before the money."

"So, let me be a father to my child." Jim said. "My father was not around for my family, and I swore to myself that I wouldn't do what my father did to us. I'm gonna be there for Natalie when she needs me."

"As you should. I just see a well of potential for you, Jim, and it's not about the money. It never was. But I didn't want you to lose everything you worked so hard for."

"Neither do I, and once the baby's born, it's gonna drive me to keep workin', and I'm going to go for the belt," Jim said.

"Attaboy, Jim! I know you can do it, and if that kid's lucky, he'll have a mean right hook like his daddy."

"But what if it's a girl?"

"Well, if it's a girl, then she'll have a mean right hook."

"You crazy." Jim made his way over to the speedbag and started jabbing away.

Jim reeled off five more wins, and after nine months, Dante Emile Shaw was born to him and Natalie. Jim visited his girlfriend and newborn at New York Community Hospital in Brooklyn. Her parents were already in the delivery room, and when Jim entered the room, to his surprise, Natalie's mother hugged Jim. Jim knew she had every right to be angry with him, even resentful, but at that moment, they were pleased that Jim stayed by Natalie's side every step of the way, and they had another reason to be overjoyed.

Jim looked at Dante sleeping in a bundle of blankets, and with Natalie lying in her hospital bed and her parents looking on, Jim reached into his pocket and took out a ring.

"There's no greater gift than to bring a child into this world, but I would love to make this union permanent. Natalie Brown, will you marry me?"

Natalie placed her hands over her mouth, unable to stop the flow of tears. "Yes, James Shaw," she replied.

Her parents and the nurses began clapping as Jim placed the ring on Natalie's finger before hugging her.

As the late 1980s gave way to the early 1990s, Jim continued his dominance in the ring although his opponents began intensifying their training before facing him. As a result, each opponent became much tougher. Jim won more of his fights by decision, and knockouts were few and far between. He was, however, paid handsomely as a middleweight boxer and was able to move Natalie and Dante out of DeKalb Street and into a brownstone in Clairmont, Brooklyn.

The first few years were some of the happiest moments for Jim whenever he was home. He relished the growth and development of his son. Dante was a very smart and articulate toddler who began reading at the age of four. From the time he began early education schooling, the teachers were impressed by his intelligence. Unfortunately, those moments were rare for Jim because he was traveling more frequently for his fights in Illinois, Florida, Georgia, Texas, and even bouts in New Mexico. He won most of the time, and even though he lost some of his fights in last round decisions, Jim wanted nothing more than to be home with his new family.

But Flip kept urging Jim to continue fighting with a promise of a title shot in the next year. But the next year would turn into two years. Then two years became three years, and the more Jim fought, the more impatient he became. His opportunity to be a recognized figure in boxing was passing him by, and he knew time was running out as he was entering the prime of his career.

One day, Jim stormed into Flip's office at Flatbush Fists.

"Yo, what's up, Boom? What can I get the man of the hour?" Flip greeted cheerfully.

Jim was not in a laughing or joyous mood. "Yo', Flip, we need to talk," he replied icily, closing the door behind him.

"Yeah, what's up, man?" Flip asked.

Jim slammed a copy of the *Daily News* sports section down on Flip's desk. "What's this shit, man? It says here that Coleman's gonna get a title shot next weekend against Ramos. Did you talk to Gus yet?"

Flip looked down on his desk, his eyes shifting side to side. Jim could tell that his trainer was looking for an excuse.

"Yeah, I talked to Gus, but he didn't want to offer us a title shot," Flip replied.

"In '86, you said we would be fightin' for the belt within three years. It's been six years, Flip, and I ain't even in the conversation for a title shot," Jim said angrily.

"I know, Boom. I'm just as pissed off as you are, believe me, but Gus is the one beatin' around the bush here. He's stallin' us from the shot he knows we deserve."

"Because he's happy makin' money off my ass for cable networks, and he don't wanna pay the type of money that a title fight will pay," Jim said.

"Well, that's part of the reason, but it's not all. Apparently, he doesn't think you're a big draw in the public. He said that you didn't fit the image of the division, and maybe if you had some more financial backing, maybe some commercial promotion, he could easily sell a title shot with you to the public."

"So, he wants me to sell out. Is that it? Look, this is who I am, and I ain't compromising for nobody. I earned my shot at the title. I've only lost four times in six years, whether it was New York, Cali, Chicago, or any other damn place. They gave Coleman a shot, and I've whipped that brotha' twice."

"I know, man, but what can I say? It's the dirty politics of boxing. When you get in this game, you gotta expect one thing. And that's for people to treat you like you ain't worth a damn. They're not gonna hand us a title shot. We gotta take it," Flip said.

At that moment, Jim'd had enough. "All these years of fightin', and all for what? Just to have a promotion group and a committee to tell me I ain't worth everything that I worked my ass off for? I'm sick of fightin' for pennies while the bigwigs are makin' dolla bills." Jim took his gloves out of his duffel bag and threw them on Flip's desk. "I got a wife and a son at home that I could be spendin' my time with right now. I'm out, man. Tell 'em to find some other fool to make millions off they back." With that, he left the office.

As Jim walked out of Flatbush, Tavion's words of warning played back in his head. The middleweight boxing committee cared about nothing more than getting millions, and Jim was done being their pawn.

I'mma show 'em. One day I'm gonna show 'em all. If I ever train someone the way Flip trained me, I'll make sure they get a title shot. We'll show 'em all.

Chapter 6

Drenched in sweat, Jim sat up in bed at three in the morning. No matter how much he tried to erase the horrifying memories of watching his son die, the scene outside the elementary school replayed in his head like a broken record. He could still see himself waving to Dante, who was nine years old and in the fifth grade. In slow motion, Jim saw another kid with a menacing look on his face push Dante into the street, and he saw Dante hit the asphalt just before another car struck him. And Jim could still hear the sickening sound the car made when it struck his only son. He remembered frantically running to his son and trying to revive him while calling for help. The driver of the car who struck him, to his credit, got out of his car and whipped out his business cell phone to call 9-1-1.

The one glaring ugly truth that confronted Jim was that he arrived at the scene too late. He couldn't save Dante. He just uncontrollably cried on the curb. The driver was charged with vehicular manslaughter, and the young boy responsible for pushing Dante was eventually expelled and sent to a disciplinary school for troubled boys due to his minor status.

Just four years after he unofficially retired from boxing, Flip offered Jim a job as the assistant head trainer and manger at Flatbush Fists. The pay wasn't as lucrative as Jim's boxing career, but he was content with working and staying around the game. It also inspired him to open his own boxing gym, modeled after Flatbush Fists. After toying around with some names, he finally came up with the name Steel Glove Gym. He was in the planning and development stages of the gym with Flip and other investors. They found an empty building in Queens, and plans were soon set in motion to build and remodel the building in the image that Jim had always envisioned for a top-of-the-art boxing facility.

But all plans were derailed in the aftermath of Dante's death. Jim often secluded himself from the public eye as he silently mourned his son. But nobody took the loss of Dante harder than Natalie Shaw. Jim's wife was a social worker who was working closely with New York's Board of Education, and she was a staple in the Brooklyn area. The hardest task for Jim was calling Natalie from the hospital and telling her that their son was gone despite the doctor's efforts to revive him. It was gut wrenching, and Jim could never forget Natalie's hyperventilated sob upon hearing the news or forget her breakdown on the other end of the phone. The unnatural foreign sound that Natalie made signified the complete grief she felt when she learned of her only son's passing.

Jim and Natalie's marriage began to suffer after Dante's sudden death. Natalie, despite the advice from friends and family, continued working, and she worked through her grief. She would be away from home for long hours and wouldn't return home. She would stay at her cousin's house in Mount Vernon, New York, for the weekends and return home just to go to work again.

Without Dante's light and energy in the home, Natalie and Jim began to drift apart. The relationship began to lose its luster, intensity, and passion. Jim didn't need to read Natalie's face or her reactions, but he knew she blamed him for Dante's death. They couldn't kiss or be intimate in any type of way because of their constant thoughts of Dante. He had been such a vibrant presence, and he'd had his life ahead of him.

The world was robbed of potential. Dante could've been anything—a doctor, a biochemist, an engineer—but now we'll never know.

Although it was excruciatingly difficult to fall back asleep, Jim faced Natalie's empty side of the bed and forced himself back to sleep. He knew she was at her cousin's house trying to gather herself and make it to the next day. Later that day, after returning home from work, Jim called Natalie, but she didn't pick up the phone. *I wonder if she's ignoring my calls.*

A couple of hours later, Natalie returned home. Her mind appeared to be preoccupied as she started placing the groceries that she purchased from Key Food into the refrigerator.

"Hey, baby, how was your day?" he asked.

Natalie just nodded her head, acknowledging the question, but she didn't reply. Since the funeral, Natalie had lost her spontaneity and jubilant personality that had attracted Jim to her.

"How was yo' day?" he repeated.

At that, Natalie sharply turned around to face Jim. "My day came and went like all the other days. What you expect?" she replied coldly.

At that point, Jim was beginning to grow weary of Natalie's flippant responses. "Okay, Nat, look. It's been three weeks since we laid our son to rest. When are you gonna stop giving me this silent, aloof treatment?"

"Ain't nobody being aloof with you. I just don't feel like talkin' right now, okay?"

"Come on, baby, sit down. You're tense. Let me rub your

shoulders for you," Jim offered.

"I'm fine, Jim."

"Okay, you know what? I don't think you're doing good. I'm tryin' everything to comfort you, make you feel at ease, and all you do is shoot me down."

"Well maybe I ain't in the mood for your type of comfort."

"Natalie, what's gotten into you? Listen, I know you're still mad about what happened, and I swear the whole thing plays back in my head. I can't sleep because I'm afraid when I close my eyes, I'm gonna see that kid push Dante into that car all over again."

"You seem to be taking it rather well then, wouldn't you say?" Natalie asked.

"Rather well? That's what you call it? I'm struggling every day, but I'll be damned if I let Dante's passing keep me from living my life."

"Jim, I don't wanna hear any of your sympathy stories right now! Obviously, you're still working at that sweat box, right?"

"If you're referring to Flatbush Fists, then yes, I'm still working there. I don't see a problem with it."

Natalie put her hands up as if she didn't want to hear anything else that her husband had to say. "Of course, you wouldn't see a problem with it," Natalie scoffed. "Jim, you're not an 18-year-old kid anymore. You can do so much more than just box and teach boxing. Why don't you go to college and get a degree or work on a trade?"

Jim rolled his eyes, hardly believing that she was having the same discussion with him over his career choices. "Natalie, we've been over this many times already, okay? I do plan on returning to school, but I gotta see the launch of my new gym through. Then, when it's established, I'll take some business courses."

"You just can't detach yourself from boxing, huh?" Natalie asked.

Jim turned to her, enraged. "This is who I am! I was born a fighter. I grew up a fighter, and I'm gonna die a fighter. Do you understand that?"

"No, I don't understand that, and you know what? I don't think I'll ever understand it either."

"What are you saying?"

Natalie then turned away from Jim, tears welling in her eyes. "This isn't working, Jim. I remember when I first met you, there was something in your eyes that drew me to you. I tried to see things your way, but it's just not possible."

"So, you're saying you want out?"

Natalie walked a few steps away from Jim and didn't reply right away, but there was no denying what she mouthed to Jim. "Yes," she said softly.

"Natalie, please don't do this, alright? I need you here. I want you here. We're still a family even though we lost one of our members. We need to stick together through this. I know it's hard, but please—" Jim pleaded.

"You have no idea what it's like for me every day, Jim," Natalie said, cut him off. "Walking to work every day as if everything is fine and having to solve issues with other people's families when you can't even solve the glaring problem with your own family...I just can't take it anymore, Jim. I think we need to take a break. Think things over, you know?"

"Natalie, no matter what happens, I still love you, and I loved Dante just as much."

"Well, if you loved him so much, why didn't you walk him to the school door? If you loved him so much, why didn't you prevent this tragedy from happening?"

"I told you, Nat, I was too late. Dante didn't want me to walk him to school that morning. He wanted to do it on his own. I couldn't hold the boy's hand forever, Nat. At some point, I had to teach him how to be a man, and I paid the price for it. I gotta live with that. But we gotta be each other's support system. You can't just up and leave."

"Believe me, Jim. I've thought long and hard about this, and I think this is the route we need to take."

"So you ain't willing to salvage this marriage that I stayed faithful for, bled for, worked for over nine years? You want to leave?"

"I can't stay here anymore, Jim. Every time I walk in here, it's like I expect my son to come around the corner of the room to hug me, and knowing that it'll never happen again still hurts me to the core."

"And it doesn't hurt me? You think you're the only one hurtin' right now?" Jim said, fighting back tears as well.

"Listen, I know you have your new gym opening in Queens, and I wish you the best of luck in all that you do there. But I think it's best if we go our separate ways," Natalie said, as she took off her wedding ring and placed it on the dining room table. "I'm going to Marjorie's house in Mount Vernon to take some well-needed time to myself, and maybe down the line, we can patch things up."

Jim lowered his head, scarcely able to believe what was happening. Natalie was becoming unglued. "I sacrificed everything for you and Dante. I gave up my boxing career for my family, and this is how it's gon' end?"

"I'm sorry, Jim. I've already started packing my things, and I went to see an attorney yesterday for the rest of our paperwork. Let's just make it a clean break, okay?" she asked.

"Ain't nothin' clean about this, and if you want to play yourself and think that what you're doin' is right, you go ahead, and you think that way," he replied.

Natalie left the dining room without saying another word, and in two days she filed for divorce from Jim. After four more days, she moved out. In that same year, Jim opened the Steel Glove Gym in Queens. Although it was a culmination of everything he had worked for, in no way did it replace the family he had lost. He would later sell the brownstone in Brooklyn and move to Queens to be closer to his gym. Natalie would never speak to him nor call him for the next twenty-two years.

Taking another sip of his wine, Jim closed the album book, stood up from the couch, and walked towards the door. "Natalie, thanks for stopping by. It was great reminiscing on the good old times, but the last time we saw each other, it didn't end very well, and going over these memories ain't gon' patch nothin' up."

"I know it won't, Jim, and I don't expect you to forget how I hurt you all those years ago. But I am so sorry about what I said. It took some strong counseling sessions to make me realize that Dante's death wasn't your fault. You loved us, and I know that if you had a chance to do it over, you would," Natalie said.

Jim went over to the front door and opened it. "I think it's time for you to go," he said.

Disappointed, Natalie took his cue and headed out of the door. "Remember, if you ever need to talk about it or get some things off your chest, I'm still here," she said, and with that, she walked away into the cool night.

Closing the door behind her, Jim walked into his living room and stared at an old portrait where a young, smiling Dante glanced back at him along with Natalie. And he couldn't help but wonder how fast time flew and how close he was to reconciling with Natalie.

The next day at the SDCC, Sylvio stopped by the boxing gym during his lunch hour to communicate with other boxers and club members. Suddenly, a hush fell over the gym as the doors opened, and in walked current middleweight champion Barry Taylor along with members of his entourage.

The gym fell silent because there so many witnesses that were present during Barry's last visit to the center where he rambunctiously challenged Sylvio to a one-round fight. Many thought Barry would beat Sylvio, but Sylvio surprisingly held his own and even delivered a few hard punches himself. Barry had not returned to the gym since the challenge, so people were surprised at his return.

"What's good, Taylor? You back fo' more?" an anonymous boxer shouted as the other gym members laughed.

"Nah, he back to try to whip Sylvio's ass. Here go da' sequel," another boxer piped in, but Barry continued walking through the gym, ignoring the hecklers, until he saw Sylvio.

He stopped. Both men stared at each other without speaking.

I ain't in the mood to fight, but if he challenges me again, I'mma embarrass this kid.

"Sup, Barry? What brings you back hea'?" Sylvio asked, expecting Barry to carry on his normal boasting. But to his surprise, Barry smiled slightly.

"It ain't what you think, Wolf," he replied.

"Oh, it's Wolf now, huh? I thought I was a bitch for quittin' the fight game. But was it a bitch that whupped yo' ass last time?" Sylvio asked.

"Whateva', dawg, you got a few lucky shots in. It's all good. But believe it or not, I ain't here for a rematch," Barry replied with a calm demeanor.

"Well, what you here for then?" Jim replied as he took his glove pads off.

Barry took out his cell phone. "I'm here to offer you a business opportunity."

Sylvio's eyes narrowed. He still didn't trust Barry, but curiosity got the better of him. "I'm listening," he said.

Barry and two other members of his entourage followed Sylvio inside the office, which faced the gym. The office belonged to Kevin and Jim Shaw and was the location where they monitored the gym and counted finances.

Once inside the office, Sylvio turned to Barry, who sat between two of his bodyguards.

"Check it out, man. First off, I wanna apologize for talkin' shit that day when we threw down. I was buggin," Barry said.

"Whateva', man, it's all good. It's psychological warfare. I knew what you was doin." Sylvio replied. "But I know that ain't the only reason you stopped by though."

"Nah, that wasn't the only reason. I've just been challenged for my belt, and I've accepted the challenge."

"Okay, good for you, but I still don't know what that gotta do wit' me," Sylvio replied.

"Look, man, after what went down, I gotta give you props. You still got a lot to give to the fight game, B. That's why I'm comin' to you now. I want you to help train me for my title match," Barry said.

"Hold up. You want me to work for you? Nah, I ain't nobody's bitch. What's wrong, you don't want to break the bank to find yo' own trainers for the fight?" Sylvio asked.

"Yo', just hear me out fo' a minute. We came out the same streets, and we both know that defending the title is much harder than winnin' it," Barry said. "This new Chinese cat just came out of nowhere and challenged me for the middleweight championship. I accepted his challenge," he said, showing Sylvio his phone, where he had the YouStream video paused.

When he played the video, Sylvio saw the highlights of the new surprise challenger, Jun Zhang. Sylvio was amazed by what he saw. Jun had quick hands and devastating punching power on both. All of his previous fights had ended in three rounds or less. Sylvio saw the sheer strength and his technique, which were combined to create a deadly knockout combination that took out opponent after opponent.

"Wait, wasn't this cat in mixed martial arts?" Sylvio asked.

"He was, but he's in our game now, and so far, he's undefeated, fifteen and zero. No one's lasted more than three rounds in the ring with him," Barry explained.

Sylvio's eyes were still glued onto Barry's cell phone screen as he watched Jun Zhang knock out each opponent with deadly ease.

"That boy got some serious power, man. Why you wanna take this fight, dawg?" Sylvio asked.

"I'm taking it cuz of all this," Barry replied, showing Sylvio his

Instagram and Facebook sites, where hundreds of boxing fans berated him, calling him the "fake champion" and accusing him of fighting little known unranked opponents. Meanwhile, Jun Zhang had worked on being a serious contender for the middleweight title by fighting ranked opponents all over the world.

"Fightin' this dude is the only way to shut all of 'em up, you feel me?" Barry said.

His words brought about a strange sense of déjà vu. That's the same way I used to think before I fought Maximo for the title.

"Barry, you da champ now. You ain't gotta give a fuck about what anybody says about you. You ain't gotta prove nothin' to them."

"I gotta prove something to myself, man. I gotta prove that I can go out there and hold my own against the world's best, and in order to do that, I need to be trained by the best," Barry said, holding out his hand to shake Sylvio, but his counterpart was not easily sold.

"Barry, I'm done, bro. I don't want nothin' to do with this situation you got with ole boy, alright? Get someone else."

"There ain't nobody else, man!" Barry said, raising his voice. "Look, you got the quick hand speed and foot speed to match this sucka'. Your stamina in the ring is crazy. As much as I try, I could never be you, man. There's only one Wolf, and I need your help. I ain't askin' you to do no public appearances or talk to my fans."

"And what's in it for me?" Sylvio asked.

"I'll give you forty percent off top," Barry replied.

Sylvio still didn't understand why Barry approached him, but he thought about the money he could bring in from the fight to help his center. "Alright, man, I'll do it. But if I help you train, you gotta be all in wit' me. No half-stepping, no shortcuts, no excuses. We doin' it my way, you feel me?"

"Okay, bet," Barry replied as the two boxers dapped and shook hands.

Just two hours after he agreed to help train Barry Taylor, Sylvio left the community center and drove to his father's apartment. It was Jacques' Dominique's birthday. The old Haitian patriarch was always busy at work, but years of failing health and old age took a toll on him. Just months before Sylvio's title fight versus Felipe Maximo, Jacques suffered a stroke brought on by an onset of diabetes. He spent weeks in a medical coma, and Sylvio believed that he would lose his father right after they'd made amends for their fallout from when Sylvio was eighteen.

With his strict authoritarian upbringing, Jacques rarely spared the rod when it came to disciplining his son, and Sylvio bore scars of the abuse that he suffered at the hands of his father. In many ways, Sylvio internalized the pain, the abuse, and the beatings. It worked to his advantage whenever he was fighting an opponent.

But on the day that he saw his father fighting for his life in the hospital, Sylvio's heart softened, and he felt sympathetic towards his father. And after a lengthy conversation with Jacques once he miraculously woke up from his coma, Sylvio realized that his father was hard on him because he wanted him to succeed in life.

When Sylvio found himself lying in a hospital bed weeks later, his father was by his side the entire time. Jacques' own health had gradually improved. For a few years, he'd lived without any incident, but just months earlier, he had suffered another unexpected stroke, which was more debilitating than the previous one. It didn't induce him in a coma, but the stroke affected his motor skills, which caused him difficulty in walking and talking at times. Although he needed a cane to walk, it didn't stop Jacques from working for MTA at the ticket booth, a job he held for over thirty years.

It was Jacques' birthday, and Sylvio wanted to make sure he helped his father celebrate another year of life since he had been at death's door once before. After buzzing his father's apartment, Jacques unlocked the door, then slowly limped back to his couch while Sylvio entered.

"Hey, Dad, what's up? *Bon Fete!*" Sylvio exclaimed, wishing his father a happy birthday.

"Thank you, Sylvio," Jacques said, hugging his son.

"So how are you doing? They're keeping you busy at the center?" he asked.

"Yup, busy all day long. Interviewed a couple workers and filled out some financial paperwork—you know, nothing major. But how you doing though?" Sylvio asked, patting Jacques' back.

"Eh, you know, can't complain. I wish I can walk like you, but you know me. I'm an old man."

"Come on, Dad. You ain't that old. You need to tell your coworkers to stop lyin' to your face," Sylvio laughed.

"Ah, I wish it were that easy," Jacques replied.

Sylvio internally debated on whether he should tell his father about his partnership with Barry Taylor, but just as he made up his mind, the apartment buzzer rang again.

"Can you push the button for me, please?" Jacques asked, referring to the buzzer near the door that allowed the visitor to enter the building.

"Just like that, Dad? You ain't even gon' ask who it is?" Sylvio asked, to which Jacques gave him a sly smile.

Then they heard the door knock. When Sylvio went to look through the apartment keyhole, he shook his head, sighing. *If only it were somebody else.*

Opening the door, his sister, Rebecca Dominique, entered the apartment, followed by a tall slender black man, wearing wide-brimmed glasses. Rebecca was two years younger than Sylvio, and she lived in Philadelphia with their mother, Anne.

"I was 'bout to say...I thought you weren't gon' let me in, big head," Rebecca joked as she hugged her brother.

"Nah, I can't avoid you even if I wanted to. What horse-hair weave you got on now?" Sylvio cracked, causing Rebecca to slap his arm. Sylvio loved teasing his sister about her hair, or fake hair.

"Shut up, boy. I still look betta than yo' lame ass," she laughed, before running over to Jacques. "Happy birthday, Daddy!" Rebecca gave Jacques her wrapped gift and a birthday card while the frail older man looked on.

"So, Rebecca, ain't you gon' introduce us to yo' new boy toy?" Sylvio teased.

Rebecca rolled her eyes. "Fine, whatever. Sylvio this is Eric Grevin, and he's my man. Eric, this is my annoying brother Sylvio."

Excited, Eric shook Sylvio's hand. "Man, what's up, Sylvio? I saw a lot of yo' fights back in da day, especially the Chavez fight. You messed ole boy up good."

"Appreciate that, B. So, since you're datin' my sister, there's a few things you need to know about her. For one, when there's a full moon, and she got a lil extra hair—" Sylvio started, before being smacked by his sister.

"Eric, don't listen to him. He play too much," Rebecca said dismissively.

"Nah, but all jokes aside, where's Mom at?" Sylvio asked.

"Well, she said she had to work, but she was gonna try to make it. I don't know."

Sylvio looked out the apartment window. I wouldn't bet on her coming. Some things never change.

Chapter 7

T hird-ranked Caron Guerra staggered against the ropes after being hit by a bone-crushing right jab. It was the second round of a middleweight fight in Albuquerque, New Mexico, against the unorthodox challenger Jun Zhang. Caron Guerra had previously been known as a smart boxer inside the ring, who was able to tactically figure out his opponents in the ring—an ability that allowed him to adjust his fight scheme. He was well in the running to contend for the middleweight crown, but he soon realized that he was out of his element against the relentless Asian boxer.

Jun has not only capitalized on Guerra's mistakes in the ring, but he also unleashed a vicious counterattack that Guerra struggled to defend himself against, and it caused worry among his trainers. With his nose partially broken, Guerra threw his best punches before the end of the second round, but Jun seemed unfazed.

When Round 2 finally ended, Jun walked calmly to his bench while Guerra stumbled and barely found his way to the bench. Taking one look at his fighter, trainer Ben Higgs knew Guerra was virtually out on his feet and worked frantically to wake him before the third round started.

"Guerra, I'm gonna call it," Higgs said, motioning to the white towel, indicating that he would end the fight before his fighter suffered more serious injury.

"No, don't stop this. I got him next round. I can't go out like this," Guerra replied, breathing heavily.

When he realized that he couldn't persuade his fighter to quit, Higgs gave Guerra his mouthpiece as the bell rang for the third round. Guerra, still groggy with rubbery legs, went to meet Jun in the center of the ring.

Jun walked calmly to meet Guerra, and both men began exchanging punches, but it became evident that Jun's punches were more affective, and his jabs were a deadly combination of speed and power.

It's like getting' hit with two million bombs at once.

Finally, Jun saw the opening in Guerra's guard and responded with a left hook to the head that dropped Guerra to the canvas. The ref began his ten-count. Guerra only slightly stirred on the floor. The ref finished the ten-count, and Jun raised his hands in victory. Running back to his corner, Jun was confident that he was now in consideration to fight for the middleweight. His trainer knew it as well.

"This was maybe one of your best performances, Jun," Chao said. "Keep this up, and you'll be the champion in no time."

After the spectators clapped for the challenger and his opponent, one of the side reporters walked up to Jun. "So, Jun, you've defeated third-ranked fighter, Guerra, and you barely managed to get hurt yourself. What does it mean to beat a great fighter such as Guerra, and what implications does this have for your next fight?"

"Well, it was a very good bout. Guerra certainly has heart, but I was determined to win quickly because my next fight definitely won't be easy," Jun replied.

"With this win, you've all but secured the opportunity to fight for the middleweight championship currently held by New York's Barry Taylor. How do you feel about him?" she asked.

Jun shrugged smugly. "I think that he's a good fighter who has fought inexperienced boys and lucked his way to a title, but now it's time to see if he can win some real fights."

"There is some speculation that Taylor has recruited former middleweight champion Sylvio Dominique to help him prepare for his title defense. Are you concerned about that?"

Jun looked at the reporter as if she had lost her mind. "I'm not concerned in the least bit because, to me, he's just a man and fighter. I don't know too much about Sylvio Dominique, but I know that he does not know my style, so I am not concerned at all."

"Strong words for a very strong contender. Thank you very much, and congratulations again," the reporter said as she closed the recording.

After watching her step out of the ring, Jun and his cornermen began to step out of the ring to make their way over to their locker rooms, unaware that Jun lied to the reporter about not knowing Sylvio Dominique.

Although he knew that Sylvio had retired, he presented the ultimate challenge that Jun had searched for. Sylvio Dominique was one of his favorite boxers growing up, and all that Jun remembered was the previous interaction with Sylvio when his idol demolished Cesar Chavez in five rounds.

Jun was only fifteen then, and he remembered asking Sylvio for his autograph, but the champion rebuffed young Jun and his friend who'd attempted to take a picture with Sylvio. At the time, Sylvio was fighting for a shot at the title. He may have been pushed by one of the members of the Wolf Pack, but to Jun, it didn't matter. He internalized the feeling he had and vowed that one day he would be in the ring with Sylvio, if Sylvio ever went back to the ring.

While the trainer took his gloves and padding off, Jun's manager, Kim Li, entered the locker room. "Great fight, Jun! One of the best I've seen out of you. Keep it up, and one day, I'm gonna be looking at the next middleweight champion."

"So, is it true?" Jun asked suddenly.

"Is what true?" Kim said.

"Barry Taylor went and got Sylvio Dominique to help train him?"

"Yeah maybe, but why should that matter to you?" Kim asked.

"It matters because he's training the same guy I'm about to fight," Jun replied.

"What does it matter? He's not fighting anymore, so he's not our concern. Our eyes should be set on Barry Taylor, alright?"

"Right. Well, I'm waiting on him. After next month, the belt is mine," Jun said, determined, as he threw his glove wraps away.

Meanwhile, Valentina Cruz was on her way home after a full day of filming. Opting to take an Uber home, she watched the Atlanta skyline lights. It reminded her of the bright lights of Manhattan. Not as busy, but the city life was one that suited her. She would've lost her mind if she stayed in the suburbs. A couple of her castmates lived in suburbs that were out into the country.

But it was too quiet for Valentina. She needed excitement and activity in her surroundings. She needed the hustle and bustle of busy cars, buses, and trains. Atlanta had MARTA train stations and MARTA buses for commute, but she preferred going home in an

Uber, whenever she could. On the ride, her cell phone rang. It was Sylvio.

"Hey, baby, what's up?"

"What's up, boo? I'm so damn tired. Anderson worked our asses off filming today. Felt like he was pissed off with every take. Imagine having to stay in character doing the same scene for over four hours."

"Well, this is the life you signed up for though. I mean, your show's got high ratings on YouStream for a reason. Gotta stay on point," Sylvio emphasized.

Valentina laughed. "Yeah okay, whatever. You ain't the one that gotta go on set to deliver an Oscar performance on queue."

"Well, I had to stay on point and in shape when I was in the ring. Perfection requires discipline. Don't sweat it though. One day, I'mma come down there, and we could chill and watch reruns of 'You Thought You Had Me.'"

"Ugh please, Sylvio, if we are eva' chillin', let's watch anything but that. I'm serious. When I see myself on screen, I cringe."

"Why? You a dope actress. Shit, your performance is so believable that, at times, I want to reach through the screen and knock Anthony's ass out for threatening my woman," Sylvio admitted.

"Okay, baby, we've been through this a thousand times. It's all made up. It's a performance meant to entertain. All the love and violent scenes in the show are not real," Valentina giggled.

"Yeah, okay. You right. I guess I let my jealousy get in the way again. I won't let it happen again," Sylvio replied.

Valentina smiled and laughed on the phone. She loved it when Sylvio admitted how jealous he was whenever she was approached by another man. She couldn't explain it, but it completely turned her on for her to know he wanted her all to himself.

"Besides, I want us to make a movie of our own," he added.

"Oh yeah, and what's the title of that movie gon' be?" she asked, as the car pulled up in front of her apartment building.

"It's gon' be called 'New York Boxer Comes to Atlanta To Surprise Actress Girlfriend,' and it comes out tonight," he said.

"What? Wait you mean…" Valentina stepped out of the car and sure enough, Sylvio was waiting at the front of the apartment entrance, holding his cell phone in one hand and a bouquet of roses in the other hand along with a bottle of Rose' wine. Valentina ran to hug her boyfriend and kissed him for the first time in months. "Oh my God, why didn't you tell me you was coming down here?"

"I didn't wanna spoil the surprise," Sylvio replied. He managed to book a flight to Atlanta for four days to rest before his grueling schedule began in New York.

Valentina had already texted him her address in case he visited, but she never expected him to visit her so soon. "Wow, this was a real surprise," she said, still lost for words.

"Well, we'll have plenty of time to talk about it ova' a drink," he said as they walked up to the apartment holding hands.

It didn't take long after she closed her door for them to make up for lost intimacy time. Valentina slid her hand down to his midsection and began to undo his zipper.

"Whoa, whoa, baby. Ain't we gon' have the drink first?" Sylvio asked.

"Baby, it's been a really long time, okay? The drink can wait," she said seductively. As she unzipped his fly, and he removed her shirt and bra, they both fell into her bed and into their passion.

After their intense lovemaking session, Valentina was lying naked on top of her boyfriend's back, kissing his glistening broad shoulders. "Sylvio, I needed this so bad. I was going stir-crazy down hea' by myself."

"Why? I thought Atlanta was about that party life. You ain't went to no clubs in the city?"

"I mean, one of my castmates invited me to go to Club Diamond, and I went there. It was cool, but after going there, I just realized that I was really over the club scene," she replied.

"Really?"

"I mean, yeah. Don't get me wrong, if they need me for promo reasons or maybe a photo shoot promoting a project, I'll still go. But other than that, it just ain't for me anymore. I mean, c'mon Sylvio, I've been working in clubs and lounges since I was seventeen years old. It gets played out after a while."

"Yeah, I see what you sayin'. But sometimes you gotta unwind too and have a lil fun while you can."

Valentina stared intensely at Sylvio, raising an eyebrow. "Funny, you should say that, Sylvio. Is that what you be doin' when you get off work?"

"Hey, it's clean, wholesome, responsible fun," Sylvio reassured her.

"Yeah, with a whole bunch of clean wholesome, skanky-ass hoes. You got a few that's using the strip club business as a come up, and I respect that, but then you got others out there that's makin' it their end-all, be-all. The happiest day of my life was when I quit Apple Kim's."

Valentina shifted her body off Sylvio's back as he turned around, and she lay under his arms. "It was just time for me to move on, and besides, that place brought back too many negative memories. Let's not forget who got me that job in the first place," she said, refusing to mention the name because it reignited her anger because the same person had attempted to take her boyfriend's life.

"Baby, listen you gotta let that go, okay? It was six years ago, and although he tried, he didn't get to me, and that man's rottin' behind bars right now," Sylvio said.

"Yeah, but I feel like I brought all that shit to you. Anyway, I'm glad we left that part of our lives behind. Now we can focus on the community center, and I can focus on finishing this series."

Sylvio looked at Valentina nervously. Should I tell her about my involvement with Barry? I might as well cuz she's gonna find out on some sports news network anyway. "Yeah, about the part of leaving our old careers behind...I agreed to help train Barry Taylor for his title fight," Sylvio confessed.

Valentina, who had been caressing Sylvio's chest, suddenly stopped. "You what?" she asked, causing Sylvio to shift uncomfortably.

"Look, Val, Barry stopped by the gym again today, and he asked me to help him train for his title defense," Sylvio admitted.

"Barry? The same busta that tried to beat your ass a few months ago?" Valentina asked.

"But he didn't, and I held my own against him. That's not the point. Look, I've agreed to help him train, and in return, he's training in the Dante Shaw Gym, which could give us a lot of publicity and some much-needed clientele," Sylvio protested.

"Yeah, but at what cost? You promised me you wouldn't get involved in the fight game again. Why are you going back to the very thing that almost took your life?" she asked.

"Don't even sweat that, Val. I'm not the one fighting for the title. Barry has his title, and he's gotta defend it, and he feels that I'm the one to help him do it."

Valentina stood up from the bed as the light from the full moon reflected upon her bare shoulders. "Sylvio, you don't need to go back to them. The boxing federation don't care about ya'll. Look how quick they gave your title away once you retired," she argued.

"Don't you think I know what I'm risking? I know what almost happened to me. I can still feel the bullet hittin' me, and I can see Omar lying in a pool of blood next to me. I still see it every night, and I don't want to get back in the ring, but that doesn't mean I can't help somebody else in the neighborhood get theirs," Sylvio said.

Valentina shook her head as she put on a red silk robe. "I'm still not down wit' this decision, Sylvio. But long as you don't get back into the ring again, I guess I'll just roll wit' it," she said.

Sylvio jumped up and kissed Valentina on the lips. "See, baby, I knew there was a reason I loved you."

"Mmm hmm. I hope you realize that this means you owe me." Valentina gushed in a tone that drove Sylvio crazy.

As they kissed passionately, Sylvio began to remove the robe that she had put on. "Really? I just put it on you for the first time in weeks. What else do I owe you?"

"I know you ain't tappin' out on me, Wolf. I got enough to go twelve rounds wit' you," she replied as Sylvio's tongue worked its way around her neck, breasts, and naval.

"We'll see about that," he said in a muffled voice as she laughed in pleasure.

Back in the Shaw-Dominique Community Center, Jim confronted his brother in his office after Natalie's unexpected visit.

"Man, look. Why you trippin' over the fact that she came back?" Kevin asked.

"Twenty-two years, Kevin. It has been twenty-two years since she last saw me and walked out on me. Took me a helluva long time to move on, and here you go bringin' her back into my orbit. You could've told me she was coming," Jim said.

"She didn't want me to tell you nothin' man. She the one that wanted to surprise you, so she looked up my info and called me. That's when I told her where she could find you. All she wanted to do was catch up," Kevin replied.

"Yeah, and when she knocked on my door, I was suddenly reminded of how she dipped out on me. Blamed me for Dante's passing. Tellin' me how she got help and worked it out, and now she thinks I need help."

"But she said she forgave you for it, and she reached out to help you. The least you can do is give her a chance, and just let her help you."

Jim paced the office. "I don't need any help, okay? Everybody grieves in their own way, and everybody compensates in their own way."

"Is that what you say when you pace elementary school grounds at random points during the day? Is that what you tell yourself when you pick up kids to try to save them from bullying so you can train them to ease yo' guilt?" Kevin asked.

"Shut up!" Jim yelled.

"Why? Because you know I'm speaking facts?" Kevin asked. "You need to seek help, Jim. What you're doin' ain't healthy, and one day it's gon' come back and bite you."

"I don't need a damn lecture from my own little brother, okay? I do what I want, when I want, and the next time one of my so-called 'old friends' want to see me, you run that by me first. You got that?" Jim asked.

"Yeah whatever, man. Look, I gotta work on keeping the books here, so is that all you wanna talk to me about?"

"Yeah, whateva', man. Go back to work," Jim answered.

Kevin left the office.

Jim walked over to his desk and sat down. *I know what I'm doing. I'm trying to save these kids out here because nobody else can save 'em. Not their parents, not the system, not their schools, or their so-called friends...I have a good reason for what I'm doing, and if anybody else can't see that, to hell with them. I don't need help. Dante needed me, and I wasn't there. Now I'm gonna make sure I'm there for any kid that needs it.*

Jim walked over to the wall behind his desk where a third-grade picture of Dante hung. In the picture, he was wearing his favorite T-shirt with the new L.A. Gear sneakers Jim had bought him just days before the picture was taken. Tears began to fill the brim of Jim's eyes. It didn't matter how long it was. The pain was still as fresh as if Dante had died the day before.

Upon returning home from Atlanta, Sylvio found himself working nonstop, from helping Barry Taylor train for his title match, to tending to his regular duties at the SDCC.

As the date of the middleweight championship fight drew near, the current champion was intensifying his training, training underwater at the local pool to improve his speed against resistance and jogging through Union Turnpike to increase his cardio and endurance.

One aspect that they discovered about Barry was the fact that he had not gone further than seven rounds in his last few matches. Sylvio felt that increasing his endurance might help him prepare for what could be a full twelve-round fight. At first, Jim was reluctant in helping Barry train because of the bad blood he previously held with Sylvio.

"Look, Jim, we're all on the same team now. He came up in Steel Gloves like I did," he said one day while Barry sparred with another boxer.

"The same team? Must I remind you that the last time he came 'round hea', he tried to bust yo' head in?" Jim asked.

"Nah, that's history, man. We got a new target now," Sylvio replied as he showed Jim Jun Zhang's highlights on his phone.

Jim took the phone and watched Jun mow down opponent after opponent with ease. "Look, man, I hate to say this, but Barry shouldn't take this fight," Jim whispered, handing the phone back to Sylvio.

"What you talkin' bout, Jim?" Sylvio asked.

Jim shook his head. "Sylvio, after all this time, haven't I not taught you how to analyze boxers on film? This Jun Zhang cat is using judo tactics in his fight. He's quick, elusive, and he's too strong. Barry ain't ready for that." With that, he handed Sylvio his phone and walked back into his office.

But Sylvio followed him. "C'mon, Jim, level wit' me. You seriously think Barry can't whup this cat?"

"That's exactly what I'm sayin'. Look at all the opponents Jun has fought. They're all top-ranked world contenders. Hell, even in the MMA division, he was fighting against superior competition. Barry couldn't even take a punch that you dished out when ya' two scrapped, and he's supposed to defend his title against that guy?"

"No, that's your opinion," Sylvio replied. "What kind of trainer puts his boxer down before he actually fights?"

"I guess I'm the only one that's makin' sense right now," Jim said. "Barry is gonna have his hands full wit' this guy. It's bad business for him, Sylvio. Ya boy's gonna have a real rude awakening on fight night."

"Look, Jim, I have my reasons for training him, okay? First off, he came askin' me for help, aight? And this place is buzzing. The media is gonna arrive soon to get some shots of Barry working out. So it's a win-win situation for everybody," Sylvio reassured Jim.

"Everybody except Barry. Look, Wolf, why don't you see the writing on the wall? You more concerned about this place's publicity more than a brotha's well-being?" Jim asked.

"Is that what you asked yourself each time that we stepped into the ring?" Sylvio asked Jim.

"No, that was different. I knew what kind of fighter I had in you, man. We don't even know Barry's boxing tendencies, what makes him tick, what he's vulnerable to—nothing," Jim argued back.

"So what, man? Barry makes up for his weaknesses with heart. Gimme a fighter with heart every day, Jim."

"Heart ain't gonna do much if he doesn't have a strategy against Jun," Jim said.

But after a few minutes, when he thought about the center, he reluctantly agreed to help Sylvio train Barry for his fight.

The next day, the press arrived at the Dante Shaw Boxing Gym. About twenty reporters, camera personnel, sports blogs, and social media reps were at the gym while Barry worked on the speed bag. The regular members of the boxing gym and the center worked valiantly to maneuver around media members.

As Barry worked on the heavy bag, he whispered to Sylvio who was holding the bag steady. "Yo', you see that reporter next to the door? Tell me she ain't bad, B.," Barry said between punches.

Sylvio glanced in the direction Barry was referring to and saw a female reporter, probably in her mid-twenties, who was wearing glasses and had a notepad and recorder in her hand.

"Yeah, she bad," Sylvio agreed.

Stopping for a water break, Barry reached over for his water gallon. "Why don't you go take a break and hit that real quick?" he asked with a sly grin.

"What? Nah, man, I'm cool. I'm wit' a jawn already, you feel me?"

"Yeah, yeah, that Latina chick on Youstream. Everybody know that shit. But she a thousand miles away, bro, and you can't tell me that she don't wanna fuck other niggas off set," Barry said.

Sylvio wasn't hearing any of it. "Nah, we don't get down like that man. What me and Valentina got is timeless, dawg. You ain't eva' gon' understand unless you got someone special, man," he replied.

"I guess not, son. I can't see myself in no monogamous relationship, man. I can't be wit' one chick, bro. I gotta have some variety in my life, man," Barry said confidently.

Not soon afterwards, two young black women—not reporters, but fans—managed to push through the media line and ran and hugged Barry.

"Oh my God, we love you, Barry."

"Yes, baby, you is too fine!"

The security attempted to remove the women, but Barry waved them off. Walking towards the locker room with a girl under each arm, he turned back to Sylvio. "See what I'm sayin', B? I need variety."

"Yo', where you goin', man? We gotta finish training!" Sylvio yelled, but Barry had already shut the locker room door behind him.

Chapter 8

In the weeks leading up to the middleweight title fight, the media attacks between Jun Zhang's camp and Barry Taylor's camp intensified. Whether it was a publicity stunt or his way to psyche his opponent out, Jun wasn't shy about smearing the champion's name and reputation. He would tell the media how Barry was an undeserving, underachieving boxer who had been spoon-fed his opponents in order to retain his place at the top of the division. He would go on about how Barry was overrated with limited skills, lacking the strength to knock out even amateur boxers. It also didn't help that Barry had a reputation of being a womanizer who always had rendezvous with women wherever he went. Jun used that as ammunition to further humiliate his opponent.

"That playboy probably spends more time having sex than he does actually training," Jun said during one sports network interview in Los Angeles.

"You talk as if you don't engage in sexual activity yourself," the reporter chuckled.

"Not before a fight," Jun replied. "A warrior must clear his mind, body, and spirit before battle so that he can focus on his opponent. Any type of physical activity that has nothing to do with preparing for a fight would be counterproductive, and I'm not the type of fighter who would hinder myself by my own personal pleasures before any fight."

"Well, Jun, I know we will be in for a great fight on May 5th. Thank you very much," the interviewer said.

Back in New York, Barry Taylor, Sylvio, and Gary Williams watched the scathing interview at the Dante Shaw Boxing Gym. The champion didn't find the interview the least bit amusing.

"I'mma break 'dis nigga's mouth for talkin' that shit," Barry said, clearly incensed.

"Yo', forget about that dude, man. It's a mind game. He's tryin' to get into your head. Gotta stay focused," Sylvio said.

Later that day, they watched footage of Jun's previous fights. "They nicknamed him the Cinderblock Tiger because when he makes impact, it's not a bag of bricks hittin' you. It's a cinder block hitting you. He has punching power for days, so we gotta keep your hands and your body moving," Sylvio said.

Barry waved his hand dismissively. "Man, I know what I'm doin'. I don't sweat that cat."

"Which is why over the next couple of weeks, we gotta speed you up," Sylvio said as he took out his boxing gear.

Over the next week, Barry and Sylvio worked diligently to counter Jun's power with speed, working on countless punch combinations, speed drills, and elusive ways to avoid Jun's effort to shorten the ring, which he loved to do against his opponents. Jun did that in an effort to not allow opponents any space to operate inside the ring. Then his wide, muscular frame and lateral movement allowed him to cut the ring off in ways that forced fighters to the ropes or the corners, where Jun would have his way with them.

Working with Barry's trainer, Tom Blaylock, Sylvio created escape strategies for Barry. On the final day of training before the weigh-in and fight, Sylvio packed his gym gear and headed to lock the gym door. Gary met him just inside the gym.

Looking at the boxing memorabilia hanging on the gym wall, Gary couldn't help but to reflect his friend's past. "Tell me you don't miss it, dawg," he said, staring at a large photo of Sylvio as a young contender in the New York Post newspaper cover. The cover read, "WOLF IS FINALLY CHAMP!"

"Miss what?" Sylvio asked.

"Being on top, man. Being that dude everybody was afraid of. Being a champ," he replied.

"Yeah, and I only had the middleweight belt for a day, Gary. So, I don't really know what I'm missing. Plus, this game took out two of my homies."

Gary stared at Sylvio like he was crazy. "Two of your homies? You almost got killed 'cuz one of your homies turned on you."

"C'mon, man, he was pressured by the Serps to do what he did—" Sylvio started to explain, but Gary cut him off.

"Pressured by who? He played us from the moment he got down wit' the Pack."

"No, man, he was paid off by the Serps to knock me off after I won the title against Maximo. He was money-hungry."

"And the reason you almost got killed, Wolf," Gary said, finishing Sylvio's sentence for him. "Look, I thought we were cool too, but when he turned on us, he stopped you at a time where you could've been dominant. Good riddance to his ass."

"Yeah, but nothin' we can do now. Everything's that happened in the past can be used to motivate us in the future," Sylvio said.

"Or it can motivate you on coming back," Gary said, raising an eyebrow upon the suggestion.

Sylvio shook his head. "No, Gary, I'm not goin' back to boxing, okay? I've already been through this. I'm done," he said.

"Look, man, I wasn't there in that alley with you and Omar, but believe me, when you were dying, I thought it was all over. Then you survived death and defied the odds. People need to see that there's hope for those who don't give up on that dream, bro."

"Someone else could give them that dream, and that someone else is Barry Taylor. He's the champ, now. He's the one who's got the burden of defending his title—not me."

"But it should be you. You should be the one going out there fighting this Jun kid. I mean, don't get me wrong, Barry's a good fighter. But he ain't you. He got your skill and power, maybe even your fan appeal, but he don't got the heart, man. You got the juice. Don't forget that," Gary said before walking out of the gym, leaving Sylvio looking at his newspaper photo.

Fight night finally arrived. For the fans in Hershey, Pennsylvania, it was not only a battle between champion and contender, but it was also an international battle of supremacy. The much-hyped bout featured the current champion Barry Taylor, who had been heavily criticized about the quality of opponents that he faced on his way to the middleweight crown, but he felt that he had a chance to quiet the critics and prove that he would be a force to be reckoned with for years to come.

But standing in his way while also providing Barry with his first title defense, was Jun Zhang. Jun had been undefeated and unchallenged in his rise to the top of the boxing ranks. There was no love lost between Jun and Barry, who had been hurling insults through social media in the weeks leading up to the fight. Jun believed Barry was a "soft pretty boy who had been fed weaker opponents for clout to ensure his ascent to the belt."

Barry responded by cruelly deriding Jun on his Chinese culture and background, even going so far as to say, "He needs to go back where he came from and cook himself a dog to eat or something."

A normally calm and collected Jun was enraged at what he felt was a racial comment, so he issued an ultimatum to the champion: "Do not fight me, or you will lose the belt. Better back down while you still can."

But talk time was finally over, and the two fighters walked to the conference room of the Hershey Park Pavilion, the site of the championship boxing match where scores of reporters were waiting for the official weigh-in. As the challenger, Jun was weighed first. Sylvio who had accompanied Barry's training team to the venue, noticed that Jun was completely all muscle. He was toned, with muscles rippling and jaw taut. Barry finally stepped up to the scale. While he was in top physical shape himself, he did not match the amount of muscles that Jun had.

Man, Barry, what did you get yourself into? This guy's gonna chew you up within the first three rounds. But Sylvio still held out hope that Barry could successfully defend his title against the foreign newcomer.

Getting ready in the locker room, Barry moved his head from side to side as he practiced his slips and jabs. "Time to separate the men from the boys, son," he told Sylvio, while shaking his hand.

"I feel you, man. But remember what we studied on him. Keep him off balance, and protect yourself at all times."

"No doubt, man. I'mma end 'dis bitch in five rounds, and I'mma see if he gon' do any talkin' then."

"Look, bro, just keep your gloves up. Don't let up for one

minute against this cat," Sylvio warned as he helped Barry's trainer lace up his gloves.

Twenty minutes later, Barry and his team came out brandishing the middleweight belt for the fight fans. Barry sat at his corner, itching to get into the ring and pound at Jun. Soon, both fighters were in the ring, and the referee was explaining the rules and warnings to them. The bell rang for Round 1. Immediately, Barry moved in on Jun, and he came out relentlessly against him, throwing wild hooks and jabs. But the former mixed martial arts fighter was not daunted or intimated, backing away as he allowed Barry to continue pressing his attack, without throwing a single punch himself.

It looks as if Barry's trying to knock him out early. He really doesn't like that guy, and he's trying to make an early statement.

But Jun blocked numerous blows to the chest and the face. At first Sylvio thought that he would let the round finish before he attacked Barry, but Jun would be proven wrong in the next two minutes. After his trainer yelled instruction in Cantonese, Jun threw a devastating right jab to Barry's face, and from the corner, Sylvio heard the impact of Jun's blow, which buckled Barry's knees. Barry retaliated by throwing a bevy of hooks, uppercuts, and straight jabs at Jun's face, but not one of them hit home. Jun either slipped the blows, ducked the blows, or thoroughly blocked them.

Damn, that boy fast. Barry can't even touch him.

At the end of the first round, Barry made his way back to his corner with a black eye that began to swell up when he sat on his stool.

"Look, Barry, you've got to move yo' head and your body, man. Quit standing there, or he'll knock you out," Tom warned while the cutman worked diligently to lower the swelling from the huge blow that Barry incurred.

Round 2 began, and from the onset of the round, Sylvio could see Barry's hopes of defending his title slipping away as Jun's elusive, unorthodox fighting style wore down the champion. Jun was one of the fastest fighters in the division, and his speed and force were on full display. He made Barry look as though he was standing still, and with each stinging blow to the champion's face, Sylvio saw the damage setting in for Barry. He had cuts on his right cheek, nose bridge, and chin. He struggled to counter, and the crowd in attendance—a majority that heavily rooted for him—sat in stunned silence as their champion was unable to respond to each punch that hit him. Jun threw a left hook that connected on his right face, and immediately, Barry crumbled to the canvas.

"C'mon, Barry, get up!" Sylvio yelled from the corner.

Fortunately, Barry survived the initial ten-count, but Jun sensed that his reflexes were too slow to fully block his punches. It wasn't too long before Barry hit the ground again, and before the referee reached the count of ten, Sylvio knew that it was over. Jun Zhang had won the middleweight title in less than two rounds and asserted his dominance.

As Sylvio and the rest of Barry's cornermen dragged the slumped defeated ex-champion to his corner, Jun decided to add more insult to injury. "See what happens when he faces a real fighter? Please drag what's left of him to the side, and wake him up from his nightmare," Jun said as he celebrated the knockout with his trainer and cornermen.

Sylvio just glared at him.

"What, you got something to say to me?" Jun asked.

Sylvio was tempted to reply, but with the cameras surrounding the victor, and Barry lying unconscious on the canvas, his face unrecognizable, he kept quiet.

After the crowd recovered from the initial shock, a mixture of cheers and boos rained down onto the ring as Sylvio and Barry's cornermen woke their defeated boxer up with smelling salts and carried him into the locker room.

That same evening in Atlanta, Valentina just finished wrapping her final scene for her YouStream series. It was an extremely intense scene where Gabrielle, after being threatened by Anthony, managed to talk him out of killing her before having sex with him. Secretly, Gabrielle intended to leave Anthony, and she needed him relaxed so she could make her next move. While Anthony slept, Gabrielle would sneak out of the house where she would go visit her cousin. There, they would call the police on Anthony.

The popular series was far from over, and although Valentina was working long hours, she was very grateful for the role that she saw as a breakthrough for her career. On her way to the trailer, she saw Robert and her other co-stars, Lewis Hayes and Nancy Dellwright, huddled together, looking closely at one of their cell phones.

"Hey, what's up?" Valentina greeted but was surprised by the air of secrecy that surrounded the small group.

"What's good, Val?" Lewis replied.

"What ya watchin'? Valentina asked curiously.

"Highlights from last night's title fight. Man, Barry got worked!" Robert exclaimed.

"Wait, hold up. Barry Taylor lost?" Valentina asked, surprised.

"Hell yeah, that Asian dude beat the shit out of him. And

they're really goin' in on yo' man right now," Robert replied as he handed Valentina his phone.

Robert had a sports network application on his phone that enabled him to receive sports-related news and updates, so sure enough, Valentina saw the highlights of Barry Taylor's brutal two-round knockout at the hands of Jun Zhang. There was no mistaking the clips, showing Sylvio's look of disbelief at the fight's outcome. The knockout was bloody enough, but Valentina was equally appalled at the sportscasters who, at large, blamed Sylvio for not preparing Barry to defend his belt, and they hurled criticism in Sylvio's direction.

"So, the city of brotherly love showed no love towards ex-champ Barry Taylor who lost in a vicious, two-round knockout at the hands of Jun Zhang. While much credit is given to Zhang as he seemingly appeared out of nowhere to win the title, at the same time, we must criticize Taylor's training team for the lack of preparation for this fight."

"There's no doubt that former middleweight champion Sylvio Dominique must shoulder some of the blame here for the loss. Barry trained at his gym, sparred in the gym, and took advice from Dominique. While most people paid to watch a competitive fight, what they saw was a beatdown of mass proportions in which Taylor did not resemble a champion, and I blame Dominique for that."

"When going up against a powerful fighter such as Zhang, an opponent has to train night and day to prepare for such a bout. I don't believe Dominique encouraged any training principles at all. The training footage at his community center and all of the selfies, and the overall lack of discipline, doomed the former pound-for-pound champion."

"Barry Taylor should have just relied on his trainers for this fight instead of distracting himself with a washed up, former boxer who quit before even entering his prime."

There was no denying who the last reporter referred to. Valentina handed the phone back to Robert. In the back of her mind, she knew that Sylvio heard all the noise from the media, and as a defense mechanism, he would shut it all off by turning off his phone and isolating himself to where he didn't have to deal with media scrutiny.

"Yo', you good?" Robert asked.

"Nah, I gotta try to call him," she replied, heading back into her trailer.

"For what it's worth, I don't think Sylvio deserves all that heat. It wasn't his fault. But you know TV media. They always gotta find their Boogeyman, and right now, Sylvio's that dude."

"I knew it was a bad idea for Sylvio to put himself back out there again. I'mma holla at you tomorrow, Robert. Lemme try to hit him up," Valentina said. On her way to the trailer, she dialed Sylvio's number.

As she expected, the phone rang several times before going to voicemail. "Sylvio, baby, please pick up. I know you're there. Look, what happened to Barry tonight was not your fault. You did the best that you could, and at the end of the day, you're not the one that got into the ring—he did. So, fuck what the media said, and just lay low for a minute. Hit me up whenever you can," she said, finishing up the voice message.

At Memorial Hospital in Philadephia, Sylvio sat with Tom Blaylock and Max Gregorio, Barry's other trainer, in the waiting room. Tom stared at the hospital room door, waiting for positive news from the doctor. Barry was so disoriented at the conclusion of the fight that he began mumbling incoherently as the trainers struggled to stem the flow of blood from his nose and his mouth. His left cheek appeared more swollen than usual, and his nose was bent at odd angles, so there was no question that it was broken.

Sylvio did not exchange words with Tom or any of Barry's trainers because, for all he knew, they most likely blamed him for the loss. He'd heard the media talks, and he knew that his name would be trending all over social media and not in a positive light.

When his phone had vibrated, and he looked and saw Valentina's name appear on his screen, he ignored her calls. He didn't feel like giving her the satisfaction of admitting that she was right and that his scheme of getting involved in boxing backfired on him.

Finally, after what seemed like ten minutes, the doctor walked back out into the waiting room. "Okay, gentlemen, thank you so much for your patience," she said.

"No problem. So, how's he doing?" Tom asked.

The doctor looked down at her clipboard. "Well, I'll tell you this much, he's extremely lucky. He has a broken nose, fractured orbital bone near his left eye, and he took some heavy blows to the right side of his head. He's very concussed right now, so we have him on some pain meds. I would recommend him not to rush back into the ring anytime soon. He will need a lot of rest and recuperation."

The doctor left the waiting area and went back into the room. Sylvio hung his head. Not only was he in a place that he dreaded the most because hospitals always brought back memories of his near-death experience, but he also realized that he might have jeopardized Barry's boxing career.

"Yo', Wolf, you good?" Tom asked.

"Nah, man. I should've prepared him more for this fight. It's my fault he ended up in here."

"Look, don't sweat that, dawg. Barry took the fight, and he signed that contract to fight Jun tonight. Don't kill yourself ova' that, B. You did good. You trained him the best way you could. They just came wit' a betta' play tonight, but trust, we'll be back," Tom reassured Sylvio.

"Yeah, I guess. I just hope his career ain't done, man," Sylvio replied.

"Yo', as long as I've known Barry, I know that dude's gon' be back. And don't pay them media heads no mind, man. They don't know how much work you put in to prepare my guy for this fight. They always want a story, and they gon' always stick wit' some bullshit-ass narrative and run with it. Block out all that noise," Tom said, dapping Sylvio.

"Thanks, man," Sylvio said.

"Yo', I'll stay wit', Barry. Get back, and get some rest, man. If you eva' wanna chop it up again, hit me up," Tom said.

Sylvio headed out the hospital. It was a long three-hour drive back to New York for him, and he knew the next few days would be a challenge. When he arrived home, he checked his phone and saw that Valentina tried to call him two other times. He listened to the voicemail message that she left him virtually offering the same advice that Tom offered him.

Kill the noise. Ignore the media and do you. They need a scapegoat to blame, and right now, I'm wearing the bullseye on my back.

Early the next morning, Sylvio drove to SDCC at his usual time, and as he'd normally done, he took a detour through the Dante Shaw Boxing Gym. The gym members, who normally greeted Sylvio and asked for pictures and selfies, stopped their activities as they watched Sylvio make his way inside. A hush fell over the gym and the faces that were once friendly to Sylvio were now indescribably tense. Sylvio knew what they were thinking as soon as he walked through the gym.

Man, this loser was the reason Barry got beat like he stole something. This bum trained one of ours, and he couldn't help him retain the belt.

"Aye, what's wrong wit' ya'? Did ya forget who 'dis man was? I know ya ain't gon' let some bums on TV tell ya who the Wolf is. Ya better fix ya' faces whenever a champ come walkin' through here."

Sylvio was relieved to hear his trainer speak up for him at that moment. His words cut through the tension in the gym, and the members resumed exercising.

"Thanks, Jim," Sylvio said as he entered Jim's office.

"No doubt, man. Look, I heard all that stuff they was talkin' about today after the fight, and all I gotta say is not one of them reporters know who you are, and that's a fact."

"Thanks, man. Normally, I'd ignore what they talkin' bout, but it seems every sports network is coming at my neck right now. They neva' grilled me this much, even when I was still boxing."

"That's because they stay trying to protect their golden boy. Look, I already knew what was about to happen. Barry was a cruiser, man. He felt like he would just walk in the ring and that Chinese dude was gon' shit his pants cuz he was the champ. He got cocky and forgot that he actually had to fight."

Sylvio paced his trainer's office. "For a moment, I thought I was you, bro. Training up a young gun like Barry, I thought it would result in the same magic."

"Nah, you could neva' be me, brotha'. There's only one Jim Shaw. You gotta get up on my level," Jim laughed.

"Whateva', man," Sylvio laughed.

Just then, Kevin walked in the office. "What's up, Wolf? I'm glad you're here. We gotta talk," he said seriously.

"What's up?" Sylvio asked.

"I wanted to review last month's figures for the center." Kevin laid out a summary of the previous month's adjusted gross income and expenses that had not cleared due to the lack of membership in SDCC's drama and the education departments.

Kevin also revealed that, due to the inability to cover the expenses of the facility, they had to take out an emergency loan that was shared by Jim and Sylvio's financial institution, which they had both vowed to avoid unless the center was in danger of being repossessed by the city of New York. Kevin could not have explained it any simpler. If SDCC failed to raise money in the coming months, the center would be in danger of shutting down.

Chapter 9

"Oh, so now you feel like talkin' to me?" Valentina answered sharply when Sylvio called her the next morning.

"Look, Val, my bad for not hittin' you back up, but I just didn't feel like speaking to anyone, okay? In case you ain't notice, my rep's being trashed by a whole lot of people right now," Sylvio replied.

"Okay, whateva'. I know that Barry losin' his title got you shook and everything, but you can't just tune me out and decide that you wanna talk to me when it's convenient for you. I've been you wit' you for over six years, and every time you feel some type of way, you wanna ignore me and those around you."

"Okay, I get it. I messed up. I'm sorry, okay? It's just that I've been kinda stressed lately—first with the outcome of the damn fight, and now Kevin's tellin' me that if we don't start getting more business at the center, we could end up losin' money, and we'd be forced to sell the property."

"Sylvio, if there's anything I know about you for the last six years we've been together, it's that you never give up when things get hard. You'll get through this. I'm sure," Valentina's calm words reassured Sylvio. She could hear his deep sigh over the phone. "But all I ask is that you don't alienate me when you're going through it. I might not be in New York right now, but we're still a team."

"Yeah, you're right. I definitely gotta stop buggin'."

"Right. So how's Barry holdin' up?" Valentina asked.

"He's a strong dude. He took a lot of damage during that fight, but he'll be back on his feet soon. He can't box for a while though."

"Damn, that sucks. So, you about to go to the center today?" she asked.

"Yeah, I'm workin' later, but I'm about to go visit A.D. at his studio. He told me that he had some heat that he wanted me to listen to," Sylvio replied.

"Okay cool. Well I gotta go to work, so I'll talk to you later. Tell A.D. I said hey," Valentina said.

After arriving at DeWitt Studios in Forest Hills, New York, Sylvio greeted his longtime friend, Alfred DeWitt, who was known throughout the area as "A.D." A.D. was an important figure in Sylvio's life. Throughout middle and high school, the two worked out at Steel Glove Gym, and once Sylvio made the decision to fight as a professional boxer, he rented an apartment with A.D., and they both worked at different manufacturing warehouses.

While Sylvio's boxing career took off, A.D. began building his reputation as a music producer and deejay, working gigs throughout the tri-state area. His impeccable gift of mixing studio beats began to attract underground hip-hop artists, and with his growing popularity came financial rewards. A.D. was able to buy a house and open a small studio in Forest Hills with a portion of the money donated by Sylvio's boxing management group.

As Sylvio walked inside the studio, he saw two other sound technicians working over a vast soundboard mixing system. A.D.

was between the technicians, and while he was playing a gritty, percussion-balanced beat, he peeped Sylvio in the room, bobbing his head to the beat.

"Yo', what's good, money?" he greeted, dabbing Sylvio.

"Chillin', man. Yo', I like what you did with the place!" Sylvio exclaimed, looking around.

"Yeah, just got the new soundboard set up, so we keep it live in 'dis piece, you know what I'm sayin'?"

"I'm definitely feelin' you. So, you got some new projects lined up?" Sylvio asked.

"All day, B. So, check it, Q-Dawg just hit me up and said he needed some beats for his new mixtape, so I've been in the lab the last couple days mixin' some stuff. Listen to this." A.D. walked over to the soundboard, hit four buttons, and played back his new beat.

Sylvio started bobbing his head again as the beat played the next three minutes.

"Tell me that shit ain't fire!" A.D. exclaimed, excited.

"No doubt, dawg. Yo', Q-Dawg gonna be spittin' some serious shit ova' that beat. You gon' mess around and get a Hip-Hop Music Award one day, man."

"Hopefully, bro. Q-Dawg's just the beginning, man. Once my beats get out there, I might get a look from the major playas in the industry. Just gotta keep grinding."

"Facts, man." Sylvio agreed.

"So, tell me what's up wit' you, man. You good?" A.D. asked.

"Yeah, man. I'm chillin'. You know that whole fight's in my rearview right now. Just gotta wait for the whole media noise to quiet down cuz you know they stay talkin'," Sylvio replied.

"That's all they do, man. Media is designed to instigate and record drama. It don't matter if you in the ring or behind this booth.

That's what they get paid to do," A.D. said, while simultaneously working on the soundboard. He stopped working on it long enough to face Sylvio.

"I heard what they said about you, man. Listen, don't even mind anything these cats are sayin'. For all the talkin' they do about you, I'd like to see their ass go in the ring and try to do what you do."

"Yeah, right? They all bark but no bite," Sylvio agreed.

"Facts. Anyway, you should be happy that the fight's over with anyway cuz yo' girl been checkin' fo' you lately," A.D. said.

"I know. I just called her back—" Sylvio began to explain.

A.D. shook his head. "Nah, bro, I ain't talkin' about Val. I'm talkin' bout Yolanda," he said.

Sylvio laughed. "Yolanda's been askin' for me?" he asked.

"Man, why you frontin' like you shocked? You know that girl feelin' you," A.D. said, smirking.

"A.D., we just friends, bro. That's it. Val and I hired her, and she's been killin' it in drama so far. But nah, I ain't even checkin' for her like that."

"Yo' quit lyin'. I know you see her across your office, wearing them thin tights where you get a clear view of that ass. Man, you better make a move on that before I do."

"Whateva', dawg. Knowing you, you probably was tryin' to holla at her, and she wasn't feeling you."

"Man, don't even try to give me that sensibility shit, B. If she knew what she wanted, she would be down for whateva'. Besides, I'mma keep it a buck wit' you. I'm surprised you lasted this long with Valentina. Before her, you was still in the game, servin' up knockouts between the sheets. What happened to that Sylvio?" A.D. laughed.

"I don't know, man. I couldn't be a playa for long. I had to settle down with somebody."

A.D. shook his head. "It sounds like to me, she got you whipped, and you've stayed whipped for six years, money. Are you sure she the one?"

The question threw Sylvio off because he wasn't ready for a response right away. "She's gotta be, man. I like the way I feel around her, and when we get down, trust and believe we get all the way down. All chill, no Netflix, you feel me?"

A.D. laughed. "I got you, man. Ya' be fuckin' like there ain't no tomorrow. I get it. But seriously, level wit' me though. I'm yo' boy. What else do ya got in common other than the fact that ya' like to get in dem drawers?"

When Sylvio couldn't respond immediately, A.D. shook his head. "Sounds like a match made in heaven to me," he said sarcastically.

Sylvio scoffed. This cat be talkin' too much for a dude who couldn't even get none until he was a senior in high school.

"Check this out. This is what I see, and I don't be all up in my boy's business or nothin' like that, but whenever she around, it sound like she the one callin' the shots. If you miss callin' her, she gets all in her feelings cuz she gotta keep you tied up. She don't want you to box anymore or do what you do, yet she's out there making movies and shit. She's settin' up for life without you, money," A.D. warned.

"What you talkin' about, man?" Sylvio asked.

"Look, I know what kind of chick Valentina is. The more you hang on the sidelines while she doin' her thing, she ain't gon' wanna stick around you. She gon' want somebody who's on her level or some old millionaire to keep her on top."

"Man, you must be smokin' that good weed cuz I don't know what you talkin' about right now."

A.D. shrugged his shoulders. "Okay, don't say I ain't warn you. I would cut my losses and drop her before she dumps yo' ass cuz the media will label you as a loser and a simp. Besides, I heard them Dominican chicks are emotional as hell, and they don't have no problem throwin' they ass out for anybody else. Didn't you say that she was an escort or something? That's just a fancy way of sayin' that she was a high-class ho."

"But what about Yolanda? I don't know her like that. For all I know, she could be a high-class ho too," Sylvio said.

"Nah, she ain't high class, but don't let her innocence fool you, dawg. She a closet freak, B. She's definitely had her share of dudes for years. You can tell by her vibe, she just down for anything. I'mma be honest. Half the reason I'm still at the center is because I'm still tryin' to holla at her. But I know she lookin' to get physical wit' you," A.D. said.

"Yo', A.D., if you keep buggin', Monique gon' tear that ass up!" Sylvio said, referring to A.D.'s girlfriend.

He laughed at Sylvio. "Aight whateva, son. But check it. Q-Dawg invited me to deejay at Club Allure tonight. It's gon' be some serious playas up in there. Mad record labels are gonna be there, and if my spin game's on point, you could be lookin' at the next big-time producer. You down?"

"Nah, I'm good, man. It's best if I just stay outta the media spotlight for now," Sylvio replied.

A.D. wasn't buying his excuses. "Bro, come on, man. While I'm in there spinnin' and winnin', you could be winin' and dinin' and just kicking back. At least look at it from a networking standpoint, you feel me? If I walk in there with Sylvio 'Wolf' Dominique, that's more publicity for the both of us."

"Wouldn't be the first time you used my rep to get yours," Sylvio said slyly.

"Yo', don't even play me like that, kid. Just have yo' ass at the club by nine tonight, boy," he said, before turning back into his soundboard.

Sylvio dapped up his friend before leaving the studio. *Maybe a night out is what I need. I haven't been to any clubs since Apple Kim's, and Valentina was still in town at the time. Just gotta overdress and stay low-key. Don't need no paparazzi stalkin' me.*

Hundreds of people were outside of Club Allure waiting for security to open the rope that blocked the entrance. Sylvio was already inside with A.D. In the club, he immediately felt accepted, even more so than in the public eye, where he had been the subject of scrutiny for his part in Barry Taylor's loss. Sylvio took pictures and signed autographs, and two orders of vodka were sent to him and A.D. from an anonymous guest.

A.D. barely had time to enjoy the party since he was so busy behind the turntables, mixing beats and spinning rap and trap mixtures the entire evening. Sylvio couldn't deny the talent his friend had as a deejay. A.D. was meticulous in his craft, switching songs on cue, and he was also a talented hypeman on the microphone.

At one point during the party, with Sylvio standing right by his booth, A.D. picked up the microphone. "Yo, yo, yo, New York! What up, what up? This is yo' boy DJ A.D. on da spin, and on my right, I got none other than Queens middleweight champ Sylvio

'Wolf' Dominique kickin' it wit' me tonight. Show him some love, ya'll!"

The crowd roared and clapped loudly as Sylvio raised his hand to take his due. For the first time in days, he wasn't criticized, and the club welcomed his introduction. Then, whenever someone came to the table to pose for a picture or get an autograph, Sylvio was left with words of encouragement.

"What's up, Wolf? You still the champ to us. Don't worry about what them chumps on TV say."

"Wolf, you the best boxer in history, puttin' on for all the zoes."

Finally, the host of the party walked over to greet the former champion. He had tattoos all over his arms and a few on his neck. He also had two women on each arm that Sylvio instantly recognized as Instagram models.

"What up, champ? I placed a bet on you beatin' Maximo that night when everybody else didn't, and I'll never forget how you tore his ass up. You made a hella lot of money for me, but you an inspiration to all these young cats comin' up," Q-Dawg said.

"Appreciate it, man." Sylvio replied.

"No doubt, money. Yo', enjoy another round on me," Q-Dawg said, nodding to the bartender before disappearing into the throng of party guests.

After indulging in another drink, Sylvio began to feel more at ease. He didn't know if it was the buzz or if he was just experiencing another level of comfort.

"Yo', Sylvio, are you just gonna sit by the table all night, or are you actually gon' walk around and do something?" A.D. asked, laughing.

"Nah, I'm good over hea'. Keep doin' your thing, man," he replied.

While he was talking with A.D., Sylvio felt a gentle tap on his shoulder. Turning around, he saw a beautifully toned woman standing in front of him, wearing a short yellow sequined dress, showing off her legs and a firm backside.

"Sylvio? Oh my God, what are the chances that we would run into each other?" Yolanda asked.

It took Sylvio a moment to fully take in Yolanda's dress, which did not leave much to the imagination. *Damn! Man, she looks like she was dipped in sparkling honey. I love honey. Okay, Sylvio, stay focused.* "Yeah, I know right. It's a small world," Sylvio replied.

"Tell me about it. To be honest, I didn't even recognize you at first. I had to come over to make sure I wasn't seein' things," Yolanda said.

"Nope, it's really me," Sylvio confirmed, his heart beating faster than normal.

"What's up, A.D.?" Yolanda greeted, waving at the deejay.

"What's good, Yolanda? Aye, lemme know if you'd like a drink. You know I got you," he replied.

"Nah, I'm okay. Thanks anyway."

Sylvio invited Yolanda to sit at his table. "So how are things going in the drama department? I've been busy and really haven't had time to check in," he said.

"To keep it real, it hasn't been goin' too well recently. Four of our kids dropped out due to financial reasons, so unfortunately, we're too many cast members short to keep rehearsing for our fall production of *Peter Pan*. So, we've just decided to do a series of comedic monologues instead," she replied.

By her tone, Sylvio knew that she was becoming deflated and discouraged. "Man, that sucks. I'm sorry that happened. The whole center is dealing with some financial issues right now. If we don't recoup the monthly cost for the center, we could end up losing it, and everybody will be out of a job. People will hate me more than they do now," Sylvio admitted, shaking his head.

"I don't hate you, Sylvio. I know what the media's been saying about you, and I don't believe any one of them. They don't know you like I do. You and Val gave me a chance to express myself in theater and gave me a job that I'm passionate about. I'll never forget that. People act like they know who Sylvio Dominique is, but nobody out there knows who he really is."

At that moment, Sylvio was suddenly grateful that Yolanda sat with him. Valentina certainly never spoke glowingly about him in that fashion. "Thanks. I really needed to hear them words."

"No problem." As she spoke, Yolanda placed her hand on Sylvio's shoulder, lightly caressing him.

"So, did you come here by yourself, or did you come wit' a dude? If it's a dude, I'm surprised he let you walk out lookin' like that," Sylvio said, not sugarcoating the fact that Yolanda's dress was eye-pleasing.

"Actually, no. I came wit' some of my girlfriends, and this ole' thing? I've had this dress for years, and I didn't originally plan on wearing it, but I wanted to show out for my homie, Q-Dawg."

"Wait, how do you know Q-Dawg?" Sylvio asked.

"We were classmates at Springfield High, and he was just Quincy Dawkins to me," Yolanda replied. "Dope lyricist, but you don't wanna be in his vicinity too long. He can smoke you out of a room, especially if you ain't a weed-head like him," she added.

"Well, I don't even smoke weed anyway, but I might be starting to develop a drinking habit," Sylvio replied.

"Yeah, you need to slow down too, Sylvio. You don't want your liver shriveling up on you."

"You ain't neva' lied. Definitely can't have that right now."

Suddenly, a popular R&B track began playing. Yolanda closed her eyes as she began dancing in her seat. "Oh my God, this is my jam. You wanna dance wit' me?" she asked Sylvio.

Looking up at A.D., Sylvio realized his friend had a smug look on his face. *I know A.D. didn't play that track on purpose. He knows he's wrong for this.*

"Uh, yeah sure, I'll dance wit' you, but I should warn you, I ain't that smooth of a dancer, you know?" he stammered.

Yolanda dismissed his excuse with a wave of her hand. "Oh, come on, Sylvio. One dance ain't gon' hurt you. I'll go real easy on you...I promise," she said, pulling him onto the dance floor.

Looking back at A.D., Sylvio recognized the look on his face. *You damn right, I'm setting you up. You betta get it wit' her, and do your thing.*

Just one thought stayed on Sylvio's mind. *Thank God, Valentina ain't here. She wouldn't be down wit' this. But it's only a dance, right? Can't hurt nobody...*

As soon as they got onto the dance floor, Yolanda started gyrating her body close to Sylvio's, moving her midsection to the rhythm and showing off her flexibility. Although she was slightly smaller in frame, Yolanda had curves, and she knew how to work them.

And with every passing minute, it became more and more difficult for Sylvio to control himself. Yolanda's movements were beginning to arouse him, and he had to back away so she couldn't feel him stiffening up. But to his amazement, she pulled him closer to her.

"How's Valentina doing?" Yolanda whispered in his ear.

"She's good. You know, doing her whole movie thing," he

replied.

"When was the last time you saw her?" Yolanda asked as she pressed her body closer to his, causing him to sweat even more.

"Um, I saw her a few weeks ago in Atlanta. It's been tough getting time to see her cuz she's always busy," he replied.

"Aww, that's too bad. You must miss her a lot."

"Yeah, I do, but she's doing okay, and maybe when she's less busy, I'll visit again." Sylvio stared down at Yolanda.

She had full lips, the most perfect cheekbones, brown eyes, and brown curly hair. "How long do you think that'll be?"

Sylvio looked around. Here he was, in what many would describe as a compromised position, with a beautiful woman who wasn't Valentina, but at the time, it didn't matter. "I don't know how long it's gon' be. But, hopefully, one day." Sylvio didn't believe his own words.

Neither did Yolanda. She inched closer. He was losing the battle.

"Has she ever danced with you like this?" she asked.

Sylvio couldn't remember any moment in time when Valentina had danced with him. "Nah, not really. I mean I'm sure she can dance too, but I guess I've never danced with her, technically speaking," he replied feebly.

"That's a shame. A woman should always share a special moment with her man on the dance floor or just anywhere."

"We do have special moments that we share together."

"Outside the bedroom?"

Yolanda's abrupt question threw Sylvio for a loop. Throughout their six years together, Sylvio realized that he had never shared an intimate moment with Valentina outside of sex. They never danced together. They never shared stories with each other...never talked till sunrise like most couples did.

The question forced Sylvio to ask himself a crucial question. Is the relationship between Valentina and me just based on sex?

Shaking away the notion, Sylvio continued dancing with Yolanda. "Damn, girl, you dance like a pro. You makin' me look bad out hea'," he laughed.

"I could never make you look bad, Sylvio. You have a certain aura about you that makes you look confident no matter what you're doing. Your vibe is really dope, and I don't mean to pry at all, but do you think Val sees that in you?"

"I'mma keep it real wit' you. I don't know if she sees that in me right now, but I'm glad you see that in me," Sylvio replied.

"I've always seen that in you, Sylvio. Ever since we first met, I used to be so jealous of Valentina because she has the most perfect man, and she doesn't appreciate what she has," Yolanda whispered.

"That's not always true though," Sylvio countered.

"Okay, so tell me something then. Does she kiss you like this?" Yolanda asked.

Before Sylvio could stop it, their lips met, and they kissed passionately.

After two minutes, they separated. Yolanda's lips had felt so soft and her smooth hands had been rubbing the calluses on Sylvio's hands.

"Nah, she ain't ever done it like that," he admitted. But in the back of his mind, he knew he made a grave mistake. "Whoa, whoa, Yolanda. Check it out. I love Val, okay? This can't happen, okay?" Sylvio backed away from Yolanda and made his way back over to his table.

But he was unable to dodge the persistent young woman as she followed him there. "Wait, where you going?" she asked.

"Um, I gotta go. I'm sorry, okay? But I got a girl, and I can't do her like this," he explained as he paid his tab.

"Yo', Sylvio, what up, son? You outta hea' already?" A.D. asked while still staying busy on the turntables.

"Yeah, got work in the A.M. You stay up, aight?" Sylvio dapped A.D. and made his way out of the club. As soon as he got into his car, he banged the back of his head against the driver's seat in frustration.

Damn, man, how could you let yourself get caught up like that? You got a girl that rides wit' you, and you turn around and do that? After silently scolding himself, Sylvio wiped his lips off with his hands and then drove away into the night.

Chapter 10

"Yeah, I know I bailed on our date the other night, but I had some unexpected company over," Jim explained over the phone the next day. He was in his office at the center when Charlene called to find out why he didn't meet her for their date to the Broadway show. Jim couldn't bring himself to tell Charlene that his ex-wife was the one who had paid him an unexpected visit. That would cause tension in the budding courtship that he had with Charlene.

"Who was the unexpected company that came over, Jim?" Charlene managed to ask, suspiciously.

"Just an old friend from back in the day. We caught up for a lil' bit, but that was it. I should've called you to let you know what was goin' down."

"Jim, I was so disappointed that night. I really was looking forward to it," Charlene said.

"I know, but I'll make it up. I'm about to go onto Ticketmaster right now and order two tickets to Jazz Night at Madison Square Garden. You know you love some jazz now," Jim laughed, knowing that if he coaxed Charlene just enough, it would ease the tension. "And maybe after the show, we can make some sweet music of our own, if you know what I mean."

"Boy, you crazy! Okay, it's a date, but please don't disappoint.

You're a sweet man, and I like where we're going, but I gotta know that I can trust you."

"You're right, Charlene. From now on, I'm gon' keep it a buck with you. No more secrets."

"Good deal. I can't wait to see you next weekend," Charlene said before they gave their goodbyes and hung the phone up.

Returning to work, Jim was back to checking inventory for sports gear when his office door opened, and Kwame Turner entered, drenched in sweat. "What's up, Kwame? How's your workout going?" Jim asked.

"It's goin' good, Jim. Check it out. I got a problem, and I need some advice."

"Yeah, what's up, son? Talk to me," Jim said.

"Okay, let's say you was feelin' this girl for a minute, and she asked you out, right? But the girl used to date yo' homeboy, and they just broke up a few days ago. Would it be right to get wit' her anyway?" Kwame asked.

"To be honest, man, I don't think there's a solid answer for that. Depends on how tight you are with yo' homie, Kwame. If he's cool wit' it, then I say go for it. She obviously sees something in you that she didn't see in him, or you might be her rebound guy," Jim answered.

"But see, that's the thing. I don't wanna come across as a thirsty-ass nigga tryin' to get with his homie's girl, you know what I'm sayin'?"

"I feel you, Kwame, but to me that's a judgment call, and this could be the situation that tests the brotherhood ya got. If he was yo' boy, he'd be cool wit' it."

"Yeah, but Tyreke ain't that type of dude. He loses his temper over the simplest stuff, and he's very territorial, especially when it comes down to his girl."

"Kwame, you think Tyreke gon' try to bust yo' ass just for datin' his ex-girlfriend? If he reacts like that, then he ain't yo' homie. But I will tell you this. You wanna tread softly on that situation. If she wanna date you, keep it discreet. But if this Tyreke starts givin' you a hard time, let me know right away."

"Nah, you ain't gotta do nothin'. I ain't askin' you to fight my battles for me, man. I'll check you later," Kwame said, leaving Jim to his work.

On his way to the center, Sylvio tried desperately to erase the events of the previous night from his mind. Feeling guilty, he'd attempted to call Valentina upon arriving home, but she didn't pick her phone up, which suggested she was working late. And she hadn't been available on Skype in weeks. Sylvio thought about leaving her a message on her answering machine but quickly decided against it. What would he tell her?

Maybe last night was a dream. Maybe I imagined kissing Yolanda, feelin' all up her booty like she was Val.

But it wasn't a dream. The moment stayed on his mind on the drive to work. I just gotta play it cool today. I had one too many drinks, and things got a lil' bit out of control. It was a harmless kiss. It wasn't as if it developed into anything else.

Despite the reassuring words that he attempted to give himself, Sylvio knew he had to see Yolanda when he got to the center. Once he arrived, he headed straight upstairs to his office. Turning to his right, he saw the drama room was still closed. Yolanda hadn't arrived yet. Sylvio made his way into the office and stared up above his desk where his middleweight belt hung. Although it was not the actual belt that he won from his fight with Dominican champion Felipe Maximo, it was an exact replica of it. The actual belt was yielded after his abrupt retirement from boxing, and top contenders frequently fought for that title. Now it was held by an unknown foreigner with extraordinary skill.

After a few minutes of working, Sylvio heard music coming from the drama room. It wasn't rap music or any speaker-splitting sound. Instead, the music was calm and soothing as melodies from harps, flutes, oboes, and other instruments filled the air.

Sylvio got up and went over to the drama room. The door was slightly cracked. That's when curiosity got the better of him, and he peered through the opening. Because none of the drama students had arrived yet, Yolanda was alone, standing barefoot over a blue floor mat on the stage, performing different stretching routines. Sylvio was entranced by her gracefulness and her flexibility as she arched backwards, her head nearly touching the floor.

God, what a body. C'mon, Sylvio, you got work to do. You can't afford to be distracted right now. You got to figure out a strategy to earn money for the center, and you gotta get your stuff together.

Sylvio started to make his way out of the room, but Yolanda saw him.

"Hi, Sylvio!" she greeted brightly.

"What's up, Yolanda?" he replied, weakly. Why was he so nervous? "So, what you doin'?" he asked.

"Oh, I'm just doing some yoga. It clears my mind and gets me ready for the day. You should try it," she replied.

"Nah, I'm good. I don't really do yoga."

"C'mon, Sylvio. Join me. I promise I don't bite," she teased.

After thinking it over, Sylvio finally gave in and stepped on the floor mat that Yolanda laid out for him.

"Uh, Sylvio, if you're gonna do this, you have to take off your shoes," she said.

"Oh, right. I knew that," Sylvio replied sheepishly, removing his sneakers.

"Okay, so whatever movement that you see me doing, I want you to imitate it, okay? And remember to clear your mind." Yolanda proceeded to perform a series of movements, where she contorted her body and stretched across her mat. "This is called restorative yoga. It's meant to soothe nerves and help you practice pose holds."

Sylvio attempted to mimic Yolanda's movements, but while his efforts were heavy and cumbersome, Yolanda's movements were swift and fluid as she transitioned from one routine to another. Meanwhile, although Sylvio was instructed to clear his mind, he thought about what the reaction would be if anyone from the boxing gym saw what he was doing. He heard Yolanda's slight giggle as he attempted one of her yin yoga routines.

"Here, lemme help you out," she said, walking over to him.

Sylvio's heart began racing again. *C'mon, man, focus on the movement, not on how she looks in them tights. Think of something else fast. Valentina. Yeah, that's who I'll think about. Wonder how her show's doing anyway...*

"Okay, Sylvio, so you do the movement like this. Arch forward with your right leg out and arms straight up," Yolanda instructed, guiding Sylvio's arms and legs in the right positions.

"Oh, okay. I got you. See I knew I could do this yoga thing. Ain't nothin' to it but to do it," he bragged.

"Yeah, I knew you could do this too. Believe it or not, back when you were still fighting, you were a lot more flexible. People could never hit you because of your quick reflexes," she pointed out.

"Yeah, I know I was a beast—hold up. You've watched my fights?" Sylvio asked as they both continued their routines.

"What? Boy, you was a killin' machine in that ring. The way you dominated Kamikaze Brown and Hernandez? I always thought you were one of the best boxers ever."

"That's refreshing to hear. Normally, I don't get a lot of boxing compliments from—"

"Women? You think because I'm a female, I don't follow boxing? Uh-uh, baby, I'm a boxin' freak. Maybe it's cuz I grew up with a lot of male influence. I got two older brothers and one younger brother, and they love sports. My oldest brother fought amateur some years back, but he ended up joining the Air Force."

"That's what's up. It's mad refreshing to talk to a lady that respects the fight game. Val doesn't get into it too much. She actually hopes I stay as far away from the ring as possible."

"Did she talk you into retiring? Because that was the worst day of my life. My brothers are still shell-shocked after that decision. There you were, on top of the world, and you gave it up. We never understood that."

"Nah, it wasn't like that. Val had nothing to do wit' my decision. It was a personal choice after everything I've been through. I felt like I gave my blood, sweat, and tears to the game, and the game almost took me out. If I knew that someone was gon' try to blast me as soon as I won the belt, I would've given it up, sooner."

Seeing Sylvio struggling to keep his posture on one of his movements, Yolanda went over to his mat to assist him. She stood directly in front of him, and her hips pressed against his pelvic area.

His heart raced again, the same way it had the night before at the club.

"You know, I never really had the chance to apologize for kissing you like that yesterday. It was wrong for me to do Valentina like that," she whispered to him. Her soft tone sent chills up his spine.

"It's all good. It happens, especially when you talkin' about the Wolf. I got that effect on everybody," he laughed, trying to make light of the situation.

"Still cocky as hell. My brothers never really rooted for you cuz they felt you was arrogant, but that's what I loved about you. You never gave a damn about what anybody else thought of you," Yolanda said, gazing at Sylvio.

"Well, confidence is half the battle. You gotta go in there knowing that you could win the fight, even when deep in your heart, you're scared as hell."

"Are you feelin' confident right now?" Yolanda teased, and without warning, she leaned in to kiss him.

Sylvio couldn't deny the sex appeal that Yolanda had going on. They kissed more intensely, and this time, Sylvio didn't hesitate.

"How many rounds do you think you can go wit' me?" she asked.

Suddenly, the feelings of guilt dissipated, and Sylvio kissed Yolanda passionately. Lowering her onto his mat, he took off his shirt, revealing his chest. Although his abs were not as defined as they were during his boxing days, he was still in exceptional shape. "Mmm, man, I can't do this, Yolanda. This is crazy. I'm doin' Val so wrong right now," he said between kisses.

"And you think she an angel? C'mon, Sylvio, she's in the Hollywood scene, and open relationships are the norm. All that kissin' that she doin' wit' her co-star on that series...do you think all that is just for show?" she asked, slowly removing the straps of her leotard.

"So, what you sayin'? You think she fuckin' behind my back?" Sylvio asked.

"I study body behavior, Sylvio, and her level of comfort is so high whenever she's on screen with that guy. Call it a woman's intuition, but I know she's sleepin' around on you too," Yolanda said, causing Sylvio to pause while she was still mounted on him.

The thought of Valentina cheating of him was unfathomable to Sylvio, but with Yolanda's pillow-like lips kissing his chest, he couldn't think straight. His mind was focused solely on tasting her as much as he could. Suddenly, a loud vibration could be heard on the mat. Sylvio's cell phone was ringing.

"Oh, come on, baby. Let it ring," Yolanda pleaded.

Voicemail will pick it up. Sylvio heeded her advice and continued kissing Yolanda's neck and breasts. But after a few seconds, his phone rang again.

Sylvio sighed. "My bad...I gotta get this," he said, putting his shirt back on as he stood up to answer his phone. He sensed Yolanda's disappointment, but he had to answer. Walking over to grab his cell, he saw that Valentina was the one who was finally calling him.

"Baby, what took you so long to answer my call?" Valentina asked as Sylvio headed back into his office.

"Sorry, Val, but I was busy this morning. You know how it is at the SDCC," he replied, feeling the sense of guilt that he had previously pushed into the back corner of his mind.

"I saw you called me yesterday. I was at the set. We were working real late again, so I'm sorry that I couldn't get to the phone," she said.

"It's okay. I was just callin' to check up on you. It ain't a big deal," he replied, with knives of guilt stabbing him. It was one of the few times that he had lied to Valentina, and it did nothing to ease his guilt. *If I was Pinocchio, my nose would've hit the damn wall by now with all this lying.*

But despite Sylvio's guilt, he felt he had to clear the air with his girlfriend. "Val, check it out. I know you filmin' wit' ole boy, and I know ya be gettin' it in on the love scenes in that show, so I'mma need you to keep it real wit' me. Was any of that real?" he asked.

"What kind of question is that, Sylvio? Course it ain't real, genius. It's called acting. You think when I'm in bed with Robert on TV, that means that I'm sleeping with him?" she asked.

"I don't know, Val. You tell me. Did you ever hook up wit' him outside the show?" he asked.

"What? Hell nah! Not like that! I mean, yeah, Robert took me to lunch a couple times, but he does that with all the actors and producers of the show. Do you think he sleepin' with them too?" Valentina asked.

"Maybe. I mean I know how ya Hollywood types get down, so I had to ask," Sylvio replied.

"You know what? You sound like a damn fool right now, Sylvio. I ain't got time for your insecurities. I'm finally getting an opportunity, and you can't handle it because of some love scenes," she argued back.

"Yo', I got a good reason for that, okay? It's all good being an actress or whateva', but I don't want you being some industry ho that gotta be on a casting couch to get roles out there."

"Seriously? And how did you think I felt when you were out there boxing, and you had all them bitches on you at Apple Kim's?

I didn't give you hell about that, but you all in yo' feelings because I'm on TV, and I'm gettin' some shine now. Tell me how that's fair," she challenged.

"Look, I'm not just gon' be the boyfriend that stands around and does nothin' while his girl's makin' all the dough. If you wanna be exploited, then fine," he said.

"Whatever, Sylvio. I gotta go. Clearly, you need some time to get your head on right cuz I don't know what's with you right now," she said before hanging up.

Sylvio sighed deeply in relief. He couldn't explain the growing rift in his relationship with Valentina. If they were not making love, they were arguing. At first he thought it was common among couples to disagree on certain aspects, but he felt at times that Valentina couldn't connect to him on an emotional level. They had little to nothing in common and were on different paths in their lives and career.

Yolanda, on the other hand, was warm and easy to talk to, and she was beautiful on another level. Not that Valentina wasn't gorgeous in her own right, but Yolanda had the innocent, yet confident, spirit about her, and she was always free to talk after before and after their workdays.

Maybe the long distance is hurting us. I don't know. I shouldn't have kissed Yolanda like I did. Maybe Valentina hasn't been messing around.

But Sylvio, like many other YouStream viewers, saw the new episode of "You Thought You Had Me," and he wouldn't admit it openly, but the sex scene that Valentina had with Robert was very convincing, from the kiss, to the scene where she undressed herself. And since the show was for mature audiences, Valentina did expose her breasts and pelvic area, and Sylvio had to watch Robert's naked body dance on top of her.

It flared up a jealousy that Sylvio never thought he could have, but Valentina always informed him that it was a TV series and that it was all just show business. So he accepted the harsh reality of the acting business, but he didn't feel any better about the situation.

"Everything okay?" Yolanda asked, stepping into Sylvio's office. She had put her leotard and warm-ups back on.

"How much of that did you hear?" Sylvio asked.

Yolanda walked over to his desk, and Sylvio felt his heart racing again. He wished she hadn't come any closer because she was not improving his predicament.

"I heard most of it. Sounded like you two were really going at it," she said, taking hold of his hand.

Sylvio withdrew his hand back. "Look, Yolanda, Valentina's still my girl, okay? I ain't gon' lie...if I wasn't involved right now, we'd be makin' more noise in the theater, but I can't do her like that," he told her although he sounded unconvinced. *Was Valentina still my girl? Or did I already lose her to show business?*

Yolanda then ran her finger seductively down Sylvio's chest. "If Valentina only knew what kind of man she had, she would never let him get away, much less cheat on him with another man."

"Look, Val said that it wasn't real between her and that Robert guy, so I gotta believe her," he said.

Yolanda rolled her eyes. "You think she gon' tell you that she doin' wrong? You didn't even tell her about us," she scoffed.

"Since when was there an 'us' though?" Sylvio asked, walking to his office door.

"Come on, Sylvio, don't front. I see the way you look at me every day when you come to work. I peep you checkin' me out whenever you take your break and talk to the guys downstairs." Yolanda said, slowly batting her eyes at him.

Sylvio stared at her eyes—the enticing brown eyes that hypnotized him.

"I see you whenever you work out, and I daydream about your muscles, your smile, your personality, and the way you are with other people. Valentina sees you physically, but I don't think she sees, or even respects, how you treat others. I still think she's using you, Sylvio, and when she blows up in showbiz, like she is right now, do you think she's gonna relegate herself to just one man?" she asked.

"How do I know you're not just sayin' that to break us up?" Sylvio asked suspiciously.

"Because I've always been up front wit' you, Sylvio. I don't hide or conceal my feelings for you. I've loved you since you were still in the ring, and I loved how you gave back to everybody in Queens, and I just don't want to see people take advantage of your nature and your generosity," Yolanda replied, holding his hand again, drawing nearer to him.

Sylvio couldn't fight his urge any longer. He pulled Yolanda in, kissing her intensely. "I wonder if this desk is made of that strong wood? How long till your students get hea'?" he asked, lifting Yolanda's slender frame and placing her softly on his desk.

"I still got about half an hour," Yolanda replied excitedly, pulling off her leotard leggings again before wrapping her arms around Sylvio.

Removing his shirt and pants, Sylvio began to let his tongue work its way down Yolanda's body, and when he touched her moist flower, he knew she was ready to be satisfied. They finally finished what they started on top of his desk at the theater.

After her tumultuous phone call with Sylvio, Valentina tried desperately to gather her thoughts. She was in her trailer while the other cast members were making their way into the studio. For the first time in many days, Valentina did not feel like filming her next scene in the series. She heard knocking at her trailer door and walked over to answer.

"Hey, Val, what's up? Can I come in?" he asked.

"Yeah, Robert, come in," she replied.

Robert walked into the trailer and sat across from Valentina. After a brief moment of silence, he said, "That last scene was real intense. Some of your best work yet."

"I hope you're talkin' about the whole episode and not that lil' three-minute love scene we shared," Valentina said.

"Oh, nah, I'm talkin' about the whole episode, Val. Shit got crazy. But I think we did better when we were preparing for that scene, you feel me?" Robert asked.

Preparing for the scene. What did I do? Valentina's mind flashed back to a few nights earlier on the eve before they were scheduled to shoot the love scene. Robert had asked to come to her apartment suite to read lines and prepare for the scene. What started out as a night of rehearsal and drinking wine, turned out to be the most intimate evening Valentina had ever experienced. She spent the night connecting with Robert, and they spoke endlessly about their starts in the acting industry.

After a few glasses of wine, Robert said, "Hey, I think we should practice the love scene between Gabrielle and Anthony cuz you know Jacobs wants the scene to look real. I think the best way to convince him is to practice it."

"What? I've never heard of practicing a sex scene before. I just thought that you just got into it," Valentina replied, suddenly feeling uneasy. She hadn't slept with anyone but Sylvio over the last six years, but she had been with countless men before when she worked as an escort in New York City.

"Yeah, believe me, actors everywhere do it more times than not. You down?" Robert asked.

Valentina was still unsure. "Yeah, why not? I mean, it's for the arts, right?"

"Exactly. It's for the arts," he said.

But as they rehearsed the scene, Valentina began to realize that what she felt for Robert was more than just for the arts. Robert was a gentleman—very sweet, kind, and funny—and he was extremely handsome. Whenever the cast traveled on promotion or press junkets, Robert was coveted by millions of women, yet was no denying his on-screen chemistry with Valentina. Although Anthony was a psychotic boyfriend involved in an on-again, off-again relationship with Gabrielle, he loved her.

Slipping off their clothes, Valentina and Robert fell into each other's arms that evening and were intimate for almost an hour, which was fifty minutes longer than the projected time of the scene. It was so intense that Robert slept through the next morning. For Valentina, it was nothing short of awkward at first, but she realized Robert gave her something that nobody—not even Sylvio—provided, and that was companionship.

"Yeah, I think we over-prepared, if you ask me," Valentina laughed.

"It's all a part of showbiz though. Gotta make it look good to keep them ratings. What did yo' man say about it though?" Robert asked, saying "man" disdainfully.

"He wasn't cool wit' it at all. He thinks we messin' around for real," she replied.

"Well, that just tells me that we doin' something right."

Valentina stood up and shook her head. "Robert, I didn't tell him about that night. It just didn't feel right to me. It felt like I was doggin' him by sleepin' wit' you."

"And he hasn't done it? You got a boxer for a boyfriend, Val. You think he hasn't messed around wit' anybody else?"

"I know he has. I mean, we met at the strip club I used to work at. That tells you all you need to know about him."

Robert stepped forward and massaged Valentina's shoulders. "Then what you did wasn't wrong. You can't continue to cage yourself for his insecurity. You gotta live too," he said as he closed in and kissed Valentina. "Damn, your lips taste good, girl."

Chapter 11

At 5 a.m. the next morning, Sylvio arrived at SDCC and opened the doors. The building was still deserted, which was exactly how he wanted his atmosphere. In the gym, he put on his red gloves, the first pair of boxing gloves that Jim had given him at the age of nine. Although they were old and had worn down over the years, they still fit Sylvio's hands. He flipped the lights on at one end of the gym and made his way over to one of the heavy bags.

Closing his eyes, he visualized his opponent before him and started working on his combinations, striking the heavy bag with a combination of force and precision. Slipping and ducking as if he was evading his opponent's blows, Sylvio quickly fell in a zone as he repeatedly hit the bag.

He did combinations for nearly forty minutes and worked up a sweat while he continued to pound away. This was Sylvio's place of solitude—the place where he could clear his head. He was so entranced by his workout that he didn't notice the gym door opening and Jim entering.

"I see you up and at 'em early today, Wolf," Jim said, walking over to Sylvio.

Sylvio stopped punching the bag and paused to take a few deep breaths, his shirt drenched in sweat. "Yeah, I just thought I'd change it up today and workout early instead of at night," he said.

"Got a lot on your mind, son?" Jim asked.

Taking a glove off, Sylvio went to drink from his water bottle. He was no longer as conditioned as he had been during the peak of his fighting days. In fact, he was already winded. Pausing to drink nearly the whole bottle of water, Sylvio shook his head. "Nah, I'm good. Ain't nothin' that I can't handle."

Putting his glove back on, he walked over to the heavy bag and began punching. Jim held the bag firmly for Sylvio so that it would not sway after his blows.

"One, two one," Jim started, and Sylvio followed his repetition pattern. Jim couldn't help but to smile as he held the bag for the boy who had eventually became his best success story. It was like the old days. "Hey, remember when you were nine, and you could barely hit the bag your first time out?" Jim asked.

"Yeah, I remember all them boys at Steel Gloves were clownin' me and didn't think nothin' of me till I started hittin' the bag wit' the quickness," Sylvio replied.

"You definitely came a long way from that shy boy who was being bullied in school," Jim said.

Although Sylvio was listening, he couldn't help but notice his fighter was distant and lost in thought. "What's goin' on, Wolf? You cool? Talk to me."

Finally, Sylvio paused, sweat pouring in streams down his face. "I fucked up this time, Jim," he said, catching his breath.

"What happened?" Jim asked.

When Sylvio didn't reply and instead gave him a look of regret, his fighter's eyes said it all for him.

"This wouldn't have anything to do with you and Valentina, would it?" Jim asked.

"Man, you know too much," Sylvio said as he and Jim laughed.

"Nah, but on some real shit, I thought what Val and I had was golden. Six years we've been together, man, and it's been a dope ride. But I don't know anymore, man. I'm still feelin' her, but lately there's been somebody else on my mind," he confessed.

"So, you've found a new fish in the pond, huh?" Jim asked.

"I guess. Man, I don't know. I mean this other chick is bad though Jim. Valentina's bangin', has a dope personality, is ambitious, and she goes after hers, but she can ill out at anytime, which pisses me off. On the other hand, this other chick is super dope, down to earth, got a nice petite body, and she bad," Sylvio replied.

"Okay, Sylvio, I'm gonna ask you a question, and I want you to keep it a buck wit' me. Did you sleep wit' this other woman?" Jim asked.

"Yeah, we got it in at my office yesterday," Sylvio replied, without hesitation.

"In the office? Damn, boy, you really are a wolf, huh? Couldn't wait till you got home to drop them drawers, huh?" Jim laughed.

"Look, man, it just happened. She came up on me wit' this skintight gear on, and I couldn't hold back, man. I gave it to her and them some," Sylvio confessed.

"So, tell me, who peaked first? You or Yolanda?" Jim asked, eyeing Sylvio slyly.

Sylvio's eyes widened in shock. "Wait, hold up. How did you know it was Yolanda?"

"Come on, man, it don't take no genius to figure out that you two been wanting to get shit poppin' for a minute. Stevie Wonder could see that a mile away. Plus, nothin' around hea' quiet when A.D.'s around," Jim added.

Sylvio was internally panicking. He did not want the news of his infidelity spreading. The media would have a field day, and Valentina would no doubt find out about his affair.

"Damn, A.D. and his big-ass mouth. So, what would you do if you were me, Jim?" Sylvio asked.

"Did you tell Valentina about it?" Jim asked.

"Man, you know I can't tell Val that shit. She'll flip out when I tell her."

Jim walked over and placed his hand on Sylvio's shoulder. "Sounds like you got a choice to make, Wolf. Do you love Valentina?" he asked.

Sylvio started to reply, but then held his tongue. Love is such a strong word. I don't know if I can really say I love Val. I love being with her, and I love fucking her, but what else do I love about her? Can I really say that I love her?

"Wolf, if you can't even bring yourself to say that you love that woman, then you ain't ready to settle down. Therefore, personally I see nothing wrong with a little sex on the side, but then again, that's me. I'm a dog, and I own up to it," Jim laughed.

"I see that, but how does that help me?" Sylvio asked, clearly irritated that Jim wasn't seriously analyzing his problem.

"Look, I'm gonna give you the same advice I should've given myself at your age. Never rush into a relationship with someone that you don't share a kindred spirit with. If you and Valentina ain't vibin' at that level, then maybe, just maybe, you weren't meant to be, you feel me?" Jim said.

"Yeah. Look, I'mma hit the showers. Then I'm goin' up to my office," Sylvio said, heading towards the exit.

Valentina sat on the couch of her penthouse apartment, drinking her favorite red wine. For the first time in many nights, the castmates wrapped filming three hours earlier than normal, which allowed Valentina to arrive home early. It couldn't have come at a more special time as she was expecting a visit from an old friend. In anticipation, she swept and mopped the floors, prepared a meal for herself and the guest, and had a bottle of wine on the table. The visit also allowed Valentina to get her mind off her complicated relationship with Sylvio, her long work hours, and the budding spark that was developing with Robert.

Suddenly, she heard four sharp knocks on her door. After checking to confirm her visitor, Valentina's heart filled with joy as she opened the door, allowing her best friend Keke Jenkins to enter the penthouse. The former exotic dancer at Apple Kim Adult Entertainment Club in New York, Keke "Passion" Jenkins, and Valentina had been friends for years.

"Ahhh what's up, Passion? Welcome to Atlanta, girl!" Valentina exclaimed, hugging her friend.

"Girl, bye! Nobody's called me 'Passion' since Apple Kim!" Keke replied hugging her friend.

"Whateva. You always gon' be 'Passion' to me. It don't matter where we at," Valentina laughed.

"Okay, that's cool, and because you ma' girl, I'mma let you rock. Cuz at the end of the day, you still gon' be my *chica*!" Passion said as she looked around the spacious penthouse. "So, this is how we livin' now? Damn, girl, I see you came a long way since Apple Kim."

"It's aight. You should see where my co-stars stay at. Some of them got big-ass ranch homes out in the 'burbs with acres of land. Girl, I couldn't do that. I need to stay by the city. I need to be wherever the action is," Valentina said, staring out one of her windows that overlooked the Atlanta skyline.

"Okay? Who you tellin'?"

"I'm so hype that you came, Passion. I should've picked you up from the airport, but I ain't know what time we was gon' wrap today."

"Oh, don't even sweat that, boo. Thank goodness for Uber cuz I wouldn't have no idea where to go around here," Passion said.

"So, what you think of yo' girl? Didn't I tell you all them years ago I was gon' make moves?" Valentina boasted, as she poured Passion a drink.

"You always did say that you had plans after Apple Kim, and you wasn't lyin'. You did yo' thing, girl. I'm proud of you," Passion said.

"So, after you left Apple Kim, where'd you go?" Valentina asked, as she and Passion both sat on the couch.

"Girl, I think I only stayed at Apple Kim for about eight months after you left, and then I couldn't take it anymore. Kim was shavin' my pay and all them other fake-ass hoes out there was backin' her stupid ass when I confronted her about my damn money. So, I up and left them bitches, and I went back to workin' escort for a minute. But I re-enrolled back at CUNY, and I got a nice lil' side gig waitressing like you used to do."

Valentina shook her head. She knew other dancers who left their former adult franchises and establishments too, and with few other options available to them, they returned to the streets, which was more dangerous than most people realized.

"Damn, so after all that time you ended up back at the Marriott on Park Avenue, huh?" Valentina asked.

"I had no choice, Val. I started the game early, before I finished college, and it was all I knew. Thinkin' back to it, I think I was the same age that you were when you started workin' the streets," Passion said.

"Ugh, don't remind me of them days. I was so green when I started. If it wasn't for you takin' me under yo' wing, I probably wouldn't have made it out there," Valentina said.

"Girl, you know we were two of the baddest bitches in Queens back in da' day, and we pulled the best of 'em. You were always a pro at getting' them athletes between the sheets. Speakin' of athletes, how's yo' fine ass man doing?"

"Girl, I don't even know anymore. Sylvio and I started out strong, and for some reason, this past year, it just hasn't been there for us. I think this long distance thing is hurtin' us."

"Girl, don't tell me you broke up wit' him!" Passion exclaimed.

"Nah, I ain't broke up with him, at least not officially."

Passion's eyes widened. "What you mean, 'not officially?' Oh, lemme guess, you gave it up to another man. Didn't you? Who was it?" she asked, raising an eyebrow.

Valentina sighed. Nothing got past her best friend. "You know my male co-star in my show? Well, let's just say, that sex scene in the last episode was more than just for show," she confessed.

Passion's mouth gaped open in shock. "You mean that Robert Yates guy?"

Valentina confirmed by nodding her head and saying nothing.

"I mean, don't get me wrong, he is a fine black specimen, and not one show goes by where I don't want that tight ass. Damn, bitch, you get all the fine men!" Passion laughed, but when Valentina only laughed half-heartedly, Passion asked the question that Valentina anticipated her asking. "Does Sylvio know about ya'?"

"He doesn't know, Passion, but he suspects something is up. I tried to tell him that it was just acting, but inside, it was more than acting. I mean, I've had great sex with Sylvio, but Robert is on another level. He knows how to love me in ways that Sylvio can't. He's just a dream, and I don't know if I ever wanna wake up," Valentina confessed.

Passion let out a slow, derisive noise. "Whooo, girl, you got a problem, but this the good problem. You gotta choose between two sexy black men. Most other women would kill for that kind of dilemma. I hate you right now, by the way," she laughed.

"C'mon, Passion, this is serious. What am I gon' do?" Valentina asked.

"I mean, if we gon' compromise, let's do this. I'll take Sylvio, and you can hang on to Yates, and whenever we get tired of our boos, we just swap 'em. How does that sound?" Passion joked.

"It sounds like we back in the lobby again, waiting on our next clients," Valentina replied as she thought back to her early escort days.

January 2010 | The yellow taxicab pulled up in front of the Marriott Hotel in downtown Manhattan during rush hour traffic. Paying the driver before opening the door, twenty-year-old Valentina Cruz stepped out of the vehicle and made her way inside the hotel. Wearing a long black overcoat over a silver sequined dress, Valentina walked over to the lobby to wait for her client. Eyeing the bar that was set up across the lobby, she wished her client would hurry so he could buy her a mixed martini before she settled in for the evening.

Valentina had checked herself before leaving the house. She didn't wear a lot of makeup because if there was one sure trait that she knew about the men she was involved with, it was that makeup turns most of them off. Instead, they loved women who bore natural faces. But Valentina applied some eyeliner, fake eyelashes, and a bit of eye shadow. Topping it all off with her favorite straight-haired red wig, she made sure the dress she wore revealed her flowing legs.

Remember what Pedro told you. Be a mystery to your client. Leave an impression, and most of all, leave him wanting more. Then leave his ass after he pays you. Not that she had any obligation to listen to Pedro Quinones, her on-again, off-again boyfriend...

They had been dating since Valentina's sophomore year in college. At first, it seemed to be an innocent romance. But later in the relationship, Valentina noticed that Pedro had secrets. He was the young leader of a crime syndicate named Legarto Inc., an underground society that banked on hedging sports bets and flipping the bets into cash. Pedro also had a crew of enforcers that roamed the streets and infiltrated workplaces. The crew was known as the 85th Street Serps, and the members were quite dangerous.

Valentina's brothers Juan and Bruno had recently joined the gang, more out of dire financial straits. Their father's moving business had bottomed out during the recession, and because bills were still due, it left the three siblings with no other choice but to join Pedro's syndicate.

Valentina also suspected Pedro was being unfaithful to her.

One day she arrived at Pedro's house and saw four women, barely dressed, emerging from the giant living room. After questioning Pedro, he told her that he was not, in fact, sleeping with the women, but they were compensating him for their escort services. Initially disgusted, Valentina walked off, vowing to leave Pedro, but he eventually persuaded her into joining his escort business. Valentina, who was not exactly a nymphomaniac but simply enjoyed the pleasures of sex, reluctantly agreed.

And after barely being one month in, Valentina had brought in more money in one month than she would have in six months working a day job. From athletes to actors and multiple TV and radio personalities, Valentina was surprised by the number of people in New York that paid huge sums of cash for escort services. Tonight in particular, she had a rendezvous planned with pro football player Andre Sorrell.

Sorrell was returning from a long road trip with his team, which was in the playoffs and was one game away from the Super Bowl. Before his intense training, he called in for Legarto's Escort Services, and Pedro felt that Valentina was the right woman for the NFL star. After speaking with Sorrell, Valentina agreed to meet him at the Marriott on Park Avenue.

But Valentina felt like a fish out of water in the high-end section of Manhattan. She was very used to working with clients in Queens, Brooklyn, even the Bronx, but never in the big city. As she waited at the lobby, another woman that appeared to be a few years older than her sat down. The other woman wore a red, silk-laced dress with red pumps. Her black and brown hair was braided and tied on the back of her head. She stared intently at Valentina, causing the young woman much discomfort.

"What you lookin' at?" Valentina asked.

"Nothin' much. I just ain't neva' seen you round dis' way before. You waitin' on somebody?"

Valentina started to grow more suspicious. She had to stay alert because, for all she knew, the woman could be an undercover police officer. She couldn't afford to be locked up.

"If you must know...yeah, I'm waitin' on someone," she replied.

"Okay, I feel you. No reason to get all hostile wit' ya girl. I'm waitin' on a jawn myself. But ain't you a cute lil' thing wit your red weave and all. What they call you?" she asked.

"Uh, my name's Valentina."

The other woman shook her head. "No, no, boo. What's yo' work name?" she asked. Clearly, she knew Valentina was an escort.

"My work name's 'Valley.' What about you?"

"They call me 'Passion' out here, boo," she said.

"Word? But what's yo' real name though?" Valentina asked curiously.

"I ain't about to tell yo' nosy ass. For all I know, you could be five-oh," Passion replied.

"Nah, I ain't five-oh. I'm actually waitin' on Andre Sorrell," Valentina said.

"The football player? Ain't he married?" Passion asked.

"I don't know. That ain't my business. I'm only here to work and get that two grand he's gon' pay me," Valentina shrugged.

Passion laughed. "I like you, girl. You a bit young, but you got swag, Valley. Guess who I'm waitin' on?"

"Who you waitin' on?" Valentina asked.

"Herbert Lenny, the Wall Street broker who's makin' up to two mill right now. A bitch bout to get paid," Passion laughed.

"So, you gon' suck off some decrepit sixty-year-old white dude?" Valentina asked.

"Girl, the money that Andre is makin' is pennies compared to Herbert. I'll walk out this bitch with probably thirty G's and buy a car tomorrow," Passion bragged.

Valentina laughed as all her feelings of apprehension withered away.

"It's Keke, by the way," Passion said after a minute of silence.

"So, you finally trust me long enough to gimme your government name?"

"Don't push it, Valley. Anyway, ain't that yo' boy?" she asked, looking at the lobby entrance.

A big stocky, well-built black man entered the hotel with a couple members of his entourage. As if by strange coincidence, an older white gentleman with neat, jet black hair and a business suit followed right behind him. The men did not know each other, but they both came for the same reason: nightly sexual pleasure.

"And there goes my piece," Passion said. Lowering her voice to a whisper, she lowered her head down to Valentina's right ear. "If you want to, we can switch dudes right now. I'll take Andre, and you can have Herbert. Either way, we cashin' our checks tonight, okay?"

Valentina thought about the proposition for a moment, and at first, she was ready to proceed with the client switch, but after seeing Andre's bulging pectoral muscles with his low trimmed beard, she declined. "Nah, I'm good with Andre. Have fun kickin' it wit' ole man Rockefeller ova' there," she laughed.

After checking their makeup and outfits, they walked over to the men and introduced themselves. Andre waved off the members of his entourage and walked to the lobby desk to check into the rooms. While Andre and Valentina made their way over to the bar, Passion and Herbert were sliding into one of the elevators to go up to their suite. *Passion damn sure doesn't waste time.*

Valentina and Andre sat on the barstool. "Mind if I buy you a drink?" he asked.

"I would love a drink. Lemme get a shot of Crown Royal," she informed the bartender.

"Make it a double for me," Andre added as the bartender went to pour their drinks. "You know, even though I travel a lot, I don't do this type of stuff in every city I go to," he told Valentina.

"You ain't gotta explain anything to me. Tonight's your night, and I'm ready to give you whatever you want," Valentina said seductively. Her eyes would frequently dart toward the ring finger on his right hand and as expected, there was no ring, but the imprint of his wedding band was apparent. "So, what team do you play for again?" she asked.

"Tight end for the Buffalo Bills. You watch football?" Andre asked.

Valentina didn't particularly take any interest in sports, but she loved the athletes that played sports. "I catch what I can. My brothers are the football fans."

"I bet they ain't Bills fans though, right?"

"I wouldn't really know," Valentina shrugged. She was already beginning to get disenchanted with Andre. Although he had a great body build, he had a dull personality. *Let's just hope he's spontaneous in bed.*

"So, you ready to go to the room? You lookin' real sexy in that dress. I can't wait to take it off," he said.

I bet you can't. I hope I get double just for blowing his mind and his dick. "What are we waitin' for then?" Valentina asked seductively as Andre paid for the drinks so they could head up to the room.

A few days later, Valentina and Passion met for lunch at Queens Grille on Farmers Boulevard, where they shared details of their intimate evenings with their clients. Apparently, Passion had an eventful evening with Herbert, and not only did Herbert satisfy her in ways that she couldn't have imagined, but he also paid her over ten thousand dollars that evening, which was one of Passion's biggest paydays yet.

Valentina, on the other hand was utterly disappointed with Andre. She couldn't understand how he could be aggressive enough to play a sport like football, yet he could not bring the same aggressiveness or passion into the bedroom. He was passive to the point where Valentina became frustrated that it took him more than twenty or thirty minutes to get aroused. Then, when he finally stiffened, he climaxed within five minutes. Pedro lasted longer on his worst day.

At the end of the evening, Valentina was just happy to get her two grand. She'd left the Marriott more dissatisfied than when she'd entered. "I'm tellin' you, Passion, Andre was nothin' but a lil' ass puppy. He ain't no dog at all. I've been with frat boys that lasted longer than him," Valentina said.

"Maybe he was buggin' over his marriage," Passion said.

"Whatever it was, he just didn't cut it for me," Valentina said.

"As long as you made that money, he could be trash all day."

"You ain't neva' lied. Ugh, girl, it was so emotionless that I just left after the fact, then went to my man's house to fuck him so I could get off. It was crazy," Valentina said.

"Girl, what you need to do is stop waiting on men to call you. Go out there, and get the man who's gon' do you right and pay you right," Passion said.

While the two girls chatted, Valentina noticed for a second that the TV hanging above the grill was tuned in to the sports channel where different highlights were being displayed. During one segment, the sports channel played highlights of the Syracuse Men's basketball team as they faced off against Seton Hall. Valentina watched as one player in particular dominated from half to half as Syracuse blew out Seton Hall.

Snapping back from her intrigue by the player's athletic output, Valentina returned her attention to her conversation. "Passion, I think I've found my next piece." Valentina's eyes were set on none other than Syracuse's star guard, Jamal Samuels.

Chapter 12

Waking up at sunrise one day, Jamal Samuels squinted his eyes as rays of sunlight flooded in through the room window. Valentina's body was intertwined with his own, and as the sunlight hit her face, she squinted and rubbed her eyes. Jamal, who stood at six-foot-five, stared at the tiny girl that slept under him. She was not the first girl that he had slept with at Syracuse, but she was the most spontaneous partner he'd ever had.

Although he'd met her only weeks earlier in a bar after a game, she was different from the other girls that he had been intimate with in the past. Jamal never considered himself an object of sexual desire, but being in a successful run with the Syracuse Orangeman Men's basketball team, he couldn't deny that he was in high demand sexually by all the college co-eds. Yet, he felt a different vibe with this Valentina woman, whom he barely knew. She was extremely beautiful but heavily coveted by multiple men.

Jamal knew that Valentina was involved with other men, and that sobering reality bothered him. The problem was that she had a way to hook and reel him in with her sexual appeal, her play of innocence, and her confidence.

As for Valentina, she was entering what she saw in her mind as a danger zone. This was not part of her plan. Jamal was supposed to be a client, just like the other men that she had dealt with in the past, but unlike the other men, she had grown attached with the star guard. And as addictive as he was with his sweaty, chiseled chest, perfect smile, and warm personality, Valentina promised herself that she would not get attached with anyone that she was intimate with during business hours. She made the same vow to Pedro and the Serps because if she didn't break it off immediately, she knew he would be in serious peril.

But here she was, sleeping with him in his college apartment a block off the Syracuse campus. By this point, she had lost count of how many times she had already slept with him. At first, it was for money, but Jamal had a kind nurturing spirit about him. He wasn't a simpleton like Andre was, but he had a quiet dominance about him that turned her on. He knew what he wanted to do, and he set his mind to accomplish his goals.

Jamal was very aggressive between the sheets, and his stamina was unlike the previous men's she'd been with, perhaps even stronger than Pedro's.

As Valentina stirred in his arms, Jamal kissed her on the forehead. "What's up, baby?"

"Hey, you sent me to heaven last night, Jamal. For real, I'm still seeing stars."

Jamal shifted his body weight in bed. "Well, I could show you the world all night long. But I gotta get up to go to morning workouts."

He slid the blanket off and rose from his comforter. Staring out the window, he said, "You know, Valentina, we could make this thing last. Who knows how far it can get?"

Valentina shook her head as she got up from bed too. "Um, I don't think that's a good idea, Jamal. To keep it real, I shouldn't even be hea' right now," she replied. *Damn why does he have to be naked in front of me? He's making it hard as hell for me to break it off with him. Now I'm debating if I wanna go another round with him.*

"Valentina, check it out. I don't care if you an escort or not. I don't give a damn if you got brothers out there gangbanging. Tell me that what you feel ain't real between us," he said.

"Jamal, listen. It ain't you. It's me, okay? I'm…I'm just not good at long-term relationships, okay? I'm the type of chick that stay in the moment, you feel me? All the other, countless dudes I've been with…and no one else has meant more to me than you have. But this can't happen," she explained.

"So, you tellin' me to throw my feelings away for a temporary fuck? Is that all I am to you? A jump off?" he asked.

Valentina walked over to Jamal and embraced him from behind. "No, baby, you're much more than that to me. You're an amazing lover, a great listener, and I'm feelin' you. But I just don't think we should keep this going. It's best if we just went our separate ways and did our own thing."

"Valentina, now's the chance for stability. If I keep killin' it at this college thing, who knows what'll happen? I might be top draft pick if I go pro, and I need a down-ass chick like you wit' me. You don't gotta keep messin' wit' that pimp or his crew for the rest of yo' life. All they gonna do is tie you down, and I know you a chick that can't be tied down."

"You damn right," Valentina agreed, laughing. "But on a serious tip though. I don't wanna be the one to weigh you down. You're a sweet guy, and you deserve to be wit' someone who's gonna make time for you and only you. Any girl would be lucky as hell to have you."

"I want you to be that lucky girl," Jamal replied. "Look, I know I ain't sittin' on billions yet, like yo' boy, and I know I ain't got hella tattoos on my body or nothin' like that, but I can offer you something that none of them shady niggas can offer you: a future for you to spread yo' wings and do you...nobody controlling you or tellin' you what to do. Please, at least think about it."

Valentina hung her head as a single tear rolled down her cheek. Jamal was making it difficult for her to leave. "I can't. Look, I know you have morning workouts, so I'mma just roll up outta here and catch a cab or something."

Jamal reached into his drawer and pulled out his towel, body soap, and toothbrush. "Aight. Well, you know where the door is. You can let yourself out," he said coldly before entering the bathroom.

Valentina watched as he closed the door behind him. Gathering her things, she walked out of the apartment.

"Damn, so you've been hard to get wit' since Jamal huh? I ain't gonna lie, I was surprised you let him get away. He was a fine thang, and he could ball! I would've been set," Passion said, snapping Valentina out of her thoughts.

"Don't get too excited," Valentina replied. "Jamal still tried to call me like ten more times after that day, and he even came over to my house, but needless to say, my brothers were less than thrilled to see him. After that, we lost touch, and he just focused on ball. He played like crap the last few games, and he ended up not getting drafted to the NBA, so he went overseas."

Passion shook her head. "Damn, girl. You were so good, that man had to leave the country. Talk about pussy power," she cracked.

Valentina glared at Passion. "C'mon, girl, it's not funny. I was in a different place in my life, and I wasn't ready for a guy like Jamal. I let a good one get away. Then I reunited with Sylvio, who was a childhood friend, and I felt that I was getting a second chance at making it right. But then he got mixed up with Pedro and his brother, and next thing I know, I'm at the ER, hoping that he pulls through. I thought I lost him that day."

"But you didn't lose him, girl. You saved his life. If you didn't call for help, he would've died," Passion reminded her friend.

"But that's just it. I don't want Sylvio to feel like he owes me anything. I wanna be with someone that I connect with," she replied.

"Ain't Sylvio that somebody?" Passion asked.

Valentina took a sip of her wine then stared out the window at the skyline. "I thought he was. I wanted him to be the one so bad, and don't get me wrong, the sex is amazing. But after six years of grinding in the industry and finally getting my break, I feel like we don't connect as well anymore. I don't think I'm ever gon' have his support as long as I'm still acting. Maybe he's bummed out cuz I'm livin' my dream, and he ain't livin' his."

"So? What you supposed to do? Put yo' life on hold while you wait for him to get up to yo' level? Girl, please. I got nothin' but love for Sylvio, but if I was doin' the long-term thing, and I had to choose between him and Robert right now, I'm goin' with one of Maxim's 100 Sexiest People," Passion replied, referring to Robert. "I mean, both of you in the same line of business anyway, and you both play toxic lovers on TV, so you might as well be dating him anyway, shit."

Valentina laughed, then put her hands over her face. "Ay Dios Mio! Why am I the one dealing with man problems?"

Passion poured herself a second glass of wine. "Girl, you ain't the only one dealin' wit' them problems, okay? You gotta decide who you vibe with more. If it's Sylvio, you work it out wit' him. If it's not Sylvio, you gotta keep it real with him, and just break it off. If you need backup for that, I got my cousin Big Lou that stay on Northern Blvd, and he'll knock a nigga out, boxer or not."

"That won't be necessary, Passion," Valentina said as she finished her own glass of wine.

Back in New York, Sylvio was lying on his back on the cold hard ground with a hole in his stomach. He could feel the blood running out of his wound, and before everything went black, a gunman with a black ski mask walked up to him, holding a pistol over his head. He was determined to finish the job.

"There's always a price for winning, Dominique," the gunman said in a muffled voice. "You lived as a champ, and now you'll die as a champ," he said, before firing the gun in Sylvio's left temple.

Waking up in a cold sweat, Sylvio panted, catching his breath. It was a vicious cycle of nightmares that began since the night he and Omar were shot. On some nights he would sleep well without any visions or nightmares, but then on a random night he would induce a new horrific rendition of that fateful evening. Running his hand across his abdomen, he traced his finger over the scar that reminded him of how close he was to certain death. The nightmares wouldn't leave his subconscious. In the past he attempted to seek professional help from shrinks, but nothing worked.

As he lay in bed, his cell phone rang. Looking at the caller ID, he realized it was Estelle Pierre, his father's caretaker. Since being diagnosed with diabetes, Jacques had been assigned a caretaker to assist him for about six hours a day. Sylvio and Rebecca paid for Estelle's weekly services, and even though Jacques declined the assistance at first, he gradually warmed up to Estelle, and she took care of his duties, from washing dishes, cleaning floors, scrubbing the bathrooms, and assisting him whenever his arthritis crippled his joints.

"Yeah, Estelle, what's going on? Why you calling so early?" Sylvio asked.

"It's Jacques," Estelle replied frantically.

By the tone of her voice, Sylvio knew something was wrong.

"I tried to call him this morning, like always, to let him know that I'm coming over to help him, but he never picked up his phone."

Sylvio's heart raced. "That doesn't sound like Dad. He always picks up his phone. Are you at the apartment now?" he asked.

"Yes, I am here, and I tried buzzing in, but he's not answering."

Upon hearing those words, Sylvio sprang up from bed and scrambled for clothes on. Now he was convinced that his father was in trouble, so he wasted no time putting his clothes on. "Okay, Estelle, stay there. I'm on my way. Did you call 9-1-1?" he asked.

"Yes, I did. They're coming right now," the elderly Haitian said.

"Okay, m'ap vini koun ya;' la," Sylvio said, letting her know he was on his way. Grabbing his keys, he rushed out the house. As soon as he cranked the car, he connected his Bluetooth headset to his phone and called Rebecca.

She answered after the fourth ring. "What?" she replied, sounding annoyed.

"Rebecca, I just got a call from Estelle. Dad's not answering his phone, and he's ain't buzzin' her inside," Sylvio explained.

That's when Rebecca realized how dire the situation was. "Oh, my God. Are you going over there now?"

"Yeah, I'm on my way. Estelle already called 9-1-1." Sylvio could hear the almost silent, muffled sobs coming from his sister on the other end. "Hey, hey, Rebecca...stop crying. We can't assume the worst right now, okay? Just try to get here as soon as you can," he said.

"Okay..." Rebecca managed before they hung up.

When he pulled up at the front of his father's apartment, Sylvio saw that the first responders and paramedics had already arrived and were rushing inside the apartment. Without even bothering to properly park, he turned his emergency lights on then left his car in the middle of the street and ran into the building. The first responders stood outside Jacques' door, apparently unable to enter inside.

Sylvio frantically knocked on his father's door, but there was no response. "Dad, open the door! It's Sylvio. Come on, answer me!" he yelled.

"Sir, do you have any way of opening this door? It's important we get to him immediately," one of the paramedics said.

"No, I don't got a key. I gotta call the landlord," Sylvio replied, pulling his phone out.

Within a few minutes, the landlord arrived at the building. Pulling out his spare key to Jacques' apartment, he handed it to Sylvio, who quickly opened the door.

As soon as he stepped in, Sylvio could hear the bathroom faucet. *Dad always made it a habit to never leave water running.* Heading towards the sound, Sylvio turned into the room that was connected to the bathroom. There, he saw a man's legs stretched out in the doorway.

"Dad!" Sylvio ran toward his father, lying motionless on the floor. He placed his head on his dad's chest to check for a heartbeat. All he heard was silence. "Guys, he's in here! Hurry up! He ain't breathing!"

The paramedics rushed to Jacques' side and checked for a heartbeat and pulse. After employing CPR for five minutes, they hurried and placed Jacques in a gurney. Sylvio jogged alongside the medical personnel until they reached the ambulance, where they placed Jacques. Sylvio jumped inside as the paramedics closed the doors and rushed off to Jamaica Hospital. Upon arriving, Jacques was immediately transported to one of the rooms, but Sylvio was forced to wait outside while the doctors worked feverishly to save his father's life.

Sylvio was too nervous to sit in the waiting room. He hated hospitals. The nurses and doctors always gave off an energy that was all too familiar to him. It wasn't long before he found himself hyperventilating. He ran to the floor's restroom and washed his hands and face.

C'mon, Sylvio, hold yourself together. This ain't Dad's first time being in a coma. Same thing happened six years ago, and he managed to pull through.

Fifteen minutes later, Rebecca arrived at the hospital.

"Did you hear anything yet?" she asked, hugging Sylvio.

"Nah, I ain't heard nothin'. The doctor's still working on him," he replied.

For five agonizing hours, Sylvio and Rebecca waited for word on their father's condition. Rebecca couldn't take it any longer. She suddenly burst into tears. "I should've stayed with him last tonight. It's my fault," she said.

"Rebecca, it ain't yo' fault. There was nothing you could've done for him. We gotta be strong for him now," Sylvio said, trying to comfort his sister.

After some time, a doctor came out of the room with an expression that told Sylvio the diagnosis even before it came out of his mouth. "Your father had a major heart attack, about eight hours ago. We've done all we can to revive him, but the lack of circulation has caused his brain functions to shut down…" his voice trailed off.

Sylvio did not hear the next words that came out of the doctor's mouth. It was another out of body experience. His father couldn't be dead. He just couldn't be. "But is he gonna make it or not?" Sylvio asked.

"He's in a coma right now. He doesn't have too much time left. If you want to say your goodbyes, now is the time." The doctor walked back out into the hall. Sylvio sank to the floor, completely numb and, for the first time in years, he was helpless.

All his memories of the arguments he'd had with his father dissipated upon the revelation that his father had passed. Sylvio's mind flashed back to the argument they had about his career choices and his option to forego college to pursue a boxing career. Jacques wanted his son to receive the education and a future that he worked so hard to attain himself. Due to Jacques' immigrant status and limited education in the states, he worked hard to ensure that his son would not miss out on the opportunity to get the education he needed to have a promising future. Although he was strict, Sylvio realized that Jacques chastised him out of love, and he never held it against Sylvio for harboring feelings of animosity towards him.

Jacques and his estranged ex-wife, Anne, never fully reconciled after the argument that caused their divorce. Anne eventually remarried, and although she reappeared by Sylvio's bedside while he was fighting for his own life, she and Jacques never fully patched the relationship. Now Anne would never have a chance to mend fences with father of her children.

Then there was Rebecca, who fought tooth and nail to reunite with her father and brother and cared for Jacques when Sylvio still harbored bitterness towards their father. Watching Rebecca break down as the doctor broke the tragic news to them was more than what Sylvio could handle. Walking over to Rebecca, he hugged her tightly as she wept uncontrollably in his arms.

"Rebecca, I'm so sorry. I'm sorry for the years we wasted being apart from each other. We gotta be strong for him now. He would want that," he said.

"I don't know what I'm gonna do without Daddy. Who's gonna pray over me? Who's gonna tell me that everything will be okay?" Rebecca sobbed.

"For the longest time, I was so angry at Dad. I would take out my frustrations in the ring. Every beating I took from that, I internalized it and used it to beat any fighter they put in front of me. But after a while, I realized I couldn't stay angry at him," Sylvio said.

"No matter what was said between you two, he always loved you. He would tell me all the time how proud he was of you," Rebecca said.

The two siblings tightly embraced as they grieved their father.

Jacques Dominique was buried in Calvary Cemetery in Woodside, New York. As much as Sylvio wanted to keep the memorial ceremony private, the funeral ended up drawing more than two thousand residents from Queens, Brooklyn, Bronx, and even other states, including Florida and Massachusetts. Jacques' relatives from Gonaives, Haiti, also flew to New York to pay their respects.

Jim also attended the funeral and even paid some of the funeral expenses, which Sylvio was extremely grateful for because he recalled that in their first meeting, Jacques was not welcoming to Jim and even shut his door in the trainer's face. But the two men had grown to show a cordial level of respect for one another over the years. Even after Jacques and Sylvio had their falling out, Jacques was never fearful that his son would be caught up in the wrong crowd because he knew Jim was a man of character.

Anne attended the funeral with her new husband, Henry LaGuerre. Sylvio could have had ill feelings toward his estranged mother, but he took the important lesson that Jacques taught him, which was to heart, learning to treat others with respect. And even if he had animosity for his mother at times, Sylvio still treated her with the same courtesy that his father would have shown her.

Sylvio was surprised that fellow former boxers attended the funeral, including Rosjan Bokavic and Ken "Kamikaze" Brown. The news of Jacques' passing had hit the airwaves and social media, so Sylvio couldn't escape the posts expressing sympathy and encouragement. While he appreciated the well wishes and the kind words, he felt that if he wasn't a sports personality that many people would not have cared enough to offer their words of condolences.

But what Sylvio was most grateful for was that a certain person came to the funeral. She was the woman who had shown her heart to him and had been able to comfort him when he couldn't keep his composure as he openly wept during the service. He didn't care if cameras were watching him or about who viewed them together.

Yolanda wrapped her arms around Sylvio's shoulder, and it meant a great deal to him that she was in attendance. She didn't know who his father was, but she knew how much of a great deal he meant to Sylvio, so she wanted to be there.

But one person that did not attend the funeral was Sylvio's girlfriend. It wasn't until the funeral that he finally came to a sobering conclusion after several years of being with her. Valentina Cruz couldn't be bothered by the news. From that moment forward, Sylvio knew that his relationship with Valentina was coming apart at the seams. There was no use trying to hold on to feelings that weren't mutual.

His phone had over six missed calls and two messages that day, and although he knew Valentina was trying to call him, he ignored the calls. Aiming to turn his phone off, he received a notification from his Instagram account. Sylvio had set his Instagram to private settings since the fallout from Barry Taylor's loss, but surprisingly the message came from the defeated former champion. It was a recording, so Sylvio listened closely to the message.

What's good, Wolf? Barry's voice resonated through the recording. Although he sounded as if he was still recovering, he was coherent enough to record the message.

My thoughts and prayers go out to you and your family at this difficult time. It's never easy to lose someone close to you, especially a family member. I don't want to make this message too long or nothin', but I wanted to tell you that you were right. I shouldn't have underestimated Zhang, and it's clear now that I wasn't as ready as I thought I was to fight him. I should've dedicated more time for training instead of messing around. Doc says that I'm makin' progress, but I ain't exactly ready to return to the ring. It kills me that I gambled away my title belt, and there ain't nothin' I can do to get it back.

But there is someone who's strong enough to take on Jun Zhang. You got the fastest hand-eye coordination, and you're stronger than you were six years earlier. The fight game needs you back in the ring again to reclaim what was taken away from you. Jun Zhang is the Tiger back in his country, and it is a symbol of pride, resistance, and strength. But it's time for the Tiger to face off against the Wolf. You might think I'm crazy recording this message, but I feel that you ain't done. Make your pops proud. Bring the title back to Queens.

The recording ended, leaving Sylvio to his thoughts. *Why would Barry tell me to come back? What is there for me to prove?* But behind the thoughts of doubt, Sylvio sensed opportunity.

I never had a chance to prove why I became champion. People are already putting dirt on my grave and labeling me as a has-been. Maybe it's time to shut people up. Maybe it's time for the Wolf to howl again.

Chapter 13

Three weeks later, Sylvio walked into Jim's office at the SDCC, where he was met by words of sympathy and encouragement from boxers, trainers, and clients. He'd taken an extensive leave of absence from work in the wake of his father's death, so Jim had taken over most of his administrative duties with Kevin's assistance.

"What's up, Sylvio? How are you holding up?" Jim asked.

Sylvio shrugged. "Just takin' it day by day, man. Sometimes I wake up, and I still wait for that occasional phone call that I'm never gonna get again."

"I know how you're feelin', son. Jacques Dominique was a great man. I know we had our differences at first, but he worked hard to provide for you and your sister. He helped you become the man that you are today. I'll miss him dearly as well."

"Appreciate that, Jim. Thanks for coming to the funeral."

"Of course, man. By the way, there's no rush for you to come back to work right away. We can hold the fort down until you make it back," Jim reassured Sylvio.

"Hopefully, we still have a fort in the next two months," Sylvio muttered. The financial status of SDCC continued to take huge hits in the weeks that followed the championship fight.

"Come on, man, keep yo' head up. We may be below water, but

we ain't drowned yet," Kevin added.

"Well, look, that's one of the reasons I came in today. I wanted you to be the first one to hear this," Sylvio said.

"Alright, what's up?" Jim asked.

After taking a deep breath, Sylvio said, "I've decided to come out of retirement and return to the ring."

Kevin and Jim exchanged looks that Sylvio couldn't read. They were bewildered by what they felt was an irrational decision.

"Sylvio, I don't think that's a good idea—" Jim started.

"Why not? Why isn't it a good idea?" Sylvio countered. "You've said it yourself, I still got moves in the ring, and I ain't old yet. The center needs money and has to rehabilitate its image, and I need to prove that I can still be a champion."

"At what cost?" Jim asked. "Sylvio, listen, you were a great fighter six years ago, but it's over. You've missed significant time in the ring. These fighters today are younger, quicker, agile, and they have increased ring sense."

"I had those things when I was fighting also, Jim. Look, man. I ain't come here to ask your permission to come back to the ring. I'm coming out of retirement, whether you like it or not."

Jim sighed. Sylvio was one step away from making the most reckless decision in the world. "Sylvio, do you have in mind the level of conditioning it's going to take to get you back into peak fighting shape? To get your timing back? Yes, you're strong, but you've gained some pounds over the years. Yes, you've been active, but you get winded after a twenty-minute routine. Even if the boxing commission board approves you in this state or any other state, the first boxer that you face off against will not be star-struck by you or intimidated by you. He will be lookin' to knock yo' head off. So, I'm tellin' you as a friend, don't make this mistake."

"It's my choice, okay? I decide what I do in my life. I got people out there tellin' me I'm washed up. I got cats out there that think I'm a quitter and have they been thinking about this only now? No, they've been thinking about this since I made my retirement speech six years ago. I don't think the game is done with me yet," Sylvio said.

"Boy, you've got to be the most hard-headed cat out hea'. Tell me, what led to this insane decision?" Jim asked.

"Unfinished business," Sylvio replied.

"Oh, that's a good one. 'Unfinished business,'" Jim replied, sarcastically. "Listen to me, Sylvio. You were one of the most gifted boxers I've ever trained in my life, but you ain't the Wolf anymore, don't you get it?"

"Who are you to tell me what I am and what I'm not?"

"Sylvio, check it. Look, I know that your father's passing got you all emotional, and you feel like you got to prove yourself as a man, but I tellin' you, this ain't the way to go about it. You really need to think this shit through."

"I already have, and this is the best time to get back in the game and prove that the Wolf ain't done yet." Sylvio got up from the chair and began walking toward the door. "I wanted to tell you first because there was a point in my life where I considered you a father to me. You've been around this game for years. If there's anyone that should understand why I want to do this, it should be you."

"Sylvio, you're still a son to me, and I don't want to lose you like I lost my own son."

Sylvio stopped in his tracks as Jim made his last appeal in his case to dissuade him from an ill-fated return to the ring.

"Man, when you fought for the middleweight title, I was so proud of you because I never got the opportunity to fight for a crown during my prime. When you won that belt, I won the belt that night too. We were both champions. But then you almost died the next day, and guess what? I almost died that day also. If that bullet had taken you out, I wouldn't know what to do then."

Sylvio went over to his trainer. Here he was, thinking about how his near-death experience scarred just him, and yet it seemed to have a psychological effect on Jim as well. "Jim, what went down that night wasn't your fault. I was the idiot that went to Valentina's house in the middle of the night without backup, and I lost two friends in the process. But I can't let that be my legacy. I can't let my life be determined by what could've been. I ain't goin' nowhere. There has to be a reason why I'm still alive and breathing, and it's to win my title back," he replied. "You helped me get a title shot once. This return won't be successful without you, Jim. I need you at my corner again. Let's shake up the world like we did when I was twenty-two," Sylvio said, extending his right arm toward Jim.

To Sylvio's astonishment, Jim didn't shake his hand. "I'm sorry, Wolf. I can't be at your corner this time. I don't wanna sit at the hospital at your bedside again trying to figure out if you're going to make it or not."

Sylvio lowered his hand. "So, it's like that, huh? We're through? Is that what you're saying?"

"Sylvio, it's not personal. You know I got love for you, but this is business we're talking about now. Boxing is a dirty business and has always been a dirty business, before you and I were even conceived. I'm done trying to kill myself for this beausiness, man."

When it was clear that Jim didn't want to train him, Sylvio began to walk out of the office.

"Wait, Wolf," Kevin said, walking over to Sylvio. Kevin had not said a word during the argument, so Sylvio was surprised that he decided to finally speak up. Extending his hand to Sylvio, he said, "I'm with you, man. I got your back, like the old days."

"C'mon, Kevin, you can't be serious," Jim interjected.

Kevin turned to face his older brother. "See, that's your problem, Jim. You're always running away from your problems instead of facing them head-on. One thing that you gotta remember is that I ain't like you. I don't run away when things get too hot like you did in '92 or like you did after Dante's death. I don't give up like you did on your marriage."

Jim suddenly rose from his chair in such a fury, that the chair flung into the back wall. "Mention one more thing about my marriage again, baby bro, and you'll be the one laying in the hospital," he threatened, his eyes burning right into Kevin's eyes.

Kevin didn't flinch. "You think I sweat you? I don't care what you do, but I'm gon' support Sylvio, and I'm gon' do whatever it takes to make sure he's back on top."

Jim just shook his head and let out a chuckle. "You just as gone as Sylvio is. How many fighters have you trained, Kevin? Your only job is maintaining the books and negotiating contracts. How do you plan to get Sylvio in shape?" he asked.

"Don't worry. I'm gon' make calls. You ain't the only one that got connections in the game," Kevin replied.

As Kevin and Sylvio walked out, the former middleweight champion said, "Door's still open, Jim, if you wanna be a part of it."

With that, both men left, and Kevin started making calls to all the sports networks to schedule a news press conference.

On Saturday, in the Nassau Coliseum press room lobby, about

seventy reporters from over thirty sports networks and newspapers were gathered with cell phones, cameras, and tape recorders in their hands. All of them were waiting to hear from former boxer Sylvio Dominique. The conference table was already in place, and people were becoming restless.

Finally, Sylvio walked out of the side door with his PR official, Hank Layman, followed by Kevin Shaw, Gary Williams, and his cutman, Harry Delmond. Sylvio was nervous when he saw the reporters. He never was a public speaker. He tightened his tie, which was tucked inside his Armani suit. As soon as everyone sat down, Sylvio reached out and pulled one of the four microphones close to him.

With cameras flashing from all directions, Sylvio started. "Thank you all for coming today. It's funny, really, that the last time I addressed the media like this was six years ago when I made my announcement to retire from boxing. Well, this morning, I have another announcement to make. I'm officially coming out of retirement, and I'm stepping back into the ring."

There was a wave of commotion as reporters from all sides of the room attempted to ask Sylvio questions about his decision. "Mr. Dominique, can you tell us what led to this decision?" a woman from Channel 4 asked.

"I feel that I still have a lot to contribute to the game today, and it's not just about winning a title but giving back to the game which has given so much to me during my early rise to the top ranks," Sylvio said.

"Mr. Dominique, there were rumors that you were pressured to return back into the ring because of financial difficulty and the eminent closing of the Shaw-Dominique Community Center. Is there any truth to that?" a man from Channel 41 asked.

"Uh, no those were just rumors, sir. The center is doing very well, and we are still serving the community and providing children and adults athletic and educational opportunities," Sylvio replied.

"Where is Jim Shaw?" a social media reporter asked.

"My brother is very busy running the center. He is well-informed of Sylvio's decision to return to professional boxing, and he fully supports this decision, and when he feels ready, the door is open for him to re-join our team," Kevin answered, although he and Sylvio knew that it was far from true.

"So, who will be training Sylvio Dominique?" another social media reporter asked.

"We have already interviewed some good candidates who will be Sylvio's trainer throughout the duration of his career. I will continue to manage and oversee his career, and we will make sure we have a good team around him so we can be successful," Kevin replied.

"Mr. Dominique, you have been away from the ring for six years. Do you think you can regain the timing that you once had early in your career?" Jillian Wells, a sports reporter asked Sylvio.

"I think I can. Um, it won't be a quick or an easy adjustment, but once we hire the trainer, we will begin conditioning work right away to get back in shape, and as soon as we are approved and certified by the Federal Boxing Commission, we will start signing to fight other opponents," Sylvio replied.

"Are you going to challenge Jun Zhang for the title? He hasn't been beaten in this division yet, and some say he won't be defeated. After his decisive victory over Barry Taylor, a fight in which you were at Taylor's corner, do you think you will stand a chance at competing against such a boxer?" *Daily News* columnist John

Fitzgerald asked.

"Our goal is to fight against some quality top-ranked opponents, and if the time comes to fight for the middleweight title, we will be ready," Sylvio replied confidently.

Other reporters wanted to ask questions, but Hank ended the press conference.

As Sylvio, Kevin, and Gary headed to the exit, Sylvio heard someone shout out his name. "Yo', Wolf!"

Turning around, he saw that it was Tom Blaylock, one of Barry's trainers and handlers. "Hey, Tom, what's up, man?" Sylvio greeted as he dapped the trainer of his former rival.

"Quite a media storm you opened up today," Tom said, glancing around as the reporters scrambled to ask Hank more questions, but the security was escorting all media personnel out the venue.

"I know, but it comes wit' the territory," Sylvio replied.

"No doubt," Tom replied. Then silently guiding Sylvio away from his group, he whispered in low tones, "I know what Barry told you on IG. Don't come back to the game because you feel you have to, but come back because that's what you want to do."

"It's exactly what I want to do. I kept trying to convince myself that I had nothing left to prove to nobody, but I got a helluva lot to prove to myself," Sylvio replied.

"Proving something to ourselves can be the hardest thing we ever have to do. A lot of us don't practice self-reflection, or if we do, we become numb and blind to it. But I gotta give you props on being real to yourself," Tom said.

Looking at his watch, he said, "I gotta bounce, man. By the way, I heard you were lookin' for a trainer. I know ya' still interviewing folks, but since Jim ain't involved, and Barry's still out the game, maybe I could throw my hat in, if you're interested."

Sylvio thought about it for a moment. The arrangement just seemed more than coincidental. *Could Barry have sent me his trainer to help me regain my title?*

"I know what you thinkin' man, and no, Barry ain't send me here to beg for your services. But I saw how you tried to help him train for the Zhang fight, and it's not about two opponents helping each other. It was two boys from Queens helping each other out," Tom said.

"So, what's your motive? Why do you wanna help me?" Sylvio asked, still unsure about whether to trust Tom or not.

"Two years ago, after I first became Barry's trainer, I promised to help him become the middleweight champion of the world. I achieved that goal eighteen months later, but I didn't help him hold on to the crown, and now he might never fight again. His injuries were worse than we thought," Tom confessed. "Maybe I got something to prove to myself too. Maybe I want to prove that I can get a fighter from the Mecca back on top. It'll be hard as hell, but I'm up to the challenge. I could get you back in shape and make you faster, stronger, sharper, and durable, but most importantly, I can make you a champion again. What you say?" he asked.

At this point, Sylvio was convinced. "Looks like I found me a trainer," he said, shaking Tom's hand.

In Atlanta, Valentina and her fellow castmates were eating dinner at Benihana's after a full day of filming. Although her relationship with Sylvio had hit the rocks, Valentina didn't want to complain because she was in the company of the people that she now considered her family. And while the spark she initially held with Sylvio began dying down, another spark was igniting between her and Robert.

After initially regretting their passionate evening, Valentina could not deny that she had feelings for the debonair actor, who had gone out of his way to treat her as a queen. He would shop with her at all the high-end spots in Atlanta and would let her buy whatever she wanted. Gabrielle and Anthony were on-again, off-again lovers whose romance was tumultuous, violent and unpredictable, but Valentina and Robert's relationship off set was vastly different from the characters they portrayed.

As the castmates ate, the television that was mounted on the wall of the restaurant was tuned onto the sports network channel. After displaying some basketball and hockey highlights, the sports reporters began to talk about the events surrounding the news conference held by Sylvio Dominique. Valentina was oblivious to the news, but she wasn't the first one who noticed the former champion's image on screen.

"Yo', Val, ain't that yo' boy?" Nancy asked as the castmates' attention was diverted toward the screen.

Boxing analyst Lee Skiers provided the report. "Earlier this morning, the sports and boxing world was stunned as former champion Sylvio Dominique announced his decision to come out of retirement and return to the ring. While some reporters were baffled by Dominique's decision, most fans are excited that the Wolf will be coming back to the ring. Dominique, who stunned the world six years earlier by knocking out former undefeated middleweight champion Felipe Maximo against all odds, will be faced with even greater odds this time around, and there will, no doubt, be questions about conditioning, rust, and punching power, which were questioned during his career six years ago. Will he be approved by the boxing commission when he undergoes the physical exams and exercises required of him? Will he be the same Wolf that we all grew to love at the height of his career? It all remains to be seen."

Valentina's heart sank. She felt a mixture of anger, sadness, and betrayal. *How could he do that to me? He promised he would never go back into the ring again, and now he made an announcement to return to boxing without telling me first? Who does he think he is?*

Excusing herself to use the restroom, Valentina left the table. After a woman walked out of the restroom, Valentina checked to make sure she was the only one in there. Closing herself in one of the stalls, she took her phone out and frantically called Sylvio.

"What up?" he replied indifferently. Normally during their arguments, Sylvio always kept the mood upbeat whenever he answered his phone. But this time, his response was unwelcoming, cold, and heartless.

"What the fuck, Sylvio?" Valentina. Her tone expressed just how upset she was.

"Val, what's your problem now?" Sylvio asked.

"Oh, you asking me what my problem is? I should be asking you that same question. I thought we made a promise that you wouldn't fight again, and now I'm watchin' you on TV talkin' bout you comin' out of retirement. Why you ain't run that by me, first?"

Out of nowhere, she heard a noise synonymous to the sucking of teeth, which was Sylvio's favorite pastime whenever he was being sarcastic or was told something he didn't want to hear.

"Oh, that's right, because I gotta run all my life decisions through you first, right?" he asked, sarcastically.

Valentina did her best to remain calm although she wished she could slap some sense into Sylvio. "Excuse me? I thought we were in a relationship, and whatever life decisions we make, we always gotta keep each other updated. Or did things change? Did Jim talk you into this?"

"Ain't nobody talked me into nothin' aight? This ain't got nothin' to do with Jim or you. I made this decision on my own. I'm takin' my career back, and I ain't letting nobody stand in my way."

"You missin' the whole point of why I'm pissed off," Valentina replied. "It's not just about coming back to a sport that nearly ended yo' damn life. It's the fact that you did so without lettin' me in on it. I thought we were a team. Ain't that not what you said?" She heard Sylvio sigh deeply on the other end, and she knew she was starting to aggravate him.

"You wanna know why I ain't tell you? There's why, right there. You think that everyone and everything revolves around you all the time. If I told you, you'd flip the hell out, like you're doing now," he countered.

"Sylvio, I can't keep playin' this game wit' you. It's like constant fuckin' guessing games wit' you. You don't return my calls for days until you feel like it. Then, you go behind my back and make a decision like this?" she asked.

"Why you actin' like you care all of a sudden? You got what you wanted. You're in your own little Hollywood now. You makin' good bread, so why you buggin' out? You ain't got time for anybody else, but you damn sure got time for yourself," Sylvio said.

Fighting the urge to cry, Valentina couldn't believe what she was hearing. The man who once took time to listen to her, talk endlessly to her, and spend time with her was starting to fade away, and a madman was taking his place.

Suddenly, Valentina realized the cause of Sylvio's irrational and seemingly misplaced anger. "Sylvio, look, I'm sorry about your dad. Rebecca called and told me about his passing, and I wanted to come to the funeral. I really did. But I was so busy, and I just couldn't make—"

She was interrupted, once again, by Sylvio. "Whatever. I guess you just can't be bothered by small shit such as real life. Not when you blowin' up, and have yo' pretty boy there wit' you."

After Sylvio said that, Valentina lost her temper. "Look, I don't wanna hear that crap, okay? I never complained when you had all them bitches on you after every fight you had," she argued back.

"Just keep it a hundred wit' me. Are you sleepin' wit' Robert? Yes or no?" Sylvio asked, intently.

Fighting back tears, Valentina decided that she couldn't keep the affair secret any longer. "Yes. Robert and I have been intimate off screen, but it wasn't supposed to go down that way," she explained, but the damage was done.

Strangely, Sylvio chuckled. "Man, Yolanda was right about you," he replied without realizing that he put himself on the hot seat as well.

"Wait, what does Yolanda got to do with all this?" Valentina asked.

Sylvio realized he said too much. "Nothing. Just forget about it, okay?" he asked.

But after six years of dating, Valentina picked up Sylvio's tendencies and knew by his tone that he had secrets of his own. "Okay, so since we on this truth tellin' tip, did you sleep wit' Yolanda?" she asked, hoping that Sylvio would vehemently deny it, but she had her doubts. Unfortunately, they were confirmed.

"Yeah, I slept with Yolanda," he confessed.

Although Valentina suspected Sylvio's playboy days would resurface, she was not ready for his answer. She angrily brushed a tear away. "So, where does that leave us?"

"I don't even know right now. I got so much on my plate. I gotta wake up in the morning to start training cuz I have to lose at least twenty pounds before my next fight, and I can't afford to be distracted."

How dare him? So now I'm a distraction to him? At that moment, Valentina knew there was no way their relationship could be salvaged. "You know what, Sylvio? Let me make it easy for you. You'll have one less distraction to worry about after tonight. It's very clear that we're going two different directions right now, and I think it's best if we just call it quits. Besides, it sounds like Yolanda knows best anyway, right?" she asked before hanging up the phone.

Valentina's appetite was gone, but she summoned the strength to return to dinner with her castmates. When she got home later that evening, Passion, who was watching television, watched as she walked through the door. They both stared at each other for a second. Unable to hold back her emotions, Valentina ran to Passion and sobbed on her shoulders. "It's over, Passion," she cried as Passion patted her head and embraced her.

Chapter 14

"Let's go, Wolf! C,mon, dig in! Final lap...let's go!" Tom bellowed as Sylvio jogged into the Kew Gardens Gym. Panting heavily, Sylvio staggered up the stairs, sweating streams of perspiration.

The previous night's events were pushed out of the former champ's mind, and he knew that there was work to be done. Sylvio's conditioning had begun, and Tom was intent on making sure that his stamina and endurance improved over the next month. Sylvio weighed over 220 pounds, so if he had any chance of successfully returning to the ring as a middleweight fighter, he was required to lose twenty-five pounds in a short amount of time.

On Sylvio's third day of training, Tom made sure that his fighter didn't miss a beat or waste any time of conditioning. Sylvio woke up each morning at six A.M. to run three miles around Union Turnpike. Afterwards, he was to make his way to Kew Gardens Gym. Tom made a point of already arriving at the gym each day, and he'd wait for Sylvio to make it to the door.

Opening his water bottle, Sylvio took a swig of water and wiped the sweat off his face as he headed into the Kew Gardens Gym. Feeling as if his lungs were burned up, he walked into the gym. The other boxers silently watched. It was the first time in years that Sylvio ventured outside of his normal confines of the community center and Steel Glove Gym.

The Kew Gardens Gym was not as crowded as other gyms were, so Sylvio was thankful that Tom allowed him to train in a completely new environment. "Come on, Wolf, take a deep breath. Relax man," Tom said as Sylvio drank more water. "Man, when was the last time you ran outside, bro?" he asked.

"Yo', don't even play me like that, Tom. Yeah, it's been a few years since I got my wind back and my lungs blazin'," Sylvio replied, panting between gulps.

"It's okay. It'll take time and commitment to get back into shape. I mean, look at Barry. I trained that dude since he was sixteen years old, and he started off being overweight, but he ran religiously, and all his hard work paid off, man."

"Yeah, but Barry wasn't coming off a six-year hiatus," Sylvio pointed out.

"Nobody said it was gonna be easy, but believe me, when it's all said and done, the title match will be within our grasp. Come on inside. I got someone waiting for you at the office. Then we're gonna jump some rope and hit the heavy bag," Tom said as he entered into gym's office.

When Sylvio walked in, there was a man sitting in his chair. He was recognizable, even when his signature ponytail was now cut off. "Yo', Shareef, what's up, man? Long time, no see," Sylvio said as he shook Shareef's hand.

Shareef James was the boxing promoter for Showtime, and during his earlier years, he was known for setting up and promoting Sylvio's fights. "You know how it is, man. I had to see it with my own two eyes...Sylvio Dominique, back in the ring again," Shareef said. "So, where's Jim? Ain't he involved in the Wolf's return to prime-time?" he asked.

"Nah, I don't think Jim's gon' be in my corner this time around," Sylvio replied. "But I got Tom here, and since the beginning of the week, he's been running my ass ragged."

"We gotta get him ready for the battery of physical tests that he'll be doing for the commission," Tom explained to Shareef.

"But Kevin's still managing me though," Sylvio added.

"Okay, cool, as long as that's the case. It can be a bitch trying to negotiate with a whole new management group cuz they always lookin' out for their cut more so than mine. At least I know Kevin's management group," Shareef said. He then reached into his briefcase and pulled out an iPad. "Gentlemen, what I'm about to show you is completely unsanctioned. But I feel like I would be doing a disservice to Wolf if I don't show him the opponents that he'll be facing on his way to the title."

Shareef opened an app that had the lineup of different boxers in the middleweight class. Each boxer was lined up by rank. Sylvio saw Barry's name and picture on the app and was stunned to see that Barry was still ranked in the top 20 percentile even after his devastating loss.

"Sylvio, forget about what you think you know about the middleweight class. The fighters that you faced six years ago can't hold a candle to this new crop. The list of fighters that I'll be showing you are younger, fierce, and are frontrunners to challenge for the belt." Shareef started scrolling through the list of contenders. "Okay, so I'm going to show you some opponents that you most likely will be facing in the coming months. He started out by selecting the headshot photo of a Hispanic boxer with toned shoulders and tattoos covering his abs."

"This guy's name is Francisco Perez. His record is twenty wins, seven defeats, and no draws. He's currently ranked fourteenth in this division. His strength lies with his right and left hooks, especially his left. Fight report says he's a southpaw, but he's ambidextrous, which makes him even more dangerous because he could knock you out with any hand. He's not a boxer that utilizes jabs effectively, so that's a weakness you can exploit."

Shareef proceeded to show highlight clips of Perez knocking down boxer after boxer before going back to his list. "Next, we have Trey 'Tiny' Morris. Don't let the name fool ya because Morris is anything but tiny."

Sylvio saw that Morris stood at six-foot-two, and he was also all muscle, but unlike Perez, he barely had any tattoos.

"Morris is currently ranked ninth in the division, and his record is twenty-eight victories and three, I repeat, three losses. Only a recent loss placed him down to ninth."

"Damn, he got a record like that, and he only ranked ninth? So, I wonder how many combined wins and losses the top five contenders have," Sylvio remarked as Shareef went through Morris' highlights.

"Strengths include a repetitive right jab that throws his opponents off balance. Morris has a long wingspan, so it's going to be difficult to get to the body. He also has incredible speed for a boxer his size, and he has incredible stamina. I believe when Barry fought him, he went the distance with Morris, right?" Shareef asked Tom.

"Yeah, we went the full twelve rounds wit' that joker," Tom confirmed. "He's also in the running to challenge for the middleweight belt as well."

Shareef selected another top-ranked fighter. The next one was another Hispanic man with low, sloping shoulders. "This is Michael Cortez. His record's twenty-six victories and two losses, and he's ranked fourth in the division. He's somewhat of a sneaky, deceptive boxer. What he lacks in strength and speed, he makes up for it with intelligence. He's a cunning, tricky boxer you gotta look out for," he said.

Shareef then closed the highlight reel and selected the first boxer on the list, the current pound for pound champion of the world. "And I believe you already know Jun Zhang," Shareef said, clicking the link under Jun's profile.

"His record's twenty-two wins and no defeats. The man has been perfect ever since he returned from China and the MMA fight game. I hate to say this, but I can't find no weakness in that man in the ring."

"What? C'mon, man, he gotta have some type of angle or an Achilles heel. No man's perfect. I don't care who you are," Sylvio said.

"Well, if you want me to nitpick the guy, I'll say this. He fights with his gloves down most of the time, so he exposes his head and chest. But the other fighters have tried exploiting it, and they have failed each time. When he hits, fighters describe it as being hit by a telephone pole. With phenomenal speed and power in either hand, Jun's jabs are just as effective, if not more effective than his hooks. Barry found out the hard way the other night," Shareef said.

"Who's this fighter here?" Sylvio asked, pointing to the middle of the chart at a fighter with a thick black beard in.

"That guy is Moses Miller. He's currently in the top twenty in terms of rank. His record's nineteen wins and eight losses. He also happens to be signed by Showtime as well, so I'm representing him too. Not much experience, but still a formidable challenger and one to be reckoned with. Sylvio, most of these fighters came after you won your title. By speaking with other promoters and trainers, they see you as easy pickins'."

Sylvio looked on as Shareef displayed boxer after boxer. By the time he was finished, a small shred of doubt started to creep up within Sylvio. *Should I have come back to boxing? These guys are nearly invincible. Sylvio, what have you gotten yourself into?*

"Alright, well, thanks for the info, Shareef. Looks like we got our work cut out for us. We'll keep in touch," Tom said as he walked Shareef out the office door.

As he was leaving the gym, Sylvio knew that his return campaign was going to be the highlight of every sports report, and the publicity was sure to catch everyone's eye, including his potential opponents.

That evening after the grueling workout session, Sylvio returned home and bathed in a Whirlpool tub filled with ice. Every muscle in his body was extremely sore. He considered it to be a miracle that he even made it home after running through the city and working on boxing combinations at the gym. Although the frigid temperatures caused every one of Sylvio's skin hairs to stand on end, the ice bath also soothed his sore muscles and helped his recovery time. He planned to take a hot shower after his ice bath. *This comeback better be worth the pain I'm going through.*

Oftentimes, Sylvio reflected quitting and going back to work in SDCC, but he was at the point of no return. He made his announcement, and everyone expected the Wolf. If he backed out, his reputation would take another hit. As he stood up out of the tub, he heard a faint knock on his front door.

"Hey, I'm coming. Who is it?" he asked.

"Yolanda," the voice replied from the other side of the door.

Wrapping his towel around his waist, Sylvio made his way downstairs and cracked open the door. "What's up? I see you ain't have much trouble finding the place," he said, smiling serenely.

"Nah, this wasn't hard to find at all. I'm kinda surprised you stay out here though. I woulda thought someone as big as you would be someplace like, I don't know, Park Avenue or something. Um, is this a bad time?" she asked, eyeing Sylvio's body, glistening wet from the ice tub and covered only with a white towel around his waist.

"Nah, not at all. Please come in. I was just icin' down upstairs. You know a brotha sore as hell after working his tail off. Gotta get my fat ass back in shape before I hit dat ring," he boasted, play-punching Yolanda.

"Stop it! You play too much," she laughed as he led her over to his couch. They had become inseparable since his split with Valentina.

"Yo', I'm 'bout to go put my clothes on real quick, and then I'll be right back with you. I was gonna take a shower, but since you here…"

Yolanda raised an eyebrow as she slowly walked over to Sylvio and kissed him. "I ain't gon' stop you from takin' your shower." Lowering her voice to a whisper, she asked, "Do you want any company?"

Sylvio smiled as he held Yolanda's waist and slowly guided her into the bathroom. Twenty minutes later, Yolanda shed all her clothes and was under the jets of water streaming from the showerhead while Sylvio was soaping her body. She closed her eyes as he made his way down from her neck and back where his hand cascaded over her petite, shapely figure. She then took her turn in soaping him down. For Sylvio, nothing healed tense muscles and sore bones like the sensitive touch of a woman. Yolanda gently applied more soap and lathered Sylvio from his head to his legs.

Unable to fight his urges any longer, Sylvio resumed kissing her while gently leaning her against the shower wall. Lifting her leg up, he softly entered Yolanda's precious flower, and she moaned out in pleasure. After the initial copulation, he began to move and thrust his waist rhythmically, causing streams of fluid to exit her crevices as her body reacted to his.

After about ten minutes, Sylvio said, "Let's get out of this tub. I ain't tryna waste water out hea'."

Yolanda laughed. "Oh my God, you're lame. But you're so damn irresistible too."

Sylvio dried Yolanda before wrapping the towel around himself, and they went to his bedroom, where they continued to make love. Once they were both satisfied, Yolanda's body lay on top of Sylvio's as they balked in their ethereal state.

Sylvio couldn't explain it, but there were more than a few instances when Yolanda was on top of him that he could still smell Valentina's hair. And her olive skin was still glistening in the moonlight while she was talked dirty to him in Spanish.

Why the hell am I still seeing Valentina when I'm in the bed with Yolanda? What is going on? While those thoughts were running through Sylvio's psyche, he never once led Yolanda to believe his mind was elsewhere. But Yolanda proved to be more perceptive than Sylvio anticipated.

"Do you still think about her?" Yolanda asked, completely catching Sylvio off guard.

"Think about who? Val? Nah, I ain't thinkin' about her whatsoever," he lied, hoping Yolanda believed him.

Although it was not the first time that he was intimate with Yolanda, he couldn't help but to feel awkward when sleeping with a woman that he worked directly with.

With her head still rested on his chest, she looked up into his eyes. "You ain't gotta lie to me, Sylvio. I know ya' been together for a minute, and it ain't easy letting go of someone you once been with. It's okay," she said.

"What makes you think I'm lying?" he asked, smiling.

"I heard your heart rate speed up after I asked you," she replied, before laughing upon seeing Sylvio's premature nervous glance. "I'm just playin', boo. I just wanted to see that look on yo' face," she said mischievously.

Sylvio then started to tickle her, and she tried to draw back, but he pulled her back towards him, playfully. "Oh, you got jokes now?"

After a few minutes of horsing around, Yolanda rested her body on top of Sylvio's again and traced her finger along his chest then down to the surgical scar on his stomach—a jagged line almost four inches long. "Is this where it happened?" she asked.

"Yeah. That's where the Serps almost took me out the night after I won the belt. I went from being the champ one night to being almost six feet under the next night. Just like that. Every time I look at this, I always think about how blessed and fortunate I am that I made it out," he replied.

"I heard about what happened to your friend, Omar. I'm so sorry that he didn't make it."

Sylvio closed his eyes for a moment, determined not to let Yolanda see him cry or get emotional over his late friend's departure. "Yeah, I just wish he wasn't out there wit' me that night. It took a long time and a lot of counseling to convince myself that it wasn't my fault."

"You can't keep blaming yourself for what happened.

Whenever we lose someone, we gotta do right by them by living the best way that we can to keep their memory alive."

Sylvio blinked and angrily brushed away a tear.

"So tell me, what was Omar like?" Yolanda asked.

"Oh man, that dude was a clown. All jokes, all the time, and sometimes, he'd get on yo' last nerve, and you'd wanna knock the shit out of him, but he was good people. He was loyal at a time where I wasn't sure who was in my corner or not. There was no questioning loyalty when it came to Omar. He was a G, straight up. Not to mention, he could ball his ass off. He was one of the best streetball players in Queens, bar none."

"Damn, I wish I could've met him."

"Well, I still believe that Omar's still around, and even if he ain't here in physical form, he's here in spirit, and I'mma need that when I get back in that ring."

"Are you nervous about going back in there?"

"At first, I was, but I don't think it's a big deal to me now. Everybody's been doubting me all my life. I shut them up before. Now I got a chance to do it again."

As Yolanda rested and drifted off to sleep in his arms, Sylvio thought about his next mission: getting back into shape and silencing the doubters in his return.

Over the next three weeks, Sylvio put all his strength and effort into his workouts. Training with a newfound energy and bravado, he ran his sprints with full force and boxed with intent and purpose. He began a twenty-day juice fast, where he would avoid eating all solid foods, especially carbs, which, as of late were his biggest weakness. The diet regimen was initially strenuous, and Sylvio missed his favorite night snacks and meals. But it was all part of the discipline and focus required of him.

As each day went by, the Wolf began to emerge as Tom began placing Sylvio in the ring with experienced sparring partners. Although the sparring partners bested Sylvio in his first few sessions, they discovered that he was becoming increasingly difficult to defeat with each passing day. Tom reserved all of Sylvio's training at the Kew Gardens Gym because, although Sylvio wanted positive press for SDCC, Tom suspected that many people who trained with his potential opponents may have worked out there in the gym. His goal was to conceal his fighter's progress so he could give Sylvio an advantage over his competition.

On one particular day, Sylvio received a visit from a surprise guest when Jim Shaw came by to watch his progress. Sylvio was elated upon seeing his former trainer. "What's up, ole timer?" he greeted jokingly.

"Oh, I got your ole timer, boy. You don't look half bad for a man workin' off six years of rust and four years of love handles," Jim laughed.

"Ah, you got jokes, man, and you better tell anyone you know to look out cuz the Wolf is in full beast mode this season," Sylvio bragged, flexing and showing off his pectoral muscles. "You know, it ain't too late if you still wanna jump in the pack and get involved."

Jim shook his head. "I don't think so, Wolf. My place is at SDCC, running operations and managing the lab and the court. Besides, someone gotta run the place during your comeback tour."

"Yeah, but it ain't like I'm gon' leave SDCC foreva' though. I'mma drop by and visit all my folks," Sylvio replied jovially, while finishing his repetitions on the heavy bag.

"Yo', Wolf, I also stopped by to apologize about what I said a few days back. Since you were nine, I've been at your corner, and you've never stopped working hard for me ever since then."

"It's all good, man. I just gotta prove you wrong, just like everybody else."

"No need, cat. You ain't gotta prove nothing to me. I know you gon' bring it. And when you do win that belt again, you betta' hold on to it this time cuz you never know, I might come back and train another boxer to go at you." Sylvio's face spoke of nothing but shock at those words.

Jim laughed. "I'm just playin' brotha. But I'm currently workin' wit some kids at SDCC. Remember the young brotha' Kwame that I was workin' wit'? You saw how he worked, right? Boy's got quick hands."

"Yeah, I mean, he's okay. He got a ways to go though. What, you thinkin' about training him to turn pro?" Sylvio asked.

"Well the kid's havin' a hard time at school, man. He got this big dude out there givin' him grief…"

"Lemme guess…you walked by his school, gave the whole, 'boxing can stimulate the mind' speech to talk him into the game. C'mon, Jim, at some point you gotta realize that they ain't all about that life. You can't force feed a kid to learn boxing."

"So, what you want me to do, Sylvio? You want me to just walk away and let him get pushed around?"

"That's not what I'm saying, man. You can't interfere every time you see someone getting bullied, dawg. Kwame's gotta fight his own battle sometimes."

"What you think I'm teaching him? I damn sure ain't gon' tell him to lie down and take it from that kid," Jim's voice rose as he became more manic. "Imagine if I didn't come by when Brandon was kickin' yo' ass in them alleyways when you were nine. Do you think you would've grown to become the Wolf?"

"No, I wouldn't have. But I worked hard as hell to get where I'm at today. You tapped a part of me that I ain't even know existed. But not everybody has that untapped potential. I understand that you wanna teach him how to handle himself. You wanna do for him what you never got to do for Dante. But you can't save everyone, Jim. You gotta get a hold of this."

Shaking his head, Jim began to walk away. But before he opened the door, he looked back at Sylvio. "If I had said those same words twenty years ago, you wouldn't have been middleweight champion of the world." He left without another word.

Sylvio shook his head in disbelief. He couldn't believe how arrogant Jim was.

Meanwhile, Kevin approached Sylvio. "What's up with Jim?" he asked.

"Yo', man, if I were you, I'd keep an eye on yo' brother and get him some serious help cuz he wildin' right now," Sylvio replied.

"Twenty-two years, and he still can't let it go. I don't know, man. But I got some news, Wolf. Looks like someone finally wants to get you in the ring." Kevin pulled out his tablet, and soon, Sylvio was staring at the first opponent that he would face in six years.

Trey "Tiny" Morris issued a public challenge to Sylvio and was waiting for his response. "Well, do you accept?" Kevin asked.

Sylvio's facial features hardened, and he wore a stoic expression, knowing full well the magnitude of the moment. "What do you think?"

Chapter 15

After weeks of promotion and fight tours, fight night finally arrived as fans from all over the East Coast filed into the Connecticut Convention Center in Hartford to watch what they viewed as a historic bout. Ninth ranked middleweight boxer Trey "Tiny" Morris paced back and forth in his locker room, working himself into a state of pure anger.

For years, Morris trained to hate whoever is across the ring from him. While it was a strategy that has worked for his success, he realized that this time he would be facing a different opponent, one that he highly respected. Just four years younger than the Wolf, Trey had patterned most of his fighting style after Sylvio, so he was quite disappointed and angered when Sylvio stepped away from boxing.

With an intimidating scowl, rippling abs, and broad shoulders, Trey worked diligently to become the ninth ranked, pound-for-pound contender for the title belt. Secretly, he felt that he let his chance to become champion slip away when he dropped a close decision to Barry Taylor, the middleweight champion at the time.

Now, another champion stood in Trey's way, and he knew that in order to earn the right to fight Jun Zhang for the belt, he was going to need another high-profile fight. It wasn't enough to fight another Top 10 contender anymore. Trey felt that the sportswriters and critics were underestimating him, and if he could defeat the man formerly known as the Wolf, he could earn back some respect.

Trey's trainer, Jordan Lewis, was an elderly man with a background of having trained over twenty fighters during his forty years in the sport. He was known for his defensive tactics that he normally equipped his boxers with whenever they faced opponents that loved to pressure them. Jordan persuaded Trey to watch Sylvio's old fight clips, but Trey confidently felt that he could defeat the fighter only returning to the sport after six years and Vegas oddsmakers felt the same way as Trey was favored 28 to 10 that he would easily dispatch Sylvio.

During the promotion tours for the fight, out of the two, Sylvio appeared to be the calmer in his demeanor and approach to the fight, while Trey spoke confidently about how he planned to "set traps for the Wolf" during the fight.

"I don't wanna get into a war of words with him, but I'm thankful for the opportunity to get back in the ring and fight at a high level again," Sylvio answered after a reporter asked him about Trey's comments during a table promotion.

Trey, who sat across from Sylvio, was beginning to get annoyed that Sylvio was being interviewed more than he was, and he was not silent about letting his feelings be known. "Yo', hold up. I thought I was the ninth ranked out here. Why you askin' him all the questions?" he asked, clearly agitated.

"Maybe cuz he was addressing me? Chill out, kid," Sylvio replied amongst the laughter from the pundits.

Trey did not approve his opponent's flippant remark. "Aight, I got a question for yo' ass then, Wolf. What's yo' favorite smelling salt?" he asked, implying the notion that Sylvio would be knocked out and would need the salts to revive him.

The reporters watched in silence as the two fighters went back and forth.

"I don't know, Trey. You tell me," Sylvio shrugged, smirking.

"You think this is funny? You got any idea what you got yourself into? You betta' say a quick prayer before I send you back cryin' to yo' mama," Trey bit back.

Upon hearing this, Sylvio became instantly enraged. But he quickly quelled his anger, although it didn't stop him from standing up across from Trey. "If you say one more thing about my mother again, we gon' have a problem."

"What you gon' do, ole washed up ass?" Trey challenged.

Sylvio balled his fists, envisioning smashing them on the side of Trey's face. "I got yo' washed up ass right hea' playboy. Come see me in the ring, and I'll show you what's up."

The reporters watched on, excited as the two fighters provided ammunition for their columns, blogs, and shows.

The time finally arrived when both fighters now had to back up their trash talk, and Trey was poised and relaxed. His opponent, however, was nowhere to be found yet. "Yo', where's Sylvio?" Tom yelled. He was almost frantic as he searched the hallway before peeking out of the curtain where both fighters would make their grand entrance into the ring.

"I don't know. The last time I saw him, he was still in the locker room getting his gloves fitted," Kevin replied.

While Sylvio's cornermen searched for their fighter, Harry, the faithful cutman and physician, knew exactly where Sylvio was. Heading toward the opposite end of the hallway, Harry entered the restroom and peeked under the bottom of each stall. Sure enough, he saw of his client's Nikes from under one of them.

Retching violently in the toilet bowl, every meal and shake supplement that Sylvio had swallowed before the fight made its way back out of his system. Harry knocked on the door of the stall.

"Get the fuck out!" Sylvio choked. He didn't want anybody to see him in a compromised position. He had not vomited since his first boxing match at age thirteen.

"Wolf, it's me Harry."

"I don't give a damn. Get out!"

Harry didn't depart from the restroom, but he stood outside the stall. "Look, Sylvio, I know how nervous you are. It's been years since you've been in the ring. I know you're anxious, and believe me, it's completely normal. But when you go out there tonight, I want you to channel that anger and rage toward Trey, and show him why they call you the Wolf," Harry said, before walking back out of the restroom.

Sylvio wiped his mouth and stepped out of the stall. Staring at himself in the mirror, he reflected on Harry's words. *Get yo' ass up, Sylvio. Time to remind the world who you are.*

The two fighters finally faced each other in the center of the ring, where both men glared at each other. Sylvio knew that Trey wanted to do nothing more than to pound him senseless, but he was prepared to stand his ground. After the referee recited the rules, the fighters went back to their corners. The roar in the building was so deafening that Sylvio barely heard Tom's instructions to him.

"Okay, Wolf, stay on the outside, and move him around. Search for an opening, and when you see your chance, crack him." Tom thrust Sylvio's mouthpiece in.

Not too long afterwards, the bell rang. The time had come.

"Make him fight yo' fight now. In and out now...let's go!" Tom yelled as Sylvio tuned out the noise of the crowd and headed toward his target.

Usually, within the first few seconds of the fight, Sylvio liked to feel out his opponents, which allowed him to study their tendencies. But Trey seemed intent on quickly dispatching his opponent as he rushed out of the corner, throwing jabs at Sylvio's head. Trey's strategy was to wear Sylvio out with continuous pressure, while piling up the points every second.

At first, his strategy worked to perfection as Sylvio seemed unable to get to Trey's body. Trey's long wingspan was throwing Sylvio off balance, and Sylvio found himself constantly on the defensive as Trey unleashed jab after jab, dropping them like missiles.

Damn, he's fast. C'mon, Sylvio, anticipate his next punch. Okay, he's throwing a right. Slip. He's gonna come in with a fast left after that. Anticipate, Wolf. Block him.

The section of the crowd that was pro-Sylvio cheered with every duck and slip move that evaded most of Trey's blows. Although Trey managed to tag Sylvio on his forehead a couple times, he was unable to inflict serious damage. Toward the end of the round, Sylvio caught Trey with a stinging left hook to the body.

Finally, I got one on him.

But Trey was unhurt. He absorbed the body blow and responded with a quick jab to the chest and left hook to the side. Sylvio winced in pain. He was hurt, and Trey knew it as he backed Sylvio into the corner, preparing to punish him even more.

Fortunately, the bell sounded, ending Round 1.

Sylvio walked over to the bench. He knew he had lost the first round, and Tom reminded his fighter right away. "Okay, shake that off. That was just them nerves, man. Gotta get your legs back under you. Right now, he's leading you in with his left and baiting you in so he can strike you with his right. Stay on him. I want you to turn on the pressure in this round."

The bell rang for Round 2, and Sylvio was back on his feet again, squaring off against Trey, who had the upper hand so far in the fight. Trey continued tagging Sylvio with jabs to the head, and when Sylvio attempted to duck the blows, Trey reacted with a jaw-jarring uppercut. Feeling himself swaying to the side, Sylvio quickly clinched Trey.

As he did, Trey whispered to him. "Come on, Wolf, how much more of this shit can you take? Give it up, my nigga. You done."

Sylvio didn't reply, but the ref came in between the two fighters and broke the clinch. Pissed, Sylvio launched his double jab, right hook combination, but Trey eagerly anticipated the blows and blocked them.

"C'mon, man, is that all you got? Where you at, Wolf?" Trey continued taunting Sylvio openly as both fighters came in full force, swinging wildly.

At the end of the second round, Sylvio's nose started bleeding from Trey's stinging jabs. Harry worked feverishly to staunch the bloodflow before Round 3.

"He's talkin' mad shit now. He's feelin' himself because he knows he winnin' right now. But let him know you ain't goin' nowhere," Tom said.

Sylvio only partially heard him as the pool of anger began bubbling within him. He wanted nothing more than to get back at

Trey for his trash talk.

Round 3 started, and Trey began to realize that Sylvio was more than was advertised. Here was a man who had been away from the ring for six years, and the public consensus stated that Sylvio was not the fighter he once was, but now he was beginning to show his heart. While Sylvio was being punched in the face repeatedly, he refused to down.

But in Round 4, when Trey threw an overhand right, it gave Sylvio the opening he needed. Quickly stepping forward, Sylvio threw a powerful uppercut. Instantly, he knew that it impacted his opponent as Trey's cheeks vibrated from the blow. The crowd roared as onlookers sensed the momentum swinging in the fight. Temporarily stunning Trey, Sylvio proceeded to throw body shots to his mid-section, causing Trey's mouthpiece to fly out of his mouth. Then Sylvio delivered another jab to Trey's face that threw his head back just as the bell rang. Sylvio watched as Trey made his way into the corner.

That's right. Drag yo' ass to your corner. I ain't goin' anywhere. I'm still here. You wanna beat me? You gon' have to knock me out.

Grinning widely, Tom welcomed Sylvio back to his corner, and even though Sylvio's face was red, marked, and swollen, he felt a surge of confidence. Out of the corner of his eyes, he saw the stunned sportswriters, pundits, and cable personnel. *Yeah, what ya got to say now? I'm back, baby.*

"It's about damn time the Wolf came back," Tom said.

"Yeah, I don't see him talkin' all that shit now," Sylvio replied.

"Cuz he thought he had it in the bag. Keep showin' him up, and knock the shit out of him."

The bell rang, and Sylvio and Trey continued trading blows. Now Sylvio appeared to be the fresher out of the two as Trey began to show signs of exhaustion. Although he'd trained to fight Sylvio, Trey never expected a drag-out brawl with the man. As the rounds wore on, Sylvio started to employ his own brand of punishment, jabbing Trey in his body, and as Trey doubled over in pain, Sylvio unleashed his patented left hook that dropped the ninth-ranked contender.

Sylvio ran to a neutral corner and watched Trey struggle to stand back up. Sylvio was sure the Vegas oddsmakers were beginning to sweat because they were losing their bets. The crowd rose, and some yelled in amazement while other cheered loudly.

The ref began the ten-count. Trey paused for a moment before getting back on his feet. After the referee checked on Trey, Sylvio closed in on his opponent, tagging him with jabs and hooks. Trey, who was already stunned by the knockdown, found himself in deep peril. Sylvio was backing him into a corner and was unleashing powerful body shots Trey couldn't quite avoid.

"Get out of there, Trey!" Jordan yelled, but his instructions went unheeded by his fighter, who was beginning to sway on his feet, clearly losing balance as the fight was slowly slipping away from him.

"Stay on him, Wolf!" Tom yelled.

Sylvio continued to follow the fight plan to a T. Before long, under a flurry of blows from Sylvio, Trey fell to the canvas again.

Don't get too full of yourself. It ain't over yet.

Fatigue, which had been hindering Sylvio at the onset of the fight, was now beginning to affect Trey. Sylvio knew from the first knockdown that Trey had lost his confidence. He could hear Jordan yelling at him from across his corner.

"C'mon, man, don't go out like this! How you gon' let a man comin' out of retirement beat you the last couple rounds? You're ahead on points. All you gotta do is outlast him and keep him off you!"

Easier said than done.

Although Trey managed to get back up, it was clear from the glazed look in his eyes that he was still out, and the referee knew that the fight was over. When Sylvio saw that he won the fight, he raised his hands up in victory.

What immediately followed was an event that he couldn't have predicted. The fans rose to their feet and began chanting, "WOLF! WOLF! WOLF!" Other fans howled just like they used to do during Sylvio's early days.

Tom ran up to Sylvio and hugged him. "That's the way to do it, Wolf! You back, baby boy!"

Sylvio stared around the arena, barely able to take it all in. Only a few weeks removed from being the most criticized figure in boxing history, he had managed to work himself back into shape, pass the physical tests administered by the New York Boxing Commission, and against all odds, defeat a top-ranked boxer. All he could do was take it all in.

As he was basking in the glory of his victory, a sports reporter walked up to him. "Sylvio, what an incredible TKO over ninth-ranked Trey Morris tonight. He was basically beating you the whole fight and was in the lead on points. What led you to this extraordinary upset?"

"Just as you said, Trey had me beat the whole fight, but in the later rounds, the fight slowed down for me, and it became a chess game very quickly. It took longer than expected for me to find a hole in his defense because he's such a great fighter, but I finally found my rhythm in the later rounds."

"Sylvio, you've made history by coming back after a six-year hiatus, and you pulled off what few other boxers did, and that is to win a fight right out of retirement. Who motivated you the most?"

Sylvio looked at the reporter and then glanced around at the crowd of fans, who were still chanting and serenading his name. "My father, Jacques Dominique, God rest his soul, motivated me tonight. My trainer Tom motivated me tonight, and even though he ain't in the ring with me right now, my old trainer Jim Shaw motivated me."

The reporter continued with his questions. "Any word on who you plan on fighting next?" he asked.

"C'mon, man, I just came off winning a fight. I ain't even think about what I'm gon' eat for dinner tonight, much less who I'm gon' fight next. I wanna enjoy this win now. Then when the dust settles tomorrow, it's back to work for me because I didn't come back just to win one fight. I came back to reclaim the belt."

"Alright, Sylvio, congratulations on your victory. We hope to see you in the championship circle again soon."

After Sylvio thanked the reporter, he went back to the locker room with his trainers. The moment the door was closed, the room exploded with cheers. "The Wolf is back! Wait till all the sports shows air tomorrow. You box office, bro!" Gary exclaimed.

"Appreciate it, dawg," Sylvio said.

Tom walked up to Sylvio and patted his shoulder.

"Good fight, man. If there was anybody else that doubted if you even belonged back in the fight game, all those doubts were put to rest tonight. You just beat a Top 10 contender out of retirement. Who does that?"

"The Wolf does it. I'm out here breakin' records, man," Sylvio replied, dapping Gary.

"Damn, man, your face looks worse for wear," Tom said,

observing Sylvio's face, which had a few cuts and bruises.

"They're battle scars, Tom. A few days of rest and treatment will clear all that up," Sylvio said. He pulled his phone out of his duffel bag. He had already received over a thousand notifications.

Many of them were Instagram and Facebook posts congratulating him on his stunning victory. Most of the posts were overwhelmingly encouraging, but among those posts were detractors that filled his page with skepticism:

"Man, you got lucky as fuck tonight. You beat a wack ass boxer. Call me when you actually beat someone like Perez or Jun, and then we can chop it up."

"Can't believe Trey lost to dude that quit cuz his bf died. Tiny better check himself and challenge that ole fool to a rematch."

There weren't too many of them, but they were enough to motivate Wolf to set up his next fight. *If they don't believe the hype, then time to silence 'em some more.*

While still checking his notifications, Sylvio received a call. "Welcome back, Wolf," a low voice greeted.

Sylvio laughed. It wasn't very difficult to recognize his old trainer's voice. "Appreciate it, old man," he replied.

"Yo', Wolf, don't think I'm tryin' to get all sap wit' you cuz that normally ain't how I roll, but I wanna apologize for not believing in you. We came up together, and I should've had your back from jump. My bad, brotha."

"Don't even sweat that, man. I shouldn't have been all up in yo' case man. What you did for me and other kids, no one can take that away from you, man."

There was an awkward moment of silence between the two.

"Anyway, did you see the show I put on tonight? Morris thought he had me early, but I had something fo' his ass," Sylvio boasted.

"Yeah, yeah, don't get too full of yourself. I thought he was gonna wipe the ring wit' your ass during the first four rounds. I was literally screaming at my TV set to back yo' chin out of there, but you kept poking it out like an idiot. That's a quick way to get laid out, man."

"But who won at the end of the day though?" Sylvio asked.

"I mean, I ain't debating the fact that you won, but I'm surprised Tom ain't seen that Morris was drawing you in with his left all night and baiting you. Had it been me, you wouldn't have taken such a beating to your face," Jim said.

"So, does that mean you wanna help train me again?" Sylvio asked.

Jim sighed. "Okay, just lemme sleep on it a few nights. I'll think about it, but I make no promises."

"Well then, I make no promises that I'll share the spoils after I win that belt," Sylvio said.

"Whatever. Enjoy this now, but don't enjoy it too much. You can guarantee that this is gon' blow up on every sports network on cable, which makes you a target. Everybody's gon' want a piece of you, so you and Tom gotta go even harder now," Jim said.

"Yeah, you right. Gotta keep my guard up each night," Sylvio agreed.

Hanging up the phone with Jim, Sylvio walked out among a throng of reporters and media members where he answered questions pertaining to the fight. But he couldn't focus on the questions that were being asked of him because, in the back of his mind, he couldn't help but to wonder if Valentina watched the fight.

No, she wouldn't wanna watch me. She hated boxing to begin with, so why would she even bother to watch me fight anymore? Besides, she's out there doing her Hollywood thing with her new boy toy anyway.

More than 40,000 miles away in Los Angeles, reigning middleweight champion Jun Zhang walked toward the other end of his room in his huge penthouse. The room was empty, except it had a heavy bag, a jump rope, and gymnastic bars, which he used to practice balance. Walking between two long installed bars, Jun got down in pushup position before proceeding to complete 100 pushups. Although he was champion, the work never ended for him. He was taught not to be satisfied to be champion because the toughest part of being champion was staying at the top.

After completing the pushups, Jun balanced his weight on his hands, standing in a perfect handstand, and in a show of athleticism, dexterity, and strength, he performed hand-standing pushups. While he worked out, he heard a knock on his door. Sighing deeply, he got back on his feet and answered. His longtime friend, Kenny Wong, greeted him.

Jun stepped back to let Kenny in and shut the door behind him. "What's up, Kenny? You know I train around this time, so I hope you didn't stop by for nothin'," Jun said.

"I know, but I gotta show you something," Kenny replied. He took out his phone and replayed the Dominique-Morris bout. "Morris was whuppin' this guy earlier, but Dominique took over and knocked him out in the seventh round."

Jun watched Sylvio intently. "So, the Wolf's back. It's about damn time," he said, smiling at the highlight footage.

"Jun, you ain't still thinkin' about fightin' this guy, are you?"

Kenny asked.

"Why not? What more could the fans ask for than the defending middleweight champion versus a former middleweight champion?" Jun asked.

"I'm sure they wanna see a good fight. They don't wanna watch another Barry Taylor. Look, we still got Perez and other higher-ranked fighters out there. We don't ne—" Kenny began.

"I don't want none of them. I want to face Sylvio Dominique. I want to face the Wolf," Jun said with a glowering look in his eyes.

"Why do you want to fight a washed-up boxer, for?" Kenny asked.
"Because we both want to be kings, and there can only be one king," Jun said, walking into his room to call his manager.

Chapter 16

The night following Sylvio's victory over Morris, thousands of people tuned in to watch the 2018 Stream Awards held at the Staples Center in Los Angeles. Among other streaming platforms, YouStream was one of the most popular. Sitting in the audience was Valentina, Robert, and the rest of the cast of the hit stream series, "You Thought You Had Me."

After wrapping up the final episodes of the season, Anderson Jacobs congratulated the entire cast on their stellar performances, and throughout the celebration, he announced that the show was nominated for the Best New Series. The entire cast was invited to the Stream Awards, where they were surrounded by celebrities, social media influencers, and movie stars.

For Valentina, it was the culmination of everything that she had worked hard to achieve for many years. Forty-five minutes into the show, the Best New Series segment finally arrived. Valentina closed her eyes, silently praying and hoping that their show would win the award. Not only would winning the reward bring satisfaction, but in many ways, it would also be consolation for Valentina since she had recently split from Sylvio after going steady for six years.

She still never fully understood how the relationship fell apart, but Sylvio didn't sound remorseful or sad during that final conversation. He was indifferent, and Valentina knew that it was time to go their separate ways.

Besides, he got his new boo, Yolanda, with him anyway. He ain't gon' miss a beat. I give it two months before he's messing around wit' some other thot.

Such thoughts constantly ran through Valentina's head, but with Passion and Robert's help, she had been able to put the situation behind her and move forward with her career. Currently, she was biting her newly manicured nails as she sat in the audience. *It's a pipe dream. There's no way my luck will change in my favor.*

But she would be in for a surprise as the hosts of the Stream Awards announced that the show "You Thought You Had Me" won the Best New Series Award. Valentina's mouth dropped in shock, and she placed her hands over her face. She knew the camera was on her, but she didn't care as the tears flowed down her cheeks.

Her other cast members celebrated their victory and pulled Valentina off her seat so she could accompany them on stage to accept the award. Valentina was speechless as the hosts handed her the Stream award. When they turned the microphone to her for her to speak, she was too speechless to reply, so Robert took to the microphone.

"First of all, I wanna thank God for this evening. I wanna thank the producers and director, Anderson Jacobs, and last, but not least, I wanna thank my co-stars. Everybody up here put the work in, and each of them deserves it. Thank you all for tuning in, and have a great night!"

The crowd applauded, and the cast walked off the stage with their award.

"Oh my God, I can't believe I froze up like that! I'm so embarrassed," Valentina groaned as Robert walked her to her hotel suite at the L.A. Marriott later on that evening.

After the Stream Awards, the cast had attended an after-party at The Mansion Club in L.A., where Valentina took selfie after selfie with different celebrities and fans. After that, the tired group headed to their suites.

"But I had yo' back though," Robert said as they went down the corridor. Robert pressed a button to wait for the elevator.

"I know...thank you, baby," Valentina gushed, kissing Robert.

Ever since she officially began dating Robert, she had begun feeling the support of a man who wanted her to succeed in the industry. He wasn't the over-protective, suffocating boyfriend that Sylvio tended to be, and unlike her ex-boyfriend, Robert encouraged Valentina to expand her horizons in the industry and helped her with line memorization and taking cues from director, along with giving her many other acting tips.

In addition to his encouragement, Robert was a very passionate lover. Although their relationship started out as a fling, it slowly developed into a romance, the type of romance that Valentina had been longing for, for years. The sex was mind-blowing, and Robert left her satisfied each time they were intimate. Valentina couldn't say the same for Sylvio, who had put in a few duds during their last years in the relationship.

"You know, the night doesn't have to end," Robert said slyly, kissing Valentina again, suggesting that she should follow him to his room where they could have their own after party.

"You are too much, Robert, but nah, I'm beat right now. I can't hang like I used to," Valentina replied.

"It's all good. We don't gotta rush. We could take it easy. We got all but four months before we head back on set."

Valentina's eyes widened. "Head back? Wait, you mean? We got picked up for another season?"

"Yeah. Anderson didn't wanna spill the tea or nothin', but he kinda let it slip that he negotiated another season with YouStream."

"Wow, that's what's up! Finally, something to stick to! No more bouncing from commercial ad to commercial ad," Valentina laughed.

"Right? Well, seein' that you ain't down with comin' up to the room wit' me, I guess I'll see you in the morning," Robert said as they rode the elevator to their floor.

"Oh, you definitely will see me in the morning. Make sure you unlock the door at seven o'clock. I wanna get some before breakfast," Valentina whispered seductively, before leaning in for another long, lingering kiss.

Entering her hotel room, Valentina prepared to settle in for the evening, but her cell phone rang. It was her agent.

"Hey, Val, what's up? Congrats on the win, but next time, prepare what you gon' say when you get up on stage," she laughed.

"Whateva', Rosa. Don't be getting' on my case now. You know it's my first major award since breaking into the industry," Valentina laughed.

"I know...anyways, guess what, girl? I got some great news. Do you know who Vickie Maxwell is?"

"Vickie Maxwell, the writer and movie director? She wrote over twenty books, and she's a bomb-ass director. Her movies are so good."

"Right! Guess what, girl? Turns out she watched you on YouStream, and she's a huge fan of the show, and she loves you. Matter of fact, she loves you so much, she's holding auditions for her new dramedy movie set to start filming this fall, and she wants you to audition for a role."

Valentina held on to the tip of her lampstand to keep herself in balance. With her breaths coming in short gasps, she thought she was hyperventilating at first, but she slowly gathered herself. "Get outta hea', Rosa! Are you for real? How'd you manage to swing that?" she asked.

"Girl, I'm so serious right now. Mrs. Maxwell had one of her assistants, who happens to be friends with another client in my agency, contact me, and she personally asked about you. She says she has a great role in mind for you for her next project. So are you interested?"

"Oh my God, yes, I'm interested!" Valentina exclaimed. "I mean, why wouldn't I be interested? Mrs. Maxwell is a freakin' legend."

"Yes, she is. Okay, so Mrs. Maxwell is holding her auditions next Monday at 8 a.m. at Columbia Studios. I need your makeup to be on point, and make sure to bring your A-game because, from what I've heard, there's about 45 other women auditioning for the role."

"Oh, trust and believe, I'm gon' be ready. Yo', I can't believe I'm auditioning for a Vickie Maxwell film. This is crazy!" Valentina exclaimed before she quickly remembered her prior engagement with her show. "Wait a minute, Rosa. I gotta fly back out to Atlanta this week. Robert just told me that YouStream is giving us a second season. What about the show?" Valentina asked.

"Look, Valentina, I don't think you get how big this is. Vickie

Maxwell's films have netted all her actors approximately twenty million and more. You're barely making a million doing the show on YouStream. If you ask me, it's a no-brainer."

Twenty million? I could do five seasons on YouStream, and I would never see that much money. But I would get that money if I sign the contract to star in the movie...given that I nail the audition, and I ain't worried too much about that.

"I mean, I know you love your co-stars of the show, especially Robert. You two make a great couple by the way, if I do say so myself. But this is an opportunity of a lifetime, Val. You can't pass this up."

"I know, Rosa, but the first season went so well, and the people wanna see a second season with Gabriella and Anthony."

"Val, c'mon, they could find another girl to play the role. It's been done all the time in sitcoms and drama shows. They'll find another Gabriella."

"Yeah, but it won't be the same though."

"Val, lemme give you some advice, from agent to actress. The one thing that you don't wanna do in show business is pigeon-hole yourself in one role. You are a versatile actress who can play different roles, and the world can finally see it. But you gotta leave your comfort zone. If you get this role, you'll be able to take care of your family."

Valentina knew that Rosa was right. There was enough pressure as a Latina American to try to make it in Hollywood but additional added pressure to stay ready for new roles.

"Okay, Rosa, I'll audition for the role. But lemme tell Jacobs about it because, in case the audition doesn't go my way, I don't wanna be left out of a job."

"Oh, girl, don't worry. Anderson will bend for you. He

understands that acting is more than a one-dimensional dog-and-pony show. He'll give you his blessings. Stay up!" Rosa said, ending the call.

Valentina thought it over. If she performed in the audition, she would have to drop out of YouStream, and she didn't want to leave Robert or any of the co-stars, but it was just like Rosa said. *It's show business.*

The victory over Trey Morris began to open doors of opportunity for Sylvio. In the following weeks, he was interviewed by various sports networks. People were intrigued by the man whom they started to dub "The Comeback Kid," and Sylvio became the center of attention in the boxing world. But to Tom's dismay, Sylvio's interviews and his speaking engagements were beginning to interfere with his training schedule, and Sylvio was beginning to spend more time outside of the ring.

As a result, Tom grew more and more concerned that Sylvio was placing more priority in the matters of media than his actual work in the ring. Sylvio saw it as a strategy to rehabilitate his image in the media and to provide publicity for the Shaw-Dominique Community Center.

One day, while Sylvio was training with Tom at the Dante Shaw Gym in SDCC, Shareef walked in. Sylvio was on the treadmill, which was slowly picking up acceleration.

"Wolf, we need to talk. Where's Kevin?" Shareef asked.

"He's in the office with Jim. What's up? Is everything good?" Sylvio asked, stopping the treadmill.

"Let's discuss it in the office. It concerns your next fight,"

Shareef replied.

A few minutes later, Sylvio, Tom, Jim, and Kevin were in Jim's office with Shareef.

"Okay, Shareef, what's going on?" Sylvio asked.

"I received a call from David Cheong, one of Jun Zhang's managers. His client has officially chosen you for his first title defense."

The whole room was silent for almost two minutes. Jim, Tom, and Kevin stared at one another.

"Cheong says that the fight will earn both fighters 70 million dollars, which is more than any other middleweight combined. The fight will be held in downtown Los Angeles at the Staples Center. Do you accept or decline this challenge made by the defending champion?" Shareef asked.

"Well, with all the media storm and the attention, it was gon' happen sooner or later," Sylvio replied.

"No. I think we need to wait on that one," Tom said. He was firmly against the challenge.

Sylvio turned to face Tom. "Wait on what? I ain't gon' duck him, Tom. I ain't come this far to lose the respect I just started gaining."

"Can you give us a minute, please?" Tom asked.

He and Sylvio walked outside the room. After closing the gym door behind him, the trainer turned to his boxer. "Sylvio, you've made great strides, but you ain't ready. I don't want you stepping into the ring wit' that guy. He's dangerous, man. You saw how he did Barry."

"Okay, well that was Barry, Tom. That wasn't me, okay? I took the heat for that loss as much as you or Barry did. Actually, I took more heat because everybody wants Sylvio Dominique to fail so badly."

"Barry is just getting out of the hospital, man!" Tom yelled. "He's trying to walk all over again and flex his limbs and joints. When he stepped into the ring with that monster, he almost died in there. I don't wanna see you go out like that."

Sylvio shook his head as he immediately recalled his first run for the title when Jim and Shareef were trying their hardest to prolong the inevitable fight with Felipe Maximo. "Okay, so you're my trainer then. Since you wanna call the shots, what do you suggest I do?"

"Let's give you a tune-up fight or two. Let's put you back out there with another ranked boxer, and if you can handle him, we'll consider the fight against Jun Zhang."

Sylvio chuckled. "So, you don't think I can beat him?"

"I never said you couldn't beat him, Wolf. But I don't want to see you in an infirmary after the fight. Your time will come, and when you're ready, we'll catch him slipping, and then we'll challenge him for a shot at the title. I want you to be at your very best when you fight him."

Sylvio thought about his trainer's words. "Okay, we'll do it your way. Let's do a tune-up, and after that, we'll decide and see if we're ready to go for it all."

Sylvio wasn't happy about turning down a challenge from anyone because he knew the media all too well, and if the media discovered that he dodged Jun Zhang, he would not hear the end of the debate of whether Sylvio Dominique was a man or a boy. Jun Zhang might even throw insults and disparage Sylvio's reputation.

Re-entering the office, Tom whispered to Kevin. After taking one look at Sylvio, he turned to Shareef. "Unfortunately, at this time, Shareef, we will have to decline Mr. Jun Zhang's challenge.

When another opportunity presents itself, we will negotiate contractual terms."

Shareef looked at Sylvio. "Are we sure about this?" he asked.

"Yeah, whatever, man. Let's just choose a consolation right now," Sylvio said.

"I've got someone else in mind," Tom said.

"And who might that be?" Shareef asked.

"Jermaine Dodson."

Exasperated, Sylvio stared at Tom. "You talkin' bout the dude that Barry beat to get the belt?"

"Yeah, why not?" Tom said.

"C'mon, man, Jermaine ain't even ranked in the top ten. Hell, I don't even think he ranked in the top twenty," Sylvio said.

"But he's a very crafty boxer and a threat to crack the top echelon of boxers. Let's fight him, and if we can contend with him, then we make a play at Zhang."

Reluctantly, Sylvio agreed, and after a short phone meeting with Jermaine Dodson's manager, Calvin Forman, the fight was set. As the men filed out of the office, Sylvio looked at the various trophies that behind a glass display in Jim's office.

One particular trophy stood out to him. It was a golden statue of a boy boxer. In the bottom of the trophy, there was a picture of thirteen-year-old Sylvio, posing with Jim after he won his first boxing match. It was nothing more than a recreational, intramural boxing exhibition between two boys from two different gyms, but to Sylvio, it was the beginning of his career.

"I remember that day like it was yesterday," Jim said. He had been quiet during the entire meeting. Since he was not a member of Sylvio's training team, he felt that he didn't have a say in who Sylvio decided to fight next.

"I wish things were this simple again," Sylvio said.

"Nothing's ever simple, man. Not in the fight game."

"Man, look how skinny I was back then. I thought I had no shot at beating Demetrious Young. He had cats all over the tri-state area shook. Hailing from the Briarwood Boxing Club, he was two years older than me, and he had most of his friends with him, but I had my crew with me," Sylvio said as he recalled the moment where his boxing career took form.

June 2002 | Two boys ran full speed, down the block to Steel Glove Gym as a part of their daily workout regimen. Sixteen-year-old Alfred DeWitt and thirteen-year-old Sylvio Dominique competed against each other daily. Since Sylvio had moved into A.D.'s apartment building four years earlier, the pair had hung out together after school and on weekends. Sylvio spent more time with A.D. than he did at home because being at home meant that he had to deal with his father. Jacques Dominique could care less about boxing, but since his son's grades were among the top in his class, he didn't have any qualms about his son going to Steel Glove.

When the boys arrived at the gym, Sylvio felt that he had won the foot race. "You a lil' slow there, A.D. Try to keep up," Sylvio laughed.

"Shut yo' ass up, man. You always got something slick to say. I got you tomorrow," A.D. replied as they went inside with their boxing gloves laced and slung over their shoulders.

"What's going on, Angie?" Sylvio greeted Angelina Peterson who worked the desk and clerical bookkeeping.

"Who won the race this time?" she asked.

"Oh, you already know who won, Angie. I'm too fast for these flat-footed fools outchea'," Sylvio bragged.

"Damn, A.D., you lettin' this lil' boy beat you on the way here?" Angie asked, laughing.

"Man, he cheated. Had a false head start from the crib. And whatever, man. Bump that! Where Jim at?" A.D. asked.

"He's in the back of the gym. I'd watch myself around him today though. He looked pissed off when he got here," Angie warned.

The boys headed to the locker room, where they changed into their Steel Glove Gym tank top and shorts.

"Over here, boys. Let's get to work," Will Timothy, one of the trainers motioned for A.D. and Sylvio to join him. "Let's get a lil' warm-up in, and after that, we'll hit the heavy bags."

"Where's Jim at?" Sylvio asked.

"He's on an important phone call outside. He wants me to get you started on warming up. Let's go, Dominique."

Twenty minutes later, after high intensity cardio on the treadmill, both boys hit the bag. Sylvio repeatedly hit it with precise combinations that Jim had taught him over the years.

"More power on them hooks, Sylvio," Will said.

Sylvio focused on the bag, throwing right hand left hooks that shook the bag's foundation. During the training session, two girls walked in. Sylvio recognized them as Angie's friends, Renee Watson and Monique Sinclair. They often visited the gym for no other reason than to talk with Angie. The girls were in high school but were nearly fully developed, both front and back side.

As they talked with Angie, A.D. stopped hitting the bag for a moment as he stared in awe at the teenagers. "Damn, Monique lookin' right. Yo', I bet you I'll get her number today," he said.

"Dream on, man. Ain't no way you pullin' any of 'em," Sylvio replied.

"How much you wanna bet?" A.D. asked.

Sylvio didn't have much money. Jacques didn't give him an allowance at home, and the little money Sylvio saved was money that he either borrowed from his friend, Kyle, or had leftover that he'd earned from a summer job selling lemonade outside the apartment. "Five bucks say she leave yo' ass high and dry," he said, laughing. "Give it up, dawg. Every time you even approach that chick, I see her backin' away like she in a horror movie."

"Okay, my ten to your five says not only is she gon' gimme some play, but I'mma have her number and her AIM," A.D. boasted. "Yo, I'mma take five, Will...water break." A.D. began making his way over to the girls.

Dead man walkin'. Sylvio shook his head.

"That boy still ain't get it, huh? If he over there tryin' to get a water break, he gon' stay thirsty," Will said, laughing.

"I tried to tell him, but that's yo' man though," Sylvio replied.

Sure enough, when A.D. stepped forward to try his luck, both girls stared him up and down as if he were an abnormal being.

"Um, excuse me, if you wanna approach me, please take a shower first," Monique said, recoiling.

"Damn, baby, I ain't even said nothin' yet, and you out hea' throwin' salt?" A.D. asked, laughing.

"Well, if someone comin' at me smellin' like rotten fish, what else am I gonna throw at it?" Renee asked.

All the girls laughed at that.

Sylvio closed his eyes. Damn, I felt that from here. I'mma give A.D. some time before I ask him to pay me.

While A.D. was being shot down, Jim finally emerged from the back door of the gym. "What's up, Sylvio. You already warmed up?" he asked.

"No doubt," Sylvio replied, dapping him.

"Good, man. Aye, step outside with me real quick. I gotta chop it up wit' you for a minute," Jim said.

Confused, Sylvio followed Jim outside the building. "What's goin' on, Jim? Everything good? Angie said you was mad about something."

"Well Angie ain't lyin'. The Steel Glove-Briarwood Boxing exhibition showcase is in two weeks, and Paul Marcel ain't gonna be fully recovered by then. I just spoke with his folks earlier," Jim said.

"Are you serious?" Sylvio asked.

Paul Marcel was one of the best boxers at Steel Glove Gym and was picked to represent the gym at the Annual Steel Glove-Briarwood Showcase, a yearly boxing match that pitted two of the best boxers from Steel Glove Gym and Briarwood Boxing Club head to head.

Since the inception of the showcase, Briarwood had been victorious, and it boasted the defending champion Demetrious Young, who won the last two annual bouts. A rangy fighter with hard-hitting hands and impeccable strength and timing, at the age of sixteen, Demetrious was considered the best boxing prodigy out of Queens. Sylvio had previously attended the showcase in 2001 and witnessed Demetrious dispatch Lloyd Gerard, the previous Steel Glove representative, within two minutes of the first round. If there was any boxer that struck fear in Sylvio's heart, it was Demetrious.

Large, fearsome, and experienced, Demetrious was already in contract with a sponsor group that would assist in kicking off his

Golden Gloves career. With new boxer Paul Marcel, Jim finally believed he had a chance of winning the showcase—until Paul broke his wrist sparring three weeks ago. With Paul sidelined, Jim had to look for a boxer to fill in the spot, but he was running out of options.

"So, if Paul ain't gonna fight Demetrious this year, who's gonna fight him then? A.D.?" Sylvio asked, secretly hoping that Jim didn't choose A.D. because he didn't think his friend stood a chance against the Briarwood Beast, as Demetrious was nicknamed.

"Nah, I'm not choosing A.D. to take his place. I want you to fight Demetrious at the showcase."

Chapter 17

The night before the boxing showcase, Sylvio tossed and turned. Until a week ago, he felt confident about his increased strength, endurance, and prowess in the ring. But he never imagined, in a million years, that he would be ready to fight the Briarwood Beast. After Jim told him the news, Sylvio wanted to tell his trainer and teacher that he wasn't ready, but he knew Jim wouldn't accept excuses. Sylvio would be entering the fight as an underdog because not only did he have to fight the toughest young boxer in Queens, but he also had to do it on the Beast' turf. The showcase was scheduled to be held at the Briarwood Boxing Club.

When word got to Demetrious about a thirteen-year-old phenom from Steel Glove Gym that he was going to face, as usual, he laughed and shrugged it off. Many of Demetrious' friends had heard the Briarwood Beast himself refer to all the boxers from Steel Glove as bums, and they couldn't hold his jock strap.

But when Jim heard the insult, he intensified Sylvio's training. Sylvio was already accustomed to many of his sparring partners, as Jim wanted him to be exposed to ring battles.

Sylvio remembered the reaction from his friend Kyle when he told him about his upcoming fight. "Damn, you gotta fight the Briarwood Beast? I heard that cat was crazy," he said.

"Thanks, bro. Your confidence is overwhelmin'," Sylvio replied sarcastically, rolling his eyes as they headed home after going to the corner store to buy some snacks.

"Yo', you could beat him. I've seen you box. You got this, dawg," Kyle reassured him.

"You sure? Demetrious has already beaten all our best boxers, and Jim wants me to go out there and put my neck on the line. I don't know, man."

"Yo', you got this," Kyle repeated.

Soon, they passed by South Ozone Public Park and stopped by the basketball courts where two boys were playing one on one.

"Yo', Omar, what's good, B.?" Kyle yelled from outside the park.

One of the boys turned his head to find out who had called him. When he saw Kyle and Sylvio, he stopped playing and ran over to dap them. "What's up, Kyle? What's good, Sylvio?" he greeted.

"Nothin', I see Jamal over there still workin' you," Kyle laughed.

"Shut up, man. I ain't gettin' beat bad. I'm only down—"

The other boy, Jamal Samuels, finished the line for him. "Ten. You down by ten, son," he replied, joining the other two boys.

"Whateva'. So, word on the street is that you gotta fight Demetrious Young this weekend," Omar said to Sylvio. "Man, good luck, and may the force be wit' you and all that because everybody that go to Hillcrest High School say that he ain't been beaten in a fight. You gon' have yo' hands full," he said, further derailing Sylvio's confidence, but at that point Sylvio decided he wasn't going to dread the day of the fight.

"Don't you mean, he gon' have his hands full?" Sylvio corrected.

"Okay, there's the real Sylvio right there. The killa'," Kyle said.

"Ya should come through though," he told Omar and Jamal.

"Oh, no doubt. You know me and Jamal gon' make it out there. We wanna see the phenom," Omar replied.

Saturday finally arrived as the Briarwood Boxing club started to fill up with neighborhood kids and boxing fans. Demetrious Young was already fitted with his boxing shorts, gym tank, and head gear. He had been in this ring many times, and the news was revealed to him only days earlier that he was going to be fighting some thirteen-year-old kid who was being called "The Phenom."

What a stupid name. I'm gonna kill this kid. His parents better come say a prayer for him.

Standing at six-foot-three with a seven-and-a-half wingspan, Demetrious was extremely smug and confident that he would dispatch the Phenom within the first two minutes. Meanwhile in the locker room, Jim was talking to a nauseous Sylvio who had thrown up the little breakfast he had forced upon himself earlier.

"Okay, listen to me, Sylvio. He's just a kid, raw like you. He's gon' try to do everything to hurt you up here," Jim said, pointing to Sylvio's head. "But that's the part you don't let him affect. Even when it gets down and dirty, keep your head, and fight intelligently. It's a chess game out there, Sylvio. Block out the noise, and focus on him. Remember all the work we put in to get here. Today, all of Queens is gon' know your name. Let's go."

As they walked out into the ring, the spectators laughed when they saw Jim jump into the ring with a skinny, small-headed boy, whose headgear appeared to be oversized. Walking to the center of the ring, Sylvio could see that Demetrious was trying to suppress his laughter too when he saw him.

After the referee read the rules, Demetrious said, "This is gon' be funny as hell. Ayo, Jim, if he get hurt, you betta' not call Child Protective Services on me. I ain't goin to jail for killin' no kindergarten kid."

"Ignore him. He doesn't know you like I do," Jim said, placing in Sylvio's mouthpiece and adjusting his headgear.

Finally, the bell rang. Both fighters came out of their corners, and Sylvio moved from side to side, keeping his gloves at eye level to protect his face. Demetrious came out and threw some jabs toward Sylvio's head. Easily dodging the headshots, Sylvio used the same tactic as one of his favorite heavyweight boxers and slipped side to side. Demetrious was headhunting early and often. He wanted to knock down this little boy, but as the round wore on, he realized that Sylvio was extremely elusive. Using his quickness to his advantage, Sylvio was able to duck all of Demetrious' punches. After the first round, both fighters headed to their corners, unharmed.

"Good round, Sylvio. Remember, stay away from his wide right hook. That's his go-to move. Find your opening, and when you do, treat him like that heavy bag in our gym," Jim instructed.

In the second round, Sylvio continued to evade the taller Demetrious, and the defending showcase champion began to show signs of frustration after hitting nothing but air for the next minute. Toward the end of the round, Sylvio watched as Demetrious missed his wide right hook. Ducking underneath the hook, Sylvio saw his opening on his opponent's flank and delivered a hard left shot. Demetrious was taken by surprise and had the wind knocked out of him before the bell rang. While the fight remained neutral with neither fighter gaining an advantage, it changed in the fourth round when Sylvio made a critical error.

Demetrious led Sylvio into his area with his right and landed a crisp, left hook on the side of Sylvio's head. After a flash of light, everything went black as the young boxer hit the canvas. Amidst the gasps of shock and the reaction of the spectators, Sylvio's vision swam back into focus as he heard the ref begin his ten-count.

"One."

Sylvio struggled to get on his knees as the gym scene still appeared foggy.

"Two."

Sylvio turned toward his bench and saw Jim frantically imploring him to get on his feet. From the corner of his eye, he saw A.D., Jamal, Kyle, and Omar screaming at him to get back up. He could hear Demetrious in his neutral corner, bragging to anyone who would listen.

"I told ya'll this would be quick. He ain't nothin', just like the rest of them," Demetrious laughed.

From the corner of his eye, Sylvio saw Demetrious make a motion of dusting dirt off his shoulder. Within the recesses of his being, Sylvio felt a pool of fury begin to bubble inside of him.

"Three."

Sylvio remembered what Jim had told him during their sparring sessions. "If you get knocked down, don't spring back up quick. Take a few seconds to breathe and gather yourself. Then gradually get back up."

Sylvio grabbed onto the ringside ropes to use as leverage to force himself up.

"Four."

Sylvio, still fighting dizziness and blurred vision, got up to a crouching position. The ref never reached the count of five as Sylvio courageously willed himself to stand up. He shook his head in an attempt to eradicate the remaining state of grogginess.

Demetrious, who had been bragging only moments earlier, appeared stunned that Sylvio rose back up to his feet just as the bell rang.

Sylvio slowly made his way back to the bench, where the young Harry worked feverishly to bring him back around with smelling salts before the next bell.

Jim stared at his protégé with a look of concern. "How you feelin', kid?" he asked.

"I'm ready to go. He ain't knocked me out yet," Sylvio replied. The look of determination plastered on his face could cut through steel.

Jim smiled because, at that very moment, he knew he had a real gem in his hands. "Okay, so when the next round begins, we're gonna work on the body. Keep ducking and slipping his shots, and get inside just enough to rip off a couple of hooks. Right and left. Remember Brandon?"

Sylvio's eyes glowered in anger upon the mention of the kid who had once bullied him in the fourth grade.

"Anticipate, dodge, and counter. Once you let them hooks rip, he's all yours."

The bell rang, and Sylvio went back out toward the center of the ring. Demetrious had recovered from his initial shock brought on by the persistence of the little boxer, and he had let off every punching combination that he knew. Yet, not one hit landed home.

Sylvio knew that Demetrious was reacting out of anger. Jim had often warned him that anger led to irrationality, which indicated that Demetrious was going to make a mistake. Sure enough, Demetrious threw an overhand left hook, but this time, Sylvio anticipated it, ducked under it, and delivered a hard right and left hook to the body.

Bang, bang! Sylvio saw Demetrious' mouthpiece protrude as he felt the force of the hooks being delivered.

With his opponent doubled over in pain, Sylvio unleashed his quick left jabs, each one snapping Demetrious' head back a notch. Now Sylvio was beginning to back him into the ropes.

The spectators, sensing an upset, roared at the sight of the short, dark-skinned boxer holding serve over his taller opponent. Finally, Sylvio unleashed his right hook, which crashed into the side of Demetrious' head, and the two-time champion crumpled to the canvas.

Boom!

The crowd chanted, and a smile crept onto Jim's face as he took in the nostalgic moment. The ref began his ten-count, and Sylvio strolled over to the neutral corner, waiting for Demetrious to rise back to his feet. Sylvio was determined to come back swinging if he needed to, but Demetrious was unable to beat the ten count. Sylvio raised his hands in victory as the Steel Glove fans chanted his name.

"SYLVIO! SYLVIO! SYLVIO!"

After Demetrious was checked, the fighters approached the center of the ring as the ref raised Sylvio's arm as a mere formality of acknowledging his victory. Demetrious even took the time to fist bump his opponent in a worthy show of sportsmanship. Although his ego was severely fractured with his loss at the hands of a thirteen-year-old, Demetrious recognized Sylvio's ability and skill.

"Good fight, B. You for real, man. You gon' be the truth in the ring one day. Keep grindin'," he said as they went to their respective corners.

"Yeah, boy, that's what I'm talkin' about! Yo', my nigga Sylvio kickin' ass and takin' names. Ya' don't want none of this!" Omar bragged as Harry removed the headgear from Sylvio's head, revealing a small lump where Demetrious' devastating hook had landed.

"Ooh, that's gonna leave a mark. Yo' face is gone swell up like a grapefruit. Let me apply some ice to that," Harry offered as one of the girls whom Sylvio recognized as one of Angie's friends, appeared at his corner.

"Yo', you gave him a beatdown. You okay?" she asked Sylvio.

"Yeah, I'm good," Sylvio replied, rubbing his head.

"Let me get that for you," the girl said. Harry handed her the ice, and she gently applied it to Sylvio's forehead.

"Thanks. What's your name?" Sylvio asked.

"Jasmine Evans," she replied.

Sylvio smiled. Oh yeah. I could get used to this.

"Seemed ages ago now," Jim said, snapping Sylvio out of his flashback. "When you got back up after that vicious hook that Demetrious threw at you, I thought, 'Yeah, this kid's got it. He's got what it takes to survive the fight game.'"

"That was the day the Wolf was born. Boxing was therapy for me in the worst way back then. I wasn't getting along wit' Dad half the time, and I was just coasting through school really. I always felt that I was born to do this."

"You were. So, you got a strategy up your sleeve for Dodson?" Jim asked.

"Yeah, Tom and I watched film on the guy. He doesn't seem too difficult a matchup. Rangy fighter with quick hands, but he ain't quick otherwise. If we stick to the strategy, we can beat him," Sylvio replied confidently as he walked out of the office.

It wouldn't take long for Sylvio to realize that he spoke too soon. Jermaine was on a tear, having won his last four bouts before his scheduled fight with Sylvio. After weeks of promotion tours and shows, the fight was finally set in Buffalo, New York. Sylvio anticipated a good but quick fight. What he discovered instead was that he was placed in the ring with a man who was desperate to recapture the belt. That was evident on fight night.

In the early rounds of the fight, Sylvio was unusually flat-footed, and Jermaine's stinging jabs repeatedly found their mark.

"C'mon, Wolf, wake up! See yo' man in front of you!" Tom barked from the corner.

Although Sylvio heard the warning, despite whatever punch he threw his opponent's way, Jermaine had a counter for it. Standing at six foot two, not only did Jermaine have height advantage over Sylvio, but he moved strangely around the ring. During their film sessions, Tom had warned Sylvio about Jermaine's unorthodox fighting style, which included side-step jabs and short hooks, both of which were punishing Sylvio that night.

By the end of the third round, the crowd, which had been mostly Sylvio supporters, was stunned into silence as it watched its favorite fighter get out-boxed. A cut had opened above Sylvio's left eye, and blood was streaming down the left side of his face. Harry rushed to wipe the blood as a dazed Sylvio sat in his corner.

Tom was beside himself with fury. "Sylvio, look at me, man. What's goin' on? You gotta anticipate his side-step jabs. You know those are his specialty. You ain't won a single damn round yet. Where your head at, man?"

"I'm good, bro!" Sylvio protested.

"Right now, it ain't lookin' like it. You lettin' Jermaine dictate the fight from the opening bell. You gotta fight smart and anticipate his jabs. It's obvious he's been studying you, and right now, he's lookin' like wants to knock you out," Tom said.

The bell rang for Round 4. Sylvio ran out toward the center of the ring, hoping to get into his rhythm, but Jermaine's clever slips and side-step jabs continued to befuddle the Wolf.

Jab's comin' from right. Move, Wolf. C'mon! Sylvio attempted to slip the jab, but Jermaine was able to tag him on his ribs.

Ah, shit! What you doin', man? You see that hit coming. Back up!

Grunting in pain and anger, Sylvio began pressing Jermaine, but Jermaine smartly maneuvered around the ring, avoiding all corners. At the end of the round, Sylvio was finally able to capitalize on an over-right hook that shook Jermaine's face, but Jermaine was still virtually unhurt.

Sylvio couldn't understand what was happening. Jermaine wasn't engaged in any trash talking. He allowed his work in the ring to speak for itself. After two more rounds, Sylvio knew that he was down in the judges' scorecards.

Jermaine threw more punches, and he also capitalized on those punches. He made Sylvio look slow and plodding while he, on the other hand, executed his ring strategy to perfection. Aside from a few marks, Jermaine was unhurt, which contrasted to the current state of his opponent. Sylvio's lip was now split open, and he was spitting out water and blood in the corner.

Unable to avoid Jermaine's side-step jabs, Sylvio was in trouble, more trouble than he had ever been in his fighting career. By Round

12, both fighters were valiantly on their feet as attrition began to set in. Sylvio was panting because, unbeknownst to him, Jermaine and his trainer, Harvey Gamble, had the blueprint on defeating him, which was to tire him out during the fight.

The crowd's awkward silence was soon followed by streams of boos from the upper deck of the Buffalo City Park Arena as onlookers saw their winning bets swirling down the drain. For the first time, Sylvio had originally been heavily favored to defeat Jermaine, but when the sports networks announced the odds, it only motivated the polarizing boxer, who was eagerly anticipating his chance to prove the world wrong.

In a dazed stupor, Sylvio barely located his stool on the corner. "What round is it?" he asked.

"It's the final round, Wolf, but I don't know how much more you can take out there. Jermaine messed you up pretty good," Tom remarked.

Sylvio's right eye was nearly shut, and the bridge of his nose was swollen. Despite Tom's reservations, Sylvio insisted on fighting the final round. Hoping for a last-minute miracle, he rushed at the larger Jermaine in an effort to land his devastating right hook, but Jermaine anticipated his movements and replied with a left hook to the side of Sylvio's head.

With that, the round ended, and so did the fight. Before the winner was announced, Sylvio lowered his head, knowing that he had lost his first fight in more than six years. Jermaine's arms were raised as he celebrated the victory that no one saw coming.

Sylvio Dominique's stunning defeat sent ripples through the sports world. The former champion, once lauded, now found himself under media scrutiny for his underwhelming performance against a fighter that most people felt he should have won against. The criticism of his performance outweighed the criticism he had received a few months earlier when he was in Barry Taylor's corner for his disastrous title defense. After the fight, Sylvio withdrew from the public eye and stayed home without taking phone calls from friends or family members.

A few days later, on a Thursday afternoon, Kwame Turner walked out of school after the final bell rang. Making his way to the bus stop, he felt his phone vibrate.

Checking his notifications, he smiled. It was Roxy, whom he had been secretly going steady with over the last two weeks. Just a few days earlier, Roxy and Kwame had been watching Netflix movies at her house while her parents were out of town. Although he didn't plan for what was to come, both kids were instantly attracted to one another, and they had an intimate moment during the Netflix session.

By the time Kwame left her house that evening, he was convinced that Roxy was his girl. But with that conviction came a problem. Roxy was currently dating Tyreke Henderson, a senior at Hillcrest High School with dangerous affiliations with the Mecca Murks, a new gang that had been silently terrorizing the area.

Kwame knew how dangerous Tyreke was because they had been best friends once, but once Tyreke became initiated with the Murks, their friendship ended. Tyreke tried to convince Kwame to join the gang, but Kwame refused. His gang affiliation also contributed to the rift between him and Roxy, and he was unaware that he was driving his girlfriend into the arms of his former friend...

Hey Kwame I had a great time the other night. We took Netflix and chill to a whole 'nother level! You ain't nothin' like Ty...it's hard to even believe that ya were best friends.

Kwame texted back. Yeah, he still my boy, we just don't kick it like we used to. Just grew apart, I guess. You doin' anything Saturday night?

Just a block before he reached his stop, Kwame was so engaged with texting Roxy that he was unaware that he was being followed by members of the Murks. When he looked up, he saw none other than Tyreke staring straight at him. With tattoos across his arms, neck, and back, Tyreke wore a smug smile that Kwame did not return.

"What's good, Kwame? It's been a minute since we chopped it up. What's wrong, son?"

"Nothin', man. I'm cool. Just tryin' to get to the bus stop to get back to the crib," Kwame replied.

"Yeah, I see that. I also see that you were too busy hittin' my girl up too. Is that who the fuck you were texting?" Tyreke asked sharply.

Kwame looked around and saw the other Murks around him. He was clearly outnumbered. But other people were walking around too, and Kwame figured that Tyreke wouldn't try anything that would get him arrested. "Man, it ain't even like that, aight? We just friends."

"That ain't what I heard. Some cat said you left her crib at two in the mornin' the other night."

Kwame shook his head as if to insinuate that Tyreke was crazy. "I don't know where you got that info, but loose lips sink ships, you feel me?" he replied, confidently. He was determined not to show fear. If he was going to die in broad daylight, at least he would not give Tyreke the pleasure of exploiting his fear.

Stepping dangerously close to Kwame, Tyreke said, "If you know what's good for you, you gon' stay the hell away from her. You got me?"

But Kwame stood his ground. "Yo', you think you can roll up on me like John Gotti wit' your boys and expect me to sweat you? Man, watch out. I got a bus to catch," he said, trying to avoid Tyreke.

But Tyreke pushed Kwame back roughly. "Where the fuck you goin'? We ain't done yet!"

"I'm done, and yo' girl done wit' you too," Kwame fired back.

Just as soon as he said it, Tyreke swung at Kwame with his left hand, but Kwame ducked the blow and struck Tyreke on the gut. Tyreke tackled Kwame, and they fell on the ground. The two other members of the Murks pinned Kwame's arms down while Tyreke got back on his feet. With Kwame defenseless, Tyreke kicked Kwame in the ribs, hard. Kwame bent over in pain.

"Now I'mma kick yo' ass till there ain't nothin' left to kick," Tyreke said, grabbing Kwame in a chokehold.

But before he struck again, a man who had witnessed the whole scene ran up behind Tyreke, twisted his arms behind his back, and threw him to the ground. Then he grabbed one of the Murks, who had tried to retaliate, by easily slipping the gangbanger's punch and then connecting with a right blow to his left cheek. The other Murk dropped Kwame and ran across the street, but Tyreke was not done.

"You one dead old man," he threatened, swinging wildly at Kwame's rescuer, but not one punch connected.

Before long, the old man's fists were tattooing Tyreke's face, chest, and ribs. "You lil' punk niggas are nothin' but scum to society!" he yelled, panting between every blow.

Tyreke's face soon became a bloody mess. Unable to stop himself, the old man was unaware that bystanders had called the police, and he was oblivious to the sirens that were blaring behind him. In no time, the police arrived on the scene.

"Freeze! Put your hands up!" they yelled as Jim Shaw, panting heavily, placed his hands in the air, surrendering to the NYPD.

Chapter 18

Thirty-six years earlier, a young Jim Shaw stared at the floor in his holding cell at the juvenile detention center, merely hours after savagely beating Grant Butler. He reflected on how his anger got the better of him and nearly cost another young boy his life. From then on, he made a vow never to allow himself to reach a breaking point to cause bodily harm to anyone else, not realizing the outlet that the sport of boxing would allow him through Flip Timothy. Jim learned to use the anger to his advantage in the ring, but Flip taught him that self-control and restraint were the keys inside and outside the ring.

For many years, Jim had kept himself under control, and he had never allowed himself to lose his head outside of the ring. But his rage once again reared its ugly head as he found himself back behind bars, this time at the Nassau County Jail. After being charged with aggravated assault and battery, Jim was booked and held on bond for $7,000.

Asking the guard for a phone call, Jim tried calling his brother, but Kevin didn't answer. Leaving a voicemail, he waited and without talking to any of the other inmates in the adjoining cells.

After Jim was locked up all night, a guard approached the cell. "Let's go, Shaw."

Jim, who had been lying on the cold bench, put his jacket back on as the guard unlocked the cell. He walked out, expecting to see Kevin, but instead he saw Sylvio sitting outside, wearing dark Ray-Ban sunglasses and a black Nike T-shirt, awaiting his trainer. They headed to Sylvio's car.

"Well, you've looked better," Jim said after looking at Sylvio's face, which was still swollen from his defeat.

"You should talk," Sylvio replied.

"Who posted my bail? Was it you?" Jim asked.

Sylvio only responded by thrusting his keys in the ignition to start the car. He spoke up after a brief moment of silence. "Me and Kevin. He told me what went down, and I'mma keep it real wit' you...you mad lucky that I'm the one that came to get you and not him."

"Man, whatever," Jim dismissed Sylvio's words.

Sylvio shook his head. This guy's never gonna change his ways.

"So ain't you gon' say it?" Jim asked, glaring at Sylvio.

"Say what?"

"Go ahead. I know you're gonna say it cuz I had to hear it from Kevin for twenty years that I needed help. Tell me, 'I told you so,'" Jim quipped.

"Man, it ain't even worth it, Jim. We could say whatever we want, but it ain't like you gonna listen anyway cuz it always gotta be about you."

"What? You think I did this shit for me? Kwame was getting jacked up by three boys, potentially gangbangers, and I'm supposed to sit by and do nothin'?"

Sylvio shook his head. His trainer never understood the repercussions of his actions. "It wasn't bad enough that I lost to Dodson, and on top of the sports media throwing dirt on my face, I gotta deal wit' more negative publicity when you pull this type of shit!" he exclaimed.

"Look, I ain't mean for it to get that far, aight? I saw Kwame pinned, and he was defenseless. Just like Dante was defenseless. Just like you were defenseless back in the day, and something went off in me. I thought I could stop myself, but I kept hitting and hitting him. I blacked out."

"Jim, they're gonna try you for assault and battery, and if you lose the case, they're gon' throw you in jail for ten years, maybe more. Is that what you want?"

Jim shrugged as if he were completely oblivious of the charges that were being rained down on him. "No, but I also want to send a message to these young fools out here. I'm sick of standing by and watching kids get bullied into depression or suicide. I'm sick of our lawmakers and police not doing a damn thing to protect these kids. I just had enough. So how bad is it?" he asked.

"Kid's got a fractured nose, some broken teeth, and couple black eyes. Word on the street is that his mama's out for blood. She's gon' want to throw the book at you," Sylvio replied.

"Maybe she should watch her lil' bad-ass kid, goin' out there terrorizing other folks just for the fun of it," Jim said.

"Okay, but you can't keep goin' out there tryna be Luke Cage, bustin' people's asses. You gotta think, man. Whatever you do reflects on me, and it reflects on Kevin. Don't you get that?"

Then Sylvio saw Jim do something for the first time that he hadn't done in front of people that weren't his own family. He hung his head, and a tear rolled out of his eye.

"I know. I hear you and Kevin warn me, day after day. But when I see kids like Kwame, I see my son being pushed in front of that car again. I see Brandon hittin' your gut while his homies laugh at you. I see all that, and it makes me mad when I can't do something about it. You don't understand what it's like to have your own offspring's blood on your hands when you could've done something about it, and you didn't. I swore to myself that I won't be too late for anybody else again."

After driving in silence for the next five minutes, Sylvio turned to Jim. "Where we goin' now?"

"Take me to the Queens Boulevard Auto Pound. They impounded my car, so I gotta sign off on it," he replied.

"I got you. So, I take it that you saw the fight," Sylvio said, changing the subject.

"Yeah, I saw it. After yelling at my TV for damn near one hour, I realized something when that bell rang."

"Yeah? What's that?"

"Jermaine was hungrier than you were that night. You lost on effort, son. He had a stronger sense of urgency, and he proved it. We need to get you back in the ring against him."

"We?" Sylvio asked, laughing.

"Yeah. If you still game, I'd like to come back in your corner, champ, unless you're happy wit' Tom now," he said.

"Well, Tom kind of went into a funk since I lost, and I ain't been able to reach him. But I'd love to have you back in my corner, old man. On one condition though," Sylvio said.

Jim stared blankly at him. "What's the condition?"

"That you go seek help. You gotta get a handle on this whole guilt trip with your son. If you go see a psychiatrist or a counselor, I'll let you back in the Pack," Sylvio said.

"Okay, deal," Jim agreed reluctantly.

Ecstatic to have his trainer back on his side, Sylvio drove to pick up Jim's car.

"Thanks for reaching out to me," Natalie said as she led Jim into her office, which was in Yonkers, New York.

"No, thank you, Nat, for clearing your schedule to see me. I wasn't sure if you'd have time to hear my problems," Jim replied before instantly regretting what he'd said.

Whenever he was with his ex-wife, his mind always went blank, or he would overthink. He couldn't help himself. She had that type of pull over him. But true to his words to Sylvio, Jim promised to seek help, and he remembered the card that Natalie gave him the night she visited him.

Natalie was dressed in complete business attire: black skirt, black blazer with a buttoned blouse underneath, and her hair was straightened with a pair of glasses to top it off. *She don't look half bad.*

Jim stepped into her office, where he saw two degrees. The first was a bachelor's in psychology from Columbia University, and the second degree was a master's degree from New York University. The one aspect that Jim never doubted about Natalie was her ambition. She was always first in her class. Even in high school, she would always manage to get straight A's with an unblemished record, while Jim had to scrape through most classes. And his reputation as a troubled child with a record didn't help matters.

"I see you've been keeping busy for the last twenty-plus years. Nice digs," he said.

"Thanks. It's not much, but it'll do for now. Dr. Favian has the office next door, and trust me, it's a whole lot bigger," she replied.

Jim chuckled.

"So, I'm curious. What made you finally change your mind

about contacting me?" she asked.

"Figured if I had to do this, I wanted someone that I actually know instead of a complete stranger," Jim said.

"Good move. Please take a seat, or feel free to lie down on the leather couch there," Natalie said.

"Thanks. I'll just sit."

Natalie walked behind her desk and sat down. Smiling as she adjusted her lens frames, she couldn't believe that her childhood friend, high school boyfriend, and ex-husband was sitting across from her. Having analyzed many minds for years, she wasn't new to the procedure, but this was a different challenge. Probing the mind of a person that she was once intimate with could be quite the task.

As he continued to scope the office, Jim's eyes fell on a photograph that was unframed but pinned to the wall with pushpins. He looked closer and realized it was an old photograph of himself with Sylvio after they won their first professional fight as boxer and trainer. Sylvio had gone up against Luis Acevedo and won the fight on a technical knockout. Jim remembered posing with Sylvio as he had his arms flexed. Both were smiling for the camera.

The photo had originally been in black and white in the sports section of the *New York Post*, but the photo Natalie held was in live color. "Yo', how did you manage to get that picture? Did you squeeze the newspapers to give you the colored version?" he asked, laughing.

"No. I know it's actually hard to believe, but I was actually at the fight," she said.

"Get outta hea'!" Jim scoffed.

"I'm so serious," Natalie said. "After some years passed, I went back to try to mend things with you, but it was clear that you moved on. I watched from a distance, Jim. I was always watching you. I even thought about stopping by Steel Glove Gym, even so much as to just step right outside the doorway, but when I got there, I would always have second thoughts and never went through with it. I didn't think you'd be happy to see me after everything I put you through. I used to walk by occasionally and watch you train the Wolf...Sylvio Dominique. I swear when I looked at him then, I saw you all over again. His arrogance...his swagger, and he had quick hands like you did. I went to watch his first fight, and when it was over, while the media took pictures, I blended in and took one of my own. I had to keep a memory of you, somehow," she explained.

Jim just sat in his seat, amazed at what he heard. All this time, he had thought that Natalie wanted nothing to do with him, when the reality was that she struggled to reconcile with him for years.

"All that time, you were right there. Why didn't you say anything back then?" Jim asked.

"I don't know, Jim. I was scared. I didn't know how you'd react, and I couldn't get my thoughts together. Then, I got in touch with Kevin, and he filled me in on you and what you were doing, and at that moment, I knew I had to get over my fear and reach back out to you in order to help you. The rest is history," she replied.

"Well, better late than ever, I suppose," Jim said.

"Exactly. Now Mr. Shaw, for the rest of this session, I'm going to be addressing you doctor to patient, okay? I'm going to ask you some questions, and I want you to be very honest with me, okay?" Natalie asked, now professional and serious.

"Got it, Doc," Jim replied lazily as he stood up from the chair and reclined on the couch.

"So, can you explain what happened three days ago in Briarwood?" she asked.

"I saw a student who goes to my gym getting harassed by another individual, who was gang-affiliated, might I add, and he was outnumbered. So, I stepped in to defend the student."

"But you ended up beating the boy senseless. According to his medical reports, he was very close to losing the vision in his left eye. If you saw what was unfolding, you could've called the police before the situation escalated."

"I had no choice, Ms. Brown. The police wouldn't have arrived on time. Kwame could've been dead by the time they arrived," he said.

"And you didn't want to lose someone the way you lost your son, yes?" she asked.

What you mean my son? He was our son! But then, Jim remembered that Natalie was treating him as a patient, and she was speaking hypothetically to him. "No, I didn't. I was too late to save Dante, and it's torn me up inside. I vowed that I would never be late again."

"That's quite a promise to keep, Mr. Shaw. Surely, you realize that you can only do so much, and at the end of the day, self-care should become paramount."

"Yeah, but if I don't help those who can't help themselves, who will? Many of these kids grew up in single-parent households, some without a mother, and some without fathers. They're confused, and without guidance, they'll end up falling into the trap of the streets."

Natalie listened intently, adjusting her glasses. "Mr. Shaw, could it be possible that your guilt and anger might have stemmed from your father not being involved in your life?"

At first Jim glared at his ex-wife. Why the hell would she put my father in this? He's a non-factor. He ain't done nothin' for me. "My father ain't got nothin' to do with this."

"I don't believe that's completely true."

"Who cares if you believe me or not? My father ain't done shit for my family. As far as I'm concerned, he ain't nothin' but a sperm donor to my mama cuz he gave her two boys that she struggled to take care of, and while he was rottin' behind bars, I was the man of the house."

"But do you think that, just maybe, you feel guilty for your father not being there? Somehow you blame yourself for his absence?"

Jim shifted uncomfortably in his chair. He didn't appreciate the line of questioning that Natalie was doling out to him. "He had two kids that he wasn't prepared to have, and he struggled to keep a roof over our heads, so he went out and did what he had to do. He hustled, sold drugs, and scraped by till he was caught," Jim explained.

While he recalled the story, Natalie continued listening.

"I mean, it didn't matter so much that he got caught. That happens to all drug dealers when they get sucked into the game, you know? But what really got me was that this man never even tried to check on his family. No phone call, no letters, no seeing if his family was okay. I mean, for all we know, we all could've been dead on the streets, and he wouldn't have known," Jim said, and although he tried to hold them back, tears flowed from his eyes.

"I'm in grade school, gettin' picked on by other kids, getting offered drugs, even experimenting at an early age cuz who the hell was there to tell me that slangin' dope was bad? I see other kids with their families, and I would think to myself, how come that can't be me and Kevin? Why can't we ever have the full functioning family?" Jim continued.

Natalie listened.

"So, I carried a chip on my shoulder, and I dared anybody to knock it off. My fists were lethal weapons, and everybody on the block knew it. I even put a bounty on my own head, betting people that they couldn't knock me cold. I made a helluva lot of money off it. Then the Grant Butler thing popped off, and before you know it, I'm arrested and sent to juvey. Like father, like son, right? I mean, my pops was in jail, so it only made sense that his son followed suit. But Flip Timothy sprung me and offered to train me in boxing. As you know, I blew up, but I didn't know that I was nothing but a charity case for him. A project, just to prove to the world that he could change a poor black boy from a thug to being accepted by society. He did what my father was supposed to do."

Natalie, who had seemed indifferent through Jim's entire account, removed her glasses, subtly brushing off a tear herself.

"Then I was given a second chance. A girl that I met at the age of fourteen allowed me to be myself and was the only girl that cared enough about me to give me the time of day. I loved everything about her, from her smile, the way she wore her hair, how good she smelled and just her vibe. I remembered thinking, 'Yeah, she the one.' My boxing career took off, we got married, and we had a son. I made a promise that I was gonna do right by Dante Shaw and not become my father. I was gonna encourage him to stay in the books because I wanted him to be a better man than me. The plan worked because Dante was in the gifted program, and he was in the fifth grade at age nine. But you know how it is out here. There's always an enemy seeking to destroy what you've built, and when Dante needed me, I wasn't there for him."

Jim was now weeping uncontrollably, gasping between sobs. "I failed him, and I failed my wife, and I knew apologizing was never going to give my son back, but I swore to his memory that I was going to do what I can to use my talent and resources to be a surrogate father to the disenfranchised kids out there and give them the protection they need from this cruel world. If I do nothing else in life, I could do that much for them."

Natalie reached into her drawer and handed Jim a tissue from a previously opened Kleenex box and took one for herself.

"Mr. Shaw, thank you for being transparent with me today. Believe me when I tell you that you've done an excellent job with the kids in your community. You've built a center where they can learn to be active members of society. You've trained fighters, and one of them won a title belt under your watch. For the nine years that your beautiful son was on this earth, you were an incredible father. Some people may not have realized it before, but now they see your worth and value. To me, you're one hundred times the man your father was, and you don't have to feel guilty or carry his sins on your shoulders," she said.

"Thank you, Doc. I hope that if my wife is out there somewhere, she knows how deeply sorry I am for putting her through the grief that I have put her through, and I hope that she can find it in her heart to forgive me."

Natalie rose from her desk and walked over to Jim. Suddenly, all professional walls broke as she embraced her ex-husband. "She already has forgiven you, Mr. Shaw."

That same day, Sylvio sat on his couch, flipping through TV

channels. Aside from some light jogging early in the morning, he decided to stay home. Soon, he landed on the sports channel. One sportscaster by the name of Newt Fitzgerald, who covered all boxing weight classes, hosted a morning show with three other sports personalities: Dwayne Rockman, Sylveena Thompson, and Jack Orion.

Sylvio sighed when he saw their first topic of discussion, which was about his bout with Jermaine Dodson. Today they were debating on whether Sylvio's time in boxing had finally come to an end.

"Well, Newt, I'll be really honest with you. It's hard to come back from a demoralizing defeat like the one Dominique suffered against Dodson. For the first time, Dominique was heavily favored in Vegas over the overrated and lightly regarded Jermaine Dodson, but unfortunately, he wasn't able to capitalize on the opportunity," Dwayne said.

"Listen, everybody has a bad day. It happens in sports, especially in the boxing world. We all recall how heavyweight champion Mike Tyson was heavily favored to beat Buster Douglas in '90, but Buster ended up pulling the upset," Newt explained.

"Yeah, but there's still a lot of controversy surrounding that fight. What about the long count that gave Buster a chance to get back up?" Jack replied.

"Was there any controversy surrounding this match? That's what I wanna know," Newt said.

"There was no controversy. Sylvio just went up against a hungry fighter, itching to get his title back. There's no question that he made Sylvio look slow and plodding while dragging his feet, and Sylvio's reaction time was off. He had no answers for Dodson," Dwayne added.

"Well, in other boxing news, defending middleweight champion Jun Zhang completed his first title defense by knocking out Frenchman Albert Finney in the second round. Now you would think that he wants to fight someone who's in his league, but take a listen to this," Newt said, playing the highlight clips from the evening of the fight.

A reporter was interviewing Jun ringside after the fight and said, "Now that you've completed title defense, what is next for you?"

"I don't feel like a champion until I get into the ring with Sylvio Dominque. We've spoken to his handlers, and at this point, it looks like he's running away from the challenge."

"Hard words from the champion right now, and it looks like he's waiting for Sylvio to reply, maybe take the challenge on. Dominique, we'll wait for your response," the sportscaster replied.

After a while, Sylvio heard knocking at his door. Checking to see who visited, a smile crossed Sylvio's face. "What's up, kid?" he said as Jamal Samuels entered the house and dapped his friend.

After a stint in the NBA's development leagues, Jamal had played overseas for over four different countries. But he never stopped trying to crack into the NBA. "Chillin', man. What's good?"

Sylvio and Jamal headed to the living room area. "You want something to drink?" Sylvio offered.

"Nah, I'm good, son. Just had a protein shake back at my crib."

The young men sat on the couch where the sportscasters continued talking about Sylvio.

"Man, don't even listen to them, B. You know how the media is," Jamal said.

"Actually, I need to listen to them. I need some motivation right now cuz I don't even know where I stand. Maybe I shouldn't have came back to the ring."

"C'mon, man, you can't let one loss determine your destiny."

"And what is my destiny, exactly?"

"To get the title back, no matter who you gotta go through. I'm sure Valentina would say the same thing. By the way, what's goin' on wit' her lately?" he asked.

Sylvio cast his eyes downward.

"I don't know, man. Val broke up wit' me months ago."

"Word? What happened? I thought ya'll were gonna be the new sports power couple or something."

"Well, turns out she never wanted me to come back to the ring, and I didn't help my cause when she found out that I was messin' around wit' this chick from SDCC. Of course, she also found another dude—that soft-ass co-star of hers on the show."

Jamal shook his head. After his brief relationship with Valentina, nothing about her surprised him anymore.

"Guess all girls can't be like Tracy. How she doing though?" Sylvio asked.

"She's good, man. She's just workin' these crazy hours, and we barely have enough time to do our thing. But yo', I heard about what yo' trainer did to yo' boy out in Briarwood. What's up wit' him, man?"

"Nah, man, Jim was just being Jim. He made a mistake, and he's getting help. He'll be okay."

"But are you gon' be okay though?" Jamal asked.

Sylvio shrugged, raising an eyebrow. "Yeah, I'm good."

"Cool...are you gon' be busy Sunday morning?"

"Yeah, I normally train at SDCC for three hours on Sunday morning. Why?"

Jamal smiled at Sylvio, and suddenly the boxer was starting to feel uneasy. "You said you need some motivation, right? Meet me outside this address at 10:30 in the morning. Dress like you goin' on a promo tour," he said, texting Sylvio the address as he walked out the door.

Chapter 19

On Sunday morning, Sylvio, guided by his phone navigation system drove to the address that Jamal gave him, but he would soon be in for a surprise. He expected to meet Jamal at a restaurant or an ad agency for promotion purposes, but instead, he was looking at a two-story building with a small steeple at the top. Just below the steeple read the words ROCK OF JACOB BAPTIST CHURCH.

Just ahead of him, Sylvio noticed an officer across the street directing traffic for those who were attending the church and those who were driving in the other lane. Following the cars into the designated parking area, Sylvio parked and made sure to put his sunglasses and fedora hat on, which matched the black suit and turtleneck that he wore with a small gold cuff link chain.

A few feet away, Sylvio saw Jamal and Tracy waving at the other churchgoers as they entered the building. Doing his best to remain incognito so he would not be immediately recognized, Sylvio walked over to Jamal.

"Yo', what's up, man?" Jamal greeted him cheerfully.

But Sylvio was anything but cheerful. If there was any place that he considered going apart from the gym, church was not that place. "Jamal, what is this, dawg? You said dress for a promo, and you got me out at a church?" he asked. "Hey, Tracy," he added quickly so that she didn't think she was being ignored.

"C'mon, man, it ain't that big a deal. Look, you said you needed some motivation, and what better place to find that motivation than in the Lord's house?" Jamal asked.

Sylvio did not agree with his friend. He was not trying to draw attention to himself, and if there was one aspect of the church that he disliked, which may have led to him not being intrigued by the prospect of attending, it was that church folks were extremely judgmental and hypocritical.

Sylvio remembered Jacques went to church with him a few times, and it didn't impact Sylvio one bit. All he remembered about church was that the pastor or whoever was directing the service talked Sylvio to sleep and would raise his voice whenever he mentioned the words "repentance" or "sin" as if he was talking down to his audience. Sylvio hated being talked down to size. He hated when his father did it, so it was no different than a fake bishop in his expensive, tailor-made suit telling others how to live when he had skeletons in his own closet.

"Nah, Jamal, I can't do this. I'm out," he said.

But before turning around, Tracy grabbed his hand. "Please, Sylvio, don't leave. You can sit by us today. Give us at least an hour. If you don't like what you see or hear, then you can walk out. Jamal and I won't say nothin'. Is that cool?" she asked, pleading.

Sylvio sighed. "Okay, fine. One hour. But if I lose interest, I'm out. You got that?" he asked.

"No problem," Tracy said gleefully.

As she walked in, Sylvio whispered to Jamal, "Yo', it's hard to say no when she look at a brotha like that."

"Oh, I know this. How do you think she hooked me?" Jamal replied.

When they entered the church, Sylvio realized that he recognized many of the members as most of them had been in attendance during Omar's homegoing service six years prior.

Pastor Mike Hillman was seated at the first pew in the front row along with his wife, Robyn. His daughter, Shania McClain, was seated behind them with her husband, Trevor, and their little daughter, Loree. Sylvio remembered when Pastor Mike visited him in his hospital bed after he got shot and provided words of encouragement to him, a stranger, that he wouldn't have known if it hadn't been for Jamal.

Sylvio was a freshman in high school when Pastor Mike's ministry had come under scrutiny when he was found in bed with another member of his church. A few days later, Omar revealed that the woman who was shacked up with the reverend was none other than Jamal's mother, Isis Samuels.

For all the talk about living right and staying away from sin, Pastor Mike fit the exact description of a heretical pastor who couldn't practice what he preached, and it all but shook Sylvio's trust in the modern-day church. But it seemed as though Jamal bore no hard feelings towards Pastor Mike. It always amazed Sylvio how Jamal still attended the church after all the drama. Sylvio wasn't sure if he could have been as forgiving as his friend.

Respecting Sylvio's wishes, Tracy and Jamal sat near the back of the church, and although he tried to stay anonymous, two small boys recognized the boxer.

"Yo', ain't that Sylvio Dominique?"

"I can't believe he's hea'!"

Great, the service ain't even started yet, and I'm ready to get up outta here. Sylvio kept his sunglasses on and lowered the fedora over his eyes as the service began.

A choir came up with a worship team and started singing "Joyful, Joyful, Lord We Adore Thee" to an upbeat rhythm from the musical department as the church rose to its feet and clapped to the music.

Then a lead singer, whom Sylvio was familiar with, approached the microphone and started singing the solo stanzas of the song. Andrea McAfee, best known as Adia, raised her voice several octaves above the other choir members. Adia had burst upon the scene as a secular artist with the controversial record label Metro, but she had rebranded and transformed into a gospel artist that was able to hit the highest of notes.

For the first time, Sylvio found himself enjoying the choir's song selections as well as the positive energy that everybody exuded. It was not the dull, boring church he remembered growing up.

After the choir's number, Pastor Mike went to the pulpit to make announcements on the church's upcoming events. "And now the time comes when we will introduce all of our visitors to stand up so our family at the Rock of Jacob Baptist Church can acknowledge their presence," the pastor said with a booming voice.

Sylvio's stomach churned. There was no way he was standing up. He attempted to turn his head sideways as if to acknowledge other visitors when Jamal lightly tapped him on the side.

"Stand up, man," he whispered.

"Shut up," Sylvio whispered, but it was too late.

Pastor Mike made eye contact with Sylvio and immediately recognized him. "Amen, praise the Lord! It looks like we got a famous athlete in our midst this morning. Church, why don't we give a loud standing ovation and a hearty welcome to our guest, middleweight boxing champion Sylvio Dominique!"

The church members turned their heads back to get a good look at the boxer.

Thanks a lot. Sylvio glared at Jamal for a second, but out of respect, he stood up and waved as the church members clapped their hands, some even chanting, "Wolf! Wolf! Wolf!"

After the cheers subsided, Pastor Mike said, "We welcome brother Dominique and all of our visitors this morning to the Rock of Jacob Baptist Church. When our offering plate goes around, there will be a visitor's card for all our returning guests and first-time guests to fill out. We would like to fellowship with you, pray with you, eat with you, and just enjoy the company we have in the Lord. If you cannot make it to church on Sundays, our services are being streamed live, and we have Bible Study every Wednesday night at 7:30 p.m."

The choir got back up in front of the congregation as Adia led them into another lively musical selection. Then Pastor Mike approached the pulpit again. "Praise the Lord, let's hear it for the Sounds of Praise led by our own Andrea McAfee!"

The congregation clapped their hands, showing support for the choir. "And now, brothers and sisters, we have come to the portion of our service where we will get into the Word and see what God has to say to us this morning."

Here we go. Here comes the overzealous, ecstatic preacher hype that I be seein' on TV. I need to get up and leave now. But after reflecting over his options, Sylvio decided to stay to listen to the message.

"This morning, beloved, the title of our message is 'What makes God the source of our strength?' Today we'll take our message from the book of Judges, where we will analyze the story of Samson," Pastor Mike bellowed in his deep voice.

As a former football player, Pastor Mike's presence loomed

larger than life with his immense stature, but to his congregation, he was a shepherd and an overbearing father.

No wonder why the ladies flocked to this guy. He'll make any woman leave their man. Sylvio thought wildly for a second, but he quickly re-adjusted his focus to heed the message.

"Judges chapter 13 introduced us to the birth of one of the strongest men on earth. Samson was gifted by the Spirit of the Lord with superhuman strength. We're talking about a brother who killed a lion with his bare hands."

Yeah, right. Killed a lion with his bare hands? Get outta here! Sylvio rolled his eyes. He couldn't take anyone who valued the words of a book written millions of years ago too seriously. The Bible had some life quotes, but the Quran and the Torah had the same life quotes or verses, and Sylvio failed to see the difference in those books.

"We're talking about a man who killed a thousand Philistine men with the jawbone of a donkey," Pastor Mike continued.

C'mon, son, a thousand men with an animal jawbone? That's virtually a whole army of dudes versus one man, and you expect me to believe that he took that many of 'em out by himself? Sylvio looked around and noticed how everyone was listening intently.

"We're talking about a man who lifted city gates on his shoulders. He was the strongest man in the world. But the source of his strength came from the Lord. What led to the downfall of this strong man?"

"Preach, pastor!" a woman shouted from the front pews.

"It was the combination of Delilah's temptation and his inability to rely on God rather than his own desires. Today, we are in the same crossroads as Samson, and although we do not share his superhuman strength, the Lord has given us strength in other areas. We are all gifted in different ways, but how many of us are grateful for that gift? How many of us thank God for what he has blessed us with?"

"AMEN!" the congregation responded.

"One day, we are on top of the world, invincible as Samson was. We defied the odds at work, at school, and at home. We've defied the odds through history. When people said we couldn't do it, God said that you can do it!"

"AMEN!"

"The enemy has to work twice as hard to bring you down because you are God's chosen people. You have been sanctified by the blood of the Lamb, and as the letter of first Peter says in the Word, we are a peculiar people. We have been driven out of darkness into His marvelous light. But many of us are still in darkness, and what do I mean by that? Samson had all the strength in the world, but the moment he relaxed, the enemy in the form of a woman and in the form of his own pride took him down. Samson lost his strength, his sight, and his freedom. The Philistines forced him to work in a millhouse. But here's my favorite part: God did not forsake Samson!"

The congregation clapped exuberantly as Pastor Mike's message reverberated around the church. Sylvio found himself reflecting on his early boxing career and how it paralleled the life of Samson. He was once a young flamboyant fighter who had everything, and at the same time, he lost everything. But although he complained, God allowed him to live another day.

"Samson's hair began to grow back, and we see when Samson had a final reckoning with the Philistines, God's strength came back into Samson, and he destroyed the enemies' city as a final act in his life. Brothers and sisters, I tell you, whenever you feel down and out, remember this: God has not forgotten you. When you get knocked down, get back up, and dust yourself off, and keep going because your journey's not over! Your fight with life ain't over! Your battle with addiction ain't over! Your battle with sickness ain't over! With God, we always have another fight left in us," Pastor Mike said with a quick glance over to Sylvio as the congregation clapped loudly.

After the service ended, Jamal smiled at Sylvio. "See, that wasn't so painful now, was it?" he asked jovially.

"Eh, it wasn't too bad. Great service," Sylvio agreed.

"So, are you down to come back next Sunday?" Tracy piped in, hopeful.

"I'll definitely think about it. If my scheduled ain't too hectic, I'll be back," Sylvio replied.

As they started to make their way to the church doors, Sylvio suddenly realized it was going to be a challenge leaving the sanctuary because kids and adults all over were flocking to him to pose for pictures with him and to ask him for autographs. If he didn't know any better, they might not have ever known that he lost his last bout. In their eyes, he was still a boxing champion, and on that Sunday, Sylvio received more genuine love than he had during the past two weeks.

Pastor Mike Hillman, who continued his tradition of standing by the door to greet all his church members, shook Jamal's hands heartily. "Great to see you here as always, Jamal. I know that I'll see you on an NBA roster this season."

Jamal laughed. "One can only hope, Pastor. I'mma keep workin' and keep prayin' for that opportunity though."

"Amen. I'll keep you in prayer. Send the family my best for me. Tracy, God bless you, sister. Thank you for coming!" Pastor Mike shook Tracy's hands. "Listen, if Jamal start actin' out, you let me know, and we'll set him straight," he added in a whisper, laughing.

"Aww come on, Pastor Mike. You gotta put me on blast in front of my girl?" Jamal asked, laughing.

"Hey, I'm just kidding around, young man. Keep taking care of her now, ya hear?"

"Don't worry, Pastor. Jamal is behaving, for now. Besides, he don't know about them stories you tell me about him from when he was little," Tracy replied.

"Wait, hold up. What stories?" Jamal asked, raising an eyebrow as Tracy led him out of the church.

Sylvio, who had been following Tracy and Jamal out the door, was next to shake the pastor's hand.

"My brother, Sylvio. Thank you for coming today. Your presence was a blessing to us, and I hope you can visit us again in the future."

"Thank you, Reverend. I needed to hear that sermon today. It spoke to me in a lot of ways."

"Amen, that's what the Word of God is there for, brother," Pastor Mike said, before suddenly reaching back behind the church doors. He then gifted Sylvio with a new Bible. "I don't like my first-time guests to leave empty-handed. This is a New International Version Bible with study references. Whenever you need to hear from Him, He's always there to speak to you."

Sylvio was taken aback. No church that he had visited in the past had ever given him or his father a Bible, let alone paid attention to him. Sylvio realized that Pastor Mike didn't play the typical, money-hungry, grubbing bishop that he saw portrayed on TV or from his early experiences. He genuinely cared for people.

"Thank you, Pastor." Sylvio was hesitant about being

transparent with Pastor Mike because he was unsure how he would be perceived. "You know, I'mma be real honest with you. I didn't plan on comin' here today, and I didn't really care much for church because so many times in my life, I felt that God never even cared about me. But I remembered you visited me in the hospital after I was shot six years ago, and I guess I owed you a visit."

"Son, I didn't visit you that day to expect anything in return. You know, when Jesus walked on this earth, He never set out to cater to a specific group of people. Jesus was about everybody, and he visited the sick, prayed with people, and he even broke bread at the same table with sinners. All I try to do is live out that example each day. If I could show the love of Christ to those who need it, I have served a purpose," Pastor Mike explained.

Sylvio looked at the Bible. It was big and bulky, and he wasn't a fan of reading. "I don't even know where to start," he said.

"I would start at the Gospel of John in the New Testament, chapter 1 verses 1 through 4. Read that small passage. It may be a bit confusing at first, but in time, it will make sense."

"Thanks, Pastor."

"By the way, can we count on a rematch versus Dodson?" Pastor Mike asked.

Sylvio wasn't sure if he was going to fight again. But not wanting to bring about uncertainty to a fan base that still believed in him, he replied, "Yeah, there'll be a rematch!" he replied confidently.

The remaining members of the congregation cheered loudly for the Wolf as he walked back to his car.

"Wait, you want a rematch with Jermaine Dodson already?" Kevin asked as Sylvio called him later that day.

"Yeah, I want another shot at him. Get Shareef and his manager on the phone, and set it up. I'll fight Jermaine anywhere, anytime. There's a middleweight championship belt wit' my name on it," he said.

"Sylvio, in case you forgot, Jun Zhang is still the undisputed champion of the world right now. You still gotta get through him to get a win that belt."

"So be it then. From now on, no distractions, no flash, no games. It's all business. Meet me at SDCC tomorrow morning with yo' brother, and if he still down, get Tom in too." Sylvio heard Kevin sigh on the phone, and he clearly knew that his manager wasn't too keen on his fighter rushing back into the ring in mere weeks after his defeat.

"Okay, I'll get everyone posted. Get some sleep tonight, champ. We'll get to work tomorrow." After hanging up, Sylvio went to his room and opened the box holding his new Bible. Turning the pages over to the book and chapter mentioned by Pastor Mike, he read carefully, but the passage didn't make sense to him.

The Word was with God, and the Word was God? I don't get it. Making a mental note to ask Pastor Mike about it on his next church visit, Sylvio resumed skimming through the Bible, until he heard what sounded like a key turning into a lock.

Yolanda walked through the door, carrying two bags of groceries. At first, it was not in Sylvio's plans to move anyone in with him. Valentina certainly never moved in with him throughout their relationship although she had frequently visited and slept at his home more than a few times. But throughout the early stages of his new relationship with Yolanda, he trusted her enough to allow her to move into his house.

Yolanda, who had been living in an apartment in Elmhurst, New York, was all too grateful for the chance to move out of it, saving herself the pain of paying the exorbitant monthly rent. And their relationship grew stronger, even with the subtle changes in their lives. Since Sylvio left SDCC, Yolanda had to extend her duties beyond the drama department to head the educational department, so she normally worked longer hours than normal, which tested her stamina.

"Hey, baby, what's up? I brought some dinner for us. I went to that new vegan restaurant on 153rd and Archer."

Here we go wit' the vegan meals.

Since she'd moved in, Yolanda had been on a vegan diet and had convinced Sylvio to embark on the same nutritional journey. But for Sylvio, parting with meat was sweet sorrow, and after a week of forced vegan meals, he was starting to have withdrawals. Yolanda insisted that the strict vegan diet would keep him in better physical shape for his fights, so although the food lacked taste to Sylvio, it did keep his energy up.

"Where you at, baby?" she asked.

"I'm in the room," Sylvio replied.

Two minutes later, Yolanda walked into the room and kissed Sylvio on the cheek while caressing him from behind. "What's that you're reading there?" she asked.

"The Bible."

Yolanda raised an eyebrow as though she didn't believe his response, and her tone confirmed her skepticism. "Really?"

"Yeah, I'm just goin' through it right now. What's the big deal?"

he asked.

"Nothin'. It's just that you don't strike me as the pseudo-spiritual type," Yolanda replied.

"I'm not, but one of my boys invited me to his church this morning, and I went and after the sermon, Pastor Mike gave me this Bible as gift."

Yolanda's eyes widened. "You went to church today? How come I ain't know about all this?" she asked suspiciously.

"Look, baby, you were at work today, and Jamal wanted me to visit after my morning workout, so I visited."

"And did you say that Pastor Mike gave you that Bible? Ain't that the same pastor that was exposed for doggin' his wife some time ago?" Yolanda asked.

"That was a long time ago, Yolanda. So, he did something stupid a while back. He still human like everybody else," Sylvio replied.

"So, what you about to tell me now? You a lil' Bible-thumping, Christian church boy now?" Yolanda teased.

"Nah, I ain't said all that now, but Pastor preached a message earlier today, and it just got me thinkin', you know, about my life, my career, and all the stuff I went through."

Yolanda took the Bible out of Sylvio's hands. Placing it on his lampstand, she began to unbutton her blouse. "Okay...baby, I've had a long day today, so do you wanna know what I'm thinkin' right now?" she asked, kissing his lips and neck while rubbing his manhood through his warm-ups.

Smiling, he said, "I mean, it don't take no rocket scientist to know what you thinkin'. But a brother hungry as hell right now, so let's eat that tasteless concoction you call food, then just chill and watch a movie or something."

"Don't be dissin' my food now," Yolanda playfully warned as she went back to the kitchen.

"I mean, hopefully, you got something that I can actually taste this time," Sylvio joked.

"Whatever! " she yelled at him.

Laying back in bed, Sylvio had already predicted what was about to happen. It was going to be another night of tasteless tofu, followed by a movie, then sex. Every night followed a pattern, and although the intimate moments were frequent and pleasurable, it was redundant. It also forced Sylvio to ask himself a question that had been slowly eating away at him. *Would Yolanda still love him if he wasn't a high-paid boxer?*

Chapter 20

To prepare Sylvio for his upcoming rematch against Jermaine Dodson, Jim took his protégé to a remote cabin in the Catskill Mountains in upstate New York. Accompanied by Kevin, Tom, Harry, and a newly hired security officer by the name of Casey Gibson, Sylvio walked into the cabin, carrying two duffel bags.

Jim advised him that they would be staying there for the next three weeks, and to get the maximum effort out of Sylvio, they needed to separate themselves from distraction. No girlfriend, no electronics, and no form of entertainment. With two bedrooms and a kitchen, the cabin was quite small, dirty, and dilapidated with no modern conveniences, and that included heat. The exception was that it had running water.

Tom, Casey, and Kevin took one bedroom while Jim, Sylvio, and Harry took the second one. There were no actual beds in the bedrooms, so the crew brought sleeping bags with an extra layer of blankets. In the cold October weather, the Catskills would regularly dip to twenty degrees, and Harry and Jim would go out and gather wood to put in the fireplace. It was all primitive to Sylvio, but he went with the program.

The crew had stocked up on food and protein supplements for Sylvio, who dedicated himself to a juice fast while undergoing intense training.

Gathered around the fire on the first night in the cabin, Sylvio sat next to Jim and put his hands close to the fire to warm them up. "So, tell me, Jim. Why the Catskills?"

Jim looked at the fire with a reflective expression. "In order to prepare me for my toughest fights, Flip would bring me here, just to get away from things and keep me focused. This place was my sanctuary in so many ways. A lot of blood, sweat, and tears were shed in this place, and I remember thinking at first like, 'We gotta train in this ole' country outhouse? I'm a city kid, you know.' I didn't understand it at first, but later, I finally understood what he was doing. He was making me stronger, both physically and mentally."

Sylvio stared at the flames dancing in front of his eyes. "It's a good idea, Jim. I wish I took Barry to this spot when I had the chance," Tom admitted.

A few days earlier, Tom had reconciled with Sylvio at SDCC, apologizing for abandoning him after his loss. Sylvio forgave him, and Tom was integrated into the team with Jim and Kevin.

"Well, that's why we're hea', Tom," Jim said. "If we're gonna get the Wolf back to prominence, we gon' have to do it this way. Let this be the place where they say Sylvio Dominique made history." He stood up to head back to his room. "Get some sleep, champ. We got work to do in the morning."

And work they did. For the next two weeks, Jim ran Sylvio through a physical gauntlet that tested his endurance, strength, and will. When he woke up in the morning, Sylvio started the day by cutting wood for the fire. He had never handled an axe before, and the first few swings were awkward, but he gradually began to gain his beat. After cutting wood, he would go on a two-hour sprint in the chartered hike path around the Catskill Mountain range where he interacted with other hikers and joggers. But he kept his eyes on the goal.

Jermaine Dodson. Gotta get him. He's mine. Ain't no way I'm letting him out of the ring with a win again.

After the run, the training team went to a local boxing gym, where they worked on speed and repetition. Jim went to the locker room for ten minutes and finally emerged with a heavy sandbag. The bag was placed on Sylvio's chest as he worked on sit-ups to tighten his core. He then did pull-ups on a weight bar while holding a 50-pound barbell between his legs. Then using the same bar, he hung upside down while doing more sit-ups.

On the first day, Sylvio could barely complete ten repeated lunges, but as the weeks wore on, he continued to increase his reps. As the days progressed, Sylvio began transforming. Because he had not shaved in weeks, the hair on his head and beard grew out. But the important change was that he'd shed the soft fat and was becoming lean while his biceps and triceps were becoming more prominent.

Jim's goal was to strengthen and lean Sylvio out, in order to not only defeat but to also obliterate his opponent. Every sparring partner that was brought into the gym to spar with Sylvio, did so at their own risk. And before long, those partners had to wear chest protectors because Sylvio had started cracking ribs.

During training, Sylvio didn't check his cell phone, and he did not call home at all while at the cabin. He didn't want to take the chance of him being tempted to check for social media notifications or the sports media gossip. None of it mattered to him. As far as he was concerned, it was all empty talk, and whatever he did hear was used to further fuel him. Besides, he already knew what the talking heads were saying about him.

Sylvio Dominique is done. After this defeat, there's no way he'll come back. He's history. He should've stayed out of the sport that he quit. He ain't nothin' but a quitter anyway. He quit on the Dodson fight, just like he quit on Barry when it came for defense of his title. He ain't ready.

But Sylvio had just one thought in his mind. I'll show 'em. I'll show 'em all. The Wolf is getting' ready to howl soon, and whoever's in his way is gettin' ripped up. Period.

Without television or any form of entertainment, Sylvio took the Bible that Pastor Mike gave him, and while the other trainers slept, he took out a flashlight and began skimming for key verses.

Upon skimming, he fell upon the Book of Isaiah, chapter 41, verse 10. It read, "Don't be afraid, for I am with you. Do not be dismayed, for I am your God. I will strengthen you. I will help you. I will uphold you with my victorious right hand."

As he turned off his flashlight to rest his sore bones, Sylvio reflected upon the words. *I will strengthen you. I will help you.*

November 1st, 2018. It was fight night. Fans made their way to the Barclays Center in Brooklyn to watch the rematch between Sylvio Dominique and Jermaine Dodson. The Vegas oddsmakers, who had picked Sylvio to win the previous bout, now placed their bets on Dodson to repeat his performance Little did they know that Sylvio was not the same fighter that he was a month earlier.

While all the fans and media were out in the arena, inside the locker room, Sylvio had his headphones on, while working himself into a mental zone. In previous fights, the moments leading up to the fights were nerve-racking for Sylvio, who literally got sick before going to the ring, but this time, he was completely settled and calm. After returning from the Catskills Mountains, he had shaved away the excess hair, but he did keep some of his beard, which astounded the spectators when both boxers were weighed in earlier in the evening. They also marveled at Sylvio's chiseled physique, the by-product of a strict regimen and a stronger force of will to refuse anything detrimental to his body. Sylvio had it in his mind that he would not address the press at all and would only retreat to his locker room before the fight.

As the time approached, Jim faced Sylvio, Kevin, Harry, Tom, Jamal, Gary, and A.D. All the men wore Sylvio "Wolf" Dominique T-shirts in support of their fighter.

"Aight, fellas, this is it. The road to redemption starts here. All of you that are in this room right now are a member of the new Wolf Pack. Not only is it our duty to protect, encourage, and hype Sylvio for the general press, but it's on us to kill the noise out there and dispel any false slander or libel that is said about our young brotha'. We're not just a crew. We're a team. Each of us had to overcome something to get to this point, and now that we're back in the ring, let's make it count. Everybody out there talkin' shit about our boy, saying that he's done and ain't no way he's gonna get back to the show. Well tonight's the night to show 'em up. Tonight's the night we prove all the talking heads wrong. Let's strike fear in our opponents each time we walk up there as a unit."

With those words firm in mind, Sylvio's team headed out the locker room and walked the corridor to enter the ring.

"Yo', check this intro track that I mixed," A.D. said to Sylvio and sure enough, on the way to the ring, an aggressive rap number played, and the people cheered loudly. A.D. had even dubbed the end of the track to record a howling wolf, and as the wolf howled, the crowd howled in response.

It was the perfect introduction as Sylvio stepped into the ring and jumped around to warm himself up. Right away, he saw the look on Dodson's face and knew that he didn't expect such a grand entrance from his opponent, and he could see his corner handlers trying to talk to him to psych him back for the fight.

Too late. You shook now. You just realized you in the wrong place, chump.

After both fighters retreated to their corners, the bell rang. As they approached the center of the ring, from the onset, it was clear that Dodson was attempting to end the fight as early as possible, throwing head shot after head shot, but Sylvio's head and shoulders were bobbing and weaving with more efficiency and purpose, causing Dodson to miss his shots.

"C'mon, man. Stop throwin' them heavy shots early! You gonna wear yourself out!" one of Dodson's cornermen warned, but his fighter remained determined to knock out the seemingly slower Sylvio.

But Sylvio eluded the blows, and with his improved quickness and stamina, he quickly went on the offensive, throwing a double jab and an overhead right that caught Dodson by surprise.

Dodson didn't back down and returned with a straight jab that pinpointed the center of Sylvio's face. Such a hit would have affected Sylvio weeks earlier, but the time that he'd spent in the Catskills had strengthened him. Now he continued pushing forward as Dodson found himself on the defensive.

C'mon, Wolf, get this nigga against the ropes. Make him defend himself against you. Push, push.

Before long, Sylvio's flurry of jabs forced Dodson against the ropes as he was on the defensive early and often. The bell rang, ending Round 1, and Sylvio confidently strolled back to his corner. He knew he'd won the first round, which indicated that he had set the tone for the rest of the fight.

Jermaine Dodson thought that his opponent would play passively to his hands and tire himself out because Sylvio's stamina was still presumed to be poor by most of his contemporaries, but Sylvio was nowhere near exhausted, and Dodson, who thought he had another easy fight, was in for a rude awakening.

"Good round, kid!" Jim said. "Keep pressuring him, and go at him. Don't let up an inch. I want that man breathin' heavy after two more rounds. You got it?"

Sylvio nodded, and the mouthpiece was pushed back into his mouth after a swig of water before Round 2.

The fighters held no punches back as they continued to strike one another. Sylvio would continue punishing Dodson with a left jab that kept snapping his head back. But Sylvio soon over-compensated. When he threw another jab, Dodson anticipated and slipped it, responding with a vicious uppercut. By the end of the second round, Dodson's left eye was nearly swollen where Sylvio's jabs had found their mark.

But Sylvio's lip was bleeding, and while Harry rushed to stop the bleeding, Tom came up to Sylvio. "Keep throwing him off balance with them jabs. Don't let up. If he senses that you're tired, he's gonna take advantage like he did during the last fight."

"That's right, Wolf. Keep that jab busy, and when you see an opportunity, drop him," Jim said.

The bell ran for Round 3, and Dodson, visibly frustrated that the fight was not going his way, began on the offensive, throwing a quick combination of hooks and jabs. Sylvio, sensing that Dodson was trying to compensate for his lack of reaction time by launching his own attack, but he was unsuccessful.

Sylvio shrugged off Dodson's blows and continued pressing him, but Dodson's punches did not have the same power that they did in their first fight. Sylvio absorbed all the blows and the body blows without harm and in return, he was dishing out punishing hooks that all but leveled the former champion. Then toward the end of the third round, Dodson made a crucial error.

He went in for the quick left hook and Sylvio anticipated the hook, ducked, and replied with a shovel hook that dropped Dodson to the canvas. As the ref began his count, Dodson knew that he was in serious trouble, and he clung to the ropes for assistance in rising to his feet. He made it to his feet that time, but Sylvio knew that Dodson had no answers for him that night.

Dodson's legs were now rubbery, and although he valiantly got back up on his feet, another quick combination of punches dropped him to the canvas again as Sylvio walked silently back to his corner. The referee began the count.

Dodson rose to his feet. By this time, both of his eyes were nearly swelled shut, and a huge bump had already sprung up on the side of his cheekbone. Yet, he still got back on his feet, but the referee did not allow him to continue, and Sylvio knew, even before the roar of the crowd and before the decision, that he had won the fight.

Sylvio raised his fists in victory as the crowd howled in response knowing that the Wolf had finally returned. As he celebrated his victory, Sylvio looked ringside, up a few rows back. Jamal, A.D., and Gary were celebrating the win, but as Sylvio gazed through the crowd, his eyes met the man who wanted to get him into the ring.

Jun Zhang was seated in the sixth row with his father and his trainer. The moment their eyes met, Jun's eyes said it all to Sylvio. *Impressive, but let's see if you can do that to me. My opponents don't even make it past the third round.*

Sylvio didn't need to speak to the man to know what he thought. Jun's eyes spoke loudly and clearly for him and even spoke of him as the champion who felt that a fight between the tiger and the wolf was imminent. Jun pretended to clap his hands for Sylvio in a show of false bravado, but Sylvio knew it was only a matter of time before they both clashed.

The reporters climbed into the ring to interview Sylvio.

"Impressive win over fourth ranked Jermaine Dodson, Sylvio. You look to be in so much better shape, and you proved it with the upset win tonight. Is it too early to ask if you're fighting for the middleweight title?" one of them asked.

Sylvio chuckled. "Nah, it ain't too early. When the opportunity comes, my trainers and I are gonna jump on it, and I believe that the best man is gonna win."

Two days after Sylvio's victory over Jermaine Dodson, he drove to SDCC for a morning workout. He also wanted Jim, Kevin, Tom, and Shareef to negotiate a deal to fight Jun Zhang for the middleweight crown.

During the last two days at home, the place had been super quiet. Yolanda was away at a resort with her girlfriends after saying she needed a vacation to relax from the long hours. The relationship between her and Sylvio had strained in the days leading up to the fight with Dodson. Truth was, Yolanda had some habits that irked Sylvio, and one of them was the fact that she pouted and whined when she did not get her way. For a woman who was all about staying balanced and centered, she was always triggered whenever Sylvio watched a program on TV or did something that she did not agree with.

Another aspect of Yolanda, which especially bothered Sylvio, was that she flirted with other men, sometimes openly in front of Sylvio. If she felt she wasn't getting the attention she needed from Sylvio, she looked elsewhere for it. When Sylvio prepared for the fight in the Catskills, Yolanda complained about being extremely bored and lamented how Sylvio was never home. Then, when he returned before the fight, she balked at Sylvio's appearance, saying that he looked like a black caveman, in lieu of the beard that he had grown out.

Although he tried his best to keep the relationship going, Sylvio knew that it was only a matter of time before she cheated on him with another guy. Sylvio would be the first to admit that he didn't know everything about women, but what he knew was that if they were always hot and bothered and frequently begged for attention for passion that they lacked, they would fulfill their desires elsewhere. And on top of that, Yolanda was a self-proclaimed nymphomaniac.

In the meantime, she had one of her drama students, Tina Jamison take over as head of drama while Jim resumed the head duties for SDCC. But despite the money that Jim and Sylvio earned from their last few fights and money donated to SDCC, the center was still losing money and owed an abundant amount of tax dollars to the state of New York. They knew they needed one more big fight, one more big payday, to keep the center going.

Therefore, it was only inevitable that Sylvio and Zhang were destined to clash for the title. As soon as he arrived at the center, he walked straight to Jim's office, but it was locked, and Jim was not in it.

Here we go again. Sylvio knew that if his trainer was not in his office, he was either aimlessly wandering through different schoolyards or visiting his dead son. Then, Sylvio heard his phone vibrate. Taking it out, he read the text message that Jim sent him.

Sylvio, what's up fam? Check it out...I won't be in my office today and no I ain't pickin' no fights with hard-headed wannabes again. I'm back in my old neighborhood of DeKalb Avenue in Brooklyn where it all started for me. I'm visiting some people I grew up with. I should be back by this afternoon. We can either train at SDCC or we can take a trip back to Catskills and train ole' fashioned again. Stay up, brother. Tell Kevin to hold it down for me at the center today.

Sylvio closed the text. While waiting for Kevin, A.D., who had been working out for over thirty minutes walked up to Sylvio.

"What's up, dawg?" A.D. greeted, dapping Sylvio.

"What's good, man?" Sylvio noticed that A.D. seemed more shifty than usual, darting his eyes left to right.

"Yo, you talked to yo' girl lately?" he asked.

"Nah, man, she out of town with her girlfriends. They went on some type of spa resort, you know, getting' a tan or massage and swimming in hot tubs, that kind of stuff."

"You sho' 'bout that?"

A.D. pulled out his phone and began flipping through the pictures on his phone before pausing on a recently snapped photo of Yolanda, clearly oblivious to the fact that she had been discovered by one of Sylvio's inner circle.

"She went swimming alright, but not in no hot tub, you know what I'm sayin'?"

Man, DeKalb Avenue has changed since the last time I was here. Jim walked around his old haunts, where he hadn't visited since his high school years. Many of the old buildings and boarding houses had been torn down and were replaced by Jewish, Italian, or Hispanic businesses. Only a few brownstones remained from the 1980s. Jim remembered the street where he bumped into Natalie for the first time on the way to the ice cream truck. He also remembered Fort Greene Park, where he beat Grant Butler and was arrested before his life changed.

Looking at his phone at the address that was sent to him after parking his car and walking for four blocks, Jim finally arrived at his destination. He anxiously knocked on the door, not knowing what to expect. The door suddenly opened, and two middle-aged men stood in the doorway.

One of the men was short in stature and completely bald with a gray mustache and goatee, and the other man was tall and well-built. It was no mystery that he was an athlete. Both Tavion and Alan hugged their old friend, whom they had not seen in more than thirty years.

"Welcome back to DeKalb, Boom! It's about damn time!" Tavion exclaimed.

"Tell me about it, Tay. Let a man loose for a couple years, and he don't say nothin' for thirty-two years? C'mon, man, you know how we do," Alan said. He lived a block away from Tavion with his wife and three children.

Previously locked up for drug possession, Tavion had spent six years behind bars, but upon his release, he married and had a daughter named Eugenia. But after Eugenia left to go to college,

Tavion's wife succumbed to breast cancer. It was a painful time for the former drug-dealer, who shared the same pain of losing a family member that Jim suffered from for many years.

Alan, on the other hand, enjoyed early success after high school, playing football for four years at the University of Pittsburgh before being drafted by the Pittsburgh Steelers. He played with them for eight years before retiring at the age of thirty.

"Yo', gimme a minute real quick," Tavion said, before walking in the master bedroom.

Alan and Jim stared curiously at each other. A couple of minutes later, their friend re-emerged, holding a deck of cards. Jim smiled. The three men hadn't played baccarat in twenty years.

"Who ready to lose their money today?" Tavion joked as he started separating the deck of cards.

Before long, three wads of cash and three beer cans were on the table, and the men were laughing and joking as the card game was underway.

"Damn, negro, you still suck at this game. Gimme all dat," Tavion said to Alan, grabbing seventy extra dollars off the table.

"You still talk shit after all them years, man," Alan replied, as they prepared to play another game.

"Man, after everything I been through, I still got a right to talk my shit. You know I ain't changin' for nobody. So, what's up wit' you, Boom? Word on the street is that you and Natalie gettin' real comfortable these days."

"Well, I don't know what you mean by 'real comfortable,' but we starting to patch it up a lil' bit. She's helpin' me get my head straight, man. I never realized how messed up I was after Dante passed."

"So, you mean to tell me that you ain't there to try to get yo' woman back?" Alan asked.

"Look, man, ain't nobody thinkin' about that. I still gotta train Sylvio for the title bout against Zhang. Once we win, then we can chill and do our thing."

Tavion and Alan stared at each other, and right away, Jim recognized their expressions. *They don't believe Sylvio can beat him.*

"Man, you sure you wanna do that to yo' boy? I mean, he good and all, but that Chinese cat ain't no joke, man. He doesn't just beat fighters. He destroys 'em. You really wanna put Sylvio's life on the line for a few more bucks?" Tavion asked.

"C'mon, dawg, haven't we been down this block before? This is the middleweight title that we're talkin' about here. Sylvio's worked too hard to pass this chance up," Jim replied.

"You know what I think? This ain't about Sylvio going for a title shot. You want a shot at something that you ain't never had in yo' own career," Tavion countered.

"No, Sylvio and I are a team. You think I forced him to come back out of retirement to try to get something that he was robbed of six years ago? He made that decision himself, and yeah, I was against it at first, but you know what? I see a fire in that boy's eyes, and he's more driven now than he was before. He's hungry, and he knows he can win it. He ain't the same fighter distracted by the lights of the big time. He ain't goin' for the okey-doke no more. He may be two years from thirty, but he's already a vet in this game," Jim said firmly as they continued playing cards.

A few days later, Yolanda returned from her vacation as the Uber driver dropped her off in front of Sylvio's house. Sylvio's car wasn't parked in the front of the house, so she knew he was training at the gym. As she approached the door, she saw an envelope with her name written by a Sharpie marker stuck between the screen door. Planning to read the letter when she entered the house, she attempted to unlock the door, but to her astonishment, her key wasn't allowing her to do so.

What's going on? She turned the key in the opposite direction, but to no avail. Exasperated that she was locked out of her house, she knew she had no choice but to wait for Sylvio to return from training. With time to kill, she opened the envelope. Inside was a letter with 5x7 developed photographs. Immediately, she recognized Sylvio's handwriting as she began to read.

Hey Yolanda what's good? You know what? You ain't gotta answer that question because apparently, you're doing great. I hope you enjoyed your vacation. You know when we first met I was feelin' you and I thought we vibed together. I went so far as to cheat on my girlfriend to get wit' you because I was a fool and I let my guard down. I don't know what it was...maybe it was how good the sex was or maybe it was the fact that I could be myself with you. I always felt that you was only getting wit' me because it improved your social status. But I never knew how toxic you were and I closed my eyes to all of it because I was focusing on getting my career back on track. I'm sure the two other guys you were kissing in these photos have no clue that they're being played by the same woman, and you know what? I ain't gonna be one of your boy toys. I don't play that and I can't have you be a distraction while I'm training for the title shot. So I've changed the locks on my door but not before moving all your stuff back into your old apartment. I talked to the landlord and she has allowed you to move back in. Plus I paid two months rent in advance for you. Some thought I was being too nice in doing that but I wanna make this a clean break. In case I haven't been clear enough in this letter, our relationship is over and I hope you have a good life.

Stunned, Yolanda took the 5x7 photos and held her hands over her mouth, as she tried to stifle the tears from seeing the pictures of her kissing her ex-boyfriend and a college fling that she hooked up with during the previous week.

Chapter 21

August 2021 | Sixteen-year-old Kenny Wong rushed back to his seat after a brief bathroom break. He made sure to be extremely urgent so that he wouldn't miss any of the action. Making his way back to the nosebleed seats in Staples Center, he was soon joined by his friend Jun Zhang. They were watching their favorite boxer, a cocky brash upstart by the name of Sylvio Dominique, who was climbing the ranks in the middleweight division.

Having followed his career since his amateur days, Jun practically had to beg his father to attend Dominique's fight against the local favorite, Jose "Cesar" Chavez. Chavez had previously defeated Dominique in a close decision in their previous bout, but he was confident that he could once again take out the younger and seemingly inexperienced Dominique. But the Wolf was on a mission to not only avenge his loss but to also earn the respect that he felt he lacked.

Jun himself had started boxing and martial arts training, and he idolized various fighters in both America and China, but none had the unique backstory that Sylvio had. Born to Haitian immigrants in lower income housing, Sylvio worked his way to become a rising contender in middleweight boxing and was primed to fight for the title against the man that everyone felt was invincible: Felipe

Maximo.

To Jun's delight and the distress of the crowd, Dominique defeated Chavez in five rounds. And in victory, Dominique had issued a public challenge to Felipe Maximo, the reigning middleweight champion.

As Sylvio confidently walked back to the locker room with the rest of the Wolf Pack, Jun whispered to Kenny. "C'mon, let's go!"

"Wait, where are you boys going?" Jun's father asked.

"I'm gonna try to get the Wolf's autograph. I'll see you at home, Father. You don't have to stay," Jun replied.

The family did not live far from the Staples Center, so returning home was no problem for Jun's dad. Kenny and Jun snuck past arena security and ran over to the visitor's locker room, where they waited for Sylvio's entourage to pass by. Jun knew the corridors and tunnels of the arena, so he was able to get ahead of the media train that was sure to follow the Wolf.

"You got your phone ready?" Jun asked Kenny.

"Yep." Kenny whipped out his I-Phone 4.

Nervously, they waited for the victor to make his way to the locker room. Within three minutes, they saw flashing cameras, and sure enough, there was Sylvio, flanked by his team. They had stopped to answer just three questions from the media members, but Jim Shaw was determined to get his fighter back in the locker room without being bombarded by media members and crazed fans.

Jun knew he only had one shot before security would escort him out. Appearing from the small hallway that faced the locker room, he said, "Hey, Mr. Dominique, great fight tonight! I'm a huge fan. I was wondering if I could get an autograph?" he asked, but not before security stepped in front of him.

"Hey, kid, get lost," one of them said.

But Sylvio patted the guy on the shoulder. "Nah, it's all good, B. Let the kid through. I got him."

The security detail stepped aside, but before Jun could get his coveted autograph, one of the members of the Wolf Pack stepped in his way, barring him again. "Sorry, kid. Yo', check it. He just got off a fight, and you ova' here bothering him for an autograph. What, tryin' to sell it or some shit?"

"Yo', Kyle back off, man. It won't take but a minute to sign it for him. You got a paper, souvenir, or something?" Sylvio asked Jun.

Jun frantically searched his pockets, but he didn't have any surface for Sylvio to sign. "No, but my friend does. Let me get him." Jun beckoned his friend to come out of hiding.

The entourage seemed uninterested and in a rush. "Look, kid, we're out of time, okay? Maybe he'll sign something next time. Let my boy get up in there," Kyle demanded as the rest of the Pack coaxed Sylvio inside the locker room.

"Hey, c'mon, Kyle. Don't do him like that, man," Sylvio said. Turning to Jun, he said, "Aight, kid, just wait out here for me. Give me bout thirty minutes, and when I shower and get changed, I'll sign something. Is that cool?" he asked Jun.

"Yeah, that's cool. I'll be waiting right here," Jun replied as the entourage entered the locker room.

"In the meantime, no fans allowed without a pass, so wait outside the arena," the security officer said.

"But he said to wait out here for him!" Jun protested, but the security guided them outside the arena and denied them re-entry. So Jun waited.

After a few minutes, Kenny found him outside the arena.

"C'mon, Jun, let's go. It's not worth it," he said.

"No, it's cool. I'll catch you tomorrow," Jun replied.

As Kenny left, Jun watched as people continued to file out of the Staples Center while he paced around hoping that his hero would come out to sign the autograph like he'd promised. But minutes gave way to hours, and after three hours, Jun began to realize that Sylvio was not coming out.

Maybe he forgot.

But the more Jun stayed around waiting, the more pointless it became to continue lingering around. He came to terms that Sylvio was never going to meet him or give him the coveted autograph.

He's the Wolf. He could've made everyone stop what they were doing so I could get his autograph, but he didn't. Maybe he's not the person that I thought he was. Maybe he's the arrogant jerk that everyone says he is.

Hanging his head, Jun dejectedly made his way back home, and as he waited for the bus on the busy intersection, one thought burned in his mind. *I'm gonna keep training, and one day I'll be a better fighter and person than Sylvio ever was. I would never be as cocky as him. I hope he gets whupped by Maximo. One day I'm gonna face him, and I'll humiliate him the same way he humiliated me. One day...*

On a cool December night, Sylvio, Jamal, Gary, and A.D. drove to Club Avalon in New Jersey to celebrate Rebecca Dominique's 27th birthday. Sylvio's fight against Jun was scheduled for January 19th in Los Angeles, and while he was training intensely, he still wanted to celebrate his sister's special day. As they entered the club, they saw the birthday girl dancing wildly with her friends.

"Damn, bro, you ain't told me that yo' sista would be on freak mode," A.D. retorted.

"I don't know, man. That ain't how she normally gets down." Sylvio said, shrugging. As they made their way to the bar, Rebecca spotted them.

"Aye, there go my brother, ladies. And, yes, he is single, so don't all rush him at once," she said.

Right away, Sylvio could tell she was inebriated. Unfortunately, her friends didn't listen to her, and they all made a beeline for him. All Jamal, Gary, and A.D. could do was watch as each woman took photos with Sylvio. Out of pure kindness, he obliged.

Sylvio finally made his way over to his sister, who was dancing with a bottle of Cristal in her hand. "Okay, sis, I think you had enough," he chuckled, taking the bottle from her.

"Boy, stop playin'! I love you and all, but if you eva' take my bottle from me, we gon' be fightin'!"

Sylvio laughed. "Yeah, okay, that'll happen. Where your man at?" he asked.

"Oh, Eric's on his way. He's just gettin' off work. He helped set this all up for me," she replied, happy.

"That's what's up. Better hold onto him cuz he the only one insane enough to drop some bands on yo' crazy ass."

"Shut up, boy!" Rebecca snapped. "You better be happy I invited yo' ungrateful, punchy ass. Guess who else I invited?" She turned to look at the club entrance.

Sylvio followed her gaze, and that's when he saw her walking towards him. Although it had been over five months since their breakup, Valentina Cruz still looked as beautiful as ever as she was adorned in a scintillating blue dress with thigh slits, a diamond necklace, and three diamond rings on her finger.

Sylvio smiled. She looks like a glamorous superstar. Man, she really glowed up since we last saw each other.

"Mmm hmm. You're welcome," Rebecca said as she turned back to mingle with the other party guests.

The music seemed to fade, and all the guests disappeared. Somehow, it was now only the two of them. The two former flames stared at each other.

"Hey, Sylvio. It's been a minute," Valentina said.

"No doubt. You look stunning. When did you come back to town?" Sylvio asked.

"I flew back last night. I still had Rebecca's number, and we talk constantly. Even when we were going through our drama, she was a listening ear. She said she was having a birthday party up hea' so I decided to come over. She never told me she invited you though."

"Yeah, well a brotha' been busy for the last few weeks. Got a title fight comin' up again, so I've been training day and night."

"And it definitely shows," Valentina complimented, staring at Sylvio's improved physique. "I love the beard. You look very sophisticated," she added.

"Appreciate it," Sylvio said, and for the few minutes they spoke, it never resonated that they were no longer an item. In his mind, they were still together. "So, how's the Hollywood life?"

"It's going good. A lot has been happening since winning the Best New Series award. A lot of doors have been opening for me."

"Is it true what they said? I read somewhere that you walked away from the show. I mean, it's probably all tabloid and shit, but I wanted to find out from the source."

"Yeah, it's true. Sylvio, I was offered a role in a Vickie Maxwell movie, and I killed the audition. She was even there herself, and she loved me. I'm currently in the middle of filming it right now, so that's why I gotta dip out after tonight to head back to L.A."

"Word? Man, Vickie Maxwell's like your idol. I remember how much you used to talk about being cast in one of her movies one day. I guess today's the day. But since you'll be in L.A. full time, I guess that means you ain't coming back to the center anytime soon?" Sylvio asked.

"I don't think so, Sylvio," Valentina replied. Sensing his disappointment, she said, "Sylvio, this is the break that I've been waiting on for a long time. I grinded through drama school, commercials, and a web show. I have a chance to make Valentina Cruz a household name now."

"I feel you, and I'm proud of you. You grinded yo' ass off for this, no question. But how did Pretty Boy take it?" he asked, laughing.

"Stop it, Sylvio. You know that ain't his name!" Valentina snapped playfully. "Actually, Robert took it pretty hard at first. I think he felt that we were gonna be co-stars on YouStream forever. But I had to follow my dream, and he had his own career to focus on. So, we decided to call it quits. We're still friends though. Why you so concerned about me anyway? Where's yo' boo thang Yolanda at?"

"Yeah, that's over and done wit' too. Turns out Yolanda had other talents with different men, and I decided to cut her loose," he admitted.

"Damn, I'm sorry, Sylvio."

"Eh, it is what it is. I just gotta focus on that title belt now. Hopefully, I can hold onto it for more than twenty-four hours this time," Sylvio laughed.

Suddenly, all the music stopped, and all eyes were facing the front stage of the club. Eric had arrived and called Rebecca on stage. Rebecca, who was still slightly drunk, stumbled onto the stage, and in front of over two hundred guests, Eric got down on one knee and took out a ring that reflected against the lights of the club. Then, he asked Rebecca to marry him.

Her jaw dropped in shock.

"Yes or no, girl?" one of the guests yelled.

"Oh my God, yes!" Rebecca replied, breaking down into tears as she allowed Eric to place the ring on her finger. She hugged her fiancée as the guests clapped.

Sylvio and Valentina joined in, and as they were clapping, Sylvio stared at Valentina, who had begun to mingle with the other guests at the party. Rebecca and Eric's moment of love nearly paralleled what Sylvio envisioned with the girl that he still saw as his angel.

Forty-eight hours before Rebecca's birthday party, Sylvio had been at home watching sitcoms when he heard a knock on his door. It was Eric, who had texted Sylvio moments earlier that day.

"What's up, man? Welcome to my humble abode, B." Sylvio dapped Eric as he stepped inside.

"Yo' spot is hittin', son. Thanks for inviting me over," Eric said.

"Yeah, no doubt. You want something to drink?" Sylvio asked.

"Um, water's cool."

Sylvio walked over to the fridge and tossed Eric a bottle of water, which he caught with amazing dexterity.

"So, what did you wanna talk to me about? How are things wit' my sister?" Sylvio asked.

"Everything's good, man. You know, we both working, but we try to go out and have some fun when we can. It's been the best three years of my life. But I wanted you to be the first one to hear this before I make it official, you know what I mean?"

Sylvio raised an eyebrow. Eric took a deep breath, and it was clear to Sylvio that he was nervous about what to say next.

"Look, Sylvio, I have deep feelings for Rebecca, aight? The way I feel about her, I never felt it with any other woman that I've been wit' in the past."

Sylvio reached into the fridge and took a bottle of water for himself. "Okay, so what are you tryin' to tell me right now?" he asked after taking a swig of water.

"I'm sayin' that she the one, man. I was waiting for the right time to pop the big one, and I figured I would do at her birthday party this Saturday." Eric reached into his pocket and took out a small box.

When he opened it, Sylvio saw that it was a ring with two small diamonds in the center. It took every effort from Sylvio to stifle his laughter because the ring barely had any shine. "Man, look B., if you gon' propose to my lil' sister, you gon' have to do better than this, son."

Eric's face fell in disappointment. "So, you're saying that she ain't gonna like this ring? It was the best that I could do, Sylvio. It set me back about fourteen thousand."

"And it shows, B. Check it, whoever gave you that lil' piece for fourteen thousand straight jacked you. Hold up, stay right here."

Sylvio walked upstairs to his room and opened the vanity drawer that faced his king-sized bed. After groping around for a bit, he found what he was looking for: an eight-karat ring worth over seventy thousand dollars that dwarfed the ring that Eric had.

But the ring bore another significance to Sylvio. He had planned to propose to Valentina before they went their separate ways, and since then, he was unable to return the ring. No one, not even Yolanda, knew about his plans or the ring. Walking back downstairs, Sylvio gave Eric the ring that was intended for Valentina. Eric's eyes widened as he saw the expensive quality of the ring.

"Here. Give her this, Eric. I think my sister would love for you to show the value of your love to her. This jawn's worth over 70K, kid, so don't blow it," he warned.

"Nah, man, I can't do that. That's yo' piece," Eric countered.

He wasn't aware of Sylvio's plans with Valentina, but he didn't want to shoulder the burden of having to pay his future brother-in-law for the ring.

"It's all good, Eric. It's already paid for, and it's never been used. You don't owe me nothin', man. Just promise me you'll treat my sister right."

Reluctantly, Eric took Sylvio's ring. "You sure about this?" he asked.

"No doubt. So please return that sorry excuse for a ring back to the pawn shop where you got it from, and give my sister something she never had."

Eric, still stunned, walked to the front door. "Man, You're a good brother, Sylvio. No matter what they say out there, you good people, man. Your sister's in good hands. Thank you."

With that, Eric left, and Sylvio watched as he made his way across the street to his car.

January 19, 2019 | After weeks of media hype, fight night had finally arrived. Unlike his previous fights, Sylvio did not join

Showtime's promotional tour with Jun Zhang, who had been quiet during his previous fights. He missed no opportunity to smear Sylvio's reputation, using words such as "ignorant," "lazy," "entitled," and "slow" among other descriptions in order to sway the media that his opponent was not ready to regain his place as champion.

Although Sylvio was grateful for the opportunity to fight once more for the middleweight title, he couldn't help but to wonder about Jun's mood. *What does this guy have against me? I don't even know him, and he's throwing my name in the dirt.*

But after some time, Sylvio stopped wondering and planned to give Jun the fight he would never forget. Scores of people filed into the crowded Staples Center in Los Angeles. Normally, the arena was reserved for the Lakers of the National Basketball Association, but they were on an East Coast road trip, which allowed the boxing division to utilize the venue for the middleweight boxing title match.

As Sylvio and the other members of the Wolf Pack made their way to the locker room, they saw Jun sitting outside the visitor's locker room. He already had his robe on with his name emblazoned in the back.

"Remember this place, Wolf? This is where you dissed me seven years ago. I never forgot that. Today, you and your crew's gon' remember my name," Jun said, rising from his spot and walking to his own locker room.

Confused, Sylvio and the others entered their locker room.

"Man, don't even sweat anything that fool says. It's a psych job—that's all. Stay focused on him," Jamal said.

"He's right, Wolf. Don't get drawn into his war of words. He wanted the smoke, and now he got it," Jim added.

Once Sylvio changed into his shorts and new robe, which was all black with the yellow, piercing eyes of a wolf, he looked around the locker room. Harry, Kevin, Jim, Jamal, Gary, A.D., and Tom stared back at him.

"Yo', today, let's not focus on the crowd or the media. We only have one target, and he's the champion right now. You want what he has. He wants to stay on top. They think you're washed, damaged goods...never to win a belt again. Let's make 'em eat their words," Tom said.

The referee appeared to signal that it was time for Sylvio to make his way into the ring. A.D.'s entrance mixtape played over the speakers in the crowded arena as Sylvio headed toward a mixture of boos and cheers. But Sylvio couldn't hear the crowd. He was extremely intense and focused on no one other than Jun Zhang. Sylvio's anxiety was non-existent. Instead, he was focused solely on his opponent.

The lights went dark as Jun's intro music began to play, and the champion made his way into the ring. Both boxers were introduced, and as the referee ordered them to touch gloves and retreat to their corners, Sylvio knelt in his corner for a silent prayer.

God, you said the battle was not mine. It's yours. Please give me the strength to outlast my opponent today. Win or lose, I want to show the world that you can restore. I'm not perfect, but I'm trying. Amen.

The bell rang for the first round. Immediately, both fighters met at the center of the ring. *The Wolf and the Tiger meet at last.*

Jun didn't waste any time throwing quick jabs at Sylvio's head. He was looking for a quick knockout, but Sylvio anticipated that his younger opponent would come out swinging.

The one thing to remember, Sylvio, is that Jun has never gone beyond five rounds. If you can outlast him for five rounds and draw him out, he may tire out. Jim's words during their film session played through Sylvio's head.

"Defense, defense!" Jim yelled as Sylvio raised his gloves to block and ward off Jun's headshots.

For the majority of the first round, Sylvio was forced to defend and was unable to land any shots of his own. But Jim had made sure that his fighter was in peak physical condition in order to keep up with Jun's blistering pace. *Do not let him press you against the ropes. Make the target smaller for him.*

Jun was three inches taller than Sylvio, and he had a longer wingspan that gave him an advantage. Unable to block all of Jun's shots, Sylvio felt his head jerk backwards when two of Jun's punches found their mark. Yet, Sylvio was not hurt, and the bell rang, ending the first round.

"Great first round, Wolf. It's important that we keep this pace going throughout the fight. He's gonna be headhunting for the next few rounds, so prepare yourself. Look for the opening inside, and break him," Jim instructed.

As the bell rang for Round 2, Jun ran into the center of the ring, and before he could continue his attack, Sylvio delivered a crisp right jab onto his forehead. The champion was dazed for a second, then responded with a quick left to the head of his challenger, followed by a punch to Sylvio's midsection.

Nope that ain't enough, Tiger. It's gon' take more than that to drop me today.

Jun scored some hits on Sylvio's shoulder, and the bell rang, ending Round 2. Sylvio knew that he was losing the fight on the scorecards, but unlike his previous opponents, who normally conceded to Jun, Sylvio never backed away from his opponent. He remained undaunted.

Sylvio courageously stayed on his feet, as Jun continued throwing shots. But by the end of the third round, he had a small cut above his right eye from where Jun had managed to find his mark.

But in Round 4, Sylvio began to methodically find openings in Jun's defense. He zoned in on Jun's rib cage, and while Jun tried hard to end his fight early, he felt Sylvio land a number of body shot combinations to his ribs. Perhaps due to underestimation or lack of preparation, Jun was not fully ready for Sylvio's onslaught on his body. Sylvio's punches were quite effective, but Jun's initial thought had been that Sylvio couldn't move his arms or legs as fast as he could.

Jun was mistaken, and for the next two rounds, Sylvio worked on his body, landing shots on Juns' chest and abdomen with extreme force. Aided by Jim's unique strength-building routine at the Catskills Mountains, Sylvio, was able to also take heavy shots and land some damaging blows of his own.

When Round 5 ended, Jun's cornermen were beginning to panic. They did not expect the fight to last longer than two rounds, and they were worried about Jun's stamina. However, Jun was also in excellent shape, so he continued to press forward with his attack.

Sylvio didn't back down though. Do not get against the ropes. If you stand still against him, he will knock you out. Keep moving, Wolf. C'mon!

Sylvio continued to move around the ring, causing Jun to miss many of the shots that he would have landed. At the end of Round 6, the fight was still up in the air, but Sylvio knew that he was still behind on the scorecards.

When Round 7 began, Sylvio felt that if he could keep the fight manageable, he would have the opportunity to win by a close decision. But the round took a turn for the worst. On one sequence, Sylvio failed to move back quick enough, and Jun caught him with a left hook that landed squarely on his jaw. Sylvio went down. Jun's fans went up into a wild frenzy.

The referee backed Jun into a neutral corner and began his count. Agonizing in pain on the canvas, Sylvio could hear the counting, and he could hear Jim and Tom's voices, urging him to stand up. He could also hear A.D.'s voice urging him to stand up when he fought for the first time against Demetrious at age thirteen.

As he struggled to rise to his feet, Sylvio looked out into the crowd, near ringside, and his eyes fell upon hers. There she was, watching his fight in person. Sylvio could see the concerned look plastered on her face.

When you were nine years old, you told her that you were going to be the champion of the world. Remember, she didn't believe you? Now you have another opportunity to be the champ. Don't let the moment slip away.

Barely beating the ten count, the bell rang and Sylvio stumbled to his corner where Tom hit him with the smelling salts. Jim struggled to get his mouthpiece out but finally managed and poured water down his throat. Sylvio gargled the liquid but was in excruciating pain as he spit the crimson water out.

Harry softly touched the sides of his face and chin and confirmed what he already knew. "Jim, his jaw's busted, man."

Jim hung his head, and Sylvio knew he was struggling to fight back tears. His worst fear had become reality. His fighter was seriously injured under his watch. "Okay, we gotta call it," he said.

"No! Don't stop this fight! I ain't done yet," Sylvio protested.

"Wolf, he knows that he broke your jaw. If you go back out there, he's gonna keep pounding on it until he takes your face off. I gotta stop this thing."

"You ain't stoppin' anything. You hear me? I'mma beat him," Sylvio said.

The referee quickly checked on Sylvio, but Sylvio indicated that he was fine and to let the fight continue.

In Round 8, Sylvio kept his gloves up to protect his face and began bobbing and weaving in and out and up and down, causing Jun to miss his headshots. Sylvio knew Jun was zeroing in on his dislocated jaw. Gulping the blood down each time it filled in his mouth, Sylvio worked hard to conceal the pain from the referee.

But he also discovered that Jun's ribs were red in the area where his gloves had found their mark, so he focused on the target. During Jun's next body clutch, Sylvio landed four hard right hooks to the area, and that's when Sylvio saw Jun's abdomen slightly cave in. His opponent yelled in pain as he clutched his right ribs. Sylvio knew that he had cracked Jun's ribs.

By now, both fighters had broken bones, and the fight would come down to a battle of attrition to see which fighter could outlast the other. By the twelfth round, each fighter was spitting up blood.

As they approached each other for the final round, Sylvio's right cheek had swelled up, and Jun was still favoring his broken ribs. In the round, Jun faked a couple of shots to Sylvio's head then threw some body shots at Sylvio as he doubled over in pain. But Sylvio retaliated with a jaw-jarring uppercut the knocked Jun back.

Both were still throwing vast amounts of punches, and toward the last minute of the round, Sylvio ignored the pain from his broken jaw and proceeded with his attack. By this time, Jun was completely exhausted after being taken to the limit. He had no gas for resurgence, but Sylvio remained almost fresh, and his jabs were landing on Jun's face as blood began pouring out of Jun's nose. Jun now had welts under both of his eyes.

Finally, the bell rang, signaling the end of the round and the end of the fight. The fans stood up and cheered after witnessing one of the best fights in middleweight history, a fight in which neither boxer gave an inch to the other.

As Jun and Sylvio stood on either side of the ref, the announcer belted out, "Let's give a hand for both of these gladiators!" After a round of applause was given, the announcer stated that it was a split decision.

"Judge Ralph Simpkins awards the fight eight rounds to Zhang and four rounds to Dominique!"

Sylvio hung his head. He had lost the first decision.

Jim approached him. "Aye, Wolf, no matter what the outcome is, you fought like a man today. You showed heart and courage that I never seen before, and I'm proud of you. You're a champion in my eyes."

Despite the effort that it took to do so, Sylvio smiled at his trainer. "Thanks, old man," he said.

The announcer continued. "Judge Matthew Kite awards the fight seven rounds to Dominique and five rounds to Zhang!"

Sylvio's fans cheered and howled loudly while Jun's fans booed.

Sylvio held his breath. His destiny now relied on the last judge. If the last judge voted a tie between him and Zhang, then Jun would remain champion of the world.

"Judge Jerome Davis has voted…"

Sylvio closed his eyes.

"…seven rounds to Dominique and five rounds to Zhang! The new middleweight champion of the world, Sylvio 'Wolf' Dominique!" Sylvio's fans cheered loudly, and Jun's fans booed.

As Sylvio looked at his corner, he saw a stunned Jun Zhang

with his cornermen, dejected as heavy favorites coming into the match. Upon shaking Jun's and his cornermen's hands, Sylvio scanned the crowd and found Valentina. Sitting next to her was her friend, Passion, who had moved out to Los Angeles.

Moving in Valentina's direction, Sylvio dapped Jamal, A.D., and Gary along the way. "Yo', Jamal, this was for Omar!" Sylvio said, as Harry helped him cut his gloves off, and he handed them to Jamal.

Valentina ran to Sylvio, and right away, he saw the tear streaks in her eyes. It was clear that she had been crying when she had seen him in pain. "Sylvio, are you okay?" she asked, hugging him.

"I've never felt better in my life," he replied, before rubbing his lower jaw. He wasn't sure if they would see each other again, but their love and support for one another was undeniable.

"C'mon, Wolf, let's go," Jim said, rejoining Sylvio's side. Together, they walked into the locker room, with Sylvio raising his hands in victory after reclaiming the title belt for the first time in six years.

Chapter 22

Two Months Later | All the residents from the five boroughs made their way to the Shaw-Dominique Community Center for the 1st Annual SDCC Basketball Tournament and Cookout that included street basketball players and pro-basketball players. The day kicked off with young kids, ages six through eleven, playing on eight-foot rims. All the games were played in the Omar Keaton Court. Among those who attended were Pastor Mike Hillman and his wife, Robyn, and various members of their church.

Omar's girlfriend, Ashley, also attended the tournament, and it warmed Sylvio when he saw Ashley and Omar's son, Cory, dominating the children's league. Cory was a natural, and whenever he shot the ball and scored, it was uncanny to Sylvio how much his mannerisms on the court mirrored those of his late father.

With the money that Sylvio made from his title bout, he was able to keep the center from being taken over by the state, and he had rebuilt the educational center and hired new tutors and teachers to aid inner-city kids that were struggling with their studies.

After their abrupt breakup, Yolanda quit as the director of the drama department. Whether it was out of spite for Sylvio, the reason was never determined, nor was it sought after. Sylvio hired Nakia Waters, a drama major from nearby St John's University, and the department saw an increase in children's participation.

Just a month earlier, Nakia had directed an African American odyssey, where each child that participated in the production portrayed a notable African American historical figure. The program was a success, and Sylvio commended Nakia for her efforts.

Sylvio recovered after the brutal fight with Jun Zhang, but his jaw had to be surgically repaired and wired shut for six weeks. After his speedy recovery, he was able to talk normally and could enjoy the day's festivities, including the musical numbers as A.D. volunteered to be the deejay and provided all his latest tracks for the event and barbecue food served by a black-owned restaurant.

After the kids played, it was time for the adult single-elimination tournaments to begin. The players were separated into different colors with jerseys baring the initials "SDCC" on the front. Before his team was scheduled to play, Jamal Samuels, the captain of the Silver squad, had come by to see Sylvio. "What's good, champ?"

"What's up, man? What you got for us today?" Sylvio asked Jamal as he looked at the court and surveyed his competition.

"Man, look. I'mma take it easy on these cats. I ain't tryna go all hard on nobody today. Besides, I gotta stay healthy for my 10-day deal."

Sylvio looked at Jamal, who smiled and showed him a picture taken on his phone by Tracy. In the picture, Jamal was signing a 10-day contract with the New York Knicks of the National Basketball Association.

"Yo', that's what's up, man!" Sylvio said, dapping his friend. He knew how hard Jamal had worked to play in the NBA. His moment had finally arrived.

"I mean, it's really just a brief contract, like a tryout really," he explained.

"Man, it don't even matter how long it is," Sylvio said, cutting him off. "One of our own is gon' be in the league. I can't wait to watch you represent, kid."

"No doubt," Jamal replied. "So, what's up wit' you and Valentina, bro? Any chance of ya'll gettin' back together?"

"Nah, man. She got a lot goin' on for her right now. Her movie's about to come out in June, and I know she mad hype about that. We both doin' our own thing, and that's good enough for now. Maybe when our lives slow down a lil' bit, we might pick it back up again."

Jamal sighed and glanced out at the court. "I know we had our differences about her in the past because we've both been with her, but I ain't gon' front, B., she really loves you man. Hopefully, by the grace of God, you guys will find your way back to each other."

"Yeah, maybe. But I'm the champ now, so ain't no slowing down for me right now," Sylvio grinned slyly.

Jamal saw a familiar face enter the gym. He had on shorts and old St. John's practice gear that he had not worn in almost a decade.

"Man, this fool coming ova here to play too?" Jamal asked as former St. John's standout, Trevor McClain, made his way into the gym, accompanied by his wife, Shania, and their daughter. Jamal tried to stifle his laughter, but he couldn't hold it.

"What's up, champ?" Trevor greeted Sylvio.

"Yo, what you doing here, McClain? You sure your knees gon' keep up wit' us?" Jamal laughed.

"Man, I'm ready to give all ya this work, Jamal. You already know how I do," Trevor said.

"Nah, I know how you did. This ain't Lefferts Boulevard Park no more, Trevor. Trust and believe you don't want this smoke now. Better sign up when I'm not playin'," Jamal warned jokingly.

"Oh, you got jokes now, Samuels? You already forgot I used to dominate you and Omar on the same court together back in the day? I don't wanna make you look bad on yo' homeboy's turf now."

Jamal and Trevor walked toward the court still trading verbal barbs, and Sylvio was soon joined courtside by Jim Shaw. He was accompanied by a woman who held his arm. "What's up, Jim? Enjoying yourself so far?" Sylvio asked.

"Most definitely. Sylvio, I'd like to introduce you to my date for this evening. Natalie Brown, this is my fighter and the current middleweight champion of the world," he introduced.

Natalie shook Sylvio's hand. "Nice to meet you, Sylvio. I'm a huge fan," she said.

"Thank you," Sylvio replied, but he soon began to make the connection. "Wait a minute, Natalie Brown. Ain't you Jim's ex-wife?" he asked, causing Jim's eyes to widen as if to say, "Why you gotta talk like that, fool?"

But Natalie laughed. "Yeah, but we're working at it. We find that we still have a lot in common. We'll just see where that takes us."

"Look, Natalie, I wanna apologize for my boy's lack of tact. Except for the ring, his timing's always been horrible," Jim said.

"Don't worry, Jim. I'm workin' on it." Sylvio winked at Natalie, who laughed.

"You're right, Jim. Sylvio reminds me so much of you."

"Hey, hey, I'm nothin' like him, okay? I was actually champion...twice," Sylvio countered.

"Aye, aye, don't forget who trained you up to be champ. I'mma remember that when you gotta defend this title," Jim threatened in jest.

"You wouldn't leave me, old man, would you?" Sylvio asked.

"I wouldn't dream of it. We got more fights to win. Now shut up and let me watch this tournament."

Jim sat in the bleachers just above Sylvio with Natalie. His arms were wrapped around her shoulders as she laid her head on his chest. Sylvio wasn't sure, but he felt that if Jim could rekindle his relationship with Natalie, then maybe there was hope for him and Valentina in the future.

Love always brings people together. It may be a few days, a few weeks, maybe some months, and perhaps some years, but love will always bring us back together. Even if I'm no longer champion, and she's no longer an award-winning actress, love will bring us back together someday. But the love for my city and my community, that's undeniable. I will always put on for Queens, New York. That's gon' be my legacy when I leave this life.

THE END

ABOUT THE AUTHOR

"Marc A. Beausejour"

Marc A. Beausejour was born on July 28, 1987 in Queens, New York to Haitian parents Jean and Lineda Beausejour. He discovered his passion for writing at the tender age of twelve, with poetry becoming his initial artistic expression. Beausejour showcased his poetic talents in various school talent shows and poetry reading events during his time at North Cobb High School and later at Kennesaw State University after moving to Kennesaw, Georgia in 2001.

Throughout the years, Beausejour continued to hone his craft, writing poems for diverse occasions such as weddings, funerals, and church events. In 2011, he took a significant step by self-publishing his first book, "Words on High," a compilation of spiritually inspired poems from his formative years. Building on this success, Beausejour released his second poetry book, "Rising Higher Than Ever," in 2015.

In the same year, he ventured into a different literary landscape by writing and publishing his first urban novel, "The Preacher's Web." This gritty morality tale marked a departure from his earlier poetic works, showcasing Beausejour's versatility as an author. Expanding his literary horizons, he created the *BlackCyrano* series, demonstrating a wide-ranging creative skill.

While continuing to share his literary work on blogs and social networks, Beausejour remains committed to his education and promotions, earning his associate degree in marketing management from Chattahoochee Technical College in 2018. As a multifaceted writer, Marc A. Beausejour continues to captivate audiences with his words across various genres and platforms.

ALSO BY, AUTHOR

"Marc A. Beausejour"

Title: The Preacher's Web | Publisher: SHE PUBLISHING LLC | ISBN: 978-1-953163-91-2 (paperback) Publication Date: February 2024 (*Second Edition*)

Set in the heart of the city, "The Preacher's Web" unfolds a gripping narrative of former All-City quarterback turned pastor, Mike Hillman, whose dedication to preaching love and forgiveness in Queens, New York is challenged by the return of an old friend seeking revenge. Amidst a community grappling with the scourge of drugs and gangs. As Mike puts his reputation on the line to testify for a young man accused of murder, the story converges with the adolescent struggles of Jamal Samuels on the basketball courts of New York City.

Now, standing at the crossroads of faith, family, and societal challenges, Mike faces a pivotal choice. Will he risk more than his reputation to uphold justice and fulfill his role as a public servant and father? The pages of "The Preacher's Web" beckon you to explore the complexities of morality and redemption. Can Mike Hillman rise above, or will he be consumed by the web of his past?

Title: Fires of Justice | Author: Marc A. Beausejour | Publisher: SHE PUBLISHING LLC | ISBN: 978-1-953163-93-6 (paperback) | Publication Date: February 2024 (*second edition*)

English professor Levell Thomas is ecstatic when he receives the opportunity to teach in a metro Atlanta high school. A native of Queens, New York, Levell moves to Georgia with his family and as they settle in their new home, Levell meets his neighbor, a mysterious girl named Raven Roberts. Despite being underaged, she doesn't hide her desires for Levell and pursues him relentlessly. Levell refuses her advances but would soon pay dearly for his decision. The spurned teenager accuses Levell of assault after a physical confrontation and Levell is found guilty in the court of law. Detective Isaac Sands leads the investigation to expose a plot of false accusation and imprisonment in a race against time. Will Sands help prove Levell's innocence by finding the conspirators, or would he put himself in harm's way?

"The controversies confronted, stirred, and then addressed in this story have no choice but to awaken you to new perspectives that might not have ever crossed your mind. Readers, all I can say is be prepared to feel the fire that Beausejour has ignited in this suspenseful masterpiece!"

—D.A. Goodwin, author of The Offender I Once Defended

Title: Adia's Ballad | Author: Marc A. Beausejour | Publisher: SHE PUBLISHING LLC | ISBN: 978-1-953163-92-9 (paperback) | Publication Date: February 2024 (*second edition*)

From the author of "The Preacher's Web", this coming-of-age story explores the life of young Andrea McAfee who struggles to cope with the tragic murder of her older sister. Then a chance opportunity lands Andrea into the music business where she shares a bond with other artists in the hip hop industry and learns she has more in common with them than she realizes. As Andrea immerses herself deeper into the life of recording, touring and partying as Adia, the new R&B princess, she begins drifting away from her family and her loved ones as her star rises too fast for her to absorb. With fame corrupting her relationships with those she loves, will Andrea find the inner peace and closure she seeks, or will she succumb to the draw of money and celebrity?

Title: Split Decision | Author: Marc A. Beausejour | Publisher: SHE PUBLSIHING LLC | ISBN: 978-1-953163-94-3 (paperback) | Publication Date: February 2024 (*second edition*)

Prepare to enter the ring as cultures clash in this adrenaline-filled drama! Under the tutelage of experienced trainer Jim Shaw, young boxer Sylvio Dominique has taken the middleweight class division by storm, winning bout after bout. Nicknamed "Wolf" for his boxing style and aggression in the ring, Sylvio works hard in the ring and plays even harder out of the ring and there is no shortage of women. Reuniting with childhood friend Valentina Cruz, the two become involved in an intense romance. But as Sylvio falls deep in love with Valentina, he realizes that she is more than what she seems. With a fight against the undefeated Dominican champion Felipe Maximo looming, secrets are revealed, and friends turn to foes as Sylvio later discovers that he may not be fighting only for the middleweight crown, but he may also be fighting for his life.

Title: Street Retribution | Author: Marc A. Beausejour | Publisher: SHE PUBLISHING LLC | ISBN: 978-1-953163-96-7 (*paperback*) | Publication Date: February 2024 (*second edition*)

New York City attorney Edward Reed harbors a secret. He was once known as Antonio Franks, a member of M.O.B., the most dangerous gang in Queens, New York. He was also the key witness in the trial that exonerated another ex-gang member, David Anderson, when he was falsely accused of murdering his girlfriend, Loree McAfee. But years later, both men's lives are in danger, as other former gang members are slain under mysterious circumstances by a femme fatale, prompting rumors that M.O.B.'s ruthless gang leader, Tadarius Hill is seeking revenge on those that turned on him and his organization. Will Edward and David survive the bounty, or will they fall victim to the code of the streets?

Title: Divine Vengeance | Author: Marc A. Beausejour | Publisher: SHE PUBLISHING LLC | Publication Date: COMING SOON!

After the murder of David Anderson, LaToya Richardson awaits her day in court while attorney Edward Reed receives a warning from Tadarius Hill, the gang leader of M.O.B. and sexy femme fatale Tina, who gives him an ultimatum. Realizing that he cannot use conventional methods to combat the tactics of his former gang, Edward pulls out all the stops to prevent Tadarius from wreaking havoc in the city. LaToya's son, Chris adjusts to his new home and new school while staying with David's family. Andrea McAfee's relationship with her boyfriend Quentin comes apart at the seams as lust and infidelity threatens to tear the couple apart. Can Edward, Chris, and Andrea summon the strength amidst the chaos in their environment to secure their futures?